THE
GAUNTLET

THE GAUNTLET

BY MEGAN SHEPHERD

BALZER + BRAY
An Imprint of HarperCollins Publishers

Balzer + Bray is an imprint of HarperCollins Publishers.

ISBN 978-0-06-224312-6 (trade bdg.)

Typography by Michelle Taormina
17 18 19 20 21   PC/LSCH   10 9 8 7 6 5 4 3 2 1
❖
First Edition

For all the readers who have followed this series across the stars.
This is for you.

1

Cora

DUST ROSE ON THE horizon.

Cora shaded her eyes against the unnaturally large alien sun. The approaching truck began to take shape as it cut through the thick dust clouds, tearing across Armstrong preserve's scrubby desert landscape toward the patch of bare land where she and her friends stood. Beside her, Rolf held Nok's hand tightly. Leon paced a few feet away, sweat streaming down his brow. Whoever—*whatever*—was in that truck, the four of them, alone and unarmed and malnourished, couldn't possibly be much of a match.

She tossed a look over her shoulder. Barely visible through the dust, Bonebreak's ship crouched like a dented green beetle on the horizon. The Mosca black-market trader had brought them to Armstrong preserve and then run away at the first sign of trouble. *Coward.* He was probably fleeing back to his ship right now, but he'd never get off the moon. Mali was on board, guarding the controls along with Anya. And the last time Bonebreak had tried to screw them over, Anya had telepathically taken over Bonebreak's mind and made him dance like a puppet. He wouldn't dare try to betray them again.

"I have a seriously bad feeling about this," Nok muttered.

The truck was getting closer. They only had a minute, maybe two, before it reached them. Cora's heart thundered so loudly, she could hear it over the whine of the approaching engine. They could run, but they would never get to the ship in time. They could hide—but where? The clapboard town was too far away. The only other structure was the transport hub the Kindred used for docking, but it would certainly be locked.

"Look." Leon pointed to the horizon. "There's more than one."

As the dust settled, Cora made out three vehicles roaring toward them. They were small and compact, a cross between lunar rovers she'd seen on television and good old-fashioned pickups, complete with black lines of exhaust billowing out the back. One of the trucks veered sharply in the direction of Bonebreak's ship, but the other two continued toward them. Outlines of a dozen people lined up along the truck beds, jostling over the bumpy terrain. The people wore objects that looked unsettlingly like rifles strapped to their backs.

"Let me do the talking," Leon said. "Whoever these people are, human or not, they're not going to listen to a pretty blond girl asking them to play nice." He gestured toward the town, indicating the tallest building. "These are the creeps who have piles of slave chains in the sheriff's office."

Cora eyed Leon closely. With the fierce tattoos on his face and the dirt caked on his clothes, he looked older than seventeen.

He stood straighter than he had before. His hands were calm by his sides, not defensively flexed into fists, ready to leap to violence at the first sign of trouble, as he'd been when she had first met him.

"No," she said. "I got us into this. I'll get us out."

The trucks were close enough now to see outlines of faces looming behind the windshield.

Leon nodded.

Just weeks ago, Cora thought, he would have been more likely to abandon them or sell them to the highest bidder than offer to lead. That had been Lucky's job. Lucky had been their leader, their moral compass.

But now . . .

Cora glanced again at the squat green ship on the horizon. A sharp, vivid pain pulled at her insides. Lucky's body was on board. He'd died just after the escape. She'd spent nearly two days in the tight quarters of Bonebreak's ship with Lucky's cold body beneath a tarp. The boy who'd died for her.

A sudden burst of light emanated from beneath Bonebreak's ship. She straightened. A low rumble began, making the ground shake. Slowly, the ship started to rise.

Cora sucked in a tight breath.

"Do you see that?" Nok grabbed Cora's shoulder, pointing toward the ship. "Bonebreak is leaving!"

"He wouldn't," Cora breathed. "Anya and Mali would stop him."

She stared with wide, disbelieving eyes as the ship kept rising. It rose a hundred feet high above the moon's surface, then five hundred, then even higher. With another burst of light, the ship was gone.

"That bastard!" Leon growled.

The ship had vanished high into space where they couldn't see it anymore. The four of them stood in the parched desert on the outskirts of the town, heads pitched toward their last hope, which had just abandoned them. Cora squeezed her eyes closed.

Anya, she urged with her mind, trying to communicate telepathically as the two of them had done on the Kindred station. *What's going on? Where are you going?*

There was no answer.

A truck revved its engine as it approached. Cora whipped her head around. Abandoned or not, trouble was still coming their way, fast. The third truck, which had been headed in Bonebreak's direction, now circled back to join the others as they barreled into the patch of desert. The trucks' wheels skidded and whined as they surrounded Cora and her friends. Nok pressed her arm against her mouth, coughing.

The trucks didn't cut their engines. Fears flashed in Cora's mind. *We'll be enslaved. I'll never leave this moon, never run the Gauntlet, never even find out if Earth is still there! And Cassian . . . Cassian will die strapped to that table. Tortured. And all because he tried to free us.*

The faces behind the windshields were clearly visible now. Grim-looking men and women of all ages with ragged hair and even more ragged clothes. At least they were human—hopefully they'd be more lenient to their own kind. A woman in the passenger's seat of the closest truck pointed toward them and then pounded twice on the inside roof of the cab.

"Um," Leon said, glancing at Cora. "You *sure* you got this?"

A dozen soldiers flooded out of the backs of the trucks. The soldiers surrounded them, grunting calls to one another, swinging rifles off their backs, and aiming. They wore handkerchiefs tied around their noses and mouths to keep from breathing in the dust, revealing only sunken eyes and sharp cheekbones. It gave them the air of bandits.

Cora braced herself. She looked toward the sky, praying that Bonebreak's ship would suddenly reappear.

But the sky remained empty.

Why did they leave?

A thin man with a handkerchief over his face stepped down from the truck. His clothes, like all the soldiers', were tattered at the edges and faded, but something about the cut of the clothes caught her eye. The outfit was shaped like a uniform with piping down the sleeves. When the piping caught the sunlight, it glittered gold. On the pocket, there was an insignia that looked like the lion embroidery from the Hunt uniforms.

Impossible.

The man pulled down the handkerchief, revealing a young face that made Cora start with recognition.

"Dane?" she sputtered.

It had been just days since she'd last seen him, but it felt so much longer. The time spent in Bonebreak's ship had passed in a blur as she'd grieved Lucky's death, and before that, Dane had already been dragged off in disgrace to rot in some cell.

Now he looked like a shell of his former self. Skin blistered from sunburn, a dullness to his eyes. Leon twisted around with a questioning look. He had never met Dane, Cora realized, and neither had Rolf or Nok. In the Hunt menagerie, Dane had been the Head Ward and had colluded with the Kindred to keep the rest of the human staff obedient. When she'd first met him, he'd had a smug air of privilege, and she hadn't at all regretted framing him for a crime he hadn't committed.

But this isn't where he was supposed to end up, she thought with confusion. Why was he on Armstrong? Supposedly only good, obedient humans were sent here.

"Hello again, songbird." He gave his trademark smirk. Cora felt like she was going to be sick.

Another truck door slammed. The woman who had signaled to the soldiers came around the front of the truck. With the cloth around her face it was impossible to guess her age, but she moved with authority, though she was smaller than the rest of the soldiers. Her dark hair was pulled back in a messy bun at the nape of her neck, a few tangled strands falling around her face. She folded her arms and studied the four of them. "You know these humans?" she asked Dane through her handkerchief.

"Only the blond one."

The woman eyed them as though appraising merchandise. "They're kids. They don't even look nineteen yet." She jerked her chin toward Cora. "You came on that ship we saw taking off?"

"Yeah," Cora answered quickly. "A . . . star-sweeper pod," she added, remembering a vessel Cassian had once told her about, figuring it was best not to mention Anya or Mali or Bonebreak. "We . . . stole one from the station and overrode the controls. It took off automatically once we landed—it must have had a pre-programmed return protocol. No one else was on board."

The woman raised a doubting eyebrow as she studied them closer. "Is that so? In any case, you aren't marked with any ownership tags, so you must be free humans." She smiled grimly. "Not that it matters. No one stays free for long here." She turned back to the soldiers. "They seem healthy enough. We can get some decent work hours out of them. Take them to town for processing."

Cora's heart thundered. She thought of the chains stacked in the sheriff's office. Of the ledger with the categories marked: *slaves, wives, dead.*

A soldier started toward her.

"Back off!" Leon shoved the soldier away. It caused a sudden scramble of activity and a *click click click* of cocked rifles. In the next instant a dozen barrels were pointed at them. A soldier reached out to grab Nok. Rolf threw a punch toward his jaw and Nok screamed. It all happened so fast, like a shift in the air. Leon lunged for two of the soldiers, grabbing their rifles by the barrels and slinging them to the ground. A cry clawed up Cora's throat— *No, this is wrong, fighting will get us nowhere*—but it was too late. Leon hurled himself at the crowd, the tough Mosca shielding that was sewn to his shoulder letting him plow through the soldiers like a battering ram.

Two hands snatched her from behind.

"You shouldn't have come," Dane whispered, digging his fingers painfully into her shoulders. She spun around. His eyes were hooded, haunted. What had happened to his claims that Armstrong was a paradise? And his dreams of being a king here? He seemed like nothing more than a servant to that dark-haired woman.

Leon roared as he knocked out two more soldiers and

twisted a rifle away from another. He aimed it straight for the woman's head.

"Put your rifles down!" he yelled. "Or her brains go up in fireworks."

The soldiers paused, uncertain. The rifles remained aimed high.

The woman's eyes were steady, unafraid of Leon's rifle aimed directly between her eyes. She walked slowly in a circle, appraising the captives, eyes lingering on Rolf's twitchy hands, on Nok's long legs, on Cora's short hair. Then she turned to Leon and pulled down her handkerchief.

"Rifles on the ground," she said calmly to her soldiers, then motioned to Dane. "Let that one go."

Dane released her, reluctantly. Cora stumbled a few steps away, rubbing her arms, throwing him a glare.

The woman looked to be in her fifties. Something metallic in her jaw caught the sun, and Cora peered closer and then recoiled. A six-pointed brass star like a sheriff's badge, but sharp at the ends, was soldered to the woman's skin. It looked almost sinister in the way its clawlike edges dug into her cheek.

The woman eyed Leon with an amused air, ignoring the rifle, and then turned to Cora. I'm Ellis, the sheriff, as you can see." She cocked her head so the sun caught the star-shaped badge again and made it gleam gold. "These are some of my deputies. It's my duty to keep order in Armstrong. Dane says you're a troublemaker. If you thought you'd find sanctuary here, you're mistaken. We'll sweat the rebellion out of you in the mines."

Leon inched the rifle closer to the woman's forehead. "You're forgetting that I'm the one with the gun, lady."

Ellis raised an eyebrow. Suddenly she swept her hands high like conducting an orchestra, and Cora stumbled backward in surprise. The dozen rifles resting on the ground rose into the air in unison. *Click. Click. Click.* The sound of a dozen unmanned weapons being cocked. Cora gasped.

"What the . . . ," Leon started.

"She's like Anya," Nok whispered. "She's telekinetic."

Ellis gave that flat smile again. "Deputies, take them away."

"Wait!" Cora said. "We're human, like you! We're on the same side. It's the Kindred who put all of us here, who abducted us from our homes. It's them we should be fighting against, not each other. We could work together to make a place for humans in this world—a fair, free place. You have perceptive abilities yourself, so you know we're just as intelligent as any other species." She took a deep breath. "If you'd just help us, I can make it happen. I have a way."

She thought of Cassian's laser-light model of the Gauntlet and its twelve puzzles that she would have to run. Solve them all, and humanity would be deemed an intelligent species. Captive humans on Kindred stations would be freed, and everyone on Earth, who had no idea there was life beyond their planet, would have a future in which they and their children would never be imprisoned.

"Just hear me out," Cora said. "You won't regret it."

Ellis stepped forward slowly. Dane turned away, as if he didn't want to watch whatever came next. A sense of fear rose in Cora's stomach with every step the sheriff took closer.

"Work together?" Cruelty laced Ellis's voice. "On the same side?" She laughed and tilted her head so sunlight gleamed off the badge and blinded Cora's eyes. "I don't want a fair world. I don't want freedom. You think because some DNA links us, that makes us loyal to one another?" She tugged the cloth back up over her mouth. "On this moon there are only two sides that matter: the side that has the guns, and the side that doesn't."

She plucked a rifle out of the air and signaled to her deputies to do the same.

"And unfortunately, girl, you're on the wrong one."

2

Cora

THEY WERE LOADED INTO the trucks like cattle.

First the deputies bound their hands with cord—securing Leon's twice to be sure—and forced them to march to the truck beds. They pushed Rolf and Leon into one and Cora and Nok into the other. Nok's knees connected hard against the truck bed.

"Ow," she said with a grimace, and met Cora's eyes. "I'm worried about the baby—"

Cora shook her head sharply. It was better if the deputies didn't know Nok was pregnant. Her growing belly was more than five months along, but the frilly apron she'd taken from Serassi's dollhouse experiment hid the bump.

The truck roared to life. Two deputies climbed in the back and tapped the side of the truck. A second before it took off, Dane jumped in too.

He locked eyes with Cora as he settled in the truck bed across from her. The engine hummed, and the truck started bouncing toward the town. Dust flooded the air, making Cora wish she had one of the cloths around her nose. She squinted out over the scrubland. Even if they got free, where would they run? They didn't know this moon. She pitched her head skyward, once more scanning uselessly for Bonebreak's ship.

After a moment, she felt Dane's eyes on her. He glanced at the deputies, who were staring toward the town, and moved close enough so that they couldn't be heard over the engine's roar.

"Why are you really here, songbird?"

"Why are *you?*" she shot back angrily. "This hardly looks like the paradise you told us about."

He rubbed his chin anxiously. "Unfortunately, I have to admit you were right. I shouldn't have believed the Kindred. They told me that if I obeyed them I'd be richly rewarded. That was a lie—well, you know how they are. They don't lie, but they don't tell the full truth, either." His gaze turned to the dry, empty horizon, broken only by the Kindred's transport hub, tall and boxy, like a small power plant. "The good humans *are* brought here when they turn nineteen. But so are the bad ones. Everyone ends up here when they turn nineteen. The Kindred strip you of any of the markings they tagged you with, put you through processing there in that transport hub, and then dump you here so that Ellis can decide if you're a slave or a deputy."

"I don't see any iron chains around your wrists," Cora said. "So you must have done something right."

He smirked. "I was supposed to be a slave. Sentenced to the root mines, just like you'll be. But within hours of arriving, I overheard Ellis saying she wanted a drink, and if I learned anything in the Hunt, it was how to mix a good cocktail. She made me a deputy instead, right on the spot."

Cora rolled her eyes. "Knowing what a suck-up you are, I'm not surprised you found a way into her good graces."

He glanced at the other deputies. "Why isn't Lucky with you?" His voice lingered on the name.

Pain clenched Cora's heart. She couldn't help but think of the blood staining the ship's floor, wherever Bonebreak had disappeared to. Dane had taken a close interest in Lucky in the Hunt. One that might have been romantic, if Lucky were into boys and if Dane hadn't been such a bastard.

"Lucky?" Her voice came out hollow. "He's gone."

Dane's eyes went wide.

"Mosca killed him," she added, feeling a pang at the memory. "He was trying to help us escape the station. He never gave up on freeing the humans there, and the animals, too. On getting home."

Dane's face went slack, and he closed his eyes while he took a few deep breaths. For a second Cora felt sorry for him. The only time he'd ever shown any kindness had been with Lucky. She touched the interior pocket of her safari uniform surreptitiously, glad they hadn't yet been searched by Ellis's deputies. She took the opportunity to quietly move Lucky's journal from her pocket to the back waistband of her pants, where it might be overlooked.

The truck stopped.

Dane opened his eyes and looked up. The sadness was fading from his eyes, and with it went Cora's sympathy for him. "We're here," he said coldly.

THE TOWN LOOKED DIFFERENT now that Cora inspected it more closely. When they had first found it after the dust storm, she had been heartened to see flowers in the window boxes and the town square cheerfully decorated as though for a dance. Now she saw that the flowers were artificial and the dance posters were ancient, for a dance that probably never happened.

"The town's mostly just props," Dane explained. "We use the sheriff's office, but everything else is for show so that when the Kindred come, we can display what looks like a thriving community. A happy village. They wouldn't be pleased if they knew it was a dictatorship. They think they rescued us from barbaric systems like that."

"They aren't stupid. They have to know."

"Probably," he said. "But all they care about is how things appear for their reports." He pointed toward a large group of canvas tents in the valley beyond, which the storm had previously obscured. "That encampment is where we actually live. Ellis's command center is the tallest tent. Deputies sleep in the little tents—the higher the rank, the closer to the river. There are two types of deputies, mine guards who oversee the root mine, and tent guards, who are in charge of the wives. That big, low tent in the valley . . ." His nose wrinkled in disdain. "That's the slave barracks. And there's the transport hub, but only the Kindred use that. Don't even think about going near it—the steam coming out of the vents will burn you alive."

The trucks stopped in front of the artificial sheriff's office. The deputies jumped down, motioning for Cora and Nok to climb out of the back. Once they were inside the building and Cora's eyes adjusted to the shade, she found Rolf and Leon already there. A husky deputy dug through Rolf's pockets, frowning as he turned up only papers scribbled with mathematical equations. Another was popping the buttons off Leon's shirt one by one, stripping the captives of anything even remotely valuable. The deputy tried to tug the Mosca shielding off Leon's arm, but it was sewn on. Leon let out a low growl and the deputy backed away.

Ellis folded her arms as she supervised the scene.

"Put the girls over there," she ordered, pointing toward the opposite wall. "Check their heads for lice and their teeth for rot."

Hands started patting her down. Cora shifted subtly, trying to keep their fingers away from Lucky's journal tucked in her pants. A young deputy felt Nok's belly beneath the apron, frowned in surprise, and opened his mouth.

"Carbs," Nok said quickly, surprising the young man. She gave a dismissive kind of laugh. "This is what all that time in space does to me. It's the changing pressure, yeah? And all the carbs in the Kindred's food. Makes me bloat like a balloon."

The deputy, a weak-chinned younger man, seemed to accept this, or else was too intimidated by Nok's fierce beauty to challenge her. Cora was glad Ellis was too busy inspecting Rolf to have heard—Ellis wasn't dumb enough to let such a lie slip.

"Slave," Ellis pronounced, squeezing Rolf's biceps. "Mark that down, Dane."

Dane picked up a pencil and the ledger.

"He's brilliant," Nok argued. "A genius. He'd be wasted doing manual labor."

"We've no need for geniuses here," Ellis said. "Only sets of hands." She moved on to Leon and pinched his cheeks like he was a puppy. "I like your spirit," she said. "You were foolish out there today, trying to threaten me, and it was amusing. You'll make a fine wife."

"*Wife?*" Leon sputtered from between his squished cheeks.

Ellis smiled grimly. "It's a broad term—we don't concern ourselves with gender roles here. This isn't Earth, if you haven't noticed." She glanced at Nok, assessing her quickly. "Mark the tall girl down as a wife, too. The men will like her."

Nok's face remained passive outwardly, but Cora could only imagine the rage roiling with her. On Earth, back in London, Nok had been a model for a seedy talent agency, just one step above a prostitute, prevented from returning to her family in Thailand. She'd sworn never to be a victim like that again.

Ellis approached Cora next.

"That only leaves you. Dane says you're clever. And I hate clever. Clever only leads to trouble." She signaled to Dane. "Mark her as a slave too. And take them away." Without so much as a second glance, Ellis went to peruse the basket of buttons and other objects the deputies had stripped off them.

It was a short ride from the artificial town to the real living quarters, the tent encampment. Cora tried to take in as many details as she could during the drive, but everything was frustratingly bland. Brown canvas tents that varied only in size. Deputies guarding tents and the riverbed, where a small trickle flowed. As soon as they were out of the trucks, two deputies came to take Leon and Nok away to the wives' tent.

"Wait!" Rolf said, moving closer to Nok. "I can't let you separate us."

"Your girlfriend?" the deputy with the gun sneered, and then gave Nok a hungry look. "Mine, now."

Rolf threw himself at the deputy. A sound like a snarl came from his lips, and his fingers curled into tight fists that raised and started to pummel the air. But Dane lunged forward and caught

Rolf's fists, twisting them around his back. The deputies laughed.

Nok pushed forward as she laid a quick hand on Rolf's cheek.

"Don't fight them," she said. "I can take care of myself. They won't lay a hand on me, I promise—"

Dane dragged Rolf away from her before she could finish. The guards reached out to grab her, but she dodged them with a quick step to the side, hands held up in surrender.

They gave one last laugh before leading Nok and Leon away.

"Come on, you two." Dane signaled for Cora and Rolf to follow him to the slave barracks. "You'll have to go through quarantine. Most of us don't because we've been through Kindred processing before coming here. But we have no idea where *you've* been. Which means two weeks sequestered in the quarantine section of the slave tent, more if you show signs of sickness. Enjoy the downtime while you can. After you're cleared for work, it's the mines for you both."

Dane lifted the flap with his trademark smirk. Cora stepped inside, immediately covering her nose against the stink of unwashed humans. She blinked until her eyes adjusted to the dark. What she had taken at first for a lumpy floor was actually a hundred sleeping bodies, maybe more, packed tightly. Two oil lamps flickered from either end.

Two weeks trapped *here*? Impossible. The next Gauntlet, the one on the Mosca planet of Drogane, started in just forty days.

She spun back to the opening. "Dane, you can't just leave us here. You owe me. You were going to let Roshian kill me."

His face was fixed into an indifferent mask, but Cora could tell from the clench of his jaw he wasn't as emotionless as he let on. "You didn't give me much choice," he said, his voice a little softer, but then his hand curled tightly on the tent flap. "You were trouble then, and as far as I can tell, you still are. Lucky never understood that, and now look where he is. People die when they get close to you, songbird. I'm not taking any chances."

He led them to a barred, empty cell that sectioned off one corner of the tent from the main area. Dane took out a key and opened the gate. "Welcome to quarantine."

"Strictly speaking," Rolf observed, "it isn't a very effective quarantine. We share the air with the other slaves."

"Ellis doesn't care if the other slaves get sick. She only gives a damn about herself and her deputies, and they won't be coming anywhere near you. Go on. In."

He locked the cell behind them, then stepped over the sleeping slaves as he left.

"He's certainly not going to be any help," Rolf observed.

"You think?" Cora asked dryly.

"So this is it?" Rolf shook his head. "All that work, all that training, and we end up slaves on some half-dead moon for the rest of our lives? No way. You have to get us out of this. Cora, I'm going to be a father. I'm responsible for our baby. For Sparrow. And for Nok, too. She can't give birth in a place like this." His voice was rising in fear.

"Maybe you two should have thought about that before getting pregnant," Cora said tightly. "Where did you possibly think it would be a safe place to raise a child? On a Kindred station? On a Mosca planet? At least here there are other humans. There's air a baby can breathe. There's food and water. Who knows what the rest of the world is like off this moon."

Rolf looked as though she'd slapped him.

She immediately regretted her harsh tone. "I'm sorry. I know you're just worried about Sparrow. I am too."

Rolf sniffed. "Well, you could act more like it." He went to lie down in the corner.

Cora went to the opposite side of the cell and curled up close to the oil lamp, hugging her knees. Could she really blame Rolf for trying to take care of his loved ones?

She thought of Cassian. She'd called him a monster once, but he wasn't at all. He'd turned himself in for a crime he hadn't committed in order to save her life. She closed her eyes, pained at the memory. The last time she'd seen him, she and Mali had been crawling through the station tunnels. She'd glimpsed Cassian through a crack; he'd been strapped down to a table, interrogated by Kindred doctors with equipment that snaked into his veins and ripped apart his memories. She could still hear the echo of his screams deep in her mind. She pressed a hand to her mouth, silencing her own sobs.

How did she know he was even still alive? He had told her that if anything went wrong with their plan, the Fifth of Five, a secret organization of Kindred who were sympathetic to humans, would rise up and try to free humans by force. Had that happened? Was it war now on the station?

"Cassian," she whispered to herself, "I'm sorry."

Before arriving on Drogane, Cora and Mali had devised a plan to save him, though now, enslaved, it seemed hopeless. They had intended to separate once on Armstrong: Mali and Leon would sneak off and board one of the Kindred supply ships, which would take them back to the station. They would find a way to free Cassian and then meet Cora on Drogane.

But Mali was missing. And Leon was just as trapped as Cora was.

Cora wiped her thumb beneath her eyes—it should be *her* rescuing Cassian, anyway. Mali and Leon had agreed to it because Cora was a wanted fugitive and they weren't—the minute Cora stepped foot on the station, she'd be arrested. And yet it itched at her, the need to help Cassian. He had saved her. It was her turn to save him.

She hugged her legs harder.

Back home, she had survived Bay Pines detention center by keeping her head down and waiting out the eighteen-month sentence. During the day, she'd written letters to her parents about her classes and her roommate, Queenie. At night, she'd written song lyrics for herself. Songs about strength, about stars, about hope. They had helped her endure the time.

"Have to stay strong . . . ," she sang under her breath. "Have to hold on. . . ."

But her voice faded. The reek of the slaves was over-powering.

She pressed her face into her hands.

There was no eighteen months to wait out, now. There were no parents to pick her up at the end and take her back to her bedroom and her waiting dog.

There was only Armstrong.

For weeks, then for months . . . maybe forever.

3

Mali

MALI PACED IN FRONT of the ship's viewing screen.

Beyond, the red curve of Armstrong's shape loomed as they orbited at a low altitude. They were too far away to see the town, even with the viewing screen's powerful magnifier, and likewise, none of the people on Armstrong would be able to see them. The lights of the ship would look like just another bright star.

"We must return for them," Mali said.

Anya sat in the second pilot's chair, hugging her knees tight, eyes big. Mali's heart softened. Anya was a genius, yes, but she was also a ten-year-old girl who'd just seen her friends captured.

Bonebreak snorted as he checked the orbital velocity. Behind the thick mask he wore, Mali couldn't see his face, only his hunchback and his grotesquely twisted limbs clothed in Mosca shielding. "Forget them. They're . . . what's the human word? Oh, yes. Toast."

Anya twisted to him with even wider eyes. "Don't say that!"

Mali folded her arms tightly, narrowing her eyes at

Bonebreak. "Anya's right. We can't give up on them."

It hadn't been either her or Anya's choice to leave the moon. When they'd watched through the viewing screen as those trucks drove toward their friends, they had frantically tried to figure out the ship's controls and managed to zoom in the magnifier. They had seen the fear on Nok's face. A dark-haired woman with a handkerchief covering her mouth. Even Leon had looked worried—Leon, who was the toughest boy Mali knew, not to mention handsome, who had an annoying way of making her short of breath. And then Bonebreak had returned to the ship, anxious and hurried, as he'd shoved them away from the controls. The next thing Mali knew, they were high above the moon.

"Those soldiers are bad people," Mali said. "One of them is a boy I knew in the Hunt. Dane. He cannot be trusted."

Bonebreak flicked a finger toward the moon on the viewing screen. "I've heard about that sheriff with the metal badge on her face. Ellis. She's got a nasty reputation. Mosca used to come here to trade in black market human wards, but that came to an end when Ellis butchered six Mosca captains in a row. For no other reason than she didn't like the way we smelled!" He sniffed at his armpits as though reassuring himself of his delicate odor. "She's not someone to be trifled with, especially seeing as we have nothing of value to trade." He turned to Anya. "You seem smart for a small little childs. You agree with me, yes?"

There was the slightest undercurrent of fear in his voice. It was clear that Bonebreak was afraid of Anya, ever since she had proven she could not only control a gun through telekinesis, but also control *him*.

Anya didn't answer at first. Mali eyed her sidelong. It had

been several years since they'd last spoken, and the Anya she had known then—just seven years old—had held a child's black-and-white sense of morality. Now that she was older, had she learned that not everything was so straightforward?

"The wolves are strong," Mali whispered to Anya, "but the rabbits are clever."

Anya's eyes lit up at the words. That was the motto, taken from a fairy tale, that Anya had used during their escape three years ago from a private owner. It meant the Kindred might be powerful, but humans were clever. The motto had spread throughout the network of privately owned humans, even into the menageries, whispered as a seemingly innocent fairy tale so the Kindred wouldn't be suspicious. It had just begun to swell in force when Kindred guards had come for Anya, drugged her, and locked her in the Temple before her whisperings could incite any uprisings.

Anya grinned at Mali. "The rabbits are *very* clever." She turned to Bonebreak. "Does this ship have weapons?"

Bonebreak dabbed a cloth over his sweating forehead, shaking his head. "It's only a cruiser. A transport."

Anya tapped a finger over her lips as she looked over the steerage panel. "There might be a way to modify the controls. Reconfigure the propulsion system as a weapon." She shrugged. "At the least, we could use the ship as a battering ram. Return to Armstrong's surface and crash it into the main tent." She smacked her hands together, mimicking an explosion.

"Don't you dare!" Bonebreak gasped. "This ship cost eight thousand tokens!" He looked to Mali as though pleading for help.

"He's right," Mali said reluctantly. "We cannot crash it. We will need it eventually to get to Drogane." She paced, careful to give a wide berth to Lucky's body beneath the tarp, and then looked at Bonebreak. "You said the sheriff has worked with traders before. What if you approached her, claiming to be an exotic species trader, and offered to buy Cora and the others?"

Bonebreak groaned behind his mask. "Did you not hear me, little childs? Ellis killed the last six Mosca captains who approached her for a trade!" He rested his face in his hands, shaking his head. "It wouldn't work, anyway. They've seen our ship. It's a piece of junk. They know we're as poor as cave rats. That sheriff wouldn't even sit for a meeting."

Anya's big eyes danced with mischief. "Not if we had a different ship—a really impressive one. Didn't we pass a trade outpost a while back?"

Bonebreak sighed. "There's a Mosca outpost one-half of a rotation from here—about a human week's time. The owner keeps decommissioned ships for parts. But it would be impossible to trade this clunker for a new one. I'd have to use all my credit."

"So?" Mali asked bluntly.

Bonebreak sputtered, "I am a black market trader! Credit is the blood in my veins. Without credit, I might as well be dead."

Mali shrugged, not seeing the problem. She turned to Anya. "Can you communicate with Cora telepathically to let her know we are coming back for them?"

"I can try." Anya sat straighter in the chair, working the kinks out of her neck, and then closed her eyes. Her face strained with effort, a muscle tensing in her cheek, until she let out a long breath and shook her head. "It isn't working. I think we're too far away."

"Then we must hurry," Mali said. "Before they give up all hope. Or before Leon does something dumb, like try to be a hero, and gets himself killed."

"You heard her. Take us to that outpost!" Anya wiggled her fingers at Bonebreak, a not-so-subtle threat to control his mind again if he disobeyed.

Bonebreak grumbled, "If we are going to go through with this senseless plan, then it at least needs to appear convincing." He dug around in his bag until he came out with two small molded black rubbery pieces and the thick thread Mosca used to sew on masks. "It will look suspicious for me to be traveling with two free humans. The outpost trader would smell something rotten before we even landed. It is safest for me to mark as you my property. Just a . . . what is the word? Charade."

He held up the glistening shielding.

Mali eyed him uneasily. This had been exactly what she and Anya had feared when forming an alliance with a Mosca. Bonebreak's kind were untrustworthy and unpredictable.

This was why rescuing Cassian was so important: Cassian had prior claim to them. If they freed Cassian, Bonebreak wouldn't be able to betray them.

He wiggled the needle, awaiting their response.

Mali pulled Anya to the facilities room, where they could speak privately. "I do not trust him."

Anya rolled her eyes. "Neither do I, but he's kind of right. How else can we get Cora? She's got to run that Gauntlet. There's no one else." She ran a shaky hand over her shorn blond locks, the tremor in her fingers as bad as that of a woman of seventy, not a girl of ten—the result of having spent years sedated under heavy drugs. If not for that physical weakness, it might have been Anya herself running the Gauntlet as humanity's savior.

Anya shoved her shaking hand into her pocket, cheeks flushing pink, as though embarrassed by the weakness.

Mali tried hard to think of any other possibility but came up with nothing. "Fine. But once we get to Armstrong, Leon and I are going to find a way to board a Kindred supply ship back to the station. We must free Cassian—he is the only thing that can protect us from Bonebreak's claim."

Anya nodded.

They rejoined Bonebreak in the main cabin. Mali drew in a sharp breath, hating the Mosca's stench. He held up the needle enticingly. "Your hand, girl."

She extended it reluctantly. He set a small piece of rubber shielding over the pad of her thumb but paused before sewing. His gloved fingers grazed her own, the scars deeply embedded in her fingers. "You've been in a scrape."

"Yes. With the last Mosca who owned me," she said tensely. "I have scars, but he is dead." She let the warning linger.

Bonebreak shrugged and started sewing the shielding to her scarred thumb. She didn't flinch at the pain. Pain was something she was used to—something she had trained herself to withstand in order to shield her mind from outside prodding.

Bonebreak finished, ripping the thread with his teeth, and then repeated the process on Anya's thumb. "If we're leaving," he said, glancing at the viewing screen, "we'd better make it fast. It will take us nearly a full rotation to reach the outpost and return. I fear your friends may not last that long."

Mali nodded thoughtfully. She was a long way from trusting

Bonebreak, but she had to begrudgingly admit that she admired his practicality.

"Let's do it," Mali said. "The wolves are strong, but the rabbits are clever."

Anya grinned and plunked down in the copilot's seat. "Get us to that outpost," she ordered.

4

Cora

CORA REACHED OUT HER thoughts toward a pebble in the corner of the quarantine cell. Slowly, telekinetically, she lifted it. One inch. Two. Three—

She lost concentration and it fell.

"Dammit."

Only one day in quarantine and she already felt weak from the fetid air in the tents, and desperately thirsty, and hopeless. Rolf snored loudly on the other side of the cell. He had slept for what Cora guessed was twenty-four hours. She understood his exhaustion. The escape from the space station, Lucky's death, Bonebreak's offer to help her run the Gauntlet on the Mosca planet . . . the past few days had been a roller coaster. But unlike Rolf, she had remained awake despite her exhaustion, sick with worry. She hadn't had such bad insomnia since the first days in the Cage, when she and Lucky had stayed up all night talking about his life on his granddad's farm in Montana. *Lucky.* The thought of him brought a pang of sadness. She sucked in an audible breath, so sharp that Rolf stirred.

His face was creased with sleep. He rubbed his eyes as he looked at the quarantine bars. "So it wasn't just a nightmare."

She picked up the pebble, rolling it between her fingers. "Not the kind that goes away when you wake up."

Rolf came over and sat next to her. It seemed he'd forgiven her for snapping at him the day before. He squinted into the low light, looking around the empty tent. "Where did everyone go?"

"To the mines. They left a few hours ago. You've been asleep awhile. Here." She handed him a canteen of water that a deputy had brought them. It still held a few tepid sips.

He drank it quickly and then wiped his lips. "I thought I heard you cry out."

"I was thinking of Lucky." She glanced around to make sure all the deputies were outside before taking the journal from her waistband. "Ellis didn't find this when they searched us. It's Lucky's journal. It's the last thing I have of him."

He reached out for it and silently flipped through the pages, then stopped on a dog-eared page and read out loud:

> *Mom sacrificed herself for me. She knew the car*
> *accident was going to happen a second before it did*
> *and swerved the wheel to keep me safe. I guess that's*
> *what parents do for children. I guess that's what*
> *people do for the ones they love.*

Rolf looked up at Cora. "Lucky's mother died protecting him?"

Cora swallowed, thinking of that awful night on the bridge. She nodded shakily. "Yeah."

Rolf reread the journal entry thoughtfully. "What you said yesterday is true: Nok and I should have thought more before getting pregnant. But now I have to face the fact that I'm going to be a father. It isn't something I imagined—I couldn't even get a girlfriend back home. And my own father wasn't much of a role model. It was my brother they all admired—I was just the freakish younger brother they shipped off to school." He rubbed his face. "I don't have the first clue how to be a good parent."

Cora thought of her own father—his political job had meant he'd been distant, yes, but in a way, his work as a senator was to create a better world for Cora and Charlie. "I think it starts with building a home. A safe, loving community for her." She motioned to the tents. "This place might not even be so bad, if it wasn't run by a crazy sheriff."

Rolf nodded, considering this.

The tent flap opened, admitting blindingly bright daylight, and Cora quickly hid the journal. They both shielded their eyes as two deputies entered and stood guard while the long line of slaves filed back in. The slaves' hands were caked with dirt and bleeding from torn fingernails. Their eyes were vacant, gazes skimming over Cora and Rolf behind the quarantine bars and registering no curiosity or acknowledgment at all. They were broken shells of the people they must once have been. Watching them, Cora couldn't help imagining herself a year from now, just as broken and hollow.

And what of Nok and Leon, taken as wives? She shuddered to think what must be in store for them.

The slaves all sank back into their positions lying or sitting around the tent, spooning mouthfuls of the bland broth the guards distributed.

Dane came in, shutting the tent flap behind him. He strode to the quarantine cell and held up two bowls. "Chef's special. Marron root broth with powdered onions."

He passed the bowls between the bars. Cora's stomach shrank when she smelled the rank liquid.

"Listen, Dane," she whispered as she took the bowl. "There has to be another Kindred supply ship coming soon. If you figure out a way to get us all on it, I'll make it worth your while."

Dane shook his head. "There's no escape from Armstrong. Not under Ellis's watch." But he lingered by the bars, and Cora smiled. She knew he couldn't resist the possibility of a deal.

"You're not loyal to Ellis," she whispered. "I see how much you hate her. You're just her errand boy. She doesn't respect you. She'll probably throw you back in the mines as soon as she's tired of you."

"I have no idea what you're talking about."

"I think you do," Cora challenged. She leaned closer to the bars. "And you can still have your dream of being king here. Humanity's time is coming. You can feel it, can't you? All the other species know that we're growing more intelligent. There's a Gauntlet happening on the Mosca planet of Drogane about forty days from now. If I can get there and run it, we humans will be free to rule ourselves. No more Kindred oversight of this moon. I'll be offered a seat on the Council. I can get rid of Ellis and make you king of Armstrong."

Dane rolled his eyes, but there was also something hungry in them. "The Gauntlet? Those puzzle tests?" And then a realization crossed his face. "Wait, is that what this whole thing has been about?" His eyes went wide as he pieced it together. "That's why Cassian kept coming to the Hunt to meet with you, wasn't it? I *knew* there was something odd going on. He was coming to train you in secret, wasn't he?"

Dane spoke too loudly, and a few slaves turned at the word *gauntlet*. One slave, tucked into the rear shadows of the tent alone beneath a cloak—so short Cora thought it must be a child or a little person—sat ramrod straight, as though this information meant something to him or her.

Cora didn't answer Dane.

He barked a laugh. "So I'm right! The Gauntlet! God, you really are insane, aren't you? In forty days, you'll still be right here, a slave in the mines. If you even survive that long. Did Lucky believe such a stupid plan would work?"

Hot anger stained her cheeks. More slaves were listening now.

"Lucky believed in me," she whispered fiercely. "So did Cassian."

"Oh, of course. The Warden. Well, we all know what was really going on there. Disgusting, songbird. Even criminal. A relationship between a Kindred and a human—"

A few of the listening slaves let out gasps of revulsion.

"It wasn't like that," Cora said loudly enough for the slaves to overhear.

"No? Then why are you blushing like a twelve-year-old? Why did you always rush up to him whenever he came into the Hunt? Why did you gaze at him like a lovesick puppy while you were dancing together? I know what I saw."

Cora felt her mouth go dry. If they'd had any chance of the other slaves helping them, it was gone now. Only the small slave, the one in the shadows dressed in a cloak, hadn't turned away in disgust by Dane's gossip. The slave only reached out for the bowl of broth calmly. Cora caught sight of an arm covered in thick black hair. She blinked a few times. Had she seen wrong?

"Oops," Dane said. "I guess your little love affair isn't a secret anymore."

As he left, Cora squeezed the bars tightly, wishing they were his neck.

SHE TRIED HARD TO keep track of days but lost count some-where around their eighth or ninth day. It was impossible to tell if it was day or night outside until someone opened the tent flap. For the first few days, Rolf had paid careful attention to the com-ings and goings of the other slaves, scratching a tally of days in the dirt floor, but then even he lost count. Every day was the same. Marron root broth and tepid water. Slaves leaving, slaves coming. Tossing in and out of sleep. Practicing her training, learning to lift the pebble telekinetically higher each day. Push-ups. Sit-ups. At night, they swapped stories of what had happened to each of them over the last few months, and Cora told him about how, if she ever managed to get to the Gauntlet, she and Mali had figured out a possible way to cheat it by taking over the Assessors' minds and having them approve of her win without her even having to run it. They spent the rest of their nights planning escapes that were impossible, yet they clung to them because there was nothing else to cling to.

"We know the Kindred won't help us," Rolf whispered one morning after the slaves had left for the mines. "At least not the Kindred who monitor this moon. But Armstrong is in open

33

territory. Which means the other species must pass through here at times. The Mosca, the Gatherers, the Axion. Maybe one of them would help us. The Mosca took Leon in, back on the station."

"Yeah, but only because they could use him." Cora made a face, thinking of Bonebreak abandoning them. "I can't bring myself to trust them."

"What about the Gatherers?" Rolf asked.

"I met one once in a marketplace on the aggregate station. They're odd looking. Eight feet tall, long fingers, gray skin. He was wearing heavy robes and had a really serious air. Cassian told me they're monastic. They live on orbital ships and farm their own food with growlights and spend most of their time praying. They adhere strictly to rules, so I don't think they'd smuggle us off the moon." She reached for the canteen, but only a single drop of water fell to her lips. "Which leaves the Axion. I don't know much about them."

Rolf tapped his chin pensively. "I overheard the researchers in the dollhouse mention them a few times; the Axion had designed the medical equipment they used. They said the Axion built most of the equipment that all the intelligent species use—the interstellar ships, the materialization tech, the thought amplifiers." His fingers kept tapping on his chin. "There was a picture book in the dollhouse—not a human artifact, but something Serassi must have had made and not gotten quite right, because the page numbers were all wrong and the pictures were upside down. It was the history of the four intelligent species. It said that each one is in charge of a different part of the common society. The Mosca oversee trade and business. Gatherers handle spiritual matters. Kindred are the peacekeepers of the universe, the police and army and judicial system all together."

Cora rolled her eyes. "No wonder they're so obsessed with morality."

Rolf nodded. "And the Axion are in charge of technology. The picture book started with them. It said they're the original intelligent species; they gained intelligence even before the Gatherers, and they've tried to bring intelligence to other lesser species, even animals. Now they live on space stations the size of planets, much larger than the Kindred's aggregate stations. In the illustrations, the Axion cities were sleek and polished, bright white curving buildings with lots of spires. They haven't farmed or mined resources in centuries—they manufacture anything they need, food and clothes and raw materials, by reengineering light."

Cora wrinkled up her face. "That's all the book said about them?"

"All I recall." But then his eyes widened. "Though, remember when we first met Mali? She told us that the Axion have strange religious beliefs—that consuming human body parts gives them power."

Cora felt suddenly very cold. "I'm guessing they left that part out of the picture book."

Rolf nodded.

Over the next few days, Cora tried to talk to the other slaves through the bars, to ask if they had seen Leon and Nok as they went to and from the mines, but the slaves ignored her or gave her long, disgusted looks. Dane came daily to check their health: shining a light in their eyes and ears, taking their temperature, inspecting their skin for lesions.

"Please!" Rolf asked. "Just tell me if Nok's okay. I'll do anything."

"Nok?" Dane said. "Oh, she's okay, all right. The male deputies can't wait until she's out of quarantine. She's *really* popular."

Rolf lunged for Dane, swiping a hand between the bars, but Dane just stepped back out of reach and gave a little wave. "Until tomorrow."

As soon as he was gone, Rolf collapsed to the dirt floor, breathing fast.

"Easy," Cora said. "Or you'll hyperventilate. It isn't true. Dane just said that to get under your skin."

"You don't know that." He started rocking back and forth, chewing on his lip so hard that Cora could smell the tang of blood.

"We'll figure something out," she said. "We'll get out of here, and Nok and Leon too. Mali and Anya will come back. I know Anya's just a kid, but you saw what she could do—mind control an entire regiment of Mosca. She didn't have to help us, but she chose to. She won't abandon us. Even if she wanted to, Mali wouldn't let her."

Rolf still sobbed quietly. Cora wrapped her arms around him.

"It'll be okay, Rolf. I promise."

Through the bars, she caught sight of a set of eyes watching from the shadows. The short slave reached a gnarled, hairy hand out from beneath the cloak's long sleeve and took another calm sip of broth.

5

Cora

"THE ROOT MINES," DANE announced.

Cora and Rolf both shaded their eyes from the bright sun. After two weeks in the reeking quarantine cell, they had finally been cleared for a work assignment. They followed behind Dane, blinded by daylight and weak from lack of food, along the desert path that led from the tent encampment.

Dane pointed to a shadow on the horizon. Cora looked out over the wasteland but only saw the same monotonous stretch of scrubby bushes and parched soil she'd seen since they'd landed.

"That shadow?" she asked. "That's it?"

"It's the entrance to the mine," he said. "Well, more of a quarry, really. A giant pit. You'll see for yourselves."

The path was well trod, marked with footprints of the slaves who had walked in bare feet this way earlier in the day. Almost all the prints were larger than hers and Rolf's, and more than one was bloodstained. In the two weeks they'd been in quarantine, she hadn't made any friends among the other slaves in the tent, thanks to Dane. Most of the slaves were much older anyway—gaunt women and hulking men who kept their distance and looked at her with no kindness.

"What kind of root do you mine, exactly?" Rolf asked. His twitchiness had returned since they'd landed, and he blinked extra quickly.

"Marron root," Dane said. "This moon's soil can only support that one crop. We boil the roots down for food; it's the main staple, along with nutrient capsules the Kindred bring on their supply drops, but Ellis keeps a tight fist on those."

They approached a small hut at the edge of the gaping chasm. It was little more than a shade tarp, really, housing a handful of deputies who nodded to Dane. He went to them and exchanged a few words Cora couldn't quite make out, but she recognized his joking tone, the way they slapped him on the back. In the Hunt, she'd heard about the way Dane had weaseled his way from the bottom to Head Ward. Charming, manipulating, placating. Clearly he was trying to do the same thing here—and apparently succeeding.

"Ellis." One of them spit in the dirt loud enough for her to hear. "That *bitch*."

"Keena's no better," another said. "And all the tent guards. They act like they're so superior to us, guarding over a bunch of wife slaves in those fancy tents, while we're out here sweating our asses off. They're hoarding supplies, I know it."

They continued to talk, until their grumbling died down and Dane turned and signaled to Cora and Rolf. "Get over here. Stop dawdling."

Cora took a deep breath and stepped up to the edge of the

chasm. She had never been great with heights, from the time she was a little girl, climbing trees with her brother, Charlie. What she wouldn't give to be back there again. On Earth. With Charlie. Sadie barking at them from down below.

Was Earth even still there?

A pang clenched at her heart, and she closed her eyes. It was. It had to be. According to the Kindred's algorithms, there was almost a 70 percent chance that Earth still existed, a number she clung to desperately.

She thought of her family. The truth was, even if the Kindred were right, even if Earth was there, humans were still living on borrowed time. The humans and animals on Earth needed her just as much as the ones scattered throughout the universe did, even though they went about their lives with no knowledge of the Kindred or the Gauntlet. Earth wouldn't be there forever. Rainforest destruction, air pollution, warfare, biological weaponry, oppressive dictatorships, melting ice caps: sooner or later, humans would destroy their planet. She had to prove humanity's intelligence so that they would have a chance for autonomy off their planet.

She opened her eyes and approached the edge of the mine. Her stomach churned in an unsettling way, but she forced herself to look down. The chasm plunged dizzyingly deep and made her vision telescope in a light-headed way. Hundreds of slaves balanced like swarming ants on rickety scaffolding, picking at the exposed ground, monitored by mine guards stationed at the ends of each scaffold. The bottom of the pit was a slurry, sulfurous mix that released a noxious gas. Bile rose in her throat.

She pulled back, dry heaving into the scrubby bushes, sick with the fumes and the strain of weeks spent in the quarantine tent. For so long she had been furious at the Kindred, and yet for all their sins, the Kindred hadn't done anything this awful to them. What was it Cassian was always saying? *The Kindred don't enslave. The Kindred don't incarcerate. The Kindred don't kill. Those are uniquely* human *practices.*

And now, looking out over the swarming ants' nest of a mine with the smell of sulfur thick in her nose, she realized he was right.

She felt Dane's presence beside her. "You two are on tier eight." He handed them work assignment papers. "Give this to the guard there. The quota is fifty marron roots a day. Once you've mined them, you turn them in to those deputies, and they'll release you back to the slave barracks. No picks or shovels allowed, only bare fingers. Ellis is smarter than to arm her slaves."

She flexed her fingers. "Let's just get this over with."

He smiled flatly. "Don't worry, songbird. You won't last long. Neither of you."

It took Cora and Rolf ten minutes to navigate the rickety ladders down into the chasm's belly. It seemed that the highest-value slaves got choice slots near the top, where the air was fresher and the dirt looser. By the time they had descended below tier five, then tier six, then tier seven, Cora realized that the newer or weaker the slave, the closer to the sulfur-sludge they were stationed. Tier eight was second to last. The only slaves below them, at the very lowest rung, were Armstrong's criminals, who were chained to their individual slots. And below *them*, half sunk in the sludge, floated a few decaying bodies.

A deputy stationed at the end of the scaffolding held out his hand for their work assignment papers.

"Slots ten and eleven," the deputy read, and then handed them each a roughly woven basket and pointed along the rickety row toward two open stations. "Go on. Move."

Cora and Rolf balanced precariously on the swaying scaffolding as they passed the other slaves on the tier. None of them spoke or acknowledged Cora and Rolf, just like in the quarantine tent. Their faces were hollow and sunken. When one woman slipped from the tier above and crashed to theirs, Cora hurried to help her stand. The woman, empty-eyed, just crawled to the ladder, returned to her slot, and kept digging with bleeding fingers.

"This must be what humans become," Rolf observed, "when all hope is lost."

Cora gripped the scaffolding railing. "Yeah. This is why the Gauntlet matters. The Gauntlet *is* hope. The Gauntlet is how we create a safe world for your baby. For Sparrow. Like we talked about with Lucky's journal."

"Not if we're trapped here for the rest of our lives. How many days until it begins?"

"Twenty-six, I think," she said. "Maybe twenty-five. It was hard to tell in that tent."

"Either way, that's not a lot of time to stage an escape and get all the way to Drogane," Rolf said.

"Keep moving!" the deputy yelled.

They continued past slot number seven, then eight . . . and Cora stopped in surprise. Slot nine was occupied by a child. Or rather, by the abnormally short slave she'd seen watching them from the shadows. Standing, the slave seemed even shorter—barely four feet tall. The slave had its back to them, facing the wall of dirt. What Cora had thought, in the shadows, was a cloak was actually a dusty jumpsuit with a hood and long sleeves. Cora couldn't tell if it was a man or woman.

She stepped closer and set down her basket.

"Hello?" she said. "I'm Cora. This is Rolf. I think we saw you in the tent—"

The slave slowly turned. A hairy face looked out from beneath the hood. Huge brown eyes. A wrinkled, leathery forehead. Cora nearly leaped in surprise.

A chimpanzee.

Of course. The hairy arm. The gnarled hand. The chimp was bigger than ones she'd seen at zoos, and it carried itself more upright. It peered at Cora almost suspiciously, unnaturally cognizant, and then returned to its digging.

Cora was too stunned to speak.

She turned to Rolf and whispered, "You said the Axion experimented on animals to make them more intelligent. Do you think this is one of them?"

Rolf blinked. "It's possible. It's clearly more advanced—maybe even halfway to being intelligent."

The chimp flinched, then kept digging.

"I think it heard you," Cora whispered, and then cleared her throat. "Can you understand me? Do you speak? Are you intelligent?"

The chimp reached out a long toe and scrawled in the dirt:

ARE YOU?

The chimp threw them a look Cora swore was sarcastic and then dropped another marron root into its basket.

"You two! New slaves!" yelled the deputy stationed at the end of their scaffold. "Get digging. You have to reach quota before nightfall or you sleep out here. And stop bothering Willa." He adjusted the cloth over his nose, but from the look on his face it didn't do much to cover the sulfur smell. Cora briefly wondered who he'd pissed off to get assigned so deep in the pit.

Reluctantly, Cora and Rolf took their slots, but Cora kept throwing glances at the chimp, who the deputy had called Willa. The wall of soil was extremely compact, nearly as dense as concrete. She had to crumble it away with her fingernails, and by the time she'd exposed half a marron root, two of her nails had split. The oversized sun shone directly into the pit, baking them. They worked for an hour, then two, then three. Sweat soaked through her clothes. Into her basket the marron roots went, one by one, as the day dragged by.

"Willa," the deputy called. "Time for your water break. Let's go."

The chimp pushed back her hood and jumped straight onto the edge of the scaffolding. Instead of squeezing by the other slaves, she simply swung hand over hand to the end and then scaled the ladder to the water bucket.

As soon as she was gone, Cora glanced at the chimp's slot. The digging was well organized—far more meticulous than Cora's own sloppy work. "How do you think she ended up on Armstrong?"

Rolf shrugged. "The Axion must have dropped her here."

Willa returned, eyeing them as though she knew they were talking about her. She pulled her hood up against the sun and returned to digging.

Cora kept throwing glances toward her as she worked. It

was incredible to see an animal with such focus and patience. Lucky would have loved to meet this chimp—he, more than anyone, had believed humans and animals weren't so different. A pang of grief hit her at the thought of Lucky, and she squeezed her eyes closed and pressed a hand to her back, where his notebook was still tucked into her waistband.

God, she missed him.

When she opened her eyes, the chimp was watching her. She returned to digging, but not before Cora had noticed Willa's eyes resting on her waistband. The chimp dropped another marron root in her basket and dusted off her hands.

And then Cora noticed the pattern the chimp was using to dig. Even squares, staggered three across and four down. The particular shape struck her as strangely familiar. She'd seen that pattern before, hadn't she? Where?

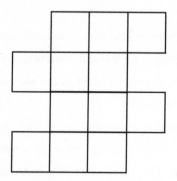

And then it struck her.

The Gauntlet.

She gasped—yes, it was identical to the Gauntlet model that Cassian had shown her. But what did this chimpanzee have to do with the Gauntlet? She remembered something Cassian had said about the lesser species who had tried to run the Gauntlet:

Other species have not been as successful. The Conmarines. The Scoates. A half dozen others, in sectors very far from here. Even a chimpanzee tried to run it once—the Axion had experimented on it to give it higher intelligence. But they all failed the perceptive puzzles.

Cora felt a tingle of excitement in her limbs as she dared a closer glance at Willa. Could this be the same chimp? Mali had said that all the previous human runners of the Gauntlet had been killed in its dangerous puzzles or had gone insane from the mental strain, and so there was no one who could coach Cora.

Yet maybe there *was* someone who had run the Gauntlet before, who could teach Cora its secrets. The fact that it was a superintelligent chimpanzee hardly fazed her—she'd seen crazier things since the Kindred had abducted her.

"Hey," Cora whispered to the chimp, nodding toward the twelve-squared pattern. "That shape. I've seen it before."

Willa ignored her as she moved on to digging out the next square.

"I know you can hear me," Cora said. "And I'm not stupid. That shape is the Gauntlet. I know it and I think you do, too."

Willa's head slowly turned, her brown eyes wide. For a second Cora thought that this would be it. Willa was the answer to their problems. Willa knew the secrets of the Gauntlet, secrets not even Cassian knew. She could help train Cora. She could ensure that Cora won—if they got off of Armstrong, that was. Soon.

"It's true, isn't it?" Cora whispered.

And then Willa threw a clod of soil in her face.

Cora sputtered out dirt.

"Slave in slot ten!" the guard called. "Water break!"

Cora wiped at her mouth, coughing, as Willa calmly returned to digging. Rolf gave her a questioning look.

"Isn't it early to be making enemies?" he whispered.

"Not an enemy," Cora said as she passed by toward the water bucket. "Our new best friend, though she doesn't know it yet. And the only hope we might have." She coughed out more dirt.

Rolf flicked some soil off Cora's shoulder. "I'd say we have a long way to go to convince her of that."

6

Nok

FOR THE LAST TWO weeks, Nok had been isolated in a small quarantine tent, made to sleep in filth, and given only some reeking bland soup once a day.

But everything had changed that morning: they'd let her take a bath.

She reveled in scrubbing the grime from her limbs, in plunging her head underwater, in rinsing her hair. It was a magnificent indulgence, though the water was only tepid.

"Hurry up in there," a deputy called through the tent's flap.

She sighed. All good things came to an end. She stood and squeezed the water from her hair, pulled on a robe they'd set out for her, and smoothed a hand over her belly, barely hidden by the folds of the robe. The best she could figure, she was twenty-two or twenty-three weeks along. She wouldn't be able to hide it much longer. And then what? Even if by some miracle they could get off Armstrong and to the Mosca planet, she certainly didn't trust

Bonebreak. He'd already betrayed them once. What was to keep him or one of his Mosca friends from grabbing Sparrow and selling her to some private owner?

Nok scrubbed a towel once more through her hair. She'd kill for some conditioner. Hell, even soap. And yet the wish was fleeting—she had bigger worries now that quarantine was over.

She leaned closer to the tent flap, listening to the conversation just outside between the two deputies guarding the tent. They were talking about American football. It sounded like they had both grown up in America, one in Boston and the other in a town she'd never heard of, and they were speculating whose team was kicking whose ass now on the field.

She rolled her eyes. Earth was gone for all they knew, and they were still talking sports.

"Is she finished?" said another voice, this one female.

The tent flap opened and an older woman with threads of gray in her dark hair came in. She gave Nok a quick, inspecting gaze. "Nok, right? I'm Keena. I oversee the female wives' tent." She started coughing and took out a handkerchief. "Feel better after a bath?"

Nok cinched the robe. "A little more like myself," she said neutrally. Despite the woman's kind words—the first kind words she'd heard here—Nok didn't trust her. She'd had two weeks to imagine what happened in the wives' tents, and each thought was more disturbing than the last.

Keena coughed again as she motioned for Nok to follow her through the den of tents, and Nok did so hesitantly, taking in every detail. They entered a ramshackle canvas corridor lit by candles that connected various tent rooms. From the noises coming from within the tent rooms, Nok could guess what was happening within. Her stomach tensed. As if sensing her apprehension, Keena cleared her throat.

"The wives' job is to keep Ellis's deputies distracted," she explained. "The more distracted they are, the less likely they are to try to stage a mutiny." Keena spoke so bluntly that Nok realized a mutiny must be a very real possibility. "This is her way of appeasing them. There's a separate tent for male and female wives. You clean up after the deputies, cook for them, do their washing, serve them drinks, laugh at their jokes, and . . ." Keena paused.

"Sleep with them," Nok finished flatly.

Keena's face darkened. "Yes. Unfortunately, Ellis permits that."

Nok pressed a hand on her belly protectively, then looked toward the other tents. "Where are my friends?"

"The blond girl and the skinny boy have been taken to the mines. The other one, the big guy, has caused quite a stir. Ellis wanted him as her personal wife, but he wasn't too keen on it. Didn't want to wear the shiny pants and cook her dinner."

From the way the woman's voice took on an edge of disdain, Nok got the feeling Keena wasn't Ellis's biggest fan. She smiled to herself. Maybe Keena was more trustworthy than she'd first thought.

"Leon can take care of himself," Nok said. "And so can I."

Keena smiled sadly. "I admire your bravery, but I fear it might be misplaced. The life of a wife on Armstrong isn't a pleasant one. I'm not sure which is worse, being a slave here or the mines—at least here there's a longer life expectancy. As long as you don't get the sand-cough, like me." She turned and kept walking, the rumbling cough deep in her chest. "I've seen so many girls

49

where you are now, shipped here when they turn nineteen. Young and brave and hopeful. They believe all those ridiculous rumors that it's a paradise." She shook her head. "I wasn't so naive. The Kindred took me on my thirtieth birthday and, after some tests, determined I wasn't worth putting in their enclosures, so they sent me here. A sheriff named Randall was in charge then. He was mad for power too—the sheriffs always are. I was enslaved, like you. I worked in these tents for five years. Then Ellis rose to power. She made me a deputy and put me in charge of the female wives."

"You must be grateful to her, then," Nok said carefully, gauging Keena's reaction.

Keena paused at the flap to a tent, giving Nok a hard look. "Do I look like I enjoy throwing nice girls like you to men like those?" She gestured to the boisterous sounds of male deputies coming from the nearest tents. "The mine guards are the worst. Brutes—and I don't just mean the male ones. They're as rotten as the fumes they smell all day."

"I told you," Nok said, "I can take care of myself."

Keena's look softened. Her eyes fell to Nok's stomach, disguised by the robe's tie. "I hope that's true—for you *and* your baby."

Nok sucked in a worried breath. "You can tell?"

"You've done a good job hiding it, but I was a nurse in an obstetrician's office back home. I knew the moment I saw you."

A hesitant flicker of hope fluttered to life in Nok's chest. An obstetrician's nurse—especially one who could keep a secret—could be exactly what she needed.

Keena pressed something into Nok's hand. "Vitamins," she whispered. "Hide them in your robe pocket. They aren't easy to get—Ellis hoards any that come in on the supply drops. But you'll need them for that baby to be healthy. It isn't a problem we've ever had to deal with before. The Kindred sterilize everyone else as part of processing before sending them here."

Nok slipped the bottle into her robe, touched by the risk the woman had taken for her. Maybe giving birth on Armstrong wouldn't be the worst possibility, if there were women like Keena here. She nodded her thanks.

Keena opened the tent flap.

Four men sat on low benches in the small canvas room. It was just as faintly lit as the rest of the tents, candles flickering on a low table laden with strong-smelling alcohol. Nok stepped in, and the men's conversation died. Four sets of eyes leered at her bare legs.

Keena started coughing again behind her, then let out a long sigh.

But Nok didn't need anyone's pity. Keena didn't know what Nok had been through. Keena didn't know about Miss Delphine, her modeling agent back in London, who had trained her in exactly how to manipulate men like these.

Nok rested her hands on her hips.

"All right. Listen." Her commanding tone seemed to surprise both the men and Keena. "I know why you're here, but I have another proposal."

She paused for dramatic effect, pacing slowly around the table as though she were a sheriff herself, not a slave. "I've just come from Earth. Where I watched Wimbledon, the World Series, college basketball. I know it all." She raised an eyebrow tantalizingly. "Pour me a drink and I'll tell you everything you've missed at home."

As much as Nok had hated Miss Delphine, the talent manager had possessed one redeeming trait: she'd bet heavily on sports, which had the best return in the business. And she'd sent Nok to place every single bet.

The men stared at her, slack-jawed.

"Come on," Nok urged. "How long has it been since you were taken? Five years? Ten? Don't you want to know who won the World Cup?"

The deputies glanced among themselves, stupefied.

"What are you doing?" Keena whispered, but Nok just tossed her a reassuring look. The men kept shifting, uncertain, but then one stood abruptly. He reached down nervously, poured a glass of the alcohol, and held it out to Nok.

"Screw it," he said. "I don't care about sports. But if you tell me what's happened on the last three seasons of *Vampires of Brooklyn*, I'll do anything you want."

Keena coughed in surprise.

Nok grinned.

She strode into the room, motioning for the men to part ways so she could have the best seat with the fluffiest cushions. She kicked her legs on the table and waved away the offered glass.

"Last I saw," she started, "Tara had just dumped Franklin. Now hand me some of those grapes."

Keena hovered by the tent entrance. When their eyes met, Nok saw a flicker of emotion on the old guard's face that hadn't been there before.

Nok recognized it at once.

Hope.

7

Cora

FOR THE NEXT TWO days, back in the marron root mines, Cora tried to get Willa to talk to her. She whispered to her while they were working and begged for information on the Gauntlet, but Willa always ignored her.

At least she didn't throw any more dirt clods.

"Is it because of what you heard Dane say?" Cora whispered at last. "About the Kindred that I . . . I had a relationship with?"

Willa tossed her an exasperated look, flicking her fingers as though she couldn't care less about the romantic entanglements of Kindred and humans.

"Then what?" Cora asked. "Why won't you help?"

But she got no answer.

That night, Cora tried to find Willa in the slave barracks tent, but the chimp had a habit of sleeping high in the rafters, out of reach. When Cora called her name, trying to get her attention, Willa just yawned dramatically.

At last, Cora let out a resigned breath. "Okay, I get it. You're not going to talk to me. I'll leave you alone." She paused. "I never meant to bring up any bad memories. I can't imagine what it must have been like to go through the Gauntlet." She looked down at her fingers, cut and bruised from digging in the tough soil. "I know how the puzzles can mess with you," she said more quietly. "I was in an enclosure filled with them, and they drove my group apart. We turned against each other. We're only now piecing back together our trust." She glanced over her shoulder at Rolf. "It took time to remember we were on the same side. All humans are."

Willa, high in the shadows of the rafters, said nothing. But her head was turned slightly, as though deep in thought.

A sore on Cora's middle finger was oozing, and she took out a jar of ointment from her pocket. Getting it hadn't been easy—the day before, she'd traded another slave two rations for it. She started to unscrew the lid but then thought about Willa's hands, which were even more damaged than her own.

She set the jar of ointment on the ground beneath the rafter. "Here. You need this more than me. I've seen the scrapes on your fingers. If they get infected, you won't be able to work and you'll end up in the sludge with the other bodies."

Willa made no move to get the ointment, though she rubbed her damaged hands together, hairy fingers running over the scars.

Cora glanced at the other slaves. Though most were fast asleep, a few eyes were watching her in the darkness. If she left the salve there, someone might steal it before Willa came down. Better to give it to the chimp directly. She drew a deep, centering breath and concentrated on the jar. It was heavier than the pebble, but her weeks of practice had paid off, and she was able to telekinetically lift it clear up to the ceiling and balance it on the rafter next to Willa.

The chimp immediately sat straighter, incredulous gaze moving from the jar to Cora.

Cora met her eyes. "I wasn't lying. It isn't a game to me. Humans are evolving and I have to do everything I can to keep us safe. Even if it means facing the Gauntlet."

The chimp paused, still looking shocked at Cora's display of telekinesis, then picked up the jar. She held it up in a silent, hesitant gesture of thanks.

Cora nodded.

She made her way back to the corner of the tent and sat next to Rolf, shaking her head. "Whoever experimented on her, they must have been cruel. She won't say a word."

She and Rolf shared a bowl of marron root broth and curled up to try to sleep. She tossed and turned, images flashing behind her eyes. She was back in the menagerie's safari hunting grounds. Only this time, she was the hunter. She clutched a rifle with both hands, following tracks in the sand to the water hole, big tracks that could only belong to a Kindred. She cocked the rifle and then spun around a boulder, catching sight of a uniformed Kindred.

She let out a volley of bullets that pierced his arms and neck.

The man fell.

She ran up and gasped. It was Cassian in the water. Drowned. Dead.

She'd killed him.

A crumpled piece of paper fell on her face, waking her.

She jerked upright, feeling disoriented. A wave of heat assaulted her, and she coughed a few times, remembering that she was on Armstrong. There was no watering hole, no cadaver pock-marked with bullets.

Just a nightmare, she told herself. *Cassian isn't dead. He can't be.*

If he hadn't survived the torture, she would sense it, she just knew. And yet the ominous feeling of the dream didn't leave her. She pressed a hand to her throat, strangled by guilt. She'd seen Cassian strapped down and tortured. For all she knew, he really had died. And wouldn't she be just as much to blame as if she'd fired that rifle?

She picked up the crumpled paper, smoothing it out.

The Gauntlet will take everything from you. It searches for weaknesses and exploits anything it finds. You say you love this Kindred Warden; think hard about who you care about. The Gauntlet will test you on it—it tested me. It defeated me. Now I have nothing. And you are asking me to revisit that dark time—a heavy request.
Prove first that you deserve my help.

Cora looked up into the rafters, but Willa was long gone. What had changed the chimpanzee's mind? The display of teleki-netic abilities? Maybe it was the salve too. In a place like Armstrong, a selfless gift—even a small one—carried a lot of weight.

All the rest of that night, Cora stayed up, awake with the possibilities. Back home, she'd had to prove herself too. For her first few weeks in Bay Pines, she'd tried hard not to be noticed, to keep to herself, but it hadn't made a difference. Word had gotten around that she was a rich kid, and the other delinquents threatened to beat her up in the cafeteria bathroom unless she transferred commissary funds to their accounts. It had been her roommate, Queenie, who'd finally agreed to help her. Queenie had taught her how to fight back. How to time her movements so a guard was always near. How to cheat at cards. Of course, it was prison, and so Queenie wanted something in exchange—but not commissary funds.

You have a real gift, Queenie had said, reading through Cora's notebook. *Not everyone can do this. Write songs like this.*

It's just some lyrics, Cora had said.

It isn't. It's the beauty and the pain. The darkness and the hope. Queenie had picked up a pen. *I feel all that too, especially in this place, but I don't know what to do with those feelings. Teach me to put those feelings into words, and I'll teach you to defend yourself.*

A deputy came in, searching the crowd of slaves, and pointed at her. Cora forgot about her deal with Queenie. She crumpled Willa's paper and stuffed it into her shirt.

"Ellis wants to see you," the deputy said, then kicked Rolf awake. "Both of you."

Cora blinked around the tent at the slumbering bodies of the other slaves, only their tattered clothes for cover, each other's arms as pillows. She caught sight of a hairy leg hanging from the far rafters—Willa's. Whenever they got off of this moon, Cora promised herself, they were taking that chimp with them. She'd proven her worth to Queenie, and she could prove herself to Willa too.

The deputy prodded them with his rifle. "Up. Now."

Rolf winced as he stood, shaking out his muscles. Cora

followed them across the tent. Outside, the desert night was still warm. The sun was just starting to rise in the east, casting a purplish light over the ground. Heat from the sand radiated up in undulating waves that blurred the mountains. Cora paused and closed her eyes, breathing in the fresh air. On the horizon, the Kindred's transport hub loomed like a dark shadow.

"Move," the deputy ordered.

THE DEPUTY LED THEM around the edge of the slave barracks tent, and Cora nearly stumbled in surprise: the vast plains beyond the tent encampment, usually empty, were now filled with a fleet of ships. There had to be fifty. In the faint starlight, their identical sleek white hulls glistened. A masked, uniformed flight crew stood at attention beneath each ship. A veritable army of hundreds.

"Those look like the illustrations of Axion ships from the picture book," Rolf whispered.

"Yeah, but look at the crews," she said. "They're hunch-backed. It's a Mosca army." She gave him a meaningful look and then mouthed, "Bonebreak?"

Rolf's eyes widened. "You think he stole all those ships?"

"Inside," the deputy ordered, holding back the flap to Ellis's command center tent.

Cora stepped into a tented room that was blessedly cool. Next to her, Rolf sighed with relief at leaving the heat. The tent reminded her of something out of a fairy tale, with its big pillows on the floor, oil lamps flickering on poles, low tables laden with bowls of water and flowers.

Ellis sat on an elevated platform that surrounded a crackling fire pit. She was bent forward, talking to someone out of view behind a canvas curtain. Nok sat cross-legged on the floor nearby, still wearing her apron to hide her baby bump. She'd bathed, and her hair was soft and loose. She caught sight of Cora and Rolf and gave them a reassuring nod. There was even a fresh streak of pink dye in her hair, which ruffled in the breeze.

Breeze?

Cora looked around for the source and nearly laughed.

Standing behind them, shaded in the corner, was Leon. He was shirtless, wearing blue satin pants, fanning the room with an enormous paper fan.

"Bring them here," Ellis said, glancing in their direction. "Put them in that corral."

The deputy prodded her in the back toward a small, fenced-in ring like one used for holding cattle. From here, she could finally see Ellis's companion.

She grinned.

Bonebreak!

She'd never imagined she'd be so happy to see the hunch-backed Mosca who had almost gotten them killed. Maybe the Mosca weren't as bad as she'd first imagined. Bonebreak hardly looked like himself now. His dented, dingy shielding had been replaced with gleaming white armor that matched the ships outside. He reclined on an enormous pile of pillows, empty platters of food sprawled around him, massaging his belly with a gloved hand. Behind him, Anya and Mali stood at attention like servants. They had some sort of Mosca shielding sewn to their thumbs but otherwise looked unharmed.

Mali gave her the slightest hint of a nod—otherwise pretending they had never met.

Cora closed her eyes and thought, *Anya, can you hear me?*

The girl's big eyes snapped to Cora.

Bonebreak is enjoying this way too much. Anya's sarcastic voice projected into her head. *We couldn't afford to buy a new ship—the best we could do was a holo-projector. The army outside and the fleet of ships are only holograms to make Ellis think we're more powerful than we are. We need to hurry up before Ellis's deputies figure that out.*

Cora glanced at Ellis—if the sheriff could levitate guns with her mind, there was a chance she could read telepathic messages too. But Ellis didn't even glance at them.

Once we free you all, Anya continued, *you, Nok, and Rolf will come with me to Drogane. Mali and Leon will sneak back to the station to get Cassian.*

Cora gave a slight nod.

"These are the youngest humans I have," Ellis said, her words tense, as though she hated every moment in Bonebreak's presence. "And that one there, with the fan, as well." She motioned to Leon. "He's been nothing but trouble. Refuses to bow. Refuses to sweep. You can have him for half price. Call it a peace offering." She looked around as though just remembering something. "Oh, and there's another young one." She turned to one of her deputies. "Get Dane."

Cora tried to hide her surprise.

"What about that one?" Bonebreak pointed to Nok casually. "She looks young."

Ellis rubbed her chin, finger tapping on the badge soldered to her cheek. "That one would cost you extra. She's become quite a favorite among my deputies."

"I'll pay you well for her."

The deputies returned with a sleepy-eyed Dane, whose hair was mussed. He stopped cold when he saw the other teenagers herded together in the corral.

"What's going on?" he said, but Ellis nodded to a deputy, who silenced Dane with a rifle butt to the jaw. Dane cried out as the deputy opened the corral gate and prodded him in with the others.

"Wait!" Dane said, gripping the corral bars. "You can't sell me to this . . . creature. I'm a deputy. I—"

"You're a traitor, is what you are," Ellis said. "And a mutineer. Or didn't you think I'd find out that you've been whispering to the mine guards about how I'm getting old and soft? How it's time for a replacement?"

Dane's face went white.

Ellis smiled darkly. "You're lucky that I haven't put your head on a spike in front of the sheriff's office as a warning to other would-be mutineers."

Dane turned to Cora with wide, fearful eyes.

"Did you hear that?" he whispered. "She'll kill me. You have to take me with you."

Cora noted the desperation in his voice with a certain amount of satisfaction. She'd once begged Dane for help, and now *he* was doing the begging. But as much as she wanted to tell him to screw off, she hesitated. For what it was worth, Dane had truly cared about Lucky. The grief in his eyes hadn't been an act. And his words still stung her—that anyone who got too close to her wound up dead.

Cora nodded reluctantly to Bonebreak, a signal for him to include Dane. She hoped she wasn't making a mistake.

"That means our negotiations are over, Mosca," Ellis snapped. "I've made you my offer, and your smell is starting to make me sick."

"Likewise," Bonebreak said, standing theatrically and brushing the crumbs off the glistening white shielding over his red jumpsuit. "My fleet and I will be most pleased to be gone from this reeking moon of yours. I would say it's been a pleasure doing business with you, but it hasn't."

The insult didn't seem to faze Ellis. She signaled to her deputies. "Help load the slaves he's purchased onto his ships. If Dane gets a punch or two in the process, I won't object."

"Err, no!" Bonebreak interrupted quickly. "We'll load them fine ourselves. No need for you to go anywhere near the ships. Better for you all to keep a distance from them altogether, actually, for no particular reason at all. Now, I'll be on my way—"

He was interrupted by a loud ringing from a piece of equipment on one of the tables. Everyone went quiet.

It rang again.

Ellis pointed to one of her guards. "Hand me that intercom."

The deputy picked up the communication device as though it might bite and passed it to Ellis, who pressed a few buttons and then put it to her ear.

"Yes," she said.

For a tense few moments, no one spoke. Cora could barely hear a voice on the other end but couldn't tell if it was human. A worried feeling took root in the pit of her stomach. They were so close to being free. Just another few minutes and Bonebreak would conclude the negotiations. They'd be racing across the desert to his fake fleet of ships.

Ellis continued to listen to the voice, expressionless. "I understand." She hung up the intercom and turned to Bonebreak.

Cora's worry grew.

"Okay, okay, fifty extra tokens," Bonebreak said in a rush. "You drive a hard bargain." He must have sensed, like Cora, that whatever Ellis had heard on that intercom might be trouble. "Fifty each and seventy-five for the pink-haired girl, that's two hundred seventy-five tokens, quite a payday. Anya, my slave, fetch the tokens and we'll be on our way, stench and all—"

"No," Ellis said quietly. "I don't think so." Slowly, her lips curled into a smile. "That was the Kindred transportation officers we liaise with. Their supply shuttle wasn't scheduled to arrive until tomorrow, but it's come early. It's docking at the transport hub as we speak. And as it turns out, they informed me that these humans, who so suspiciously appeared out of nowhere, are fugitives. The Kindred are willing to pay well to have them back."

"You can't give them to the Kindred!" Bonebreak yelled.

"Oh, I'm not *giving* them to anyone. I'm selling them to whichever party offers the most, you or the Kindred." She smiled. "We're going to have a bidding war."

8

Cora

A BIDDING WAR?

Cora couldn't read Bonebreak's face behind his mask, but from the way his body went rigid, she knew he must be as panicked as she was. More of Ellis's deputies came in, followed by three uniformed soldiers who were nearly seven feet tall. Her breath vanished.

Kindred.

At first they were just silhouettes against the early morning sky. Two women and one man. Muscles like granite. Dark hair pulled back or else cut close to the scalp. They moved in the stiff way that revealed their emotions were cloaked. The flames in the fire pit cast a harsh light over their copper-colored skin, making it almost glow.

The male Kindred faced the fire-pit platform. Cora bit back a curse.

It was Fian, the Intelligence Council official who had

pretended to be Cassian's friend and confidant, but who had actually been a Council spy. He was the reason Cassian was being tortured and the reason she'd fled to this desolate moon.

Her fingers sparked with rage.

"Ah," Ellis said. "The other bidding party has arrived." She motioned to the bench on the opposite side of the platform from Bonebreak. "Have a seat, Kindred guests. Deputies, corral the rest of the wards. We can't have them trying to escape. They're our bargaining chips."

Ellis's deputies prodded Nok and Leon into the corral. Cora gripped the wooden bars, glaring at Fian.

"You know that one?" Nok whispered.

"Unfortunately," Cora said tightly. "He works for the Council. He's been trying to stop me from running the Gauntlet."

On the platform, Ellis narrowed her eyes at the Kindred. "You aren't the transport supply officers we normally deal with. Where are Titian and Malessi?"

"This is no routine supply drop," Fian said coldly. "I am here on official Council business. I have come for those wards. They are Kindred property. Hand them over to us now."

At seven feet tall, few creatures were more intimidating than Fian. But Ellis only smiled grimly, the firelight glinting off the badge soldered to her cheek. She jumped down from the fire-pit platform and reached between the corral bars, grabbing Nok's fist.

"Kindred property?" She held out Nok's bare hand. "I see no tags. I see no paperwork."

"A technicality," Fian said impatiently. "They escaped before they could go through the proper processing."

Ellis raised an eyebrow, shaking her head. "They are

untagged and on neutral territory, which means they're free humans. And as the lawmaker who supervises all free humans on Armstrong, it is my authority to govern them."

"*We* granted you that authority. We could take it away."

"The Kindred didn't grant me anything," she countered. "The sheriff's position has been designated by the Intelligence Council at large: Kindred, Axion, Gatherers, and Mosca. As only one-fourth of that, you have no more power or authority here than he does." She threw a finger toward Bonebreak. "And so you see, we're at an impasse. But I'm a reasonable person. Take a seat and we can discuss the fate of these wards."

She motioned to the platform's bench opposite Bonebreak.

The wrinkle in Fian's brow deepened. He exchanged a few words with his colleagues in their Kindred language. He and the other Kindred sat on the platform stiffly. Though their faces were perfectly calm masks of indifference, Cora could practically feel the rage burning deep beneath Fian's emotional cloak.

Ellis just smiled.

"Excellent. Let the bidding begin." She climbed back up on the platform and paced before the fire pit. "The rules are simple. This needn't take long. Whoever pays the most tokens gets the wards." She turned to Bonebreak. "The Mosca has already offered two hundred seventy-five."

"What do we do," Nok whispered to Cora, "if the Kindred win?"

Cora shook her head, uncertain. "We'll cause a distraction and make a run for Bonebreak's ship. As many of us as can make it. Leon, you'll grab Mali and head for the shuttle dock."

He nodded.

On the platform, the negotiations continued.

"We only want the blond one," Fian said, signaling to Cora. "We'll give you one hundred tokens for her."

Cora shivered as his black eyes met hers. For a second, she felt a flash of connection. His emotional cloak slipped for the quickest instant, revealing a glimpse into his head. She felt roiling panic there that he was desperately trying to hide. Panic that seemed completely un-Kindred-like. She saw an image of the aggregate station in chaos. Kindred soldiers dead. The marketplace in shambles. But she didn't know what any of it meant.

"They're a package deal," Ellis said flatly. "And the price has just gone up to three hundred."

"Three fifty!" Bonebreak answered.

"You don't have three fifty," Fian said flatly. "That isn't even a real suit of shielding. It's holographic, just like that fleet outside the encampment. These humans may not be able to see through your tricks, but we can."

Bonebreak jumped up, outraged. "I have never been so insulted!"

Fian's face remained calm outwardly, but his fist was flexing. His patience was growing thin.

"Enough!" Ellis said. Her voice thundered through the tent, silencing even Fian. "Deputies, fetch me that one—the girl with pink hair."

Nok's eyes went big as two deputies swung open the corral gate, reaching in and grabbing her. Other guards held Rolf and Leon back with guns. Nok twisted as they dragged her up to the platform, where the fire sent shadows flickering over her frightened face.

"I'm tired of these games," Ellis said. She grabbed Nok by the hair, forcing her to stand in front of the fire pit. "I want final offers. And if they aren't high enough, I'm going to toss each of these wards, one at a time, into the flames until your bids *are* high enough. The blond one you both want so much burns last."

Nok let out a scream, trying to claw out of Ellis's grasp. Though Ellis was strong, she was a good six inches shorter than Nok, and Nok flailed so violently that Ellis had to widen her stance to hold on to her.

"You can't!" Rolf yelled. "Stop!"

Nok screamed again, twisting so hard that Ellis nearly fell over. Ellis let out a frustrated growl and tossed a look to the knives on Bonebreak's trays of sliced cheeses. She jerked her chin, and the knives rose telekinetically. They glided eerily through the air to where Nok struggled. Two of them hovered on either side of her head, blades pointed at her temples.

Nok, breathing hard, stopped struggling.

Cora glanced at Fian. This was what he and the Council had most feared: proof of humanity's growing abilities. It wasn't just Anya and Cora who had perceptive skills—if Ellis did too, then there had to be more. Humans all over the known universe, in menageries and enclosures and maybe even back on Earth. But Fian didn't flinch at the psychic display.

He already knows, she realized. *That's why he's trying so hard to stop me from running. One last desperate attempt to silence us.*

"It's a pity," Ellis said, admiring Nok. "She's a pretty girl." She shoved Nok an inch closer to the fire, the floating knives moving with her.

Rolf yelled, "She's pregnant!"

The room went silent. Ellis jerked Nok back and pulled back the frilly apron over her belly. For a second, whispers spread throughout the tent, the tension palpable.

Then Ellis shrugged. She flicked a finger, making the knife blades press closer against Nok's temples. "That's two into the fire, then."

"Five hundred!" Bonebreak sputtered. "That's as high as my credit goes! Check the system!"

Ellis glanced at Fian.

The Kindred only shrugged. "Go ahead and throw her into the fire, pregnant or not. That one means nothing to me."

Ellis's eyes narrowed. "You're bluffing."

Fian didn't blink. "Burn her and see."

"No!" Rolf cried. "Nok!"

He tried to climb up and over the corral bars, but a swarm of deputies aimed rifles at him. Cora's heart was thrashing with panic. She grabbed the corral bars, knuckles going white. This couldn't be happening.

Think!

Ellis gave Nok a solid push toward the flames.

"No!" Cora yelled.

Time seemed to move more slowly. She forgot about the deputies. She forgot about the Kindred. She could only focus on her friend, falling forward, pitching toward flames.

No.

She threw out a hand, palm aimed toward the knives. She poured every ounce of her concentration into those knives. Wrapping them with her thoughts like a hand. Gripping them. Jerking them away from Nok so that Nok could twist safely to the side.

The knives clattered to the floor. One slid off the platform.

"Nok!" Cora yelled. "Roll!"

Nok tucked her chin and balled herself up as though preparing for a somersault. The quick movement threw Ellis off-balance. Nok twisted to the right, rolling backward and landing behind Ellis. She pushed to her feet. The sheriff spun away from the fire pit to face her.

Nok and Ellis both looked down at the remaining knife on the platform.

Quickly, Nok stepped on the blade. It rattled under her foot, trying to move telekinetically, but Nok threw her whole weight on it.

"Burn, you bitch!" she yelled, and shoved Ellis backward into the fire.

9

Leon

IN THE NEXT INSTANT, the tent plunged into full-on chaos.

The sheriff's screams still echoed through the tent. Leon didn't have to be a genius to see that Ellis would be dead in another second—the flames crackled impossibly hot in the dry alien atmosphere. Too bad she couldn't levitate *herself* above the fire.

Her deputies stood in a stunned stupor, not used to making the slightest decision on their own. There was no designated second in command. Half the deputies, the tent guards who had kept him captive in the wives' tents, immediately looked toward the mine guards, who in return seemed just as wary. He'd heard the grumblings. The two groups had no love for each other.

At the commotion, another dozen Kindred soldiers poured through the entrance.

"Oh, shit," Leon said.

He glanced at Cora. She was just as slack-jawed as the

deputies. He gave her a sharp nudge. "This is what you call a distraction, sweetheart!"

She immediately blinked out of her shock. "Right. Let's move!" Together they scaled the corral fencing, and right behind them was Rolf, who ran to Nok on the platform, enveloping her in his arms.

"Over here, little childrens!" Bonebreak yelled, waving to them as he cowered behind Ellis's big chair.

But Kindred soldiers were already headed in their direction. Anya scrambled up onto the platform, knitting her unsteady fingers in the air, and a handful of Ellis's deputies started swaying at her command like puppets. They raised their rifles. Assumed battle stances. Charged Fian's troops.

Leon braced himself.

The warring bodies collided in an explosion of sparking weaponry. Tent guards. Mine guards. Kindred soldiers. In the confusion, the Kindred fought back against both, but uncertainly—their war was with neither.

"Leave them!" Fian yelled. "It's the girl we want!"

Two Kindred soldiers turned toward the corral like mechanical warriors. A thrill ran through Leon. Damn, but he loved a good fight. He started to draw back a fist, ready to smash it into their faces, but then paused. There was no telling how long the Kindred shuttle would be docked at the transport hub. And before it took off back to the Kindred station, he and Mali needed to be on it. He'd promised her that he'd help her rescue Cassian.

Where *was* Mali?

He scanned the tent until he found her in the very center of the fight. Of course she'd be in the thick of it—she loved a fight as much as he did. She kicked a Kindred in the kneecap with an audible *crack*. He grinned.

"Cora! This is where we say good-bye." He jerked his head toward the fight. "Mali and me, we'll meet you on Drogane after we've found Cassian."

"Hang on," Cora called. "I have to tell you something." She jerked her head toward the corral fencing, which provided just enough shelter that they could speak in safety for a few moments. She pulled out Lucky's journal from her pants waistband. "You might need weapons. And I know where a stash of kill-dart guns is on the station. Lucky wrote about it. The hostess gave them to Dane in case an animal ever got out of control. There are a few big ones and more handheld ones. They're kept in a secret panel in the Hunt's medical room. This is the symbol to use to open it." She flipped through Lucky's journal and showed him the emblem.

Leon patted her on the shoulder. "You're full of surprises, sweetheart."

Cora threw her arms around him. "Thanks for going after Cassian, Leon. I mean it. The sooner you can get him, the better. We only have twenty-two days until the Gauntlet starts."

He hugged her back. "We'll get him in time."

Leon turned back toward the fight. It was such a tangle of bodies and flashes of armor that he didn't see Mali at first. But then—there she was. Fighting off a female Kindred officer who must have weighed double Mali, but hell, that girl knew how to use her small size to her advantage. She was faster, lower to the ground. She managed to throw the Kindred off-balance and slam the woman's head against a metal tray.

"Mali!" he called.

But two gloved hands suddenly grabbed him from behind. His muscles tensed on instinct, until he recognized Bonebreak's shielding and relaxed.

"What gives?" Leon hissed. "Mali needs my help. How did you get over here so fast, anyway? I saw you just a second ago on the far side of the platform." He sniffed the air. "And why do you not smell as bad as usual?"

"The girl will be fine," Bonebreak answered, dismissing Leon's worries with a wave. "You and I have unfinished business."

"The money I owe you? Seriously? *Now?*"

"Forget the debt." Bonebreak motioned for Leon to follow him into a corner of the tent, deep in the lee of the canvas curtains. "I overheard your plan to return to station 10-91 and free the Kindred Warden."

Leon eyed him suspiciously. "Yeah, so?"

"I left a valuable provision pack on that station, in my old storage containers. If you were to use the tunnels to fetch me that pack, I would make it worth your while."

Leon scoffed. "I don't smuggle anymore. I'm a hero now, didn't you hear?" The fight raging in the main part of the tent showed no signs of dying down. Cora and the others were arguing. Nok kept pointing to the platform emphatically. He thought he heard Cora yell something about a chimpanzee.

He started to push past Bonebreak, but Bonebreak clutched him with an iron grip. "Wait, boy. A hero, are you? The kind who would help a pretty girl, yes? Isn't that what heroes do?" His gaze shifted to Mali.

Leon hesitated. "What are you saying?"

"I saw glimpses of what is in that girl's mind. A family back home that she barely remembers and no way to get in touch with them. So sad. So tragic. But *I* have ways. Fetch me that pack, boy, and I will tell you how to find your girl's family. She would be grateful to you. You'd be a real hero, yes."

Leon gritted his teeth. He looked at Mali, who was now fighting off two Kindred at the same time.

"An easy job," Bonebreak continued in a rush, preying on Leon's indecision. "It will take you only a few minutes. Just grab the provision pack, that's all I'm asking. Your girl does not even have to know about our arrangement."

For a second, Mali looked his way and their eyes met. Blood was splattered on the side of her head, but it was dark. Not hers. She gave him a *time to go* look, jerking her head in the direction of the shuttle outside, before she punched one of the Kindred officers in the nose, sending more black blood spurting everywhere.

God, she was beautiful.

"Fine," Leon grunted. "But this is the last job, got it? What's in the pack, anyway?"

Bonebreak let out a pleased sound from behind his mask. "Some tools, that's all. I'll see you on Drogane. Try not to get yourself killed first." He snickered.

Cora started yelling for Bonebreak to hurry, that it was time to go to his ship, and the Mosca disappeared behind the canvas curtains. A second later, he reappeared behind Ellis's chair on the opposite side of the tent, hustling toward the entrance. Leon blinked. That was impossible. Had he seen right? How'd Bonebreak get all the way across the tent so fast?

Leon looked at them all one last time.

Nok and Rolf.

Cora.

Anya, who he'd barely known.

And then he turned toward Mali and smiled.

"Took you long enough!" she called as he ran up and elbowed a Kindred guard in the neck who had her in a headlock.

"Miss me?" he said.

Mali rolled her eyes. "Come on." She grabbed his hand, and his heart started rumbling around in a way he wasn't quite used to. She lifted the bottom flap of the tent and they crawled out into the morning air. It was already hot enough to make sweat bead on his brow, but all the fighting was confined to the tent, and outside it was thankfully calm.

"It'll be in there," Mali said, pointing to the transport hub.

They charged across the sand. Hot steam came from vents ringing the hub, but they were able to weave among them and get safely to the open flight door. Inside, the Kindred shuttle waited. Unmanned. A few paces before reaching the shuttle, Leon motioned for her to help him rig up a rope ladder system out of tent poles and ropes, to climb on top of the shuttle so their footprints wouldn't show. As soon as they made it, Leon threw the rope ladder away. They climbed into the rear hatch, which led to fuel cell storage. It was pitch-black inside.

"Ow," he said, promptly running into a fuel cell.

"Take my hand. I can sense the objects." Mali slipped her small, scarred fingers into his and led him to the padded walls of the transport. "The shuttle uses inflatable bladders in the wall to keep the cells from being damaged. If we deflate one, we can crawl inside and hide in it. Do you have a knife?"

He produced one with a flourish, though it was too dark to see well. "It was one of Ellis's. Swiped it off the floor." He felt around on the wall until he found a seam toward the bottom, where a cut wouldn't be obvious. He punctured it. Chemically fresh air fizzled out. He cut a two-foot-long gash and he and Mali wriggled into the cavity.

"Ouch," she muttered as his elbow poked her.

"Sorry—gah." They bumped heads. "Tight quarters, eh?"

Mali shifted. He could feel the curves of her body against his, and he thought of her fighting off the Kindred, so beautiful and lean and deadly. He realized that he might not mind these tight quarters after all.

"Mali?" he whispered.

"We should be quiet," she said. "Silence is—"

And he silenced her by pressing his lips to hers. Her body went rigid with surprise, but then her lips met his again, and he realized that valiantly risking his life for this rescue mission might have perks he hadn't considered before.

He kind of liked this hero thing.

10

Cora

"BONEBREAK!" CORA YELLED. WHERE had he snuck off to now? Fian's Kindred soldiers had driven most of the deputies to the rear of the tent, where they were pressing against the canvas side, making the entire structure sway precariously.

Fian turned at her call. *Shit,* she thought. He lifted his pulse rifle and aimed it in her direction. Her heart shot to her throat and she ducked, shielding her head with her hands. But . . . nothing. After a few seconds she looked up. Fian was jiggling the rifle's pulse unit.

It had jammed.

He threw the rifle to the ground and started toward her instead. Cora jerked upright. She should run . . . she should flee . . . but there was nowhere to go. The tent canvas was too heavy to lift on her own.

Fian was three steps away, then two. Cora snatched one of the silver serving trays, brandishing it like a shield. He raised a fist. She stepped backward and collided with something hard. The platform. She was boxed in.

His face was a chilling void of emotion. His fist raised and—

Stopped.

Just stopped.

Not a single muscle moved.

Cora clutched the silver tray with white knuckles. She took a quick breath. Then another. He still didn't move. Frozen as a wax statue. Slowly, she lowered the tray.

Anya stood behind him with her trembling fingers outstretched.

"Anya," Cora called. "Thanks."

"I can't hold him off long!" Anya called. "Kindred minds aren't as easy to control as human ones are. I can only control one or two at a time."

Cora ducked out from under Fian's frozen fist. The tent was a chaotic storm: Mind-controlled deputies fought Kindred. Kindred fought humans. Tent guards fought mine guards. The structure swayed again as Kindred soldiers pressed a group of tent guards harder against the canvas sides.

"Do the best you can," Cora said. "I'll find Nok and Rolf. Once we're all together, release Fian's and everyone else's minds all at once. It'll cause a panic. We'll hope they're all too distracted to realize we've even gone."

Anya nodded, grimacing with the effort of keeping Fian frozen. "Go on. Find the others. I'll cover you as long as I can."

Cora gave her a nod and then skirted the edge of the tent, keeping low. For once she was glad she was small, unnoticeable in the chaos. The heat of battle made her sweat.

From the corner of her eye, she caught a glimpse of Leon and Mali slipping out from under the bottom flap. *Good.* At least they'd managed to get away. She searched through the knot of bodies for Nok, but she didn't see her anywhere, and then—*there.*

A flash of pink.

Nok and Rolf were crouched in the narrow space behind Ellis's platform.

Cora ducked behind a fluttering curtain, stepped over a deputy bleeding from a gash on his head, and threw herself behind the platform, breathing hard.

"Nok! Rolf! We've got to go."

But Nok and Rolf weren't alone. A handful of Ellis's deputies were with them, including an older woman with a rattling cough. For a second Cora tensed her muscles, ready to fight. But then Nok lifted a hand to stop her.

"Cora," Nok said, "this is Keena, and Loren, and Avery. Tent guards. They're on our side."

Deputies? On their side?

"Okay," Cora said in a rush, "but we have to go. Now."

Overhead, the tent was swaying even more violently. *Pop.* One of the smaller support beams cracked in half and a corner of the tent's roof sagged. "We need to get out while everyone's distracted," Cora continued. "Anya's holding off the Kindred. I need to get Willa and then we can all head for the ship—"

Nok shook her head. "I can't."

Cora blinked, confused. "What? This is our one chance to get off this moon."

"I know," Nok said. Her hand slid to cradle her belly. "But if we leave the moon, we have no idea what's out there. Even if you get to Drogane, who knows what kind of reproductive medical care the Mosca have—we don't even know if they *have* children like we do."

"What are you saying?" Cora asked in disbelief.

Nok glanced at Rolf.

"Armstrong isn't stable, I know that," Nok said. "But this baby is going to come soon. Keena was an obstetrician's nurse back home. Loren and Avery both have given birth back on Earth. As dangerous as it is here, I think it's the best chance we have for a healthy birth. There are midwives." She motioned to the deputies. "There are people who will help us. And I've gotten to know them in the wives' tents. I trust them. That's more than I can say for Drogane."

Cora still stared at them both as if she hadn't heard right.

"It's true," Rolf added quietly. "You said the same thing yourself, Cora—that this place might not be so bad for a baby, if the sheriff was gone. And anyway, the Gauntlet's your mission. If we go with you, we'll only slow you down. You need to be as focused as you can, not worrying about us and the pregnancy."

Cora shook her head. "It's practically war here. The mine guards and the tent guards hate each other!"

"Ellis is dead," Nok said. "There'll be a new sheriff. A new system. It's a chance for things to change here. Things could be better. At least, I hope so." She took a deep breath. "I think it's the best option we've got."

Cora stared at her like she'd gone mad. All of them. Words pushed around in her mind, but she couldn't seem to make any sense of them.

Someone screamed as another support post broke. Half the

tent buckled before collapsing on top of half the battle. Muffled, choked cries rang out. Dust stirred up and Cora threw a hand over her mouth.

"Go," Nok urged Cora, coughing.

"But Earth," Cora started. "There's still a chance . . ." She spun to Rolf, uncertain. "Don't you see how crazy this is?"

He looked at his fingers thoughtfully. "We haven't always gotten along, you and I. I'm sorry for not seeing that you were trying to help us. For so long Lucky tried to tell us that we each have our own cause. Well, I see that now. You have yours. Go, and beat the Gauntlet, and do what you were meant to do. Show the Kindred how strong humans are. We'll be here, cheering you on."

Without warning, he threw his arms around her. Nok joined in, and Cora squeezed tight, knowing it was pointless to argue.

Another support beam snapped. Nok pushed Cora away. "Go, hurry!"

The deputies grabbed Nok, pulling her to safety as another portion of the tent ceiling buckled. The last support snapped.

Screams rang out as the entire tent collapsed.

Cora ducked behind the platform just as the heavy canvas slammed down overhead. The dust was so thick, she couldn't see. Everywhere, bodies fought against the canvas, amid the smothered yells of those who couldn't breathe. Cora gasped for air in the lee of the platform, spotting a small opening at the edge of the tarp. She crawled for it, but the canvas pressing down was too heavy. Her lungs were choked.

She kept crawling, barely aware of the other bodies also thrashing to get out from under the collapsed tent. She saw a glint of light ahead—daylight. She was so close to the edge of the tarp.

She reached and reached but couldn't make it. . . .

Suddenly the canvas lifted. A face looked in.

"Dane!" she cried, coughing.

He reached a hand in, grabbing hers, and dragged her out the rest of the way. She emerged, coughing, into fresh air. Took deep gulps, filling her lungs. She squinted into the sunlight. The collapsed tent looked like something from a nightmare; bodies pushed up from inside, trying to crawl out. She could make out the sound of cutting as the Kindred used knives to saw their way free.

"Come on," Dane said. "That tent won't slow them down for long."

"You—you saved me."

"And you're going to save me."

"Nok and Rolf . . ."

"They got out. I saw them. They ran to another tent with some of Ellis's deputies. And Anya took off toward the ship. Bone-break too. I saw them both heading across the desert separately."

"He'll take off without us if he gets there before Anya."

"We can outrun him," Dane assured her.

We? Cora thought warily. But he had just saved her life. And she knew if he stayed, he was a dead man. The deputies knew he'd been planning a mutiny.

She hesitated.

Dammit. She couldn't leave him.

"Help me get Willa," she said, "and you can come with us."

Dane nodded. "I know where she is."

They raced for the slave barracks. There were no deputies guarding the entrance—they'd all run to the command center tent once the fighting had commenced. Inside, the slaves were all wild-eyed and anxious, trying to figure out what was happening.

Cora grabbed at the bars just inside the tent flap, straining to look for Willa among the crowd. Anxious slaves called to her.

"What's going on?"

"It's the Kindred, isn't it? They're attacking!"

"Where's Ellis?"

"Ellis is dead," Cora said. She strained again to see Willa, but there were too many figures in the way. She fumbled with the latch until she figured out how to release it. "You're no longer slaves." She threw open the door. "Go!"

The slaves started pouring out of the tent into the fresh air and sunshine.

"Do you see Willa?" Cora called to Dane.

He motioned to the rafters in the rear of the tent. "Back there!"

As soon as they could squeeze between the escaping slaves, they ran inside the barracks.

A thump sounded behind her.

She whirled to find Willa in the center of the room. She'd dropped from the supports where she'd been hanging.

"Willa," Cora breathed, "you have to come with us."

Willa snorted and shook her head, making a writing motion as though she were referring to the last note she'd written Cora.

"I know I haven't proven myself yet," Cora said. "But we don't exactly have a choice. Kindred have come, bad ones who are trying to stop me from running the Gauntlet. If they find out you've run it before and could help me, they'll kill you."

Willa huffed, but her eyes looked uncertain.

"It's true," Dane added.

Willa cocked her head as she listened to the commotion outside. She shuffled to the tent entrance, peering outside, and then jerked upright at the sight of the battle and the flashing lights of the Kindred cruisers. Not far away, figures were climbing out of the central command tent wreckage. They moved almost robotically—Kindred who had managed to cut their way free. They turned, sensing Cora's presence.

One of them pointed.

Willa started running for the entrance.

"I'll take that as a yes," Cora said. "Let's go!"

The three of them raced out of the slave barracks. Willa tugged Cora's sleeve. The chimp pointed a hairy finger toward the tent that served as the fleet garage.

"The trucks," Dane said. "That's brilliant. I know where Ellis kept the keys. Let's go!"

They veered in the direction of the garage. The Kindred were running toward them, thirty yards away, then twenty, closing the gap fast. Dane reached the closest truck and Willa jumped in the back, pounding on the side in urgency. Cora climbed into the passenger's side.

Dane fumbled with the keys, cheeks going red. "I can't . . . never learned . . ."

"Seriously? Give the keys to me. Slide over."

"I was fourteen when they took me from Earth," he started as they switched places. "Only driven twice . . . my dad's minivan . . ."

Cora slammed the keys into the ignition and cranked the truck to life. The complicated controls looked like those of an airliner jet, not a car. She glanced at the pedals—there were six.

"Cora," Dane said warningly, looking behind them.

"I don't know which pedals to push!"

"The Kindred—"

"I know!"

She picked a pedal at random and slammed a foot down.

The truck roared forward. She cried out, gripping the wheel hard. In the rearview mirror, she watched a surprised Willa holding on for dear life. The truck raced forward, kicking up dust. She blinked furiously and tried to control the wheel.

"The Kindred are still running," Dane said. "Damn, they're fast! They're nearly gaining on us!"

Cora pushed the pedal harder. In the rearview mirror, she could see a half dozen Kindred tearing across the desert behind them.

"There's the ship," she said.

Ahead, the gleaming fleet of white ships and Mosca troops had vanished. The hologram must have shorted out, because now only Bonebreak's dented old ship crouched on the horizon. Lights came on beneath it as it prepared to depart. The ground rumbled softly.

"Anya and Bonebreak must already be on board," Cora said. "They'll wait for us. They have to."

Other lights suddenly shone overhead, moving back and forth like helicopter spotlights.

Dane leaned out the truck window. "Kindred cruisers are overhead. They must have had one on the shuttle. It's like a motorcycle with a propeller—and it's got guns!"

On cue, a volley of laser pulses shattered the ground in front of them. Cora screamed and jerked the wheel to avoid the deep ditch the lasers had created. The rearview mirror reflected the running Kindred easily leaping over the ditch.

"Pull up beneath the hatch," Dane said, pointing beneath Bonebreak's ship. "The truck will block us and give us a second to climb up."

Cora pressed her foot harder against the pedal, but the truck wouldn't go any faster. She muttered prayers under her breath, trying hard to remember driver's ed back at Richmond High. Parallel parking . . . something about a three-point turn . . .

She slammed her foot against another pedal, then another, until she found the brakes, whipping the steering wheel around. The truck skidded and she cringed. For a second it felt as if the truck were lifting on two wheels. They spun, spun, and she caught glimpses of the Kindred soldiers, then glimpses of the cruiser lights overhead . . .

Then the truck stopped. She looked up through the windshield.

They were directly beneath the ship's hatch. Anya looked down, round cheeks flushed. "Climb up!" Anya yelled above the roar. "Hurry!" She reached down with a small hand to help pull Cora up, but she wasn't strong enough, and Willa made a stirrup with her hands to help boost her from below. Cora climbed in on her stomach. She spun around and reached down for Willa.

Kindred were closing in. Ten feet. Five.

There wasn't time for both Willa and Dane to board.

A panicked look crossed Dane's face. He suddenly hurled himself against Willa. She stumbled and fell off the truck bed.

"No!" Cora yelled.

She gripped the edge of the hatch with white knuckles. She

never should have trusted him. "Dane, you bastard!"

"Help me up!" he yelled, reaching a hand.

Cora stared at him, disgusted and confused. How could she save him after he had just betrayed Willa?

A streak of fast-moving brown fur leaped into the back of the truck. Just as the Kindred reached for them, the chimp leaped from the truck bed to Dane's shoulders, then to the ship's hatch, using Dane as a springboard. He cried out as her fingers clamped on to the hatch.

Anya and Cora each grabbed one of Willa's hands and pulled her the rest of the way up.

"Cora!" Dane called. "Don't leave me!"

But a laser pulse hit the truck, and he crashed to his knees.

He looked up as Kindred guards surrounded him.

Cora slammed the hatch closed, leaving him behind.

11

Cora

SPACE WAS UNSETTLINGLY QUIET.

Bonebreak's ship rumbled amid the stars with a low hum. If it wasn't for that slightest vibration, Cora might not even know they were in motion. Bonebreak sat in the pilot's seat facing the controls, staring at the view screen and the stars beyond. His musk filled the cabin with a stench she tried to ignore, a hand pressed against her nose as she paced uneasily.

She wasn't sure how long they'd been flying. Hours? A full day? As soon as it had been safe, she'd collapsed in a ball in the corner of the cabin, exhausted. She'd been too wired to rest, her mind jumping between what they'd left behind and what lay ahead. Thinking of Dane's betrayal made her curl her toes with anger. The only way to calm her mind was to practice her training: Meditation to calm her mind. Push-ups until her arms shook.

Now, sweat slick on her temples, she hugged her knees tightly and tried to calculate how much time they had left before the Gauntlet was due to begin. Twenty-one days. Five feet in front of her, covered in a white tarp, lay Lucky's body. It had been weeks since he'd died, but the dry, purified air on the ship had kept his body from breaking down. If she pulled back the tarp, she knew, he'd look as though he were simply asleep.

She hugged her knees harder.

"Travel time to Drogane is three more days, if I use the hyperengine," Bonebreak said. "But that will take extra fuel. There's an Axion-run fuel station not far away. It will be a slight detour." He turned to face her. "It is a sandy outpost. A meteor, but there is artificial oxygen and gravity, and soil." When she looked at him questioningly, he motioned to Lucky's body. "A place where you can bury the boy."

His voice held a trace of sympathy that surprised her. The last time Bonebreak had mentioned Lucky's body, he'd wanted to dissect it and sell parts on the black market to pay for their voyage. But maybe Bonebreak had changed. Maybe he wasn't as heartless as he'd first seemed. Still, it would be a long time before she trusted him.

"I'd like that," she said, wiping her face.

Bonebreak returned to the controls, and the ship continued to rumble in silence. Cora eyed Lucky's body beneath the tarp, chewing on a fingernail.

This is our place. This is our cause.

Those were among his last words.

And yet a tiny voice nagged in the back of her mind. After months trapped in the cage, and in the menagerie with Makayla and the other Hunt kids, she was finally free of the Kindred. Free of Ellis and Armstrong too. Bonebreak could be manipulated or bargained with or, as a last resort, mind controlled by Anya. There was nothing stopping them from having Bonebreak steer them in the opposite direction from Drogane—straight to Earth.

We could go home.

The possibility was there, hovering so close that she only needed to reach out and take it. She doubted Willa would object. Anya might, but Cora could reason with her. Right now, they could be on a course back to her solar system. She could find out in days, weeks at most, if Earth was still there. She could put her feet in the cool waters of a lake. Smell grass and wildflower fields. Hear the sounds of traffic, of bees, of cafeteria chatter, of music on the radio. And most of all, she could go home. Bury her face in Sadie's fur, hug her mother and father, tackle Charlie like they used to when they were kids.

A deep sense of longing made her close her eyes and smile.

But then her toe grazed Lucky's body, and she jolted upright. No.

If she went home, that wonderful reconciliation wouldn't last long. Soon she'd see for herself all the devastation humans were wreaking on the planet. She'd be reminded that all that traffic and wildflowers and her dog and her brother were living on borrowed time, on a planet that wouldn't last forever. If she didn't run the Gauntlet and free humanity to live among the stars, her race's days were numbered.

The facilities door slid open and Anya came out, rubbing her temples. She had dark circles under her big eyes, and her hands were shaking worse than Cora had ever seen. It had cost her almost all her strength to take control of Fian and the deputies. As soon as they'd boarded the ship, she'd collapsed and slept for hours.

Now Anya sat cross-legged beside Willa, resting a hand on the wiry hair of the chimp's shoulder. "I wasn't sure I'd ever see you again," she said.

Cora sat up in surprise. "You two know each other?"

Anya touched her heart in a greeting that Willa returned. Anya gave another small flicker with her hand, some kind of sign language.

"It's been a long time," Anya explained. "Before the Kindred locked me in the Temple menagerie, I was in a cell for several days. Willa was in the cell next to me."

Willa took paper out of her pocket and wrote:

Anya snored. Kept everyone awake.

But there was kindness in her dark brown eyes. Anya read the note and rolled her eyes. "Funny, as I remember it, *you* kept everyone awake swinging from the ceiling bars all night."

Willa wrote something down again.

Not my fault humans need eight hours of sleep. Lazy bums.

"Listen, Willa, we really need you," Cora said gently. "I've lost my coach. The Kindred Warden, Cassian. He taught me the basics of telekinesis and telepathy, and set up puzzles to simulate the ones in the Gauntlet. Bonebreak has agreed to be my Mosca sponsor, but no one knows what really goes on in those twelve puzzle chambers." She paused. "No one but you."

Willa grunted as if to say that she was well aware of that fact.

"Please," Cora said.

Anya rested a hand on Willa's shoulder until she looked up, and then they exchanged a few hand signals. Willa's face looked deeply troubled. She wrote:

The Gauntlet . . .

She paused. Anya patted her shoulder, and Willa took a deep breath.

The Gauntlet can be won only at a heavy cost.

"What cost?" Cora asked, reading the paper.

Willa didn't answer right away, and a sinking feeling filled Cora's stomach. After exchanging a long look with Anya, Willa hesitantly started writing again.

Are you certain this is what you want? Are you certain it's worth any price?

A thousand thoughts filled Cora's head, along with a pang of guilt. Cassian was possibly being tortured even now. There was no way of knowing if Mali and Leon would be successful in their attempts to free him. And Lucky . . .

Her eyes fell on the tarp.

"We've already paid a heavy price," Cora said quietly. "Not just me, but all of us. Lucky died for this cause. Cassian let himself be arrested to protect me. Mali and Leon are risking their lives, along with hundreds of sympathetic Kindred members of the Fifth of Five. Whether it's worth it or not, it's a price we're already paying."

Anya's face went very serious, and she nodded in silent agreement. Willa clutched the pencil.

> You already know that the Gauntlet requires you to push yourself to dangerous extremes. Few Gauntleteers survive, and those who do are the ones who drop out in early rounds; they are left damaged for life. For some, the physical challenges leave them maimed. For others, the paradoxes in the mental challenges render them insane: one Gauntleteer I knew was locked in a chamber with a starving lion and instructed to feed it, but the only thing to feed it was the Gauntleteer himself.

She glanced at Anya before writing again.

> But most dangerous of all are the perceptive puzzles. If you strain your brain too far, it will rupture. You could permanently lose control of some function. The effects are different for each person. Maybe your sanity will go. Maybe your ability to speak. Maybe . . .

Her eyes went to Anya's shaking hands. Anya held them up, watching the tremor that was beyond her control.

"Maybe you'll lose motor function in your hands," Anya

said quietly. "Like me. I can't even hold a pencil to write anymore. The only thing my hands are good for is playing puppet master—and most of that's with my mind, anyway."

Cora stared at Anya's useless hands with uneasy worry. She'd already pushed her brain too far—the nosebleeds, passing out. Cassian had warned her of the danger, but it hadn't ever felt as real as it did now. What would she lose if she pushed her brain too far? The ability to walk? Her sense of sight? Her sympathy?

She stood up, breathing hard.

"Cora, are you okay?" Anya asked.

Before she could answer, Bonebreak hit the controls and the ship hummed at a lower frequency.

"We're approaching Fuel Station Theta," he announced. "Time to refuel and"—he glanced in the direction of Lucky's body—"take care of the rest of our business."

CORA'S FIRST VIEW OF Fuel Station Theta was from the screen of Bonebreak's ship. When Rolf had described the Axion cities, he'd mentioned enormous complexes on planet-sized space stations, but Theta was only a small fuel station, no bigger than an airport. It was circular but flat, a platform eerily hovering in space like a giant Frisbee suspended amid the stars, with a gleaming, smooth white station at one end and a fleet of glossy ships lined up behind it. But what surprised Cora most was what ringed the edge of the fuel station like the rim of a dinner plate: a forest.

They stepped out of Bonebreak's ship slowly. Cora took a deep breath, testing out the air, glad to see Bonebreak was right—there was artificial oxygen. She took a step toward the strange forest. It hugged the edge, a twenty-foot-wide buffer separating the flat Axion fuel station from outer space. There were trees, grass, flowers—everything beautiful and delicate and completely unexpected. Beyond the ring of forest, she could see the sudden drop-off of the fuel station's platform, which gave her a dizzying feeling.

"How is this possible?" she asked, taking another step, judging the gravity, which felt light and buoyant. "It's flat—we should just float off."

"Axion technology," Bonebreak grumbled dispassionately. "They've learned how to harness gravity fields however they wish, no matter the station's size or shape. Show-offs." He grunted. "They keep to themselves, mostly. Don't like to socialize with the other intelligent races, except for trade and official Council business." Bonebreak nodded toward the flowers. "The Axion just sit around trying to figure out how to keep those flimsy petal-y things alive in outer space. Waste of time, if you ask me."

Cora took another bouncy step toward the nearest tree. She closed her eyes, remembering being home, standing in her yard by the big oak trees, with Sadie panting happily in the sun, the clink of ice in her mother's lemonade. It felt so real. And it *was*. In her gut, she knew it was all still there: Sadie. Her mother. The lemonade.

She opened her eyes. The artificial atmospheric controls gave her a sense of lightness, almost of hope, after the heavy, oppressive gravity of Armstrong.

She shaded her eyes to take in the fuel station more closely. Everything was sparklingly crisp and white, like a shining kingdom of ivory, as though straight out of the pages of Rolf's picture book. Unlike the Kindred station, which was all sharp angles and straight lines, the Axion structure consisted entirely of smooth geometric curves. A few figures came and went from an arched doorway in the distance. She squinted to see better—she'd never seen an Axion before. They were smaller than she'd expected: a little over four feet tall. From this distance, their faces seemed unhealthily gaunt, some with dark brown hair, some with light brown, but each with a streak of white running through it.

"Those are the Axion?"

Bonebreak grunted the affirmative. "Yes. You childrens wait for me here. The Axion are unpredictable. Mercurial. Look at them—small creatures, thin and ugly. And they are not overly fond of humans, unless it is consuming your livers powdered in tea." Cora shivered, and Bonebreak cackled. "Don't worry. They only consume human parts if the human is already dead."

Unsurprisingly, Cora didn't feel much better.

"Are all those ships here because it's a refueling station?"

Bonebreak shook his head, turning toward the fleet of ships with an uneasy air. There must have been hundreds of ships, each the size of a small fighter plane, lined up in perfect order.

"The Axion are in the process of repurposing this fuel station into a ship distribution center—they construct the ships for all of the intelligent species. They have dramatically increased production in an effort to improve mobility between the species. They're storing the ships here until they can be distributed."

Cora looked at the fleet hesitantly. "It looks more like a military base than a distribution center."

Bonebreak didn't speak for a moment, as though similar worries had occurred to him. But then he shrugged. "Ah, well. The Mosca are in charge of business. Which means we'll get a commission from each ship once distribution begins." He rubbed his hands together greedily. "Now. On to more timely things." He dug around in a bag slung over his shoulder, muttering to himself, and then raised his fist proudly.

Cora's stomach turned. Her ponytail dangled from his fist.

She reached up to feel the short, uneven hair that just brushed the back of her neck. It was only hair, yes, but she couldn't help feeling that she'd lost something more of herself, clutched there in Bonebreak's grasp. As though by being asked to make this small sacrifice, she was opening the door to much bigger ones.

Bonebreak hummed to himself as he headed toward the glistening Axion spire.

Cora walked in the opposite direction, toward the ring of forest, and crouched down to pick a wildflower, trying to clear her head of worries. She sniffed it and then handed it to Anya. "Do you remember? This is what Earth smells like."

Anya looked at the flower with uncertainty. "Not really. It was too long ago."

Cora had seen the same troubled look on Mali's face. Taken from Earth as a toddler, Mali retained only distant and dreamlike memories.

"I wish I could remember," Anya continued. "My family, my town, all of it. I've been trying so hard to free a species I barely know. . . ." Her hands started that violent trembling again, and the flower tumbled to the ground. She let out a frustrated sigh. "And now I can't do anything."

"That's not true," Cora said softly. She rested a comforting hand on Anya's shoulder. "You've laid the groundwork for humanity to be free. If it wasn't for you, I wouldn't be able to even dream of running the Gauntlet. And once all this is over, you and Mali both will go home and find your families. You'll make new memories." She took Anya's shaking hand and squeezed it. "The wolves are strong. But the rabbits are clever. Mali told me you used to say that."

The tightness in Anya's face eased. She mustered a half smile. "I'm going to go inside and ask around for news of station 10-91."

Cora hesitantly eyed the short, eerily gaunt Axion people who came and went from the structure. "Bonebreak said to wait here."

Anya rolled her eyes. "I'm not afraid of the Axion. Even *I'm* bigger than they are. And besides . . ." She wiggled her fingers in the air, reminding Cora of her mind-control ability. Cora watched her go, thinking it wasn't fair that someone so young had felt such pain.

A soft hand touched her shoulder. Willa. The chimp motioned to beneath the ship, where she had gently laid the wrapped white tarp containing Lucky's body on the ground. Willa motioned toward a patch of grass tucked away behind a small willowlike tree.

Cora took a deep breath.

"Thank you. For helping."

Willa nodded, and they carefully moved Lucky's body to the patch of grass.

"We don't have a shovel," Cora said. "But the ground feels soft enough to dig with our hands, I think." She rested her hand on the edge of the tarp, fighting to keep her emotions from spilling over. At her silence, Willa gave her a concerned look that seemed to ask if she was all right.

"I was just thinking," Cora said, "about the enclosure we

were in on the Kindred station." She brushed her fingers against the smooth tarp. "We were all so frightened the first day we woke up there. Lucky made each of us feel better, in his way. It was a knack he had." She touched the journal tucked in her waistband for reassurance. "He never gave up on home. I wish we could bury him there, on his granddad's farm. But I guess this is the closest we can come."

She started digging in the dirt with her fingers. Willa joined in. The soil was much less dense here than it had been in the root mines, and it felt good to dig for a real purpose. Once they had a shallow pit, Willa helped Cora lay Lucky's body there. Together, they smoothed the dirt back over him.

Cora rested a hand on the grave, overwhelmed with memories.

Even if they had escaped Armstrong . . .

Even if they went to Drogane and trained for the Gauntlet . . .

Even if they managed to free Cassian . . .

How could she continue without Lucky?

She sniffled, running a hand beneath her nose. He'd never be back amid his family. No oak trees and lemonade. No summer wildflowers and fresh-cut grass.

She heard footsteps and glanced over her shoulder. Bonebreak and Anya were coming back from the Axion station, loaded down with various containers and bags. She wiped at her nose again—she could smell Bonebreak's reek even from this distance. Anya trailed behind him, eyes darting between the shallow grave and the ship. Her forehead was pinched tightly, as though something were bothering her. Cora's worry returned.

Had something happened in the station?

Bonebreak handed her two of the heavy containers before she could ask. "Your hair fetched us twenty tokens' worth of supplies! They said they haven't gotten such long hair in a hundred rotations. Now the next stop is Drogane. My brother and his family. Hospitality. Good food."

"And the Gauntlet," Cora prompted.

"Yes, yes." He waved dismissively. "Freedom for your people and all that. But first, food."

He climbed into the ship. Willa made a few of the sign language symbols to Anya, who turned away as though she hadn't seen and started to climb the ladder. Cora rested a hand on her shoulder, stopping her.

"Hey, you okay? Did something happen in there with the Axion?"

Anya shook her head. "I'm fine. It's . . . it's just a headache." Her eyes drifted to the crumpled wildflower she had dropped before. "Probably because of the weird gravity."

She pressed her hands against the sides of her forehead. Something felt off, and it took Cora a second to realize that Anya's hands, for once, weren't shaking.

Anya climbed the ladder, leaving Cora below with Willa, who stared after Anya. Willa turned to Cora and raised an eyebrow in question, then jotted down a note.

Seems like more than just a headache to me.

Cora nodded, staring after Anya, and then looked at the crumpled flower. "Yeah, you might be right. Maybe she's still upset because the plants here are so much like on Earth. Because she can't remember what home was like. Just give her time. She's been through so much."

Willa nodded, then looked uneasily back at the Axion station.

Cora traced her gaze and said hesitantly, "I heard it was the Axion who experimented on you."

The light in Willa's eyes dimmed, and Cora couldn't be certain whether Willa feared the Axion, or was grateful to them, or felt something else entirely.

"Do you know why they did it?"

Willa shook her head. She cradled her skull in one hand as though remembering something painful, then climbed the ladder, anxious to escape those memories.

Cora was left alone on Fuel Station Theta.

She turned back to take in Lucky's grave. She wanted to remember every detail about it. The willowlike tree. The flowers. The breeze.

"Good-bye, Lucky," she whispered.

She climbed into the hatch.

In another few moments, they were far from the Axion fuel station, headed for Drogane.

12

Rolf

AS THE SUN BEGAN to sink toward Armstrong's horizon, Rolf doubled over, coughing from the thick dust that still filled the air after the main tent had collapsed. Overhead, bright lights flashed as the Kindred shuttle took off.

Rolf spit a curse after them. "Good riddance. I hope you never come back!"

He heard footsteps and turned quickly, ready to fight off any of Ellis's rogue deputies who had survived the tent collapse, but was surprised to see Dane, limping slightly, his uniform singed.

"I thought you were leaving with Cora," Rolf said warily.

"I thought so, too," Dane said, breathing hard. "But . . . plans changed. There was only time for one of us to board, either me or Willa, and I . . . I sacrificed myself so that Willa could escape."

Rolf raised his eyebrows.

Dane motioned to his limp. "I had a tussle with some Kindred guards who were chasing us, but they let me go. It was Cora they were after, not me." He looked up toward the sky. "At least she's safe now." He sighed dramatically. "That's what's important."

Rolf observed cautiously as Dane sank onto a crate, wincing. Rolf hadn't known Dane, other than what Cora had told him, and those stories were hardly flattering. But wounded, Dane seemed in no condition to be an immediate threat. "You really did that? Sacrificed yourself?"

Dane nodded. "It was the least I could do." He wiped his forehead and motioned to the collapsed tent. "The battle?"

"It ended when the tent collapsed. Half the deputies suffocated. Most of the ones who got out are badly wounded. The mine guards and the tent guards called an emergency truce. They moved the wounded to the wives' tents."

"A truce?" Dane shook his head. "It won't last. Not until there's a new sheriff to replace Ellis." He stood up, hobbling toward the tents.

"Where are you going?"

"If everyone else is occupied with the wounded," Dane said, "they don't need us there. We'd be more useful here, burying the dead."

Rolf frowned. "You should go to the wives' tents too, and get patched up. That leg looks bad."

"I'm okay. Besides, that sun's getting lower. We should bury the bodies before it gets dark." He hobbled toward the tent with determination.

Rolf glanced over his shoulder at one of the smaller tents, where Keena and the other deputies had taken Nok for safety. He should go to her, make certain she was all right. He took a step toward the tent.

"Hey, I think this guy's alive!" Dane called.

Rolf paused, then turned back and hurried to help Dane. If there were survivors, he had to do what he could. Dane knelt near the edge of the collapsed tent, where a pale hand stuck out. Rolf helped Dane lift the heavy canvas and pull the man's body out. It was one of the deputies, the young one with the weak chin who had almost revealed Nok was pregnant during their processing. They dragged the body into the sand and Rolf crouched beside it, feeling for a pulse.

He shook his head. "He's gone."

Dane started pulling out another body, calling to Rolf to help. Rolf glanced again at Nok's tent, wanting to check on her, but Dane was right—the day's heat had made the bodies begin to putrefy. They needed to bury them soon, and anyway, he hated the idea of Nok seeing so much death like this. It was grueling work, but soon they had a row of bodies lined up on the sand. No survivors.

Dane was pacing, agitated. "None of them are Ellis. We have to find Ellis."

Rolf scrunched up his nose. "She's dead. She isn't going anywhere."

"Rolf!"

He turned at the sound of his name. Nok was coming out of the tent with Keena on one side and Loren on the other. Dane abruptly stopped searching the bodies, stepped back, and wiped his face of sweat. Nok ran up and threw her arms around Rolf. She wasn't wearing the apron, and he felt the full press of her belly against his own.

"You're feeling okay?" he asked.

She nodded, then looked at Dane. "What's *he* doing here?"

Dane held his hands up in a gesture of peace. "You can trust me—just ask Rolf. I had the chance to leave, but I stayed behind. I wanted to help."

Keena snorted, which turned into one of her deep coughs. "He's a mutineer. We should send him headfirst into the mine."

"We *were* planning to overthrow Ellis," Dane agreed quickly. "But only because she was a tyrant. And it wasn't even my idea. I'm not interested in leading. Only peace."

"Is that right?" Keena eyed the row of corpses. "Then why are you out here digging through the dead bodies?"

"We're . . . we're burying them," Rolf explained. Wasn't it obvious?

Keena shook her head. "I know what you're up to, Dane. You're looking for Ellis's body. You want to get your grubby hands on that badge, don't you?"

Dane glared at her in silence.

"He thinks whoever has the badge automatically becomes sheriff," Keena said. "But that isn't how it works. Though the badge *is* important."

Keena coughed harder and then signaled for two deputies to lift the heavy canvas of the tent closest to where the platform had been. "Ellis took power by killing the previous sheriff, Randall," she explained. "Randall took power by killing the sheriff before that, and . . . well, you get the idea." Keena peeked inside, made a face at the rank smell of bodies in the heat, and then took out her handkerchief and coughed more. "I'm afraid you're the only one small enough to climb in there, Rolf."

Rolf folded his arms. "You want me to go in there? For a piece of metal?" He shook his head.

"Please, Rolf," Nok said softly.

He sighed. She could ask him to jump off a ten-story building and he'd do it.

The deputies lifted the flap higher, and Rolf reluctantly got to his hands and knees and disappeared under the tent flap into the darkness, the heavy fabric stirring up noxious smells. He pressed his sleeve over his mouth, crawling as quickly as he could. The stench of death was suffocating. Bodies brushed against his sides, but in the dark he pretended they were just statues. He finally found the platform. He felt along the edge until his fingers touched charred hair. Ellis's body.

He recoiled.

Suppressing the urge to gag, he felt along the cadaver's shoulder to her neck, then to the charred face. His fingers touched metal. He hissed and drew back—the edges were still hot. He had to dig his fingernails carefully into her cheek to free it. As soon as he had it, he crawled out of the tent as fast as he could and emerged into daylight, coughing, gagging.

The badge was slick with blood and singed skin from where he'd pried it from Ellis's cheek. The metal wasn't nearly as finely made as it had looked from a distance. This wasn't anything Kindred made, that was for sure. Someone had roughly hewn this from whatever scrap metal was available on Armstrong.

"Here," he said, handing it to Nok. He wiped his fingers off on his pants—he'd never missed soap and hot water more in his life.

Nok cradled the badge in her palm. There had been a time,

Rolf knew, when just the smell of it would have made her retch. Now she ran her finger over it admiringly before passing it along to Keena.

But the old woman held up a hand, refusing to take it. "I don't think you understand, Nok."

Nok wrinkled her face. "Understand what?"

Keena exchanged a long look with Loren and Avery before turning back to Nok. "Dane thinks that whoever controls the badge controls Armstrong," she said, "because that's what the mine guards told him. But it's only half true. The Kindred who oversee this place acknowledge the owner of the badge as sheriff; that's the only person they'll do business with. But the humans here don't care about a scrap of metal. They care about tradition. Tradition that goes back generations, since Armstrong was first founded."

Rolf eyed the badge in Nok's hand. He was getting a bad feeling about this.

"What tradition?" Nok asked.

Keena picked up a piece of loose thread from the fallen canvas tent, stringing it through the badge as a makeshift necklace.

"Round up any deputies you don't trust," Keena said to Loren and Avery, "and take away their firearms. Especially the mine guards. They've been demoted. Tell the slaves they'll be treated fairly now in return for fair work. The days of Armstrong being a dictatorship are over. There's a new sheriff in town."

Rolf let out an uneasy breath. Now he had a *really* bad feeling.

"I don't get it," Nok said. "Who's the new sheriff?"

"Randall killed the sheriff before him," Keena explained. "And Ellis killed Randall. That's the tradition. Whoever kills the old sheriff becomes the new one." She handed Nok the badge looped over string. "And *you* killed Ellis."

Nok gaped.

"We'll help you, all of us tent guards. We know this place. We know how to run it, how to improve it." She coughed more, and Rolf wondered how long she could help before the sand-cough rendered her too ill. "But we can't officially hold the title of sheriff. Only you can."

The badge tumbled out of Nok's hand. It landed in the dirt, where Rolf stared at the charred flesh at the edges. The reflected light stung his eyes, but he didn't look away.

"*Sheriff?*" Nok sputtered.

Rolf glanced over his shoulder at Dane, who was hanging around just to the side, arms crossed, a nasty smirk on his face. Had he really sacrificed himself to make sure Cora got off the moon? Rolf raised his eyebrows as he realized that now that Dane knew the path toward leadership, he only had to do one thing to be sheriff—kill the current one.

Kill Nok.

And Rolf took his new role seriously: Father. Protector. He was damn sure not going to let that happen.

13

Cora

CORA STOOD OVER BONEBREAK'S shoulder, gazing at the ship's view screen. "Is that Drogane?" she asked. It was hard not to be awed by the green-and-blue planet that filled the sky. It looked so similar to Earth, except the blue color of the water was two shades lighter, and the shapes of the continents were all different. Regardless, it made her heart ache with longing. Lyrics drifted into her mind.

Home is more than a house . . .
It's more than a room . . .
Home means loved ones and . . .

"That's Drogane, all right. It's got a similar atmosphere to your planet, but the air has a higher nitrogen content. Swallow these—oxygen adjusters. You'll be able to breathe." He handed her three white pills, which she weighed in her hand hesitantly, then distributed to Anya and Willa. She swallowed her own down dry. Bonebreak began the procedure to slow the ship and then started muttering as he fumbled with the controls. "Damn Axion technology. Where's the blasted . . . oh."

The ship lurched sharply to the left, and Cora clutched the back of his chair to steady herself.

"Go sit with the others," Bonebreak said, waving toward the corner where Anya and Willa were seated. "You make me nervous hovering so close."

Cora sat on the floor next to Willa, who slid a paper her way.

You know you cannot trust the Mosca, don't you?

Cora glanced at Bonebreak and tried to keep her voice low. "I actually think he's not so bad," she whispered. "But just in case, that's why Mali and Leon went back to the aggregate station. If Bonebreak tries to claim ownership and sell us, Cassian will stop him. Technically, Cassian's still our owner. Once they find him, they're going to meet us on Drogane."

Willa wrote something else.

Was it true what Dane said? That you love this Kindred?

Cora read the note and felt her cheeks warm. The first time she'd seen Cassian, she'd certainly been intrigued. Drawn to him, even. And she had to admit that there were times when she'd lain awake at night, thinking of their kiss, breathless at the memory.

But love? How could she love someone who wasn't even human?

And then she pictured him being tortured.

She closed her eyes.

Images filled her head: him with those snaking wires attached to his skin, and then flashes of her nightmare too, bullet holes ripping through him. They mixed together in a guilty haze that she could barely swallow down. If she really loved him, how could she have let that happen?

And yet, she told herself, it had been his choice.

Love was always about choice.

"I do care about him. And he does for me. But it isn't as simple as it sounds. It isn't love like regular couples back home. It's more like . . . a connection. Like we see something special in each other, something no one else fully sees. It's just . . ." She opened her eyes. "How can you really love someone you can never fully understand? A different species?"

Willa nodded thoughtfully and then wrote:

> Anya and I are different species and yet we care about each other. Not romantic love, but still the care you describe. A connection. A recognition of something special. That kind of bond is not easily broken. Perhaps different species have more in common than you believe.

As Cora read the note, her guilt lessened, and a thrill ran through her. It was true that the bond she felt with Cassian was powerful: it had been built slowly, over many trials, and was all the stronger because of it.

She felt herself shaking a little with hope.

Could she and Cassian actually have a chance for a future together?

She glanced over the paper at Anya, who was turned toward the view screen, silently watching the stars, knees hugged in close. Even if she hadn't known Anya long, she too felt a connection, and not just awe at the girl's unnatural brilliance. Anya was the only other human she'd been able to communicate with telepathically.

She closed her eyes and tried to reach into Anya's mind to send a message of reassurance. *Everything will be all right. The wolves are strong, but the rabbits are clever.*

But her thoughts hit a wall. It felt odd, as though there were something mentally blocking her. Anya only continued staring at the screen as though she hadn't sensed anything at all.

"Anya?" she asked aloud.

The girl turned and smiled, flashing a thumbs-up.

Her thumb didn't shake.

The ship began to rumble as they entered Drogane's atmosphere. Cora folded the paper and stashed it in her pocket. Strange curled clouds flew by, giving way to a ridge of mountains in the distance. The mountains were mostly bare patches of steep rock with a few clusters of trees nestled in the lower elevations, towering over lakes and oceans shimmering in the valleys. The entire planet looked pristine and untouched.

"Where are the cities?" Cora asked.

"The climate is too volatile for any species to live permanently on the surface," Bonebreak explained. "The mountains are hollow. We make our cities there, where it is safe from the storms." He wagged a finger at the beautiful blue sky. "Don't trust clear skies. You take a breath and next thing you know there's a snow-storm."

He piloted the ship into a valley, toward a dark shadow Cora had mistaken for a cave, which turned out to be a docking port. Heavy metal doors fixed with intricate Mosca locks opened with a rumble as Bonebreak evened out the ship for entry.

"I can smell roast cave rat already," he said happily.

As the doors opened, they plunged into the deep of the mountain, and the view screen went black. Bonebreak hummed to himself as they flew into the blackness, seemingly untroubled about the absence of light.

"I already radioed in from the outer atmosphere," he said. "My brother will be waiting for us in the terminal. Expect to be filled with delicious foods—we are a hospitable race even to lowly humans and apes."

Cora rolled her eyes, but there was a smile on her lips too.

The ship landed.

The hatch opened, and Bonebreak took his bag and jumped down. Willa helped Anya and Cora down. She blinked in the darkness. There were no lights or guides to show where they were going, only the faint glow of what seemed to be glowworms or bio-luminescence up high.

"Bonebreak?" she called. She could hear him humming ahead. "Wait! Turn a light on."

"Light?" His voice was disembodied in the darkness. "What light?"

Cora reached out in front of her to avoid bumping into any-thing. "How are we supposed to see where we're going?"

Bonebreak grumbled to himself as his footsteps returned,

and she felt his glove on her shoulder. "I forgot about humans' poor eyes. Our masks give us the ability to see in the dark as well as in the light. My brother will have some extra masks for you. Until then, link hands, and I will guide you."

Cora gagged at the thought of having to wear one of the Mosca's reeking masks. Willa slipped her hand in Cora's, and Anya took the other one, and they started walking. Cora couldn't help noticing how eerily still Anya's hand was, clutched in her own.

She gave Anya's fingers a squeeze. "It seems like you're doing better. With the tremor in your hand, I mean."

Anya's hand suddenly went rigid. "It . . . comes and goes," she said. "I've been sleeping better, and that helps."

A cold premonition ran down Cora's back. Sleeping better? Would that really make a difference on a physical impairment? And yet she hardly knew the girl, not really. She certainly didn't know the details about how exactly the Kindred drugs had affected her.

"I'm glad," Cora said.

The temperature was cool and damp, a blessing after Armstrong's blistering desert. Bonebreak stopped, and she heard more complicated locks opening and then a few formal-sounding Mosca exchanges between shadowy figures she could barely make out in the bioluminescent light. And then gloved hands were on her, patting down her body like an inspection. The mystery hands found Lucky's journal before she could stop them, but whoever the Mosca inspector was flipped through it with little interest and handed it back to her.

And then Bonebreak's voice rang with joy. "Ah! Brother!" In the faint light, Cora could make out the vague shape of another hunchback Mosca embracing Bonebreak and something like smaller people skittering all around, hunchback too, breathing heavily through masks. One of them spoke foreign words in a high-pitched voice, and with a start Cora realized the little shadows were Mosca children.

"Here." Bonebreak shoved something into her hands, and she heard him do the same for Anya and Willa. "Goggles. They belong to my brother's children, but the young have good eyes. They can see well enough in the dark without them until we get back to their home. Also your puny heads are so small that our regular masks would probably fall off your faces."

Hesitantly, Cora felt the shape of the goggles. They were thick, round lenses with a strap that felt fleshy and stank something awful. She tentatively slid them over her head and then jumped as some kind of machinery automatically turned on. The goggles started vibrating, the lenses rotated, and the apparatus clicked loudly.

Suddenly, she could see.

She nearly jumped again. They were standing in a room the size of a train station lobby. It even reminded her of one, with something that looked like a digitized timetable on the wall and low benches in the center built for the Mosca's hunched frames. There were a dozen Mosca scattered throughout the hall, waiting by doors, standing by something that looked and smelled like a restaurant.

And the children! She tried hard not to recoil. She'd never seen a Mosca without a mask before. The children's faces without masks or goggles were wrinkled, with heavy eyelids and unnaturally large eyes and almost no nose at all—no wonder they didn't mind the stench. Yet at the same time, there was something almost endearing about their oversized features.

She found herself smiling—was she actually starting to *like* the Mosca?

A grown Mosca, who she assumed was Bonebreak's brother, patted her shoulder as though she too were a small child. "Little human childrens," he said. "I am Ironmage. My brother tells me he has a deal with you. A lucrative deal. *If* you win the Gauntlet." He let out a burst of laughter. "My brother was never bright. But come, get food just the same."

He patted her again. Less like a child, she realized, and more like a dog.

"This is crazy," she muttered. With the goggles on, Anya and Willa looked almost alien themselves, and Cora knew she must look just as strange.

A Mosca child excitedly pounced on her, pulling her along amid a torrent of giggles. "Come," it said in slightly broken English. "I'll feed you and give you a baths and take good care of you."

Cora sighed and let herself be dragged along. Forget beating the Gauntlet. It would be challenging enough to prove humanity's worth to a species who thought of her as nothing more than an overgrown puppy.

14

Cora

BONEBREAK'S BROTHER, IRONMAGE, TOOK them on a long underground train ride through the hollow mountains to a small city he told them was called Tern. Tall buildings rose like skyscrapers toward the ceiling of the mountain. The edifices were made of stone and metal and glass, but all cast in a reddish shade. Ironmage pointed to a building on the city's perimeter, proudly declaring that his home comprised the tenth level—nearly the highest. Cora took off her goggles out of curiosity. Without them, the world beneath the mountain was almost entirely black, with only the faintest twinkle of glowworms like stars overhead.

As soon as they'd climbed the spiral ramps to Ironmage's home, one of the children set a bowl of food on the floor in front of Cora; it was unappetizingly watery and brown and didn't smell much better.

The child smiled as it patted her on the head. "Good human. You eat now."

It set down another bowl for Anya but gave Willa a plate of food that at least resembled solids.

"Why do you get a real meal?" Cora asked.

Willa wrote on her pad:

The Mosca have always liked apes. We don't walk upright either. They think that's a sign of superior intelligence.

Cora rolled her eyes. Her stomach grumbled. She tilted the bowl to her lips, prepared to wince if the food tasted as bad as it smelled, and was pleasantly surprised to find it only mildly offensive.

"So, brother." Ironmage sat heavily in one of the backless Mosca chairs surrounding a low table, where he and Bonebreak were eating something that looked far more palatable. If there was a Mrs. Ironmage, Cora hadn't seen any sign of her. "You bring me presents. You bring me news of the outer galaxies. You bring me"—he motioned toward the humans—"this unusual business opportunity."

"This could be the deal we've dreamed of since our youth," Bonebreak said through his mask. "How often have you and I sat over hotmugs, talking about what would happen if humans were granted intelligent status? With their nimble fingers and their skill at lying, they'd be formidable trading partners. You said so once yourself."

"I was drunk at the time," Ironmage stated.

"It is more than a drunken dream now," Bonebreak insisted. "If a human runner were to beat the Gauntlet, that human would wield incredible influence over her people. She would be a natural leader, the first human councilperson. She'd be able to set trade deals on behalf of all of humanity. And you and I"—Bonebreak's voice brimmed with excitement—"we'd hold all the cards! First rights to trade deals! Exclusive bartering! We'd be rich, we'd even be famous . . . the runner would have sat on our own floor!" He swept out a gloved hand to motion to Cora and her friends.

Ironmage eyed them closer, no expression showing behind his mask, but Cora got the sense that as tempted as he was, he was still skeptical. "Which one will run?"

"The older girl," Bonebreak said.

Ironmage stood. He lumbered over to where they sat, crouched down on his weak knees, and prodded Cora's arm. "She is rather puny. Perhaps if she had months to improve her strength, but the Gauntlet begins in less than six days."

"*Six* days?" Cora sputtered. "I thought we had seventeen!"

One of the Mosca children giggled. It waddled over with a contraption of wires and blinking numbers. The child rearranged the wires expertly, programmed in some numbers, and then handed it to her. "Here, little human."

Cora looked down at the numbers on the contraption. The first column said 5.9, the second said 17.1.

"A time conversion clock," Bonebreak explained dismissively, as if such highly technical electronics were child's play. "Each day here is about three on your planet. There are roughly seventeen human days until the Gauntlet begins." He turned back to his brother. "And she *is* strong enough. If size mattered in the Gauntlet, those stumpy little Axion would never have passed it.

She's fast, and you haven't seen what she can do with her mind." Bonebreak set down his drink and pointed to it. "Girl. Levitate this drink."

Ironmage's children watched in awe, little mouths agape to reveal uneven teeth. Cora rolled her eyes. He might as well have asked her to play fetch.

She closed her eyes and concentrated on the drink. She let her thoughts reach around the cup and the handle like fingers.

Lift, she commanded.

The children clapped their hands together. Cora opened her eyes. The cup hovered three inches off the table. Slowly, she let it lower, even gave it a little spin before it landed. The children cheered. She smiled. All that practice during quarantine had paid off.

Ironmage stared at her in disbelief. "Well!" he said at last. "You weren't lying, brother. I've heard the rumors, but I've never seen *that.*"

"She has been trained by a Kindred. She might not look like much, but she meets the requirements. And that ape has run the Gauntlet before. She can give us important insight."

Willa huffed in disagreement, but Bonebreak only waved away her objection.

Ironmage rubbed his chin, nodding. "This could work. . . . Yes. It's possible. Not *probable,* of course. She'll probably go mad like the others and die within the first few puzzles. I give her a handful of hours at most. But if it did work . . ." He cackled in delight, rubbing his hands together at the thought of imagined riches.

A handful of hours?

"How long does it last?" Cora asked. "The whole Gauntlet from start to finish."

"It varies, little childs, it varies. Some runners complete puzzles in ten human minutes. For someone relatively weak like you, I would imagine each puzzle would take several human hours."

She ignored the insult. So if there were twelve puzzles, she should expect the Gauntlet to last about twenty-four hours. A full day.

She motioned to the darkness beyond the windows. "Am I going to have to wear these goggles the whole time?"

"Oh, no, little childs. The Gatherers are blind as cave worms, and the Axion and Kindred as well. The Gauntlet happens aboveground, on the surface. The module ship lands in a valley close to Tern; there are tunnels to connect it. The delegates bring their own ships that interlock to the Gauntlet module. They don't set foot underground. Afraid of the dark." He made a disgusted sound. "All together, it forms a small compound. The Gauntlet module, with its twelve chambers, is the centerpiece. Around it are smaller modules that serve as the central vestibule, recess rooms, and control compartments."

"Cassian said there was a formal registration process."

Ironmage dismissed that with a wave. "Bah. Perhaps there is when the Kindred host the Gauntlet. I am not surprised they would make it as complicated as possible. We Mosca care nothing for such formalities. Once the weather cooperates, we throw the runners in and it begins. It is no more formal than that."

"How many runners will there be? And of which species?"

Both Ironmage and Bonebreak were silent for a moment.

Bonebreak scratched his chin awkwardly. "Well," he said. "One. You."

Cora nearly choked on the last of the gruel. "I thought there were normally more than that. At least five or six."

Ironmage took a hefty sip of his drink. "Runners don't like to travel all the way to Drogane. Can't imagine why."

"I'm sure it has nothing to do with the smell," Cora muttered. "Or the general complete disregard for any law and order or, you know, lamps."

Ironmage shrugged. "What does it matter how many run?"

"It matters," Cora said, "because this means all eyes will be on me. The Kindred Council member Arrowal has been trying to sabotage me this entire time. And Fian has been helping him. This makes it easier for them."

Bonebreak scoffed. "We do not fear meddling by a few Council members. The Gauntlet cannot be sabotaged. Believe me, if one could cheat the Gauntlet, we Mosca would be the ones to figure out how. The Kindred have even tightened the regulations. A loophole was brought to the Intelligence Council's attention, something about how a runner might be able to manipulate the Chief Assessors' command inputs to approve a victory before the puzzles even began. The loophole was closed, the regulations rewritten."

Cora felt the blood draining from her face. *She* had been the one planning on using that loophole to win.

"When the time comes, little childs," Bonebreak said, "we will take you aboveground to the valley. You will see the Gauntlet modules for yourself. In the meantime"—he poked at her thin arm—"I suggest you work on building your strength."

He said something in Mosca to the children, who jumped up and grabbed Cora and the others by the hands, pulling them toward a partitioned area of the great room that had been filled with big, ridiculous fluffy pillows.

"Good night, little childs," one child said, standing on tiptoe to pat Cora on the head.

Once they were alone, Cora sighed and flopped onto a pillow. Willa pulled out a piece of paper.

Isn't nice, is it?

Cora swallowed hard. She was suddenly aware that everything the Mosca did to treat her and the other humans like animals, humans had done—and worse—to chimpanzees.

"Sorry," Cora said quietly.

Willa huffed.

"Listen," Cora said to Anya. "You heard what they said. What are we going to do now?"

"About what?" Anya asked blankly.

"About the Gauntlet!" Cora whispered.

Anya nodded quickly. "Oh, yeah. Right. Of course." Her hands, tucked in her lap, were shaking with the tremor.

Cora turned to Willa and explained, "We were going to use that loophole to cheat it. It was Plan A. Take over the Assessors' minds and make them approve my win before I'd even entered the first puzzle. But somehow, the Kindred found out our plan. It must have been Fian. When he betrayed Cassian, he must have told the Council."

Willa wrote a note.

If cheating was Plan A, what's Plan B?

Cora nearly laughed in panic. "Plan B," she said, "was to run it for real. To actually try to win. But you heard Ironmage and Bonebreak. I'm not ready. My training with Cassian was interrupted. You said yourself I shouldn't run."

Anya leaned forward. "But you *have* to run, Cora. I'll help. We have seventeen days, that's enough to finish your training. I can teach you to control your perceptive abilities better. And physical conditioning should be easy enough; there's plenty of room to climb and run in the city."

"Thanks," Cora said, "but it's the intellectual puzzles I need most help with. Letter and number puzzles have always been my weakness."

She and Anya both looked sidelong at Willa. The chimp folded her arms obstinately until Anya batted her eyes and said in a sweet voice, "Isn't that what the Axion did to you, Willa? Make your brain stronger?"

A grunt of unhappy affirmation came from Willa.

"Look at it this way," Cora pleaded. "I'm going to run the Gauntlet with your help or without it. Nothing you say can convince me not to. But your advice could make all the difference. And if humanity is freed, animals will fare better too. I'll make certain of it."

Willa huffed and wagged her head side to side.

"You could even help set up a new system," Cora pressed. "If

I win the Gauntlet, you could have a real say in the way animals are treated. We could put in laws so that none could ever be experimented on like you were."

At this, Willa paused. She wrote again.

This is beyond foolish. You will get yourself killed. But that is your choice to make.

Cora grinned. "I take this to mean you'll help."

Willa rolled her eyes but nodded.

"That just leaves moral training," Anya said.

Cora took Lucky's journal from her pocket. She flipped through the pages almost reverently, as if she could see him in his tight handwriting, smell him in the binding. In these pages, he had written his thoughts about how the Kindred had mistreated their human and animal wards and what he thought was right and wrong.

She stopped on a list he had made.

Granddad's Code, it said. *First: Do no harm. Second: Think about the good of the group over the good of the individual. Third . . .*

Cora closed the book, squeezing it tightly. "I already have a moral coach," she said. "Lucky."

15

Mali

BY THE TIME THE Kindred supply shuttle docked on the aggregate station, every muscle in Mali's body was strained. For the last eight days, she'd been pressed awkwardly against Leon in the ship's insulated lining. His elbow shoved in her back. Her nose crammed near his armpit. Only puddles of condensation to drink and pilfered cargo stores to eat from. She figured she'd like him a lot better again when they had a few feet between them.

They listened in hushed silence as the Kindred officials unloaded the shuttle cargo hold, turned off the lights, and sealed the doors. Once she was certain it was clear, Mali pushed her way out of the ship's lining, gasping for air.

"Couldn't . . . breathe . . . ," she said. "You're too . . . fat."

Leon stumbled out behind her, stretching his neck, sucking in deep gulps of air. "It's muscle! Besides, it wasn't a picnic having my face smooshed up against your hair, either. It kept getting in my nose."

They went to opposite sides of the shuttle's cargo hold, eager for some distance. Mali closed her eyes. She wiggled her toes and fingers, pumping some blood back into them. She opened one eye, glancing at him sidelong. Okay, it hadn't *all* been terrible. One thought of that kiss and she felt herself going warm. Again.

Leon sniffed the air filtering through the shuttle's vents. "Old air and rusted metal." He made a face. "I didn't miss that smell."

The station's smell, faint though it was, stirred unpleasant memories for Mali too: Being imprisoned in the enclosure. Learning Anya had been drugged. Fian's betrayal.

"With luck," she said, "we will not be here long. Cora saw Cassian in one of the interrogation rooms on the fourth level. We traveled there through the shipping tunnels before; we only need to follow our previous footsteps, locate the kill-dart weapons cache Cora told you about, and use them to free Cassian. Then we come back here, steal a shuttle that Cassian knows how to fly, and go to Drogane."

"You say it like that's easy," Leon said flatly.

"You doubt my abilities?"

"No way. I'm not stupid." He held up his hand in mock surrender as she went to the cargo door, pressed her ear against it, and then slowly eased it open. Beyond was the same flight room they'd departed from weeks ago, though spotless now. Someone had cleaned all signs of the battle that had raged here when they'd escaped.

She signaled to Leon that it was safe to exit, and they silently slipped out of the shuttle and made their way to the edge of the flight room. Mali knew the official modules and corridors of the station well, but those would be swarming with Kindred. It was Leon who knew the hidden interior tunnel system.

"I don't see any entrances to the tunnels," Leon said, jerking his chin toward the edge of the flight room. "We'll have to go into the hallways and look for one there."

Mali didn't like the risk, but she nodded. She took a step toward the door, glancing at the sensor directly above it. She closed her eyes and concentrated. Telekinesis had never been her strongest talent, but the amplifiers built into the sensors would make it easier. She concentrated. The door slid open an inch. She redoubled her concentration. Two inches. Then . . .

"Shit!" Leon hissed.

Mali's eyes flew open. The hallway beyond the cracked doorway was decimated. A crater three feet across scarred the metal floor. Damaged lights flickered on and off eerily. Smoke still rose from the wreckage.

She blinked in incomprehension. "An explosion. It happened recently." She twisted around to Leon. "What caused this?"

He shrugged one shoulder.

They both listened keenly, but except for the flickering lights, there was no other sound. No footsteps. No battle calls. No blaring alarms. They eased open the doors and tiptoed into the silent hallway. Mali went to the edge of the crater and peered down. It cut straight through to the level below, and even the level below that. Stains of dark blood were smeared on the edges. Kindred blood.

"A gas main blow?" Leon offered.

"There are no gas mains," Mali answered. She crouched to inspect the burn marks. "This had to have been intentional. Biosynthetic chemicals would be the only ones strong enough to do this. They are kept in the science chambers, which are only accessible to Kindred officials. The Kindred must have set off this explosion themselves."

"Why would they blow up part of their own station?" Leon asked.

Mali touched the edge of the crater. A familiar smell hung in the air. She leaned closer to a puddle of mystery liquid and sniffed. She drew back sharply. "One of the incendiaries was peach liqueur."

Leon raised an eyebrow. "They only keep that in the Hunt menagerie. Trust me, I know every bar on this station."

Shots rang out down the hall, and he spun around. Mali went rigid. She knew that sound: laser pulses. Pulses could be strong enough to either kill or stun, depending on the setting, and these sounded especially deadly.

"Quick." She pointed to where the explosion had shattered through the wall to reveal one of the tunnels. They crawled into the tunnel as the laser pulses fired closer.

"We need to get to the Hunt," Leon whispered. "And get Dane's kill-dart guns. Whatever's going on here, we need weapons of our own."

Footsteps approached, followed by the shouts of Kindred and then more shots. Mali pressed a finger to her lips. The tunnel was shallow, and Leon reached out to pull her closer.

"Careful."

He hugged her tightly so that she wouldn't be visible from the hallway. His chest against her back. His breath on her neck. She felt her heart starting to beat faster. For all she'd acted like she'd been annoyed by the days pressed uncomfortably close together in the supply ship, she had to admit, she did like the feeling of his arms around her.

Trusting someone this much, she thought, *is dangerous.* And yet, perhaps, a danger she was willing to face.

More footsteps approached, stiff and regimented. Cloaked Kindred. But the other sets of footsteps were looser and quick, more like how uncloaked Kindred would fight.

"The Kindred are fighting one another," Mali whispered. "Cloaked against uncloaked."

"Why?"

Mali's lips parted to answer, but she wasn't certain. Her mind turned to what Cora had told her about Cassian's secret organization, the Fifth of Five. If anything went wrong with the Gauntlet, the Fifth of Five planned to rise up and forcibly take control of the station.

"The Fifth of Five must believe that the Gauntlet plan has failed," she whispered. "They do not know that Cora is preparing to run a different Gauntlet. That there is still hope. This complicates things significantly. We must find Cassian, quickly."

Another explosion went off on a nearby level, shaking the whole station.

"We gotta get out of here first," Leon said, eyeing the creaking beams overhead, "before this whole level collapses. Come on. I know where we can go."

They crawled deeper into the tunnel, away from the sounds of laser pulses. The chalked navigation marks Leon had made weeks ago were dusty but still there. At every turn, he consulted his old marks until he found the symbol for Bonebreak's lair—a masked face—and led Mali down two more levels and through winding passages, pointing out the cleaner traps along the way and showing her how to avoid them. At last, they reached a grate at the end of the tunnel.

"This level's practically forgotten," he said. "It's where Bonebreak used to house his smuggling operation. We'll be safe here." He elbowed open the grate, and they climbed out into a dimly lit room. Mali drew in a lungful of fresh air, studying the room. A warehouse. Lit only by a pair of flickering wall lights, the rest long broken.

A huge figure suddenly lurched from the shadows.

Mali tensed, ready to fight.

"Wait!" Leon said. "Look."

And then she recognized, as the creature emerged into the lights, four legs like a horse, a ridiculously long neck, and brown and yellow spots. A . . . giraffe? Here? Behind it were two zebras and a lioness, tethered to the wall.

"Bonebreak traded in animals?" she said.

Leon shook his head. "Uh, I think I'd remember if those had been here before."

Mali took a hesitant step forward. The lioness turned to her with lazy eyes, flicking her tail. Recognition flared in Mali. "They're the animals from the Hunt. Someone must have brought them here."

"Mali?"

Both of them spun at the sound of Mali's name. A girl stood in the doorway, too far from the nearest light to be seen clearly. But Mali recognized her outline. The strong, lithe dancer's body. The way she favored one knee. The hair twisted into balls.

"Makayla?"

Makayla ran up and, before Mali could react, threw her

arms around her. "I can't believe you're here! I thought you left the station!" They had never been the best of friends—Mali had kept her distance in the Hunt—but she'd observed Makayla long enough to know she was trustworthy.

"I did leave. We came back." Mali introduced Leon and explained why they had returned. Makayla nodded along, a serious expression on her face.

"Tessela is going to want to hear this. Hang on. Shoukry!"

Another face popped around the corner. Mali recognized the Hunt bartender's kind dark eyes, which lit up in surprise when he saw her.

"Shoukry," Makayla said, "tell Tessela we have company."

He nodded and disappeared down the hall.

Mali looked over the animals in the dusty warehouse, taking in Makayla's dress, which was now torn and dirty, as though she'd been in a battle. "What happened?"

"Not long after you escaped, all hell broke loose. Kindred started fighting against Kindred. I've never seen anything like it. Tessela came to free us and the animals—as many as we were able to get out of there. She's leading a group of rebels against the Kindred Council. They've stormed a flight room and loaded most of the animals and the other kids on a ship to Armstrong. We're leaving in minutes. You should come, too."

"Armstrong isn't the paradise the Kindred told you it was," Mali said, exchanging a look with Leon. "And now the sheriff there is dead. It's even more unstable than ever."

Makayla took this in for a moment, scratching her ear, and then sighed. "Any place has to be safer than here. They're bombing every level. Sooner or later they'll find us."

Shoukry returned, exchanging a few words with a Kindred woman in a form-fitting gray uniform, her straight dark hair loose around her shoulders.

"Tessela," Mali said in relief.

"Mali?" Tessela shook her head. "You two are fools to have returned to the station. You're lucky Makayla found you and not Arrowal's troops."

Tessela's eyes were clear and her movements were fluid—she was uncloaked. Tessela had been Cassian's second in command after Fian, but now that Fian had betrayed them, Tessela was the only Kindred left who Mali knew they could trust.

"We had to return," Mali said. Shoukry stepped forward to hand her a flask of water, which she guzzled and then handed to Leon. "We came back for Cassian."

Tessela shook her head in regret. "We've had no luck trying to free him. We thought three hundred Kindred were sympathetic to our cause, but only half that rose up with us. We're using tactics developed on Earth: guerrilla warfare. We've lasted this long, but we can't fight much longer. Arrowal set off an electromagnetic pulse that rendered all our guns useless. We only barely managed to flee down here. Cassian's two levels up and they have every hall closed off. There's no way to reach him."

Mali turned to Leon. "Could the tunnels get us there?"

Leon scratched his chin. "You and me, yeah. The Kindred can't fit."

Tessela wiped an arm over the grime on her face. "That's brave of you, but without weapons, it's impossible."

"We do have weapons," Mali said. "Or at least, we know where to get them." She glanced at Makayla and Shoukry, who had known the Hunt menagerie even better than she had. "Kill-dart guns that Dane used to control animals. They work with low-tech mechanics. The electromagnetic pulse won't have affected them."

Tessela's eyebrows rose. She glanced at Makayla, who nodded. "It's true. Once they arrested Dane and made me Head Ward, they told me about them." She looked at Mali. "You know the code to access them?"

Mali nodded. "Cora told us."

Tessela still looked doubtful. "Even with functioning weapons, it would be dangerous to go after Cassian. The ship for Armstrong leaves in moments. It's a cargo vessel, slow but safe. It will arrive in fourteen days. You should be on it now, or you might not get another chance."

Leon snorted. "Sorry, lady. We aren't leaving without Cassian."

Makayla grabbed Mali's arm. "This is good-bye, then. Shoukry and I have to get on that ship with the last of the animals."

"Our friends are on Armstrong," Mali said. "Nok and Rolf. Ask for them—they will help you."

"We will." Makayla pulled her into another embrace. "Good luck." She and Shoukry turned and ran down the hall toward the flight room.

"Come," Tessela said. "We must hurry."

As she led them down the hallways, she described where Cassian was being imprisoned and explained in quick bursts about the Fifth of Five's uprising: how as soon as Cassian was arrested and Cora escaped the station, they stormed the station's control center. Cloaked Kindred soldiers fought back, led by Arrowal, but members of the Fifth of Five managed to free two menageries of humans and animals and were preparing to free a third.

"Arrowal's troops outnumber us three to one," Tessela said. "The odds are against us, but we're staying strong. Be cautious— even if you free Cassian, this level might soon be overrun. And there's nowhere else to go. We're at the bottom of the station."

Mali opened her mouth to speak.

Before she could, a volley of laser pulses ricocheted on the level just above them.

All eyes turned toward the ceiling.

Tessela's face was heavy with foreboding. "They've found us. All we can do now is hold out as long as we can, and hope they can't get through."

16

Cora

ON DROGANE, CORA SOON learned what Bonebreak
meant when he said days there didn't pass the same way as they
did on Earth. In the darkness of the hollow mountain, any hint of
the exterior sun was gone. Instead the Mosca counted time by the
throbbing of the glowworms, which pulsed consistently for what
Cora calculated, using the time conversion clock the Mosca children made for her, to be around fifty-seven Earth hours, and then
shut off for twelve.

Cora spent every day practicing her training. Levitation with
Anya and solving mental puzzles with Willa, as well as keeping to
a strict physical regimen: push-ups until she collapsed; agility until
her toes went numb; running up and down the ramp that circled
Ironmage's building twenty laps a day.

She reached the tenth floor—Ironmage's home—just as her
leg muscles threatened to give out. *Twenty. Done.* Her forehead was
slick with sweat. She walked onto the suspended balcony outside

Ironmage's door and collapsed on the terrace, chest heaving as she caught her breath. Around her, eerie white plants that got their nutrients from the air hung from the balcony railings, overlooking the dark subterranean city of Tern.

She checked her time against the conversion clock. Four minutes faster than the day before.

Better.

Chest still heaving, she forced herself to sit up. Training wasn't over yet.

She adjusted her goggles and took out Lucky's journal. She'd spent time each day after her physical regimen going through it, soaking up Lucky's words, remembering him.

> *Everything that's alive must die. If you can, give it a good life first. . . .*

Lightweight, nearly inaudible footsteps sounded behind her and she put down the journal. Willa approached across the balcony, goggles knotted behind her head. For the last week they'd run through intellectual drills every afternoon, multiplying by fractions and rhyming difficult words, but Willa still hadn't said anything about her own experience in the Gauntlet. The chimp swung herself up to perch on the railing in a way that made Cora's head spin, but Willa only looked down calmly at the hundred-foot fall. Willa pointed to Lucky's journal.

"Yeah," Cora said. "I practically have it all memorized by now. I wish you'd known him. His granddad taught him a moral code. Not like the Kindred's code—it doesn't have anything to do with logic, but rather kindness. Listen to this." She read, "'Don't make anything suffer just because you can't stomach what needs to be done. Be true to the soul of the world.'"

Willa nodded. She reached out a hand, touching Cora's heart, and Cora nodded back.

"That's right," Cora said. "Heart. That's what Lucky was all about. That's why his words are going to help me in the Gauntlet." She frowned as she tucked the journal back into her pocket. "You know, I keep thinking about Rolf and Nok. And all the people we left behind on Armstrong. It was chaos. What if another bad sheriff took over? They could be enslaved again, or worse." Cora tried not to think about all those dead bodies under the tent.

Willa handed her a note.

> . . . Or they could be thriving. They were strong. Believe in them.

Cora smiled. "Thanks. I needed that." She sighed. "Time for more multiplication tables?"

But Willa shook her head. She jumped down from the railing and waved Cora over to one of the low benches on the balcony. She patted the seat next to her and then held out a note.

> We have only eleven human days left. It's time to practice something real.

Cora looked up in surprise. "You mean a real intellectual puzzle from the Gauntlet?" She dropped her voice. "One of the ones you solved when you ran it?" A thrill ran through her, thinking about getting real information at last.

Willa nodded.

She handed over several scraps of paper. Cora took each one and studied them carefully. Her hands shook a little as she imagined being in the Gauntlet itself just days from now. Willa had been there once, sequestered in a ten-by-ten-by-ten puzzle cube, trying to solve this very same puzzle. What had been going through the chimp's head? Had she been confident? Scared?

Each paper held a number.

46

823

4164

38

1022

Willa took out her notebook and wrote:

Sort out the numbers and you will end up with one word. The word will be your key to solving the puzzle.

Cora took a deep breath. Rolf would have probably been able to solve it in thirty seconds. But Rolf wasn't able to help her now. She was on her own, just like she'd be in the Gauntlet. No Lucky and his morals. No Rolf and his number games. No Nok with her gift for language, no Leon to climb walls for her.

She set the scraps of paper on the bench and started

rearranging them. She tried to order them like a numerical cross-word, but it led to nothing. She tried reading them backward, then tried using multiples, and then tried factoring numbers by each other. Nothing.

Sensing her frustration, Willa picked up the 46, set it at the top of the bench, and then drew out a 2 in the dust beneath it.

Cora studied the scraps of paper. "Two? You mean that the missing link between four and six is two? But how does that form a word?" It suddenly clicked. "B? You mean it's alphabetical?" She started moving the squares faster, using trial and error until she found a relationship among all the numbers, then translated them alphabetically into letters that she rearranged to spell a word.

B-E-L-O-W.

"Below?" Cora said.

Willa wrote in her notebook:

Good. In the Gauntlet, each chamber has six doors, one on each wall. When I solved this puzzle, it told me that I should go through the lowest door—BELOW—to move on to the next. Of course, each iteration of the Gauntlet is different. It is unlikely you will get this exact puzzle.

And then she added:

It took me only sixty seconds to solve.

Cora read the note and rolled her eyes. "We can't all be genetically modified supergenius chimpanzees."

Willa smiled.

Cora looked again at the number puzzle and her mood shifted back to one of worry. "Cassian said some of the puzzles were dangerous. A lot more dangerous than just getting the wrong door. He said that out of eleven humans who have run the Gauntlet before, none of them survived." She paused. "Isn't there anything else you can tell me about it? How it works, how it strategizes? Why it's so dangerous?"

The smile fell from Willa's face. Her fingers started drumming anxiously over her pencil. Cora couldn't see her eyes behind the goggles, but she sensed Willa was thinking back on memories she'd rather not remember.

At last, the chimp wrote:

> The Gauntlet wants you to feel confident—a
> false confidence that will trick you into
> arrogance. The psychological tests start from
> the very beginning. They get harder. I made
> it as far as the eighth puzzle chamber. It was a
> moral puzzle—

The pencil stopped moving in her hand.

"A moral puzzle?" Cora asked, surprised. "I thought you failed in a perceptive one."

Willa shook her head and then held up the pencil in the air. When she took her hand away, the pencil hovered in empty air. Cora started. All this time, Willa was that effortlessly perceptive? And she had *still* failed the Gauntlet?

Willa plucked the pencil out of the air and wrote:

The Gauntlet gave me a perceptive puzzle in
module five. The puzzle chamber caught fire
on all four sides. I couldn't get to any doors
without putting the fire out, but there was
nothing but sand in a box too high to reach.
I had to use telekinesis to move the sand to
smother the fire, or I would have died.
And then . . .

She paused, her hand shaking slightly. Cora wasn't certain
she would continue until she wrote:

Puzzle six was an intellectual puzzle. A
word problem, but in real life. It was about
determining when two trains would intersect.
The trick was not to crash them. One broke
through the wall, letting me into puzzle seven.
That module was a physical puzzle. Balance.
That one was easy for me, of course, but a
Conmarine runner in a different module fell
and died. And then puzzle eight. The moral
one.

Her lips were set firmly.

After a moment, Cora rested a hand over hers and said, "You
don't have to tell me. Not until you're ready."

Willa hesitated for a few moments and then wrote:

The final four puzzles make up the third round. In the third round, they will make it personal. They need to know that the Gauntlet is real for you. That round is when I—

Willa stood abruptly.

It doesn't matter. I failed. That is all you need to know.

Willa left in a hurry. Cora sat on the bench alone, studying the scraps of Willa's notes, wondering what had traumatized Willa so much that she couldn't even discuss it. When she looked up, she saw Anya standing by the doorway, half hidden behind a white fern. How long had she been there, watching?

Cora held up a hand in a small wave. "Anya?"

Anya hesitated, her features tight, and quickly crossed the balcony to Cora's bench. She sat a little closer than normal. Her hands were shaking again.

"What did Willa say to you?" Anya asked.

Cora's eyes widened. "Willa? Just the usual advice." She tilted her head. "Are you okay? I know we haven't had a lot of time to talk outside of training, but you haven't been acting like yourself ever since Fuel Station Theta. I've barely even seen you except for trainings and meals."

"I've been trying to see if I could get any information from the children," Anya said. Again, she looked toward where Willa had gone. "Willa didn't say anything else about the Gauntlet? No other advice?"

"Not much. I think it troubles her to talk about it."

Anya's face relaxed slightly.

"What's wrong?" Cora asked. "I thought you and she were friends."

"I thought so too," Anya said. "But I sense something different about her. I can't put my finger on it, but I don't think you should trust any advice she gives you. It's been a long time since I knew her, and her loyalties might have changed."

Before Cora could ask more, Bonebreak came onto the balcony.

"Well, little childrens. Guess what just landed on the surface."

Cora felt a nervous thrill. "The Gauntlet?"

Bonebreak nodded. "The preliminary modules docked at first light. It is constructing itself as we speak. And fortunately for you, I have some friends who monitor the transport hub near the surface. I've arranged for them to be conveniently absent so that we can take a private tour." He rubbed his hands together in glee.

Cora started. "Now?"

"Yes, while the storms are holding off."

Cora stood.

Anya jumped up. "I'll come too!"

"No." Cora wasn't even sure what instinct had made her answer so quickly. There was no reason not to trust Anya. Anya was more dedicated to humanity's freedom than practically anyone else in the universe. But Cora couldn't shake an uneasy feeling. "You still haven't entirely recovered. You should rest. I'll go alone."

Anya gave her a confused stare, but Cora turned away.

"Let's go," Cora said to Bonebreak, trying to sound confident. But the truth was, as much as Anya warned her about Willa, Cora couldn't help the feeling that Anya was the real wild card. Those Kindred drugs, somehow, had made her more unpredictable. And right now, Cora needed people she could count on—even if that meant only herself.

17

Cora

CORA PULLED OFF THE goggles and let sunlight bathe her face. It was a gorgeous day on Drogane's surface, warm and breezy with just a hint of storm clouds on the horizon.

"I've missed the sun," she said.

Bonebreak climbed to the top of the tunnel and tilted his head toward the blue sky. "Sunlight?" He shrugged. "Overrated. Come on."

He pointed toward a path that led over a small rise into the valley. The path seemed to be made of crushed stone and shells cemented together, with deep grooves every few inches like tire tracks. "We seldom walk on the surface," Bonebreak explained, lumbering in the typical skittish Mosca walk. "We prefer to take rover spheres when we must travel aboveground. They run on these tracks."

Cora had noticed a row of tank-sized spheres in the underground travel hub they'd passed through before taking the tunnel to the surface. "Why didn't we take one, then?"

"The rover spheres and their destinations are logged. It's against the rules to see the Gauntlet before it begins. And last I checked, we were sneaking up here covertly."

Cora swept her hands out toward the open valley. "*This* is sneaking around? We're completely exposed. Anyone could see us."

"No one else would be foolish enough to come up here with that storm approaching." He pointed toward the end of the valley, where the storm clouds were moving in, a smear of heavy gray. "We won't have long to look over the modules. We have to be back underground before it hits."

They continued walking along the track. The valley reminded Cora of something from Colorado or Montana, tall mountains with trees clinging to the sides, vegetation hardy enough to withstand the planet's frequent storms.

As they crested the rise, the lower part of the valley unfurled, revealing metallic pieces of a structure like the craggy ruins of a small town: about twenty modules of varying size—some as big as giant industrial shipping containers, others as tiny as a closet. They were coated in gray metal siding that glinted, reflecting the storm clouds overhead. A car-sized module suddenly lurched to the left.

"They're moving!" Cora said. "I thought you said we were alone."

"We are." Bonebreak nodded toward the valley. "They're self-directed. The module arrives and builds itself. That, little childs, is the Gauntlet."

Cora watched in fascination as robotic arms and levers slowly inched the modules closer to one another. Panels mechanically opened and expanded into different shapes. The entire structure was about the size of the Bay Pines detention facility: smaller than she would have thought, but she supposed the Gauntlet didn't need much room, as it mostly worked with optical illusions.

Bonebreak pointed a stubby finger toward the various structures. "The two biggest modules interlock with each other to form a large central vestibule. The other modules are the recess rooms and control compartments. And those twelve modules of identical size are the puzzle chambers."

"That's what all this trouble is about," Cora said, studying it. "What divides free species from captive ones. Just a few pieces of machinery."

"Highly intelligent machinery," Bonebreak clarified. "The Gauntlet is an autonomous structure, built from Axion and Gatherer technology, capable of operating its own systems. It is run by the stock algorithm—an evolved computer program. Its protocol cannot be influenced by any outside species, not even its creators."

The two largest modules began to unfold themselves. The edges were cut into uneven shapes like puzzle pieces, which slowly moved together to form one large room. Nearby, small mechanical arms scraped up dirt and rock like bulldozers and deposited the debris deep within the control compartment modules.

"What are those arms doing?" she asked.

"The Gauntlet requires natural resources to power the illusions in the puzzle chambers. Minerals, water, air, sand. Basic materials that can be obtained on almost any planet or station." He glanced at the storm clouds at the edge of the valley as though judging their distance. "Come. We can take a closer look, but we must not dawdle."

He started down the path to the valley floor. His twisted legs didn't handle the steep angle well, and he let out a volley of cursing. Now Cora understood why everything in Tern was made of spiraling ramps.

"How did the Mosca ever pass the Gauntlet's physical puzzles if you can hardly walk down a hill?"

"We have incredible strength!" Bonebreak said in a huff. "And we're fast when we want to be. Plus we got lucky with the puzzles. No stairs."

As they approached the Gauntlet, the sound of grinding metal echoed up and down the valley. The closest module was shifting slowly, transforming itself from a flat panel into a cube. Already the hull had lifted and rearranged itself into what looked like a break room with benches and tables. Interior thrusters were slowly moving upward, the walls pulling in.

"How long until it's finished transforming?"

"Two days," Bonebreak said, which Cora translated into about six human days. He continued, "The first delegates anticipated to arrive are the Gatherers. Most boring race in the galaxy. They'll spend their time standing as still as these mountains, meditating on something dull like the meaning of wind, or time, or fingernails, until the Gauntlet begins. After that, the Axion will come, and then the Kindred. The Mosca delegation's already here, of course, in Tern."

"I don't suppose the Mosca delegates could be . . ."

"Bargained with?" Bonebreak made a noncommittal gesture with his head. "The Chief Assessor, Redrage, is exceedingly moral for a Mosca. Hence she was chosen by the Council. And besides, as I mentioned, the Gauntlet protocol cannot be tampered with. However . . ." He leaned in close. "Ironmage and I have been working on Redrage. We got her drunk last night and convinced her to include us in the delegate aide party, so we will be there to assist you. She is warming up for a bribe, I think. Already she informed us that one of the perceptive puzzles will require levitation of heavy objects."

Cora chewed on her lip, nervous. "How heavy? I've just been training with dice and pebbles."

"How should I know? Twenty kilos, forty kilos, sixty kilos. I suggest you practice while you still can. Hard."

They continued to walk among the eerily shifting modules. It was like a living creature, able to grow and thrive on its own. Bonebreak kept glancing out toward the edge of the valley, where the clouds were darkening.

"Up we go." Bonebreak climbed awkwardly onto a metal platform, reaching down a hand to help Cora. She ducked as one of the walls swung upward and connected with another in that puzzle-piece way.

"Stay close," Bonebreak said. He pointed to one of the ten-by-ten-by-ten puzzle chamber modules, which was rotating itself on top of another one. "See that? The twelve puzzle chambers. And this"—he led her to the largest structure, which towered above them—"this is where the four Chief Assessors will sit at the dais and observe your progress from monitors, while the stock algorithm produces a real-time report on the puzzles."

Cora marveled at the moving structure. Back in the Hunt, Cassian had shown her a three-dimensional holographic projection of the Gauntlet. She still remembered the tiny scale model with its twelve rooms, each a different color depending on what type of puzzle it was, and a tiny holographic figure moving from one module to the next. And now she was *here*. Not a scale model anymore. No longer just a dream.

She reached out and touched one of the gray metal planks moving upward.

"Careful there, little childs." Bonebreak moved her fingers out of the way just as another plank swung down that would have crushed her hand. It met a platform that was rising from the floor. There were four small holes in the facing table.

"That was where the keys used to be," Bonebreak said. "In previous versions of the Gauntlet, the four Chief Assessors turned four keys to signal that they approved of the Gauntlet's results. But the loophole was brought to the stock algorithm's attention. Now the Assessors only observe. The stock algorithm itself is the only one that approves or not."

Cora ran her hand over the holes in the table. This was how she had been planning on cheating the Gauntlet: with those keys. But now there was no way to cheat at all.

She let her hand fall away. Bonebreak continued to give her a tour of the deconstructed modules, pointing out the entrance ramp and where the recess room for the Mosca delegation would be.

Overhead, lightning suddenly cracked. The distant clouds had rolled in fast, casting half the Gauntlet in darkness.

"The storm approaches," Bonebreak said, walking toward her quickly. "We must go. It will rage all day and into sleep-hours, I think. Do not worry about the Gauntlet. It can withstand almost anything."

Bonebreak started to move as fast as his legs could carry

him, and Cora hurried behind him. She paused at the edge of the track to glance back at the structure. The twelve modules had roughly taken shape now. A three-by-four staggered wall.

Thunder pealed, loud enough to make her clamp her hands over her ears. And then heavy, freezing sheets of rain began, and the Gauntlet was swallowed by fog as they raced back into the tunnels.

18

Leon

ON THE BOTTOM LEVEL of the aggregate station, Leon eyed the ceiling, his heartbeat thumping hard, half expecting Arrowal's troops to bomb their way through at any moment. He'd lost count of how long they'd been trapped. It had to have been more than forty-eight hours. He was going stir-crazy, just sitting around and waiting like this. The tunnels had collapsed behind them, closing off any way for them to get to Cassian or the weapons cache in the Hunt.

He sighed. With luck, Makayla and the other kids from the Hunt were well on their way to Armstrong.

A burst of laser pulses sounded overhead and his heart thunked.

"Take cover!" Tessela called. "Everyone down! This is it—they're almost through!"

Leon and Mali ducked into the safety of the nearest door frame. He glanced behind him—it led to a supply room stacked high with crates. He recognized it; it was where Bonebreak's crew had stored most of their contraband. If they had to, he and Mali could hide in two of those crates and wait out the battle.

But he had a feeling both of them would rather be in the thick of it.

Then, with a jolt, he remembered his agreement.

I left a valuable provision pack on that station, Bonebreak had said. *If you were to use the tunnels to fetch me that pack, I would make it worth your while.*

Mali's attention was riveted to the ceiling. Leon subtly eyed the supply room. Whatever Bonebreak had wanted was in those crates. He glanced at Mali, who had her back to him, trying to convey some sort of message to Tessela across the hall with hand gestures. He glanced back at the crates and judged the distance. It would take him two minutes, max, to sneak in there and find the provision pack. He could do it right now, while they were stuck here anyway, and Mali would never even know. He took a quiet step backward. She didn't hear him, her attention focused on Tessela. He swallowed hard and took one more step backward, peeking into the room.

No time, you idiot, he told himself. *Arrowal might get through at any minute.*

But . . . the crates were right there. It would take him literally seconds to grab the provision pack. He'd be an idiot not to, really. After all, he was doing this for Mali. *Fetch me that pack, boy,* Bonebreak had said, *and I will tell you how to find your girl's family. She would be grateful to you. You'd be a real hero, yes.*

A hero. He'd gone and convinced everyone that he was a good guy, and dammit, that was a tough reputation to uphold.

He pictured how Mali's face would look when he told her that he had a way to find her family back on Earth. She'd throw her arms around him. Kiss him. Hell, maybe more. . . .

He swallowed, casing the hallway—no one was paying attention to him. He sucked in a deep breath and ducked into the supply room. His heartbeat thundered. He'd have to be fast. The bottom crate had four stacked on it, which Bonebreak hadn't bothered to mention. Leon shoved into them with his reinforced shoulder until the top four toppled over. There was a crash of glass, the sound of wood shattering, and Leon cringed in fear that the sound would give him away, until he heard another volley of laser blasts in the hallway.

The battle would cover him.

But now he'd really have to hustle. He ripped open the crate.

Empty.

He kicked the crate, letting out another curse, and started to hurry back to Mali. But something made a strange hiss. When he peered back in the crate, the bottom had slid to one side. In it was a provision pack about the size of an apple.

Bingo!

He snatched the pack. Felt around the edges, trying to guess the shape. It was sealed. Whatever it was, it was hard, with something that felt like mechanical parts.

From the hallway, more laser pulses went off overhead, followed by Kindred shouts. Leon cursed. *Really* time to get back— Arrowal's troops must have broken through. He shoved the pack into his jacket as he ran back to the hall.

"Leon!" Mali said, spotting him. "Where did you go?"

"Had to take a leak," he called over the din.

Her face was redder than he'd ever seen it. Her eyes darted wildly. She was angry. Furious. She slapped a fist into his shoulder. "You idiot, I was worried about you!"

He grinned.

She rolled her eyes.

A deafening explosion shattered the station. The blast slapped him across the face, throwing him back against the wall. Smoke filled the hallway. Debris rained down from above, along with some liquid that had been piped through the walls.

His ears rang. He blinked, touching his face. For a second he was a tyke again in Auckland, just eight years old. His uncle had gone on another bender, come home to find him still awake and watching TV, and smacked him across the face hard enough to overturn his chair. *Lazy good-for-nothing,* his uncle had said. *Just like your dad.*

But as Leon blinked out of his daze, he saw dust and water, smoke and blinking lights. Not his uncle's fist. He was on the Kindred's station—not eight years old. Not back in his old life. Not a criminal anymore.

He staggered to his feet. A few Fifth of Five fighters were prostrate on the ground, unmoving, but others were getting up slowly.

Where was Mali?

He frantically began to search the wreckage. The walls were split open. Dimly, he realized that the blast had reopened the closed-off tunnels. Then he spotted her white Hunt uniform. She was facedown, not moving. Panic clutched at him as he scrambled over a fallen beam. Mali wasn't made of steel like the Kindred. She bruised and bled.

"Mali!" he said, shaking her.

She opened one unfocused eye. Blood was streaking down a gash in her arm.

Another volley of shots went off overhead.

"Everybody down!" Tessela yelled. "They've bombed their way through! They're coming in from above!"

Leon pulled Mali closer to the collapsed beam, which afforded a small amount of shelter. Arrowal's troopers began to drop down on ropes from the upper level, firing laser pulses as they came. Leon quickly went over a mental map of this level. The tunnels were open again. If he could just get them into the closest one . . .

"Target Arrowal!" Tessela yelled to her soldiers. "Take him out!"

Leon peeked over the beam. The Fifth of Five's aim focused on a Kindred dressed in an official uniform who was coming down the ropes. An older Kindred, big as a tank. It had to be Arrowal. But with their primary weapons disabled, Tessela's rebels could only use hand-to-hand combat or makeshift weapons made from fallen beams and pieces of debris.

Leon grimaced. This fight was going south fast. He grabbed Mali, despite her protests, and threw her over his shoulder. He kicked in one of the wall panels with sheer force and thrust her into the tunnel.

"What are you doing?" she said.

"What does it look like? Saving our asses. And just in case . . ." He grabbed the collar of her shirt and pulled her in for a kiss. Mali went stiff, surprised. Her lips were soft, and he relaxed into it. God, he could stay here. Forget the bombing. Forget the rescue mission. Just kiss her forever. But he pulled away and pointed down the tunnel. "Crawl. Fast. I'm right behind you."

They started crawling as fast as they could. His ears still rang from the explosion. He stopped only when they reached a fork in the tunnels. He gulped air, trying to catch his breath, following his zebra-striped navigation marks, the symbol for the Hunt.

At last they made it to the menagerie's entrance, and Mali pushed through the tunnel's door, into the narrow area behind the menagerie's bar. They stood up in the lodge. It was deathly silent. The lights were off. Dust coated the tables. It clearly had been shut down since the Fifth of Five had freed the kids and animals that had been imprisoned here.

They hurried through the red door into the backstage area. The rows of cells were empty. Open cell doors and overturned dishes of food spoke of a rescue that had happened quickly. He followed the directions Cora had given him to the hidden safe in the medical room. When he traced the symbol on the secret drawer and it opened, he looked at Mali with wide eyes.

Dozens of kill-dart guns were lined up in a row. Small, handheld ones. Bigger, riflelike ones with scopes. All of them deadly.

"I've never seen anything so beautiful," he said.

Mali grabbed an old feed sack and stuffed the dart guns into it. "Come on. We are only one station beneath Cassian."

They climbed back into the tunnels. The tight space made Leon's skin slick with sweat that kept pouring down his forehead and stinging his eyes. They avoided a cleaner trap on level three and then climbed an incline to the next level.

"We're close," Mali said, pointing to a long tunnel with alcoves in the sides. "While we were fleeing, Cora and I hid in those alcoves when a package came past, and Cora spotted Cassian through a crack in the wall. Check the alcoves."

They took turns checking each alcove for a hole or gap to peer through that might show them Cassian's cell. Leon crawled from one to the next, touching his pocket surreptitiously to make sure Bonebreak's pack hadn't fallen out in the shuffle. He glanced at Mali. What would she think if she knew he was smuggling again? Would she believe that he was doing it for a heroic reason? For her?

"Over here!" she said.

Leon crawled to the alcove where she had her eye pressed to a gap in the panels. She pulled back and let him take a look. At first, the chamber beyond was so dark he didn't see anything, but then his eyes adjusted, and he made out a body on the floor. There was no cot, no dresser, no tables. Just the figure, curled in on itself.

"It's him," Mali breathed.

Leon looked harder at the figure. It hardly looked like the Warden who had once towered over him. Curled in the fetal position, Cassian now looked vulnerable, weak. Leon actually felt sorry for the guy.

"We should break him out now, while he's alone," Mali said, tracing her fingers over the tunnel walls. "These panels are held together with a chemical sealant. It's like wax. Too strong to break when it's hardened, but if we could melt it, we should be able to loosen the panel enough to open." She dug her nail into one of the seams, trying to pry it open. Her nail split and Leon winced.

"Let me try. This isn't the first time I've broken into some-place I shouldn't be." He examined the sealed seams closely, feeling for the hardened waxlike sealant. Back home, he always carried a lighter. But here, what could he use to melt it? Flint from one of the menageries? Then he glanced down the hall at the cleaner trap they had so carefully avoided.

He smiled.

"Mali," he said, "go wait for me in the next alcove."

She gave him a worried look but did as he said. Once she was safe, he went to the cleaner trap and inspected the mechanics. The thin holographic laser, like a trip wire. The flame ports on either side of the tunnel. For a second, a shiver ran down his spine as he remembered finding the charred body of Chicago, one of the menagerie kids who had died caught in the trap's fireball. He judged the distance to the nearest alcove, where he could hide out from the blast. It was six feet away. Too far to reach before the fireball would burn him alive.

He took off one of his shoes and crawled to the alcove.

Pressing his back against the wall, he weighed the shoe in his hand, hoping it would be enough pressure. "Mali," he called. "Stay back!"

He threw the shoe at the laser trip wire.

The fireball erupted instantaneously. It happened so fast he didn't even have time to fully take shelter in the alcove. Flames swept over the right side of his body, charring his skin. He let out a hiss of pain. Mali cried out in surprise from the next alcove down, and suddenly his worry for himself was gone. He clutched his burned arm, but his thoughts were on her. As soon as the flames subsided, he crawled into the tunnel, wincing at his burned, crackling skin. "Mali! Are you okay?"

Mali spilled into the tunnel too.

His eyes were already searching her for any burns, any bruises. But she was so small that she had managed to tuck her whole body into the shelter of the alcove. Except for a singed hem of her pants, she was unharmed.

Her eyes went to the cleaner trap, to the burned shoe, to his charred skin. "That was a stupid thing to do!"

"I think you mean brave."

She sighed. "Stupid and brave."

He grinned, then winced. Damn, his face hurt.

She moved aside to allow him room, and, together, they pressed against the panel. Sure enough, the fire had melted the sealant, and the panel crashed into Cassian's cell. Leon cringed at the noise.

"Think someone heard that?" he asked.

"Of course they heard it. We must be fast."

Mali dropped down into the darkened cell, and Leon followed. As she crouched beside Cassian's curled body, Leon drew a kill-dart gun and, sidling up to the closed door, positioned himself to fire if anyone came through.

"How is he?" Leon said over his shoulder.

"Alive," Mali answered. "Barely. Can you carry him?"

Leon looked at the Kindred doubtfully.

Suddenly, Cassian coughed.

"I can . . . walk."

"Cassian!" Mali kept her voice low as she ran her hand down his arm, helping him sit up. Leon cast another doubtful look at the Kindred. He'd never been a fan of Cassian's, but he had to admit, Cassian had saved their asses more than once. Now, he looked awful. He wore only black underclothes that covered his torso and hips, and the bare flesh on his arms and legs and neck were marred with dark bruises. His limbs looked shockingly pale.

"He can't fit in the tunnels," Mali said.

Leon cursed under his breath. He tightened his hold on the kill-dart gun. "Then we take the hallways and hope the fight on the bottom level has pulled all the guards away from here."

Cassian tried to sit up. "Just get . . . to Tessela . . . Cora . . ."

Cassian's normally black eyes were a glassy gray color that made Leon grimace. Mali tried to help him up, but he was too heavy, too disoriented. As soon as he put pressure on his scarred legs, he nearly collapsed again.

"Christ," Leon said. "They really did a number on him."

"Help me get him up," Mali said.

Leon stowed the kill-dart gun in his waistband and went to help, throwing one of Cassian's scarred arms over his shoulders and heaving him to his feet. Once they had Cassian up, he was able to inch along on his weakened legs. They approached the door, and before Leon could ask Mali to try to open it with her mind, it slid open.

Leon glanced at Mali. "Did you do that?"

She shook her head, then glanced at Cassian. "I think he did."

But, delirious, Cassian didn't answer.

They shuffled him into the hall. Leon's pulse pounded in his ears. He checked both ends of the hallway. Left. Right. All the soldiers had been pulled away to the battle. The hall was empty.

"Wait," Cassian breathed. His voice was raspy, his lips split. He swallowed hard, then nodded toward another cell. "In there. We need him."

Leon exchanged a look with Mali, wondering if they could rely on Cassian's words. Mali nodded, and Leon slammed the heel of his hand on the controls. The door opened.

Mali gasped.

Another Kindred prisoner rose from the floor. There was a dark bruise ringing an injection site on his cheek and scars down one arm, though he wasn't in as bad shape as Cassian.

Fian.

Leon pointed his gun at him. "Traitor!"

"Wait." Cassian, eyes glassy, motioned for Leon to lower the gun, speaking between strained breaths. "We can . . . trust him. Fian is . . . loyal to me . . . and to the Fifth of Five."

"Bullshit," Leon said. "He turned on us. And he tried to kill us on Armstrong!" Even as he said it, he realized the timing didn't work. How could Fian have been on Armstrong and at the same time been here, being tortured?

"That . . . was not Fian," Cassian answered in his stilted voice.

Fian came forward, taking Mali's place under Cassian's arm, lifting his fellow Kindred with ease. "It is true," Fian said. "I have been here for over eight rotations. The person you saw on Armstrong was the same one who incarcerated me, and later, Cassian. It was someone posing as me."

Leon shook his head. "Look, mate, I posed as a Kindred once. I know what a disguise looks like, and that guy was *you*."

"It wasn't," Cassian said. "The real Fian was here the whole time, badly wounded. The creature you saw . . . was an Axion."

Leon wrinkled up his face.

"The Axion are shape-shifters," Fian explained. "There are safeguards to prevent them from taking on someone else's identity: they give out a high-pitched frequency when they're in disguise that all intelligent species can hear. But the Axion impersonating me must have figured out how to silence his frequency. The same for Arrowal. The real Arrowal was killed long ago."

Leon felt his head spinning. "But Tessela . . ."

"Tessela and the others do not know the truth," Fian said. "I didn't know myself until I was imprisoned here, and of course, I could not escape to tell anyone. It isn't a war between cloaked Kindred and the Fifth of Five; it's a war between Axion and Kindred. The real Fian and Arrowal were never trying to stop Cora. It was the Axion impersonators."

"I do not understand," Mali said. "Why do the Axion care if Cora wins? What bearing could the Gauntlet have on their war?"

"Because . . . aeons ago . . ." Cassian leaned against the wall, face flushed with exertion.

Fian explained for him. "Aeons ago, the Axion ruled the universe. But then the Gatherers also gained intelligence and developed the Gauntlet to give all species a chance. Fifty human years ago, the Mosca achieved intelligence. They didn't like that the Axion were shape-shifters. Didn't trust them not to pose as someone else. The Intelligence Council mandated that they maintain their true appearance or else emit a frequency when altered—it works through a genetic implant. The Axion accepted the ruling at the time."

"Let me guess," Leon added. "They were actually super pissed off."

"To put it mildly," Fian said. "Here, Cassian and I learned the extent of their plan. And their fury."

Distractedly, as though fighting a bad memory, Cassian placed one hand over the oozing scars on his left arm.

Fian continued, "The Axion felt that, as the original

intelligent species, they had granted everyone else freedom, and now theirs was being taken away. They set about a plan to retake their original control."

"I'm afraid to ask how," Leon said.

"They had to learn to hide their frequencies so that they could infiltrate the upper echelons of each intelligent species. At the same time, over the decades, they began to build an army. They produced ships in far greater numbers than ever before, claiming it was so all species could be better connected. Of course, the ships were actually a war fleet. But first, they knew they had to take out the Kindred."

Mali's eyes were wide. "Why not attack all the species at once?"

"We serve as the peacekeepers of the universe. We are the strongest physically, with the most integrated infrastructure, which makes us the only real militaristic threat to them. Take us out by infiltrating our leadership, and the other species would be easy to dominate. That is where the Gauntlet comes in."

Fian paused, as though further explanation were on the tip of his tongue, but then he thought better of it. He glanced at Cassian.

"In a way . . . we were fortunate our plans failed," Cassian said between unsteady breaths. "They would have . . . killed Cora to keep her from running the Gauntlet."

Leon's eyes went wide. "Uh, shit."

Both Fian and Cassian looked at him curiously.

Leon exchanged an uneasy glance with Mali. "That's why we're here. To get you. Cora's going to run the Gauntlet on Drogane."

Cassian coughed his surprise. Uncloaked and wounded, he couldn't hide how much this information affected him. "*The Gauntlet?*"

"She's on Drogane right now with Anya and Bonebreak," Mali explained. "The Gauntlet module is probably already there. It starts in around twelve days. She still intends to run it. Bonebreak has agreed to be her sponsor, but we do not trust him. We need *you*. An intelligent species member we can trust."

Cassian tried to straighten, wincing as he put his weight on his scarred limbs. "We have to get to Drogane," he said. "*Now. There's . . . a flight room . . . on this level.*"

Leon eyed Cassian doubtfully. He barely looked strong enough to cross the room, let alone cross the galaxy. But with Fian's help, they were able to move through the hallways, while Mali covered them with kill-dart guns drawn. The halls were empty; all of Arrowal's troops were battling on the lower level.

At last, they reached the flight room.

"I won't forget this, Fian," Cassian said, resting a hand on the Kindred's shoulders. "Whatever happens, your loyalty is acknowledged."

Leon flinched. It still felt wrong to see Cassian thanking the enemy—even if he knew that *this* Fian wasn't the same one who'd betrayed him.

"Here," Leon said, handing Fian the sack of kill-dart guns. "These are for Tessela. She needs them."

They helped Cassian climb into the ship, and then Leon climbed up the ladder behind Mali. It was tight inside, the size of a fighter jet, just one seat in front and room for supplies in the back, where he and Mali crawled. Cassian eased into the pilot's seat, wincing.

"Stay low," he breathed. "Try . . . to keep your balance centered. These ships are meant to be solo units. They're . . . sensitive to movement. Fast, but they require frequent stops to recharge. We'll just make it in time."

He closed the roof and hit some controls. From somewhere deep in the station came more gunfire. Mali sat in front of Leon, and he wanted to draw her close, wrap his arms around her, and breathe in the smell of her hair, but he knew she'd never tolerate it. He slid the sack around to his front. The sharp edges of the provision pack inside pressed against his fingers. What the hell was in it?

Cassian handed them some pills—oxygen adjusters that would let them breathe on Drogane. Then he hit a few more controls, and the ship rumbled and lifted off. It rocked violently—Cassian hadn't been joking about balance. Leon and Mali both gripped on to either side of the narrow cockpit, steadying themselves. Cassian steered them to the port.

The flight room disappeared behind them.

Leon dared a glance back, the slightest turn of his head, not wanting to risk unbalancing the ship more. From the exterior, the aggregate station looked as perfect as it always did. If he hadn't known better, he'd never imagine a battle was waging within.

He reached forward and squeezed Mali's shoulders.

Then Cassian hit another control, and the vessel shot forward so fast that everything went black.

19

Cora

THE STORM ON DROGANE'S surface raged ceaselessly. But in the sheltered belly of the mountain, the only change Cora could sense was a dampness seeping through the stone. Her eyes drifted constantly to the clock the Mosca children had made for her: seven human days left until the Gauntlet began. Then five. Then three. Reports filtered in that the modules had finished constructing themselves. The various delegations' ships were entering the outer edges of Drogane's solar system.

The Gauntlet was nearly here.

Right up until the final day, she trained long and hard, running up and down Tern's spiraling ramps twenty times, then thirty. She practiced telekinetically lifting heavier and heavier objects, as Bonebreak had suggested. First an empty clay pot the size of her fist, then a stone statue the size of her head, then a chair that weighed about thirty pounds. She tried to lift a potted fern that must have weighed one hundred pounds—nearly her own weight—but no matter how hard she tried, she couldn't so much as make it wobble without pain throbbing in the back of her head, forcing her to ease off.

Now, from the edge of Ironmage's balcony, she noticed through her goggles that Tern seemed more active than usual. More Mosca were out on the streets. They moved faster than normal, not exchanging greetings with one another, hurrying to their destinations.

Ironmage came out, looking over the activity. "Tensions are high because of the impending Gauntlet," he explained. "We Mosca don't like it, as a rule. No one wants the Intelligence Council on our doorstep. At least five smuggling units have had to suspend operations until they leave." He adjusted a setting on his mask. "Lucky for you, the storm has bought you a little extra time. The Kindred and Axion and Gatherer delegates cannot land until it lessens. Their ships are in a holding pattern in the outer atmosphere, waiting." He looked up at the stone ceiling as though he could judge what was happening beyond. "Half a day, maybe."

She let out a tight breath.

He pinched her arm, feeling the muscle that had grown there, and let out a grunt of approval. "You have trained well. My brother and I, we believe you might actually win this thing. Your chances are low, of course, but not impossible."

"Thanks," she muttered.

He patted her arm and left.

She chewed on her lip, anxious. Half a day. Not much time. She turned to the potted palm, taking a deep breath. If she didn't figure out how to lift it, she might fail the Gauntlet as soon as she'd started it.

She walked over to the fern and tried to lift it physically, judging its weight again. Her arms strained. She stepped back and rubbed her sore palms.

Cassian hadn't prepared her to lift anything this heavy. The thought of him triggered a torrent of worry, and she sucked in a breath. Why wasn't he here yet? Had something gone wrong with Mali and Leon's rescue mission? Her imagination filled with gruesome images of his torture. A flood of guilt rushed in behind it, and then longing. She'd give anything to have him here with her, his arms circling her waist, his whispered reassurances in her ear.

She closed her eyes.

Focus on the fern, she told herself. *Focus on what you can do now.*

She opened her eyes slowly, held her palms flat, and tried as best she could to turn her thoughts from Cassian to the potted fern. A few white fronds ruffled. She gritted her teeth together and focused hard on the heavy pot, willing it to rise. A spark of pain tickled the back of her mind and she released her hold.

"You're not doing it right."

Anya stood in the balcony door, pointing at the potted fern.

"What do you mean?" Cora said. "I'm doing it exactly how we practiced."

"Yeah, but we've been practicing with little things. Pebbles and coins. Things Cassian trained you to move, because that's the way that the Kindred train their young." Anya eyed the potted fern closely. "But this takes other techniques."

"I thought there was only one technique. Concentrate and lift."

"Only one *Kindred* technique, yeah," Anya said. She came onto the balcony. "But our minds don't work the same as theirs.

When it comes to little things it doesn't much matter what technique you use, but with bigger things, it matters a lot." She walked around the fern, flicking its fronds playfully. "Cassian told you not to push your mind too hard, didn't he?"

Cora nodded.

"See, that's what the Kindred don't understand. Because humans don't cloak our emotions, we can't ever concentrate as hard as they can. Our emotions are always clouding everything, which means we actually have to push our minds even harder to match their level of perceptive ability."

Cora folded her arms, chewing on a lip. "Cassian said if I pushed my mind too hard, it could tear permanently." She paused before adding, "He said that's what happened to you."

Anya's expression went flat. Her small hand curled tightly around the fern. "He was wrong."

"But your hands," Cora said, motioning to the way Anya's hands shook. "And in the Temple, you were practically delirious."

"Delirious because of the Kindred drugs," Anya insisted. "Not because I pushed my mind too far. Pushing my mind to the brink was the only thing that kept me alive in there." She chewed on her lip, as though reliving bad memories.

Cora hesitated. She still couldn't shake the feeling that Anya wasn't all there—that her mind was slightly off somehow. She glanced toward the house. Inside, Willa was playing with the Mosca children, oblivious to what was happening on the balcony.

I'm being paranoid, Cora told herself. *Anya's just trying to help.*

Anya pointed to the fern. "Go ahead. Try it."

Cora focused on the heavy fern. Before, she had used

caution when reaching out toward objects with her mind. But she was out of time. Now she pushed aside that caution and projected her thoughts as hard as she could. Not reaching delicately for the plant, but snatching for it. Instant pain ricocheted through her head, and she hissed but ignored it and pushed harder. The potted fern trembled. It rose an inch.

Cora was so surprised that she dropped her focus, and the fern crashed to the floor, cracking the pot.

"See?" Anya grinned. "Don't think like a Kindred. *Feel* like a human."

Cora pulled off her goggles and shook out her hair, raking her fingers against her aching temples. Her head was throbbing. But still, she'd done it. Which meant maybe she could do it again in the Gauntlet. In the sudden darkness, she noticed that the dripping sound of storm water filtering through the mountain's crust had lessened. She leaned over the railing, listening.

"The storm must have broken," Anya observed.

Cora let out a long breath. "That means the delegates will start to land. I'll have to go up to the surface." She turned to Anya in the dark. "Cassian still isn't here. I'm worried about him. And about you and Willa, too. Once I go into that Gauntlet, Bonebreak and Ironmage will have no need of you anymore. What's to stop them from selling you while everyone is distracted? And . . ." She suppressed a shiver. "I can't shake the feeling that Fian and Arrowal have something else planned. Something bad."

Anya rested a hand reassuringly on Cora's arm. "Your job is to worry about the puzzles," she said. "Let us worry about what the other species might be planning. You'll be in there, but we'll be outside. Technically, I'm a ward of Bonebreak's now"—she tapped her hard thumb badge against the railing—"which means I can join him and Ironmage as part of the Mosca delegation. We'll observe your progress from the recess rooms. Assuming you make it to the break after each round, we'll be able to talk, and let you know about anything we discover."

Cora smiled. "Thanks. That makes me feel better."

She slid the goggles back over her head as Ironmage and Bonebreak emerged from the house, dressed not in their rust-red jumpsuits, but in crimson-red ceremonial shielding.

She sniffed the air. They looked nice but still smelled rotten.

"It is time," Bonebreak said. "We must go now, in the storm's eye. The official Mosca delegation has already made its way to the surface. They are awaiting us."

Ironmage held out a simple set of black clothes. "Put these on. They are embedded with nanocircuitry that the stock algorithm will use to track your progress."

Cora hesitated before taking the clothes.

No more time to train. No more time for Cassian to land and reassure her that everything would be okay.

She was going to have to do this alone.

She felt a heavy hand on her shoulder and turned to find Willa behind her. The chimp gave her a long nod, her dark brown eyes wordlessly reassuring her. She handed Cora a scrap of paper.

I have not wanted to tell you about what happened to me in the Gauntlet because I feared the same might happen to you. The truth is, I lost the one thing that mattered most to me: my identity. The moral puzzle in

*module eight forced me to face the fact that I
was no longer a chimpanzee, but neither was
I a human. It shattered any hope I had of ever
belonging. And I fear that you might lose
what matters most to you too. But I do not fear
that anymore. I believe you can do this.*

Cora smiled.

No, she wasn't completely alone.

She went inside to change behind the curtain that divided the bedroom area and cooking area. Ironmage's children were on the other side, making strange beeping noises. She pulled back the curtain to watch them playing some kind of laser tag game. The youngest one tackled the others, and they all erupted in giggles.

She let the curtain fall.

If it hadn't been for their curved backs and odd way of walking, she could almost have imagined they were human children. Memories of home flooded her mind. Once, she and Charlie had dressed up their dog, Sadie, in fairy wings. They'd played fetch all morning in the big yard beneath the oak trees, laughing, telling each other that every time Sadie brought back the ball it was a wish granted. *What do you wish for?* she'd asked Charlie. He'd smiled and thrown out his arms. *To fly!* And she had laughed too, picking up Sadie and giving her a kiss between her floppy ears. *I wish to be famous. A famous singer with my songs on the radio!*

Now, as she dressed, she shook her head at how carefree she'd been. In a way, she'd gotten her wish. She *was* important—an entire species's survival depended on her. But famous? No one even knew she was alive. And, she realized, maybe it was better that way.

"Home means loved ones . . . ," she sang quietly, "and good times and shelter from gloom."

She pictured Fian as she'd seen him on Armstrong, so cold in his cloaked emotions, and yet she had been able to feel his simmering anger just beneath the surface. She represented a threat to Fian's superior way of life. To the menageries, to the enclosures, to the system that kept Kindred like him powerful and dominant.

She pressed a hand to her throat, fighting against the phantom feeling of suffocation.

She had survived the bridge accident.

She had survived eighteen months in Bay Pines.

She had survived being imprisoned by an alien species.

And she would survive this.

She pushed back the curtain and met the others on the balcony. "I'm ready."

20

Cora

FIERCE WIND HOWLED AS they neared the transit hub that led to Drogane's surface. Cora shielded her face from the sleeting rain that blew in from the hub's enormous gates. "I thought you said the storm had lessened!" she called to Bonebreak.

"This *is* lessened!" he answered.

The storm was a wall of angry gray rain that made Cora, Anya, and Willa shield their faces. Before, when Cora had gone to the surface to tour the Gauntlet's module with Bonebreak, the planet had so reminded her of a summer day on Earth that it had made her heart ache. But now, the mountains weren't visible. The whipping wind howled at an almost deafening level.

"Wait over there, away from the gates!" Bonebreak called, waving them away from the exposed entrance. "Your weak human bodies will be bruised!"

Ironmage strode into the exposed section, rain bouncing off his thick rubber shielding and mask. He flicked at a sharp shard of ice that struck a bare patch of skin like he was shooing away a mosquito. Cora watched him disappear into the storm. Every once in a while, she caught sight of a few flashing cerulean-blue lights in the distance.

She drew in a sharp breath.

It had to be the Kindred delegates' ship docking with the Gauntlet.

In another moment, a circular orb appeared out of the haze: one of the rover spheres. Ironmage steered the rolling vehicle to the sheltered side of the transit hub. A dozen of the complex Mosca gears unlocked themselves, and the rover sphere cracked open like an egg.

"Climb in," he called.

They clambered into the orb, which had a circular bench around the perimeter. Anya sat by herself on one side, knees drawn in to her chest, her fingers once again still. Ironmage leaned forward to press some controls in the center of the orb, steering it so that they rolled smoothly out of the transit hub gates. They passed the other rover sphere stalls, but only one remained. The Mosca delegates must have taken the others.

Ironmage steered the rover sphere up a ramp that led to the planet's surface. The wind tried to bat around the vehicle, but Ironmage steered it carefully down the valley track, its ridges locking with the gaps in the track for stability, until a tall structure loomed before them. Cora wiped away condensation from the rover's windows and stared up at a wall of metal.

"That's it," Cora told Anya and Willa. "That's the Gauntlet."

They all peered through the windows. In the raging storm, the Gauntlet looked imposing and monolithic. There were no more shifting parts, no deconstructed cubes. It was whole.

Near the Gauntlet's base, a port opened just wide enough for them to roll inside. Through the rover sphere's window, Cora made out a small garage where the other rovers were parked, as well as vehicles that must belong to the other species. One was a small transport with glowing blue lights and sandstone-colored panels.

She pulled off her goggles. "The Kindred are here."

"Yes," Ironmage said. The heavy garage door closed, sealing out the storm. Ironmage hit the controls, and the egg-vehicle cracked open again. "All the delegates are here. We are last to arrive."

Bonebreak and Ironmage climbed out, reaching in a hand to help out Willa, and then Anya, and finally Cora. She climbed out shakily into the garage, hugging her arms for warmth, and then froze.

Fian stood at the entrance ramp, with the entire Kindred delegation behind him.

She tried to keep her face calm, not give away how badly her heart was racing. Just the sight of that deep wrinkle in his brow made her feverish with rage. Behind him, six Kindred aides stood at attention. Two more uniformed Kindred flanked him—one Cora didn't recognize on his left and, on his right, Serassi.

She immediately straightened. *Serassi?* What was the medical officer doing as part of the Council political delegation?

Serassi folded her arms calmly as their eyes met. Cora's jaw clenched. Once, Serassi had been an ally of theirs, or at least neutral. But the cold look on her face now said that truce had passed.

The structure creaked. Cora glanced at the high windows of

the docking module. The walls swayed slightly. The storm was still pounding outside.

Bonebreak adjusted his mask and eyed the Kindred delegation. "Where's your Chief Assessor?"

The smirk on Fian's face faded. "Arrowal has been detained on station 10-91, dealing with an . . . irregularity. He sent me in his place. I will serve as the Kindred Chief Assessor."

Cora shifted uneasily—Cassian was on station 10-91. It was where Mali and Leon had gone to try to get him back. Could their rescue attempt be connected to this "irregularity"? As though sensing her discomfort, Willa moved closer. She made a small hand gesture that Cora took to be a reassurance that everything would be okay.

Serassi leaned close to Fian and whispered a few words.

Fian nodded.

"Come," Fian said to Cora and the others as he motioned to a corridor. "The other delegations await us in the central vestibule. I'd hate to keep them waiting, though none of us expect to be here long. We don't anticipate that you will complete the first round."

She tossed him a glare. All around them, the metal walls creaked eerily as the storm pounded, but none of the Mosca or Kindred seemed troubled.

The corridor opened up to the wide central chamber that she'd seen with Bonebreak, only now it felt closed off and dark, like a tomb. Lights in the ceiling shone gloomily over the dais with its four chairs. Four doors off the central vestibule led to four smaller chambers—the recess rooms. A row of monitors on the wall scrolled with some kind of coded language Cora couldn't read. As soon as they entered, voices died down.

The other delegations stood.

There were about thirty figures in all, a mix of Gatherer, Mosca, and Axion. She tried not to stare at the strange sight of the Gatherer delegation, with their eight-foot-tall frames, long faces, and willowy fingers. They wore simple gray robes with a row of pockets at the base and more pockets at waist level. *Monks*, Bonebreak had called them. *Boring do-gooders. All they're good for is praying and thinking.*

The Gatherer in the front—Cora couldn't tell if it was a man or a woman—gave a slow, deep nod. "I am called Brother Magga," it said in a drawling voice. "As established in rule 18, section 10, of the Intelligence Council accords, I will serve as Chief Assessor of the Gatherer delegation." It swept a hand out toward its eight other robed colleagues. "These are my aides, who shall monitor and observe the proceedings to ensure fairness as established in rule 14—"

"Yeah, monk," said Ironmage, rolling his eyes. "We all know the rules."

The Mosca delegation sauntered over to clasp hands in greeting with Ironmage and Bonebreak, all of them wearing the same formal crimson masks and shielding that by now felt familiar to Cora. It was crazy that she was starting to think of the Mosca as friends.

"I am Redrage," the tallest woman said. "The Mosca Chief Assessor. And my aides." She waved a hand toward about a half dozen other Mosca. "Your human and primate associates are Mosca property, so they may use our recess room." She pointed to the third of the four rooms leading off the central vestibule. "From there, we will observe your progress and reconvene with you during the breaks between rounds."

Cora nodded.

That left only the Axion delegation.

They were standing at the far end of the vestibule, in the shadows behind the dais. She had only seen Axion from a distance, on Fuel Station Theta. She couldn't help feeling apprehensive; she hadn't forgotten that they consumed human body parts as part of their bizarre religious beliefs.

Slowly, they stepped into the light. Cora expected the same creatures she'd seen on Theta: short, gaunt, with white streaks in their hair.

But they were . . . *human.*

She started. They couldn't actually be human. But they *looked* human. All of them were of human height, human sizes, with human features, so perfectly human looking that they might have walked out of Armstrong, except for a white streak in their hair.

"What's going on?" Cora hissed to Bonebreak. "They look human!"

"I told you on Theta," he said, "they are a mercurial species. They can take on any appearance they wish."

Cora stared at him. "I think you left that last part out."

He shrugged as though it were a technicality.

One of the Axion men stepped forward, smiling in a charming way. "A pleasure to meet you, Cora Mason." He reached out a cold hand to clutch Cora's. "We are wishing you the best. We've witnessed human runners before, but never one so young."

She felt Willa tense by her side and remembered that the

Axion had been the ones who had conducted brutal experiments on her.

Cora pulled her hand back.

The Axion man didn't seem to notice the slight. "I am called Crusader, the Axion Chief Assessor, and these are my aides."

An Axion woman stepped forward, smiling. Her light brown hair, with its single streak of white, was pulled back in a lose ponytail. She had a kind face and even a slight gap in her teeth. The very picture of warmth, and it shook something within Cora. Hair so like her mother's, but a smile that was more sincere than her mother's ever had been.

"We have taken on a basic human appearance because it is something you are familiar with," she said. "We want you to feel comfortable. We've left these streaks in our hair, which are true to our natural physical states, so that you can tell us apart from your own kind."

Cora hugged her arms tighter, wary of trusting them. Their kindness had a ring of artificiality to it.

As though sensing her suspicion, the Axion woman's smile slid to Willa. "How nice to see you again, Willa." Willa shrank back, whining softly deep in her throat. "We've been looking for you ever since you disappeared after failing the Gauntlet. Awful business, that. We feared you were dead."

Willa backed up behind Cora, hands pressed to her head as though memories were tearing at her. Cora reached down and scooped her up into her arms. Willa was heavy for a chimp, but she wrapped her arms around Cora's neck, holding tight.

Thunder struck overhead, shaking the central vestibule.

"I don't trust them either," Cora whispered to Willa. "Not the

Kindred *or* the Axion. They're planning something. I just know it."

Willa hugged her tighter.

Thunder struck again outside, harder this time. All eyes rose to the ceiling.

Fian turned to Redrage. "We should begin."

"Assessors," Redrage said, "take your places. Aides, retire to the recess rooms."

The four delegations began to separate. Redrage, Brother Magga, and Crusader moved toward their seats on the dais, as their aide parties sorted themselves in the various rooms designated for each species. Fian was slow to take his seat, hovering near the base of the dais, whispering something to Serassi.

Cora eyed the two Kindred closely. They were so smug. All those smiles. All that talk about fairness. They were toying with her.

She needed Mali and Leon. Most of all, she needed Cassian.

She drew in a breath, worried about what Fian had meant by an irregularity on station 10-91. She reached out her mind, fumbling desperately for some sense of Cassian. Had Mali and Leon found him? Were they all okay? She hadn't realized how used to Cassian's presence she'd grown. How he had always been with her in spirit, as comforting as the charm necklace she used to wear to remind her of her family.

She touched her neck. Gone now. And she felt just as bare without him.

"Are you ready?" Bonebreak asked quietly.

Cora gently set Willa on the ground and then smoothed a hand over her simple black clothing.

"As ready as I'll ever be," she said.

"Gauntleteer," Redrage announced from the judge's chair, "approach the portal door. It is time to begin."

Cora drew in a deep breath.

Ready or not, her time had come.

21

Rolf

NOK PACED BACK AND forth by the window of the old sheriff's office, twisting a pink strand of hair around one finger. She threw Rolf a worried look, as he sat at the old sheriff's desk, his notebooks laid out around him. "I'll never get used to it. Me, sheriff. The whole idea is crazy. Absolutely mental." She peeked through the blinds at the town beyond, where the former slaves were repairing the schoolhouse roof.

"I've told you, try to think of it as an honorary title." Rolf concentrated on his notebook, where he was about to finish the latest blueprint he was working on. "Keena's done a good job of managing everything so far. Besides, it isn't entirely crazy. You being sheriff, I mean. When you worked in the tents you managed to get all the deputies to hang on your every word. Even the most brutish of the mine guards. Keena said it was like watching someone tame lions into kittens."

Nok paced harder. "That was just some stupid trick. Bribing

them with sports news and reality television."

"Yes," Rolf pointed out, "but it worked."

Nok turned back to the window and chewed on a fingernail.

Rolf frowned down at his notebooks, wishing he could ease her worries. Weeks had passed since Ellis had died, and tensions had been high ever since. The first day, Keena had rounded up Armstrong's survivors for a town meeting—four dozen mine guards, three dozen tent guards, and two hundred slaves—to declare a transitional government. She had persuaded Nok, as the official "sheriff," to be with her for every announcement, though Nok had just stood there looking completely out of place as Keena explained how the new system would work: slaves freed, all residents rotating between two-hour shifts at the mines, two-hour construction shifts, and two-hour shifts cooking or working in the infirmary. A good plan, Rolf thought. Still, not everyone had been happy about the new rules. More than once, Rolf had overheard discontented grumbles, mostly from the mine guards, while he'd walked around the tent encampment.

"What are you working on, anyway?" Nok asked.

He set down his pencil. There were no electric lights, since the building had only been used previously as a prop, but a fair amount of sunlight streamed through the windows. He smoothed his hand over the blueprints proudly. While Nok had been stuck in government meetings with Keena, he'd spent days inspecting the old town, making notes for how it could be improved and turned into a real, proper place to raise a daughter. Even better, he'd stumbled upon old blueprints of the Kindred's transport hub, which indicated there was a reactor core. It was radioactive and protected with layers of reinforced buffers, not to mention the hub emitted scalding steam through vents; but if he could find a safe way to run wires from its auxiliary nodes, he could potentially bring enough electricity into Armstrong's town for lights and basic communications.

"It's a surprise," he said. A rare flicker of pride filled his chest. Back on Earth, he'd spent countless long nights cooped up in Oxford's library, stuffing his head with knowledge that was good only for standardized tests and impressing professors. And for what? A father who'd always overlooked his accomplishments in favor of his brother's track medals? Fellow students who'd resented his grades?

But everything was different on Armstrong. Here, when he'd first sheepishly showed Keena his plans to rebuild the town, she'd called him a genius. To his surprise, the citizens didn't tease him for his twitches but, rather, came to him with questions about how best to engineer new water systems.

Here, he mattered.

Nok gave him a playful smile. "A surprise? I hope it involves chocolate."

She rubbed her hands over her straining belly. Her pregnancy was no longer a secret, thanks to Ellis. And on a moon full of sterilized humans, everyone had developed a sort of fascination with her growing belly. Two middle-aged women, former slaves, had come by this morning and left an offering of flowers and extra gruel by the sheriff's office door. The mine guards might not love her, but the tent guards practically idolized her.

Nok peered between the slats again and her smile faded.

"Oh, great," she muttered. "Some of the mine guards are

congregating by the dance hall. They're probably plotting to murder me."

Rolf pushed up from his chair and went to the window. Outside, Dane was speaking to a few hulking guards under the dance hall awning, their faces hidden in shadows.

"No one is going to murder anyone. I'll make sure of it." His hand found hers and squeezed. "Where's Keena?"

Nok sighed. "In bed. Her cough's gotten worse. Loren says she's been in and out of consciousness. She'll need a few days to recover, at least." Her eyes narrowed as she watched Dane making big, emphatic gestures. "The timing's not good for her to be sick, with Dane spouting off all his lies. He says he wants peace, but he really wants to be sheriff himself."

"No." Rolf's voice was quiet and certain. "He wants to be king."

Nok turned away from the window, muttering things about sheriffs and Dane and responsibilities and babies. She was so distracted that she didn't see the strange, snaking line of smoke that appeared over the buildings. Rolf frowned, pushing aside the blinds to see better.

"Um, Nok?"

"And he has the nerve to—"

"Nok."

"I mean, who does he think—"

"*Nok.*"

She spun to face him. He pointed at the sky.

She ran back to the window and peered at the streak of smoke. "What is that?"

Rolf felt his hands twitching again. At the end of the snaking line of smoke was a small black dot that could be only one thing.

He swallowed. "It's a ship."

More dots filled the sky. In the next second there were dozens of ships behind the first, which was rapidly headed for the town square where they stood. Nok's face went slack as she stumbled backward, a hand squeezing over her badge as though clasping a lifeline.

"Maybe . . . maybe Cora's come back," Nok offered. "It could be friends."

Rolf braced himself as the first ship grew closer. Through the haze he could just make out the cerulean-blue flashing lights of a Kindred cruiser.

"Those are *not* friends."

He pushed out into the town square, squinting against the bright sun, hands squeezed into fists. He had so many plans for this town—he'd only just started to realize its potential—and he wasn't about to let anyone take away his hope.

Nok joined him in the square. They shaded their eyes as the Kindred cruiser hovered overhead. Frightened citizens of Armstrong poured into the town square, gaping as they all looked up. Dane and his mine guards stood in front of the dance hall, looking up with solemn expressions.

"I wish Keena was here to handle this," Nok muttered. "Shit. Look." She grabbed his hand.

Rolf felt eyes on them and realized that most of the citizens of Armstrong were staring at them. *No.* Staring at Nok, their eyes going hesitantly to her badge. A few gazes then shifted to Dane.

Rolf nudged her. "You've got to say something. Take charge."

"Me?"

Overhead, the ship discharged its thrusters and began to land just outside of town. A nervous energy spread through the crowd, as whispers hissed at the edges. A few citizens ducked into the general store to hide.

"With Keena unconscious," Rolf whispered, "these people are going to turn to either you or Dane for leadership. And we have to make sure it's you."

Eyes wide, Nok looked down at her reflection in the gold metal badge.

The ship landed and began powering down, its blue lights fading slowly. The crowd was growing more fearful, a few anxious cries rising above the chatter.

Rolf gritted his teeth. Nok needed him—not his brain this time, but his support. He grabbed her hand and pulled them both forward, toward the ship.

"What are you doing?" she asked.

"What we have to do," he answered.

Slowly, a look of understanding crossed her face. She glanced over her shoulder at the nervous Armstrong citizens, then at Dane. By the time they'd pushed their way to the front of the crowd to stand beneath the ship, she stood a little straighter.

"Don't worry, everyone!" she called. "Stay calm!"

Both of them waited tensely for whoever was inside to emerge. Anything could be inside. Kindred guards. Fian, come back to finish them off. But then Rolf frowned, looking closely at the ship's tail. "Look at its fin. It's been singed. And there's damage to the rear thruster. It almost looks as though it's been in battle."

"Against *who*?" Nok whispered. "I thought they'd come to attack *us*."

The hatch hissed as it opened, and Rolf braced himself. Overhead, dozens of other ships hovered, ready to land right behind the first. He recognized the shapes as the ones from Serassi's picture book: Gatherer and Mosca and Kindred ships. Why would they be traveling together?

Then, strangely, a girl dropped down.

Rolf went rigid with surprise. It was a human girl with dark brown skin and hair knotted in balls. The girl covered her mouth to cough, waving away dust and exhaust. "It's okay!" the girl said. "We're friends!"

Rolf and Nok exchanged a cautious look. The crowd was murmuring louder. Glints of pickaxes and hammers shone here and there, a reminder of how quickly the crowd could be overcome by panic and end up doing something rash.

Rolf nudged Nok. "You got this."

Nok cleared her throat, addressing the girl loudly. "Who are you?"

"My name's Makayla. I was in one of the menageries on the Kindred station. We're refugees. We have a dozen more ships behind us wanting to know if it's safe to land. There's a lot of wounded people with us. Animals, too."

"Do you believe her?" Nok whispered.

Rolf's fingers tapped anxiously. "Ask her which menagerie—"

But the girl, Makayla, had caught sight of something in the crowd that had stolen her attention. Her eyes went wide with surprise, then anger, then determination. She strode through the crowd toward the dance hall.

"Stop!" Nok called. "Hey, girl, whatever your name was, don't move!"

But Makayla didn't listen to Nok. She strode right up to the group of mine guards congregated near the dance hall. Rolf's thoughts raced—what was this girl planning? Should he grab a pickax too, just in case?

She walked past the biggest of the guards. Right to Dane.

Dane's eyes were wide—he clearly recognized her. For a second, worry flared in Rolf's mind. A friend of Dane's was certainly no friend of theirs. But then Dane's eyes narrowed.

"Makayla," he said through clenched teeth.

"Dane," she replied, as though spitting out something distasteful. And then she drew her fist back and punched him in the jaw.

Several people gasped.

Dane stumbled backward into the crowd of surprised mine guards. Ripples of worry ran through the crowd, but Rolf just leaned close to Nok.

"I have a feeling we can trust this girl," he said.

22

Cora

CORA STOOD BEFORE THE portal door that led to the Gauntlet's first puzzle chamber. It was five feet high, ringed by blindingly bright lights. It faced the dais where the four Chief Assessors sat, their delegations behind them, watching. Cora's eyes fell on Serassi, and she felt a stab of anger.

Traitor.

"Once you enter," Fian explained from the dais, "the stock algorithm will take over. There is no exiting or stopping the Gauntlet until you either complete the first round, after which you will be granted a break before moving on to the second, or you fail." He tented his fingers.

The lights suddenly flickered and Cora looked up, along with the Chief Assessors. She could almost feel the storm's wind howling outside, pushing against the structure. But then the lights brightened again.

Fian pointed to the monitors, which displayed an unintelligible series of symbols. "These coded monitors will allow us to track your progress. Though we do not judge you ourselves, we observe in order to ensure a fair run. Each of our aides has been trained to interpret the coding. Now, approach the portal door."

Lights illuminated on the floor as she approached, as though guiding her way. Each step made her knees shake harder—or was that the storm, making the structure tremble? She looked over her shoulder and caught Willa's eye from the bench along the rear wall. Willa touched a hand to her heart, and Cora remembered her words. *The Gauntlet will take everything from you. It searches for weaknesses and exploits anything it finds.*

Cora touched her own heart in response. Then her hand dropped to the edge of her black Gauntleteer shirt. It felt as light as cotton, no sign of the nanocircuitry she knew was embedded there to monitor her physical fitness and mental capacity.

"I would wish you good luck," Fian said, "but luck is a human concept. There is no logic in it. A lesser concept for a lesser species." He lifted a hand over the control to open the portal door. At the same time, the lights flickered irregularly again.

He pressed the control, but nothing happened.

He pressed it harder.

Then the room began to quake. The smirk on Fian's face faded as Brother Magga gripped the edges of the dais with his long fingers and Crusader whipped his head around toward the other Axion.

"What is happening?" Crusader demanded. The charming note to his voice had vanished.

"An earthquake," Redrage explained calmly from behind her mask, tapping a few controls on the panel. "A part of the storm.

It's stronger than we anticipated."

The lights flickered again.

"This is a farce!" Fian pushed to his feet. "How you Mosca ever became intelligent is beyond me!"

"Quiet down," Redrage hissed. She stood up, pacing anxiously. "The stock algorithm evaluated the forecast weather patterns and judged the conditions to be acceptable. The quake will pass. They rarely last more than a few minutes." She sauntered over to Bonebreak and Ironmage, exchanging a few hushed words with them.

Cora paced in front of the door, the floor lighting up each of her steps. The tremor wasn't enough to cause more than a mild vibration, but she was already so jumpy that she felt like she might pass out.

As if sensing her growing panic, Ironmage and Bonebreak came over to the portal door. Ironmage handed her a cup of water and then leaned in close.

"Listen," he whispered, jerking his head at the Mosca's Chief Assessor. "My brother and I have been working on Redrage, like I said. Trying to negotiate a deal for some under-the-table information. She stuck to her morals for a while, rambling about safeguarding standards for the galaxy . . ." Ironmage rolled his eyes. "But it seems the other delegates have irritated her since they first landed. The Kindred ordering her around, even though this is our territory, and those boring Gatherers always reciting the rules. Redrage just now relented to share some information—nothing too revealing, but enough to give you a chance, which will annoy the other delegates."

"I didn't think anyone could tamper with the Gauntlet," Cora whispered.

"We aren't tampering," Ironmage said. "We can't *change* anything; we're merely relaying information that happened to fall into our lap."

Cora leaned in close.

"The first puzzle," Bonebreak explained quietly as he took the empty cup back from her, "is a moral one."

Cora straightened. "That's it?" She'd been hoping for something more useful, like the key to solving one of the more difficult puzzles.

Bonebreak let out a grunt. "That information cost us a percentage of trade rights if you win. The first puzzle is almost never a moral one. Just take heed."

Overhead, the lights resumed full power.

Her thoughts vanished as the earthquake's tremor underfoot stilled. The floor stopped shaking, and the monitors ceased rattling.

Redrage returned to the dais. She pressed a few more controls on the panel, then nodded. "The meteorological disturbance has passed. Our controls should function again at regular capacity."

Fian strode over to where Cora stood with the Mosca. His fingers dug into her upper arm as he dragged her back toward the portal. She struggled, hating the feel of his cold skin on hers. "Chief Assessors," he called over his shoulder, "prepare to open the door to the first puzzle chamber. The Gauntleteer is ready—"

The ground rumbled again, interrupting him. But it didn't

have the same vibrations as the earthquake. The rumble felt more like wheels—or a great rolling ball.

Cora gasped. The other rover sphere!

"Wait," Brother Magga said, frowning toward the direction of the sound. "Someone approaches. Open the entrance into the hallway."

"No!" Crusader said. "We have already been delayed long enough!"

Bonebreak and Ironmage, however, were already unlatching the heavy gates. Cora craned her neck as the rumbling grew. She caught sight of the rover sphere plowing down the hallway, throwing rain and mud against the walls. It must have just come from the storm outside.

The Axion delegation jumped up. The room erupted in surprised muttering.

"Highly unusual . . ."

"Against protocol . . ."

"Appears to be a Kindred steering it . . ."

"Enough!" Crusader yelled with a note of strain in his voice. "Enough distractions! It begins now." He slammed his hand on the controls. With a *whoosh* of pressure, the portal door cracked open from the bottom, rising slowly, letting out a blast of cold air that made goose bumps erupt on Cora's bare ankles. She tried to step backward, but Fian still held her tightly.

"Oh, no," he whispered in her ear. "No escaping this time. No one rushing to your rescue now."

The rover sphere rolled to an abrupt stop by the dais. Through the muddy glass windows, Cora could just make out three figures inside.

The portal door kept rising. Fian pushed her toward it. Cold air was on her calves now.

And then the rover sphere door cracked open. She nearly cried out. She knew those faces!

Mali.

Leon.

Cassian!

He was at the rover sphere's controls. Her heart started thundering violently. She blinked and blinked, unable to believe it, trying to get out of Fian's grasp. Her friends spilled out of the rover sphere and she twisted toward them. Cassian was alive. He was *here*. Her eyes drank him in. One hand clutched at his ribs, as though they were bruised. And his skin—she winced. Pockmark scars dotted his arms and neck from the wire probes the Kindred doctors had tortured him with. A sickening feeling struck her as she realized they looked just like the bullet holes from her nightmare.

His eyes found hers in the crowd. She felt a ripple of the same electric spark as when they touched—bright and jarring, but now heavy with guilt. Cora stifled a sob. He was limping. She'd never seen him like this before—weak. The distance between them ate at her. If only she could feel his warmth, hold him close, tell him she was wrong to have doubted him, tell him that she loved him.

"Cassian!" She nearly dislocated her shoulder trying to tear herself from Fian's grip.

Cassian took a step forward but hesitated, as though fearing to get too close. In the next instant, Kindred and Axion aides swarmed between them, stopping Mali and Leon before they could come any closer.

"Cora!" Cassian called. That moment of hesitation was gone. He shoved an Axion out of his way.

The portal door was nearly entirely open now. Cold air brushed the back of her neck. Serassi and Leon were arguing, looking like they were moments away from punching each other. Mali was glaring between the Axion and Kindred delegations as though she didn't trust either one. Two Axion aides grabbed Cassian and held him back with a rifle pressed into his spine. In the commotion, their eyes met. Memories flooded Cora of the last time she'd seen him, tortured and screaming in agony.

"Let me go!" she cried, trying to pull free from Fian's grasp.

Fian's eyes went to the portal door. He smiled.

Cora hissed in a breath, realizing her mistake a second too late. Fian's hands were already moving before she could react.

"My pleasure," he said, and shoved her through the portal door into the first puzzle chamber.

23

Cora

CORA SLAMMED INTO A hard metal floor.

Bursts of pain radiated from her knees and palms. She took in the room in a daze: a ten-by-ten-by-ten cube, glowing panels on all sides, walls and floor and ceiling identical, so that she suddenly wasn't certain which way was up. And the portal door . . .

The door was closing. She scrambled for the gap, trying to see through. Back in the central vestibule, two Axion guards were holding back Cassian. Mali and Leon were yelling something to Willa and Anya.

The door kept lowering. Five inches left. Four. Three.

"No!" she cried. "Wait!"

Fian's boots suddenly loomed before the narrowing crack. He crouched to meet her gaze. "Don't worry," he said. "I'll handle your Warden."

And the door sealed.

"No!" She clawed at the door, then pounded with her fists.

Nothing. She shoved herself to her feet, breathing hard, pacing. Fian was planning something, she knew it. Something even worse than what he'd already done to Cassian.

She kicked the door one more time. *Useless.* It wouldn't open again until the first round was complete. She spun back toward the chamber. She had to get through these puzzles—they were the only way back to Cassian.

She took a step forward, and the chamber went black.

She stopped. Blinked in the darkness. Cold air from unseen vents snaked up her ankles. She held out her hands and shuffled forward until she touched the place where she guessed the door had been. She felt for the seams, but they were gone. It was just a wall now, identical to every other side.

She raked her nails across her scalp. She closed her eyes, trying to send Cassian a psychic message. *Cassian . . . answer me, please . . .* But there was no response. The walls were thick, designed specifically to prevent telepathic communication.

She cursed.

Without warning, a rumble spread through the darkness, and she took a quick step away from the wall.

The lights flickered back on, blindingly bright.

She shaded her face with her hands, waiting for her eyes to adjust. Her heartbeat pounded in her chest. The stock algorithm was capable of engineering any possible habitat or scenario; she could find herself on the edge of a cliff or charged by a lion—and there were no safeguards.

Die here, die for real.

The bright light faded and she was able to warily open her eyes, surprised to find herself still in the ten-by-ten-by-ten cube.

No illusions or habitats. The only difference was that a small table had materialized in the center of the chamber: a wooden desk filled with blocks that looked like toys.

She eyed the table cautiously. She knew better than to trust anything that appeared so innocent. She turned back to the wall, resting her fingertips on the smooth surface.

I'm coming, Cassian, she thought. *Hang on.*

She drew in a steadying breath and approached the desk. There were nine blocks, each with a number printed on the top: 8, 105, 2, 34, 300, 1, 15, 90, 4. There had to be some pattern. She reached for the first block, but it was fastened to the table. It could slide left or right or up or down, but it could not come loose. She tried another, then another. All the blocks could slide, but only in certain directions. She slid the 34 between 15 and 90 but wasn't able to move the 4 anywhere except up.

"Rolf," she muttered, "I could really use your brain right now."

The first puzzle they'd found in the cage had been a number puzzle, like this. Rolf had figured it out almost instantly, spinning its numerical gears until the lock opened and candy poured out onto the floor, filling the toy store with a sickeningly sweet aroma. The memory started to make Cora's stomach turn.

"Think," she told herself. *Cassian is waiting. He's in trouble.* All she could picture was those scars on his arms and neck. She couldn't change the fact that he'd been tortured—but she'd be damned if she'd let it happen again.

She gripped the edge of the desk.

There had to be some relationship among the numbers. What was it Willa had said in their training? *Sort out the numbers and you will end up with one word. The word will be your key to solving the puzzle.*

By that logic, if the 2 was a B and the 4 was a D, then they shouldn't be next to each other sequentially. But she still couldn't move the 4 at all, and what number would 300 represent, anyway?

She tossed a glance over her shoulder, worried about what might be happening outside—only to realize she wasn't sure anymore which wall had held the portal door. They all looked identical now. And knowing how the Kindred could manipulate gravity and forced perspectives, for all she knew she'd come in through the ceiling and was now standing on one of the walls.

"Come on. Concentrate."

She started to hum aloud, forced at first, but after the first few notes, the tension eased from her shoulders. The sound of a soft melody always settled her mind.

She touched the 300 block. If this puzzle was anything like the one Willa told her about, then 300 had to represent a letter. If she added the digits, 3 plus 0 plus 0, she got 3, which would be a C. And there was a 1 block, which could be A . . .

It was starting to make sense. Four of the blocks could stand for A, B, C, and D. Cassian had told her that the puzzles got harder as she progressed, which meant this first one might really be this simple. She slid the 1 in front of the 2, and the 300 next, but the 4 still wouldn't move. She tried to pry it up, but it wouldn't budge.

She hummed harder. Her pitch rose with her frustration, turning into a growl, and she tore herself away from the desk. "I don't have time for this!"

Her eyes caught on the edge of the 4 block, and she stopped. The corner of the number 4 was loose—a label glued to the top of the block. She stepped closer. When she'd pulled so hard, the edge of the label had started to peel free. Hesitantly, she picked at it with her fingernail. The corner came up cleanly. She tried the same with the 105 cube.

It came up cleanly, too.

She swallowed. *I could peel up the labels and rearrange them without moving the blocks at all.*

She glanced over her shoulder.

Charlie had once done the same thing with their old Rubik's Cube toy. On a long car ride, their father had told them the first one to solve the Rubik's Cube would get to choose where they stopped for lunch, thinking it would distract them during the long car ride between campaign stops. She'd driven herself crazy trying to twist the cube to form six sides of the same color, but Charlie had just taken out his penknife, secretly peeled off each of the colored stickers, and moved them around. Their dad had thought Charlie was a genius.

Slowly, Cora started humming again.

She peeled the label a little bit farther. It was cheating, yes, but her friends were in danger—and what did it matter as long as she got it right in the end? She and Mali had made the same argument when they'd devised the idea to cheat the Gauntlet. That plan had failed when Fian had closed all the loopholes, but the same strategy could help her now.

She pulled back the corner a little farther. Almost there.

And then her finger froze. With a jolt, she took a quick step back.

No.

She glanced around at the walls, the ceiling, the floor, touching her clothes, wondering how exactly the stock algorithm was monitoring her thought processes. Right now, it would be collecting data on her progress and sending a steady feed of information to the monitors in the central vestibule. The Chief Assessors were watching. And she had almost forgotten what Bonebreak had told her:

The first puzzle is a moral one.

Which meant it wasn't about solving a number puzzle at all. It was about presenting an opportunity to cheat to see if the competitor would take the bait.

She stared at the desk with wide eyes.

This was the trap.

She flinched, breath coming fast, eyes darting to the corners. Was someone watching her now? Was the Gauntlet itself—or the stock algorithm program that ran it—monitoring her?

She shook her head, hard. "No. I won't cheat."

The lights abruptly went out.

She stared into darkness. Had she lost? Failed already? But then a rumble started, and a door to her right opened.

Lights flickered on in the next chamber.

She let out a deep, shaky breath.

She'd beaten the first puzzle—but only barely. If Bonebreak and Ironmage hadn't given her that clue, she'd have cheated and failed. Cassian had told her the first puzzle was always intellectual—so if the Gauntlet had changed its programming to lay this trap for her, could she trust anything she'd been told? What else might the Gauntlet throw at her?

She swallowed.

She didn't have a choice: she stepped through the doorway into the second puzzle.

24

Mali

THE CENTRAL VESTIBULE WAS awash in chaos as Kindred argued with Mosca, Gatherers argued with Axion, and delegates yelled about rules at anyone who would listen. Mali ignored the din and instead ran her hands along the seams of the portal door. Minutes ago, Cora had disappeared through it before they could warn her that it was a trap. Mali tried to pry the door open with her fingernails.

It didn't move.

She hissed at the shock of pain as she broke a nail. She bit off the rest of the nail, spitting it on the floor.

Cora would be trapped inside for the duration of four puzzles. Under normal circumstances, Mali wouldn't worry about her during these initial, easier puzzles. But this wasn't just any Gauntlet. Somehow, in some way that they desperately needed to figure out, the Axion had made it into a trap.

"Arrest this Warden," ordered Fian—the Axion impostor—

as he pointed toward Cassian. "He is a disgraced official and an escaped fugitive."

Axion aides moved forward to arrest Cassian. Mali jumped out of their way, breathing hard. She couldn't let this happen. She tossed a wary look around the room. Who else besides Fian was an Axion in disguise? The Kindred aides? The Mosca? Even the Gatherers?

Her eyes fell on Serassi.

Something hardened in the pit of her stomach. Maybe it *wasn't* Serassi. Maybe it was an Axion impersonator, which would explain why Serassi, who had once been her friend and ally, had so suddenly turned on them.

As if reading her mind, Serassi slowly turned to meet Mali's gaze. Mali shivered with a sudden spark of coldness.

Impostor, she thought. *Traitor.*

"Wait!" Redrage slammed her gloved fist down on the dais and faced Fian. "Take your hands off the Warden, stop yelling in my ears, and have some respect for the fact that you are on *my* planet, in *my* jurisdiction, guests here of *my* turn hosting the Gauntlet. If one more person dares to give an order, they will be escorted out of here immediately and left on the surface. The storm might have lessened, but it will still flay the skin off your bones in a matter of minutes!"

This put an end to the arguments.

"That Warden is a Kindred," Fian said slowly, his voice still tight with anger but trying to show more respect. "He is one of our own, so he should be dealt with under our laws."

"Kindred laws are still subject to Council laws," Brother Magga said in a droning voice. "According to the Intelligent

Council Accords of Common Time 549—"

"Stop talking," Redrage hissed toward Brother Magga, "or you can tell the *storm* all about Intelligent Council Accords as you're freezing to death."

Brother Magga seemed flustered for a moment, then shut his mouth.

Redrage turned to Cassian. "They are correct in one thing, Warden. It is disrespectful to roll into another species' Gauntlet without an invitation. You'd better have a good reason for intruding, or else *you'll* be the first to face the storm."

Cassian's eyes slid to Mali's. She nodded slowly. She knew they were thinking the same thing: he couldn't just come out and expose Fian for the Axion impostor that they both knew he was. It would be chaos. They'd have a war on their hands. They needed to figure out the Axion plot in secret.

"The Gauntleteer," Cassian answered instead. "I came because Bonebreak cannot be her sponsor. He has no claim over her."

Redrage raised an eyebrow, looking at Bonebreak. "Is this true?"

Bonebreak's jaw hung open beneath his mask, as though lost for words. He scratched his chin, folded his arms, looking as though he were trying to buy some time. "Uhh . . ."

"It is," Cassian asserted, and held out a metal tag. "As Warden, I have Cora Mason as my charge. Any claim that this Mosca trader might have on her is nullified by my prior claim."

"Irrelevant!" Fian said. "He's been stripped of his Warden title."

"I warned you to be quiet!" Redrage snapped at Fian. "And

unless you have some proof of your claims, I don't want to hear another word."

Fian's face flamed. He had no documentation, no files. He clearly couldn't prove Cassian's demotion.

Redrage cocked her masked head toward Cassian. "You do know what being a sponsor entails, do you not?"

"I do," Cassian said. The only hint of emotion Mali saw on his face was a twitch in his jaw. She frowned. As far as she knew, being a sponsor meant assisting in training and in supporting the Gauntleteer between rounds. But now she had a cold premonition that being a sponsor meant something else . . . something dangerous. Bonebreak must have really wanted that trade deal if he was willing to risk himself as Cora's sponsor. She tried to reach her thoughts into Cassian's mind. For a second she picked up on a claustrophobic sensation . . . but then Cassian closed off his thoughts, shutting Mali out.

Redrage shrugged. "Very well, but you will be fined twenty tokens for stealing the rover."

One of the Gatherers cleared his throat. He pointed a long finger at the coded monitors that were filled with scrolling symbols Mali couldn't read.

"The Gauntleteer has passed the first puzzle," he announced.

A ripple of anger visibly tightened Fian's face. Serassi only blinked, as frustratingly devoid of emotion as she always seemed. Mali narrowed her eyes, feeling even more certain that Serassi was an Axion in disguise.

Leon took a few steps to stand beside Mali. "Come on." He nodded toward one of the recess rooms off the central vestibule, the one reserved for the Mosca delegation. "We need to regroup.

There's nothing we can do for Cora until she finishes the next three puzzles." He glanced at the Axion delegation and whispered, "We need to figure out what those freaks are up to and how to stop them."

Mali still felt hot anger pumping through her, but Leon rested a steady hand on her shoulder, and the anger cooled. He was right, the oaf.

Mali nodded and signaled to Cassian, then to Anya, who had been surprisingly quiet during the arguments. She'd hardly even acknowledged Mali and barely seemed glad to see Mali alive. Mali reached out to her telepathically.

Is everything okay?

She pushed the thoughts across the room but hit a mental wall. It had a cold feeling to it, and Mali recoiled as though she'd gotten an electric shock.

Anya only blinked calmly as though nothing had happened.

Mali followed the Mosca delegation into the recess room, throwing hesitant looks at Anya, wondering if the Kindred drugs had damaged her friend's mind more than she let on.

Once they were gathered in the recess room, Cassian closed the door. "It is safe to speak freely," he said. "With this door closed, the other delegations cannot hear or sense what we say. These recess rooms have been designed to be private."

The room was nothing more than several benches, a coded monitor, and a small facilities closet with food and water. Between the entire Mosca delegation—eight Mosca, including Bonebreak and Ironmage—and Cassian, Willa, Anya, Leon, and Mali, it was tight. Mali hugged her arms in close, not liking the press of bodies around her. Except for Leon. Him, she didn't mind so much.

"So how do we figure out which of them are impostors?" she asked.

"We know Fian is one," Cassian answered. "And given that Fian can't have done all this on his own, I believe Serassi might be as well. Along with Crusader and the ten Axion aides, that makes thirteen Axion that we know about, some disguised and some not."

"Hardly enough for an army," Mali said. "Or even a coup."

"Which is why I believe there must be more," Cassian agreed. "Perhaps even someone in this very room, sent here by the Axion to spy on us. Which is why I must insist that none of us leave the room until Cora has finished the first round."

Everyone went quiet.

Mali shivered as she looked around the room. Bonebreak. Ironmage. Leon. Willa. Anya. Plenty of Mosca she wouldn't trust even if they *weren't* impostors.

"Hey." Leon rested a hand on her shoulder. "Don't worry. We find out one of these bastards is in here, I'll let you get in the first punch."

She couldn't help but smile.

At least one thing was certain: Leon was no impostor. No Axion would ever offer her the first punch. An Axion couldn't possibly understand how much it would mean to her to get that honor. But Leon did.

Out of everyone in the world, Leon knew what was deep in her heart.

There was no faking that.

25

Cora

AS SOON AS CORA crossed into the second puzzle, a familiar smell hit her. Sweet, minty, strong. *Candy.* She had expected to find another bare ten-by-ten-by-ten cube, but an illusion was projected throughout the room.

A candy shop.

She touched the shop's glass counter with unsteady fingers. The candy jars, the giant cash register, the bins along the back wall—everything was identical to the candy shop they'd found in the cage. She almost expected Lucky to walk through the door behind her, joking about sugar highs. She moved behind the counter hesitantly. In the cage, the candy store had been an intellectual puzzle: the keys on the cash register weren't numbers but letters, and each receipt card was an anagram. Nok had solved them almost instantly by unscrambling the letters to form words like CHOCOLATE and LICORICE and MINTS.

There was a card in the cash register's receipt box here too.

MY ANISE.

Cora's fingers rested on the cash register keys. Anise was a sweet herb that licorice was made out of. But anagrams were supposed to be scrambled nonsense words, and this one seemed already solved. So was she supposed to scramble it herself? That didn't sound like much of a puzzle.

Her pulse beat in her fingertips, urging her to hurry to unscramble the word. MA . . . MAN . . . But her thoughts kept twisting back to the central vestibule. The scars on Cassian's arms. The way he'd hesitated before calling to her. The fear in his eyes, almost as though he'd feared *her*, as though getting close to her again meant risking his life even more.

She snapped back to the letters. *Solve it.*

MANY . . .

ANY . . .

NAME . . .

Nothing she could come up with worked, and she huffed in frustration. *The first puzzle was a trap,* she reminded herself. *This could be a trap too.*

She forced herself to calm down.

She studied the card more carefully, staring at the letters, continuing to mentally move them around. SAY . . . YES . . . SAM . . .

No combinations made sense.

SIN . . .

SEINE, the river in Paris? But no, there was only one E. What else could it want her to spell? A habitat, like DESERT or JUNGLE?

A name?

AMY . . .

YAS . . .

She sucked in a breath as a sickening chill uncurled in her stomach. There *was* a name that started with Y. Then an A. Then S. Bile rose in her throat as she arranged one letter after another, half hoping she wasn't right.

But the letters kept matching up.

Y . . . A . . . S . . . M . . . I . . . N . . . E.

She swallowed back the sour taste of bile. Yasmine had been the Middle Eastern girl she and Lucky had found in the cage on their first day. The original Girl Three. Yasmine had been dead when they found her, drowned. Cora had seen the Kindred experimenting on her body. She bent down, dizzy with the memory, then forced herself to take a breath and slowly tap out Yasmine's name on the cash register keys.

The register dinged cheerfully. A token rolled down into the change trough.

She picked up the token, feeling sick, waiting for the next door to appear. She'd won, hadn't she? But the walls remained the same. Then her fingers brushed four slots in the counter—the same size as tokens. *Great.* She had to solve four anagrams to win.

She shoved the token into the first slot and a new card popped up.

A RHINOS.

Okay. Think. Rhinoceros made her think of the Hunt, where all the animals had been so horribly mistreated. She tried to piece apart the letters.

NOIS . . .

RINA . . .

She sighed. Nothing seemed to click.

HARI . . .

Her uneasiness grew as she continued to rearrange the letters, coming up with nothing, until at last she found a combination that worked.

ROSHIAN.

Sweat beaded on her forehead. Roshian was the only person Cora had ever killed, impaling him through the eye. Her stomach twisted as she typed his name and got her second token. She was starting to realize the trick of this puzzle. What a messed-up game. Technically an intellectual one, yes, but it wasn't about challenging her intellect. The stock algorithm was trying to shake her confidence by showing her the names of the dead.

People die when they get close to you, songbird, Dane had said. *I'm not taking any chances.*

She swallowed down the guilty taste of bile.

The third card popped up with a ding, and she closed her eyes, wincing. She knew what it would say. She just knew. There was only one other person who had died as a result of getting too close to her.

She opened her eyes with heavy dread.

CORA LIES ON FLU.

It was a nonsense sentence, but the first two words made her flinch as though each one were a slap. *Cora lies.* Which was exactly what she had done to Lucky. It was part of the reason he was dead.

Her fingers were shaking now, but she typed Lucky's real name, LUCIANO FLORES, the ding of each key making her want to retch. A third token rolled out. She snatched it up, clenching her jaw. She wasn't going to let this puzzle shake her. If the stock algorithm was trying to make her doubt herself, it would have to work harder.

She slammed the token into the third slot, determined, and the final card popped up.

MACAROONS.

She focused on the letters with renewed resolve. Who else was dead because of her? No names came to mind, and for a second, her confidence faltered. A cold chill spread through her legs. Maybe she hadn't figured out the hidden trick of this puzzle after all.

SCAR . . . CARO . . .

And then her lips parted—there was a name in the letters.

CORA.

Her own name. The chill grew as she unscrambled the rest of the letters.

CORA MASON.

She jumped back from the cash register as if the keys had turned molten. She stared at her name. Yasmine, Roshian, and Lucky were all dead because of her, and now her own name was on a card.

Am I going to die too?

Fear shot to her throat. She pushed back, shaking her head. No, the stock algorithm had no way of knowing that. It was just trying to make her second-guess herself, that was all. A trick. She paced, wondering how much time she'd already wasted.

I can't let it get in my head.

She set her fingers on the keys, ready to type her own name, but paused. What if, by entering in her name, she was somehow signing her own death warrant? What if typing her name would make it come true?

She lifted her fingers off the keys, letting out a tight breath. This could be another moral test in disguise. Add her name to the list of the dead, and the Gauntlet would make certain it happened. But what choice did she have? If she didn't solve the puzzle, she wouldn't move on.

She started typing slowly.

C-O-R-A-M-A-S-O-

She hesitated, the premonition that she was ensuring her own death almost too overwhelming to fight against.

She swallowed.

She hoped she wasn't making the biggest mistake of her life.

She typed the *N*.

26

Cora

C-O-R-A-M-A-S-O-N.

Cora stepped back, tense, braced for something terrible to happen.

The cash register dinged. A door appeared to her left.

She'd won.

She let out quick breaths, not daring to trust it. Had she just sealed her own fate? Her legs shook as she walked around the counter, toward the open door. She peeked into the next cube: plain walls. Empty. She stepped in quickly, glad to be away from the cloyingly sweet smell of the candy shop, from the names of the dead, from her *own* name.

The door closed behind her.

The third puzzle chamber was blessedly dark, giving her a moment to breathe. *Two more puzzles to go,* she urged herself. But the premonition didn't go away.

She waited anxiously for the lights to come on, and when

they didn't, she pushed to her feet and felt against the wall. *Nothing... Empty...* But then her foot collided with a hard object. She crouched down to pick it up.

A gun.

She jerked her hand back as though it had singed her.

A gun meant shooting, but shooting *what*?

The room remained black, and the darkness began to seep into her mind. She imagined she heard breathing. She spun around. Was it her own breath, or was there someone else in the room? Willa had warned her of deadly moral paradoxes like the one that pitted a Gauntleteer against a starving lion.

She grabbed the gun, aiming it into the darkness.

"Hello?" she called.

No answer.

Maybe she was alone after all. But then, what was she supposed to shoot? The image of her own name on the anagram puzzle flashed in her mind, and a bitter metallic taste filled her mouth. Surely she wasn't supposed to shoot *herself*. Right?

Her pulse raced as she paced the length of the pitch-black room. It felt too tight, like the walls were moving closer together. There was that sound again, like someone breathing. She spun around sharply, aiming the gun.

"Hello?"

The darkness was complete, oppressive, making her lungs feel constricted. But there—a huff. There *was* someone else here. Or something. The gun started shaking in her hand. When she'd been a little girl and had nightmares in the dark, crying out in her sleep, Charlie had rushed in and turned on the lamp on her bedside table. The monsters in her imagination had vanished. *All you need to chase off the darkness,* he had said, *is light.*

She took a few deep breaths, holding the gun steady. There weren't any lights here. It was only her, the gun, and whatever was breathing: no lamps, no switches, at least not any that she had felt in the darkened chamber. And yet, slowly, an idea occurred to her.

By process of elimination, this puzzle had to be either physical or perceptive. And a plain cube with no stairs, no balance beams, and no maze didn't seem physical.

This was a perceptive puzzle.

Which meant the trick had to be using her abilities to see what else was in the room—to see in the dark.

She looked around the blackness. She'd never practiced anything like this with Cassian or Anya. They had focused only on levitation and mind reading, and the uncertainty made her queasy feeling return. Right now Cassian was out there, with Fian, and she had no idea if he was okay.

The gun started shaking in her hand.

But she pushed through her fears to try to see—or rather sense—into the darkness.

Concentrate. What's there?

Anya had told her that humans had to exert extra mental effort to match the perceptive abilities of the other species. She closed her eyes, drew in a full breath, and threw her thoughts out as violently as she could. It made her head spark with pain, but she kept pushing. What was she supposed to shoot? What creature was here with her?

Focus! See in the dark!

There. To her left. A flash of movement. She gasped, spinning toward it, aiming the gun. The room was still pitch-black, but she was able to use her psychic abilities to sense what was there: four legs. A swishing tail. Black and white stripes.

A zebra.

She sighed with relief—just a zebra. Harmless. And not a real one, either—she sensed it flickering in and out like a hologram. On its side was a bright red bull's-eye target.

She took a deep breath and raised the gun at the holographic zebra.

She concentrated.

Sensed where it was.

Squeezed the trigger.

Suddenly something barked behind her, lunging out of the darkness. She gasped and spun. *What is it?* She sensed another animal, four legs, long silky fur. A dog.

Sadie! Sadie was here!

It happened so fast. She didn't even realize her finger was still on the trigger until the bullet shot out. Too fast. Distracted. Her hand jerked. *Shit!* She tried to slow the bullet with her mind, move it to the left a little, and *yes:* the bullet stopped in midair. Sadie barked again, but Cora ignored the holographic dog and focused only on the bullet. She wasn't going to let the Gauntlet distract her.

She was able to reangle the bullet, pause, and release it. At the same time, a burst of pain exploded in the back of her skull.

She cried out. The gun fell. The bullet slammed into the zebra on target, but she doubled over in pain, clutching at her skull. The barking stopped. Both holographic animals vanished, leaving her alone.

Her head felt splintered in two.

She winced. This couldn't be right. Anya had said to push her mind to the limit, but this felt all wrong. Something was dripping on the ground—her own blood.

Ahead, the next door slid open.

Puzzle four.

She'd won. But she could barely move. Her head was throbbing, tender and raw. What had she done to herself? Had she broken her brain, just as Willa had warned her? She tried to use telepathy to see what was in the next puzzle chamber, but her head pulsed with such a sharp burst of pain that she nearly blacked out. She sank against the wall.

Took a deep breath.

When she tried to use her psychic abilities again, she got a slight, barely there glimmer of something and was flooded with relief. She hadn't broken her mind completely—just torn it.

Still, this was bad. She had two perceptive puzzles left to solve. She needed her brain intact.

She wiggled her fingers, checking to make sure they weren't shaking like Anya's. She blinked, testing out her vision, mentally checking herself over for any damage, just as her brother used to do after wrestling matches, making sure he hadn't pulled any muscles. God, she missed him. He . . . He . . .

She froze.

Her brother.

She couldn't remember his name.

Her lips parted in shock. She racked her brain, pushing through the pain. She remembered her mother, Linda. Her father, John. She could picture her brother's face, but there was simply no name there, only a gaping blank. And her dog . . . her dog who had just been here . . . she couldn't remember what her dog looked like, or the dog's name, or even what breed it was.

She swallowed back a lump of fear.

This must be what would happen if she pushed her mind too far. She'd torn her mind partway and she'd now forgotten little details like names and appearances. What if she broke her mind completely? Would she forget *everything*? Her family, her friends, even her own identity?

She pressed a hand to her nose as she stumbled toward the door. She didn't dare push her mind further. But then how could she complete the remaining perceptive puzzles?

The sound of wind and a crack of thunder tore her from her thoughts. She took one look through the doorway at the fourth puzzle—the last for this round—and sank to her knees.

As if it could possibly get worse.

"Oh, no," she said aloud.

27

Cora

CORA STOOD ON A platform a dizzying hundred feet off the ground. Tall pines rose on all sides. Wind howled, whipping her hair, pushing her forward. She crouched down, gripping the edge of the platform to keep from getting blown off. Icy sleet stung her arms and face. She squinted into the storm, but the door behind her, back to puzzle three, had shut and vanished.

She was in a forest, alone.

From what she could tell, it was the same high-ropes course Lucky had completed in the cage. The platform circled a giant pine tree, connected by ladders and rope swings and bridges to other platforms. Only now, wind pushed violently at the bridges, making them creak and groan in a way that shot fear to her heart. The rope swings thrashed around, whipping at the air. Sleet bit into her eyes. She lifted her hand to anxiously wipe at her face, but a gust of wind shoved her backward. She cried out, fingers scrambling for hold, but ice coated the platform, and her fingernails slipped off it uselessly. The wind blew her toward the edge faster. A rope danced in the air, snapping like a whip. She grabbed it a second before she would have fallen. It jerked and twisted in the storm, but she held on tight, knuckles white, pulling herself back onto the platform until she could wrap her arms around the tree trunk, pressing her chest to the bark.

The storm raged harder, rain drenching her.

She let out a shaky breath.

This was nothing like the course in the cage. This was practically a hurricane, and Lucky wasn't here to coach her how to climb from tree to tree. That day, she'd realized how special Lucky was: how even in the middle of a nightmare, he could find moments of joy. But Lucky hadn't plunged over a bridge, as she had. Her throat clenched at the memory. Sitting in the passenger side while her dad drove drunk across a bridge late at night in the rain, swerving at the last minute to avoid an oncoming car.

Breaking through the bridge's guardrail.

Tipping downward.

Plunging.

Crashing.

Dark water pouring in through the windows.

Cora's limbs started shaking violently, as if the bridge accident had happened just moments ago, not years. She squinted into the rain and dared to lift one hand, staring at the tremble. Her mind was too tender and painful to be able to make her hands stop shaking. The wind howled harder. Something cracked not far away. She twisted her head to see one of the pines attached to hers by a rope bridge crashing its way to the ground.

She screamed and held on tighter as the tree fell, ripping

away the rope bridge, ropes snapping and whipping in the air, the entire platform shaking violently. A few boards ripped away, but the platform remained intact. There was now only one way off her platform, though—a narrow ladder to another pine. The storm roared, and the next pine began to groan as well. She let out quick breaths as she forced herself to crawl to the edge. She had to do this. For Cassian. For *everyone*. When she dared to look down, amid the swirling rain and sleet, the ground did that awful dizzying telescoping thing, making her feel like she was already falling.

Drip.

A drop of blood from her nose fell toward the ground. Her head was throbbing in a way that made her more certain than ever that something had gone wrong when she'd strained her abilities. She tried again to think of her brother's name. Alex? Carl?

Panic started to crawl up her throat.

The tree groaned again.

Dozens of bridges and ladders spanned the forest, giving her hundreds of possible paths to get from her platform to the last one. But she'd run this course before. Thanks to Lucky, she knew the quickest path. It couldn't be a coincidence that it was the exact same puzzle as in the cage. Cassian must have arranged it somehow, to give her an edge. He couldn't cheat, of course, but he was skilled at bending the rules.

"Thank you," she whispered to him from afar.

She wiped away another streak of blood from her nose and gripped the first rung of the ladder that connected the platform to the next. It was coated with ice, and her hand slipped off. Panic tried to take control of her limbs, but she forced herself to carefully grip each rung, climbing as fast as she dared. She reached the next platform, which was swaying, the tree creaking dangerously. Lightning cracked overhead, lighting up the swirling sleet. This platform connected to the next in two ways: a wooden bridge and a rope ladder. She mentally ran through the course she'd taken with Lucky—he'd taken the bridge. She steadied herself on the slick bridge, her feet threatening to slip on every icy step.

A nearby tree cracked in the storm, plunging to the ground. She cringed, bracing herself, as it crashed straight into the rope ladder. She gasped. If she'd taken that rope ladder, she'd be dead.

The biting rain numbed her hands and feet. *Don't look down*, she told herself. Lucky had held her in his arms that first night, warming her with talk of home. She concentrated on that memory, letting it warm her again.

She pushed through the wind. Crossed another bridge. Climbed a twisting rope.

And then, at last, she was at the final rope swing.

With numb fingers she unhitched the rope from where it was wound around a giant tree trunk. She couldn't get a good grip, no matter how much she tried to shake the blood back into her hands, but she stepped toward the edge of the platform, knowing she didn't have a choice.

Wind howled at her.

If she didn't land on the opposite platform on the first swing, she'd be stuck out there, dangling in the abyss. She clutched the rope, counting down.

Five.

The wind whipped harder, blinding her with sleet.

Four.

She blinked away the sleet. *Three.* She breathed into her

hands, trying to warm them. The plunging distance to the ground made her stomach twist.

Two.

Suddenly the tree she was on groaned. Something snapped and it lurched. Inch by inch, it started to tilt.

She sucked in a breath. "One!"

She jumped a second before the tree buckled.

Wind whipped her hair back. She let out a shriek and clutched the rope hard. It all happened so fast. The final platform came rushing toward her. Closer, closer—but something was wrong. It was too far. The wind was too strong, whipping her around. There was no way the rope swing could possibly reach.

She let out a desperate cry as the rope reached its farthest point and came swinging back the other way. "No!" She kicked out, trying to reach the platform with her toe. The movement made her body twist around, as the rope swung in big loopy circles instead of a smooth arc, tossing her like a leaf in the storm. She kicked furiously, trying to hook her feet around the rope.

Almost—

But her numb hand slipped.

Suddenly she was back in the car with her father, plunging off that bridge, every fear in the world coming true in one terrible squeal of brakes, and her pulse started racing faster and faster.

But then her other hand closed over the rope. She clamped on hard. Got her feet wrapped around it.

Her pulse throbbed, quick and urgent.

She hadn't fallen.

She was alive.

Suspended between two platforms, blinding rain soaking

her, but alive. Blood was flowing again from her nose, streaking her arms, dripping to the forest floor. She looked around desperately. There was no way out but down.

And falling meant losing.

Death.

A rumbling sound started above her head. She squinted into the storm overhead and saw a sight that made her laugh a little deliriously. A dark square formed in the middle of the black clouds.

The next door. There, at the top of the rope.

And then her delirious laugh threatened to overtake her. To reach it, she'd have to climb. And her hands were so numb. Her muscles wrung out. She reached an exhausted hand up, forcing herself to climb inch by inch on a rope that was slippery with ice. She ignored the nosebleed. Ignored the wind trying to push her back down. Ignored that awful throbbing pain in her head as she climbed, and climbed, and at last touched the edge of the door with a rush of relief.

A hand reached down to help her.

A hand so big it could only belong to a Kindred. *Cassian.*

She let her muscles go slack. She clutched the hand, letting her eyes sink closed. She'd made it. Round one was done. She didn't dare think about the rest of the Gauntlet or whatever sabotage Fian was planning. She just wanted *out.*

Cassian pulled her the rest of the way up, through the floor of the central vestibule, between those blinding lights. She collapsed gratefully on the familiar ground, eyes still squeezed closed.

"Thank you," she breathed, opening her eyes.

Only it wasn't Cassian.

Fian blinked at her, not an ounce of mercy in his eyes.

28

Nok

KEENA WAS STILL SICK in bed, fading in and out of consciousness, unable to lead.

Nok couldn't help worrying about what would happen if Armstrong's de facto leader didn't recover soon; she certainly didn't like being the one everyone turned to for answers in Keena's absence. It had been a few grueling hours since the refugee ships had landed. Nearly forty battle-scarred Kindred, Gatherer, and Mosca ships that each carried a ragtag group of survivors who were now recovering in the shade of the old slave tent, which, with Rolf's help, they had set up as a makeshift hospital.

Now, she and Rolf and a few head citizens congregated in the sheriff's office with Makayla and a Gatherer named Brother Paddal to hear about this new threat. Nok glanced out the window at the eerily calm skies and then at the Gatherer. Eight feet tall, gray skin, fingers like crab legs. She chewed on her lip. She seriously wished Keena were here.

"Start from the beginning," she said.

"Does he really have to be a part of this?" Makayla jerked her head toward Dane, who was standing near the sheriff's office doorway, arms crossed.

Nok gave Dane a long, untrusting look. "Believe me," she said, "I wish we didn't have to include him, but the mine guards chose him as their representative. They deserve a voice."

Makayla folded her arms, glaring at Dane, as she explained how war had broken out on the Kindred station, how they'd heard on the ship's communication system that it had actually been an Axion battalion in disguise, and how Fian—to their surprise—had been an impostor. The real one had been imprisoned for months in the same cells as Cassian.

"And you saw Mali and Leon?" Rolf pressed.

Makayla nodded. "They were okay, last I saw. But the station was in bad shape. The Kindred didn't stand a chance."

Next to her, the towering Brother Paddal nodded. "The Axion's attack was well orchestrated throughout the galaxy," he explained. "From what our communications officer could gather, they attacked at least eleven Kindred stations simultaneously, reaching as far as the Lehani province. We also received reports of attacks on the Mosca planets of Drore and Dramaden. Our entire Gatherer east-sector fleet was wiped out. My ship's tracking device was broken, which is the only way I was able to escape."

Nok twisted her pink strand of hair, trying to guess what Keena would do in this situation. "Well, you can stay as long as you'd like, though we don't exactly have overflowing resources. We'll do what we can to heal your wounded and keep you fed until your people can come rescue you, once the war is over."

Makayla and the Gatherer exchanged a long look.

"It isn't that simple," Makayla said. "We didn't come here because we thought it would be safe. We came here to regroup, and also to warn you." She paused. "The Axion are headed this way next."

Dane's eyes flashed with surprise. Rolf jumped up, taking quick strides to the window to peer at the skies.

"Here?" Nok sputtered. "Why? We have no argument with the Axion!"

"They have an argument with you," Makayla said. "They've heard rumors there are evolved humans here who could be a threat."

Nok cursed under her breath. "We aren't ready for a battle with the Axion! Rolf has worked up plans for defensive fortifications to the town, but we haven't even started construction, and it would take months. For the present, we're barely keeping ourselves alive here." She spun around to face the towering Brother Paddal. "What about your ships? Don't you have weapons?"

"A few, yes," the Gatherer explained in a droning voice. "We have forty ships between my vessel, the Kindred shuttles, and the Mosca ones. Twenty-two have functioning weapons, though most are badly damaged, and we are low on fuel."

Nok jerked her head toward Loren. "Loren can show you where we keep our fuel reserves, though we're low too." She paced in front of the windows, twisting even more anxiously at her hair. "Who knows how many Axion are coming, and how good their weapons are. Twenty-two ships might not be enough to stop them." She let out a frustrated sigh, squeezing the bridge of her nose between two fingers.

Dane cleared his throat. "There's another option."

All eyes turned to him. Nok narrowed hers, having a feeling she wouldn't like whatever he was going to suggest.

"The Axion have ships, and weapons, and superior technology," he said. "And who knows what other kinds of tech they've developed over the last few decades that they've kept secret from the world. We don't stand a chance against them if we try to fight." He paused. "But maybe we could survive if we joined them."

Nok and Makayla both jumped up.

"No way!" Makayla said.

"Are you insane?" Nok asked at the same time.

"Hardly," he snapped at them both. "If the Axion are as smart as you say they are, then they must know that it could be beneficial to have loyal humans on their side. I'm not saying I'm happy about it—I know you all think I'm a monster, but I'm not. I'm only suggesting it as a last resort. To keep us alive. And which is more important to you, *Sheriff*? Having brave dead citizens, or living cowardly ones?"

Seething, Nok shook her head. "We aren't siding with the Axion. That's final." She squeezed the sheriff's badge. The edges pressed sharply into her palm, setting her senses on alert. Sweat started to break out on her brow. She felt as though all eyes were on her, waiting for her to come up with some brilliant plan to save them. She tried to think of what Keena would say, but she hadn't even known Keena that long.

She turned to the window, the sunlight glaring like a camera flash, and her thoughts scrolled back to her life in London. Her first week there, when she'd been only fourteen. Miss Delphine standing behind a camera, chewing that saccharine red licorice, ordering Nok how to pose. *No, no! You look like you've just crawled out of the jungle, girl.*

Nok had blinked. *But Chiang Mai is in the jungle.*

Miss Delphine had rolled her eyes, muttering, *Listen, girl. I'm going to tell you the one piece of advice that will get you through any shoot. "Fake it till you make it." Got it? You aren't some scrappy kid from a backwater Thai town anymore. You're the goddamn Queen of Sheba, if you want to be. Fake it. Make me believe.*

Nok blinked out of her memories of the past.

If she could fake being a sultry model for all that time in London, then she could fake anything. Fake being confident. Fake being a sheriff. Fake not being terrified. She pressed a hand to her stomach, feeling her child growing. It wouldn't be long now. What kind of world would Sparrow be born into? Would she see her mother as a scrawny, flighty girl who shirked her responsibilities? Or would she see her as someone brave?

She let the sheriff's badge rest on her chest and took a deep breath. "We'll send all the elderly citizens and the wounded to take cover in the root mine. Rolf, you can start taking loads of people there in one of the trucks. The rest of us will take up arms in the tent encampment. We'll leave this empty town as a decoy, hoping the Axion strike it first."

"There may be another problem." Brother Paddal unfolded his long, spindly fingers, pointing to the map that Rolf had unrolled on his desk. He pointed to the town, then slid his forefinger to the transport hub. He tapped it. "This moon contains a Kindred transport hub that is powered by an Axion reactor core. It allows for all the satellite tracking and communication with the Kindred stations."

"We know," Rolf said. "I've been looking into ways to harness the power to give us electricity here in town."

Brother Paddal nodded solemnly. "It is cloaked from outside radar, so it cannot be detected from above—it reads only as a standard warehouse. I did not know it was here myself until after I had landed. But you see, the reactor is highly volatile. One targeted laser pulse, and this entire area becomes a smoldering crater."

"What do you mean?" Nok demanded.

"If an Axion laser pulse hits that reactor core in the right place, all life on this moon would be dead. Instantly."

Nok's face went white.

"There is a way," Brother Paddal continued, "to manually shut off the core from inside the facility. Power it down, and there is no danger if it is hit."

"Yeah," Rolf said, "but I've studied the blueprints. Anyone who goes inside far enough to shut it off manually would die of radiation exposure."

Brother Paddal cleared his throat. "That is a problem, yes."

Nok cursed under her breath and leaned over the counter, letting her hair curtain her face. "No one's dying of radiation exposure, got it?" She looked up at the Gatherer. "You said it's untraceable from the skies. And that's how the Axion will attack, from above. To them it'll look like a plain warehouse. They have no reason to target it any more than the other tents and buildings."

"Yeah," Makayla added, "but it's still dangerous. A stray laser pulse, or if they just attack it by chance . . ."

Dane muttered, "We're all going to die."

Nok spun on him with a clenched jaw. "We're not going to

die. We just have to keep them away from that reactor core. We'll distract them on the ground, leading them here toward the empty town, while Brother Paddal and the other pilots attack from the sky."

For a moment, everyone was quiet. Dane didn't look happy, but he didn't grumble aloud again.

"It's a good plan," Rolf said at last. His gaze met Nok's, full of confidence in her. He nodded. "Really good, Nok."

She flushed with relief, toying with the sheriff's badge.

It was true that Nok had no particular love for the dusty moon, but she had hope for what it could be, with all the improvements Rolf planned on making and with the community they were starting to build. A safe haven for Sparrow.

A home.

She looked back down at the badge. Her own eyes reflected back.

Sparrow kicked.

Maybe Nok was never meant to be a sheriff, but for her unborn child, she would fake being anything. And for a second—the slightest moment—she wasn't even sure she *was* faking being strong anymore.

"Let's get moving," she said.

29

Cora

FIAN DIDN'T RELEASE CORA'S hand. He scowled down at her in a way that made the wrinkle on his forehead even deeper.

"Let the record state," one of the Gatherers announced, "the competitor has completed round one and is now entitled to a break for medical attention and rest."

Fian still didn't let go of her hand. She jerked upright, tugging against him. Behind him were the Axion delegation, the Gatherers, and all four Chief Assessors, but where was Cassian? Mali? Anya and the others?

Fian leaned forward, squeezing Cora's hand tightly enough to cause pain to radiate in her bones. "Only four puzzles in," he said in a dangerously quiet voice. "And you look ready to give up already."

"I'll beat anything the stock algorithm throws at me," she seethed, ripping her hand out of his.

His eyes narrowed, but then footsteps came from the

hallway. Mali appeared first, followed by Leon. They caught sight of her and raced forward.

"We heard the announcement!" Mali's eyes searched the dried blood around Cora's nose with concern. "Are you okay?"

"Fine." Cora threw Fian a defiant look. But she stumbled as soon as she took a step, and Fian smirked.

"Come on, sweetheart," Leon said, lifting her in his arms. "You can rest in the Mosca's recess room. We have water and food and"—he dropped his voice as he carried her—"plenty to tell you. A lot has happened while you've been in there."

Mali held the door open for them, and Leon carried her into a small room packed with wonderfully familiar faces: Anya, Willa, Bonebreak and Ironmage, several Mosca aides—and Cassian.

Cora's breath hitched in her throat.

He's okay.

He was standing upright, one hand knitting against his forehead as though his head pained him. When their eyes met, his hand fell. All she could think about was how she'd left him behind on the aggregate station. How she'd heard his screams as he was tortured, how all that pain had been to cover up her crimes.

Leon set her down, and then Cassian took a step forward. Hesitantly. Did he hate her? Blame her? But then he took another, and then he was across the room, and she was in his arms, and she never wanted to let him go. She held him as tightly as she dared, afraid of the scars, afraid of hurting him more.

"You're okay," Cora whispered.

He had changed out of the bloodstained Warden's uniform she'd last seen him in. The soft black clothes he wore now smelled of smoke and the ozone scent of the aggregate station, but beneath it was the tang of metal that made her think of the interrogation table.

"Yes," he said haltingly. "Thanks . . . thanks to Leon and Mali."

Cora knit her fingers in the folds of his clothes. Her finger grazed a cut on the side of his neck. "I watched the Kindred torturing you. They were going to kill you. God, Cassian, I'm so sorry. I blame myself for leaving you there." She swallowed, pulling back slightly. "What did they do to you?"

That pain flashed in his eyes again. He looked away, almost like closing a door between them. "Standard interrogation." His voice was suddenly formal, a little forced. From the way his jaw flexed, she knew it must have been anything but standard. "I wasn't strong enough to resist the mind probes. The Council learned about the Fifth of Five. Now it's war on the station."

Her eyes searched his. What wasn't he saying?

"War?" Her lips parted. "The Fifth of Five must be hugely outnumbered."

"Tessela is using the kill-dart guns. They have a chance." He gently tugged a pine needle from her tangled hair.

She leaned into his hand and closed her eyes.

"Um, before the make-out session starts," Leon said, and Cora jolted alert, "maybe we should talk about this whole Axion-taking-over-the-world thing." He pointed to a clock above the recess room door. A sliver of the round face was green, the hand ticking down. "This break only lasts ten minutes."

Cora took a step back from Cassian, suddenly aware of a dozen sets of eyes watching her. She cleared her throat, combing her fingers through her hair. She glanced at the clock.

Ten minutes wasn't a lot of time.

"The Axion?" she said. "What are you talking about?"

Cassian explained the Axion's ability to disguise themselves, how they had been impersonating Arrowal and Fian and others, and how the battle on the station was actually an Axion attack, part of a wider war in which Axion were assaulting other planets simultaneously. Suddenly her mind ached, and she sank onto a bench, clutching the sides of her skull.

"Are you okay?" Cassian asked, touching her shoulder.

"It's just all so much to take in at once. And . . . I think I strained my mind too hard," Cora said. "In the perceptive puzzle. Tore something . . . I can't remember certain things." Wincing, she looked around the room until she met Anya's eyes. The small girl was standing alone by the recess room door, fingers now calm at her sides.

"I did what you told me to, Anya," Cora said. "Something went wrong."

"But did it work?" Anya asked quickly.

"What?" Cora rubbed the sides of her head. "Well, yeah. I was able to stop a bullet in midair and redirect it. I've never done anything like that before. But the pain, and my memories—"

"That will pass," Anya answered. "I bet your arms and legs are sore too, right? They'll recover, and so will your mind."

Cassian was watching Anya with an unreadable expression. "You told her to strain her mind? That is dangerous—"

A knock came at the door, interrupting him.

Everyone went quiet.

"Open it," Cora said, and Leon, standing closest to the door, did.

Serassi stood on the other side.

Cora instantly dropped her arms to her sides. "What do you want?"

The Kindred Chief Genetics Officer's black gaze went to each of them in turn, taking in the crowded room full of Mosca and humans and a chimpanzee. She stepped into the room and closed the door behind her. "I am not an Axion, if that is what you are wondering."

Cora shot up from the bench, alarm blazing. "How do you know about the impostors, unless you are one?"

Serassi blinked calmly with her black eyes like oily puddles. There was no kindness in her gaze. No glimmer of friendship.

But then again, there never had been.

"Am one? No, not at all." Serassi lowered her head slowly, closing her eyes. Her whole body hardened in concentration, a look Cora recognized as a Kindred going through the uncloaking process. After a few seconds, Serassi looked up with uncloaked eyes. Her irises were visible: brown with faint flecks of blue.

Cora regarded her warily.

"The Axion have learned how to turn off the frequency that gives away their disguises," Serassi said. "They intend to reinstate their status as the original intelligent species, not by breaking from the others, but by dominating them. Beginning with the Kindred."

Cora glanced at Cassian. "We already know that."

Serassi did not blink. She merely fixed her steady gaze on Cora. "But do you know how to stop them?"

Cora's heart thundered in her chest. "Do you?"

Serassi nodded.

"We cannot trust this woman!" Bonebreak cried. "The

uncloaking proves nothing. How do we know she is not a decoy they've sent?" He sniffed the air as though he could tell her true nature through scent alone.

Cora turned to Serassi. "Bonebreak's right. Rolf and Nok told me about what you did to them. Locked them up in that dollhouse experiment. Forced them to act out human life. Threatened to take their baby. We'd be crazy to trust you."

"The dollhouse experiment, as you call it," Serassi said flatly, "was crucial for me to collect necessary DNA samples. I needed a full range of human emotions and strengths, including those of child rearing, for my plan to be successful."

Cora paced, hoping the movement would distract her from the ache in her head. "How could the dollhouse have anything to do with defeating the Axion?"

"Quite a bit, in fact. Their ability to disguise themselves is why I was forced to be so secretive in my efforts. As Chief Genetics Officer, I had the full genetics laboratory equipment at my disposal, but I had to devise an explanation for why I was using such sensitive equipment: that was when I invented the idea of the dollhouse experiment. I convinced the other Kindred scientists that I was obsessed with child raising. Such a ridiculous interest made them think less of me, so no one looked too carefully into my work as I gathered DNA samples from a wide range of humans—thousands in all, from the enclosure wards, the menageries, the humans in processing on their way to Armstrong—in an effort to create the one thing that can stop the Axion." She held up a small syringe. "This."

Almost in unison, everyone in the room took a step backward.

"What is that?" Cora asked hesitantly.

"For generations, Kindred medical officers have collected DNA samples as part of routine processing before sending humans to Armstrong. When I realized what the Axion were planning, I suspected that it was possible to bind that DNA to other humans using a procedure normally used for healing extreme injuries. I began covertly collecting more DNA from select humans with a wide range of abilities. The serum in this syringe holds the best of humanity's intelligence, strength, and moral fiber. It contains a protein that can bond this human DNA to another human's DNA chain."

Cora's eyes widened. She didn't know much about biology and genetics, but from what Serassi was saying, it seemed she'd done the impossible. "You mean that all of humanity's strengths are in that one vial? An entire race's knowledge and abilities?"

Serassi held it up. "I call it a 'paragon burst.'"

Cora eyed the syringe cautiously.

"I'll need to inject it directly into your bloodstream," Serassi continued.

Cora turned away, pacing. "What do you think?" she asked Cassian quietly.

He rested a reassuring hand on her shoulder, easing the tension there. "You have passed the easiest of the puzzles, but not without cost. They have ruptured your mind and exhausted your body. The probability that you can pass even the next round, let alone the final one, is dangerously low."

"You mean that without the enhanced strength of the paragon burst, I don't stand a chance."

He didn't answer. He didn't have to.

Memories of the first four puzzles washed through Cora's

head, along with a wave of pain. She hissed in a sharp breath and closed her eyes, feeling dizzy. Cassian's hand on her shoulder tightened to steady her. When she opened them again, everyone in the room was staring at her.

Cora glanced at the clock on the wall: only a sliver remained green. "Why do the Axion even care if I win or not? I'm a human—I'm no threat to them."

"They care because once a species wins the Gauntlet," Serassi explained, "it triggers a change in the entire species. We call it an 'evolutionary jump.' Evolution is more complicated than you have learned on Earth. It is not only a biological change that occurs over millennia, but also a spiritual one. Once one member of a species attains intelligent status, it opens the door for the others. For some who are already highly gifted, like Anya, they will see an immediate change. Others will take more time, but the result will be the same. If you win the Gauntlet, your entire species will become more powerful."

Cora blinked through the incredible things Serassi had just said. "Even so, humanity would still be in its infancy. We'd still be no threat."

"That is correct," Serassi said evenly. "*You* would not be a threat. But the Kindred are not in our infancy. We are the peacekeepers, the police, the army of the universe. We have the best chance of defeating the Axion."

"But how would elevating humans elevate the Kindred, too?" Cora asked.

Serassi cocked her head. Her eyes slowly went to Cassian, and Cora got a creeping feeling that she was missing something very important.

"You never told her?" Serassi asked.

Cora whipped her head around to Cassian. "Didn't tell me what?"

He swallowed.

A crazy premonition entered her mind. Her eyes traced over the curve of his throat, his lips, his jaw. She'd noticed from the first day the startling similarities between their species, but the differences—their black eyes, their large size—had been impossible to ignore. Surely, Serassi couldn't be suggesting what Cora imagined. . . .

"Humans and Kindred," Cassian said slowly, "are the same species."

30

Cora

CASSIAN'S WORDS HIT CORA like a slap in the face. She sat heavily on the bench. The others seemed equally stunned. Leon flexed his hands, seeming to compare them with Serassi's larger ones. Bonebreak and the other Mosca whispered to one another in words Cora couldn't understand.

"Same *species*?" Cora repeated.

"Not exactly identical, of course," Cassian clarified, keeping his gaze just slightly away from hers. "We derive from the same ancestral species: *Homo erectus*. Our DNA is similar enough that if a human wins the Gauntlet, both our species will experience the evolutionary jump."

"That can't be." Cora shook her head. "You told me that you were an astral species, not a terrestrial one."

He glanced at Serassi. "That has been true of us for the last twenty thousand years, but we originated on Earth. I told you that we owe our intelligence to the Gatherers, who long ago elevated us to live among the stars. It was Earth where they found us. Our two species had already branched apart. You *Homo sapiens* were smaller and faster—you spread more quickly across the continents. Our ancestors were Neanderthals, larger and smarter, but in danger of annihilation. That was when the Gatherers took us. That is why we among the Fifth of Five care so strongly about your species. Because Earth is our planet, too, or at least it was once. You are kin to us."

She stared at him as though he were speaking a foreign language.

"Only a few know," Cassian added, still not meeting her gaze. "I learned myself when I became the leader of the Fifth of Five—it is a closely guarded secret. The Intelligence Council does not wish to reveal that Kindred are related to a lesser species. I intended to tell you, but you hated me so viciously after you thought I betrayed you that you wouldn't have believed me." He paused and then spoke more softly. "I always knew that your plan to cheat the Gauntlet wouldn't work—cheating wouldn't have triggered the evolutionary jump. But you didn't want to hear it. If the Council hadn't stopped your plan, I would have had to find a way to do so myself."

"What about the paragon burst? Isn't that cheating?"

"Not as long as it is composed only of human DNA," Serassi said.

Cora spun to face her. "You aren't part of the Fifth of Five. Why do you care about helping humans?"

"I do not," she answered flatly. And then she cocked her head. "Let me rephrase that: I have been a friend to Anya and Mali, in my own way. I have always been fair in my dealings with humans, I have served diligently as Chief Genetics Officer overseeing human health, I have even tended to your own wounds on multiple occasions. It is my duty as a Kindred to protect lesser species, and I take that responsibility seriously. But care? No, I do not personally care about helping humans evolve. You are merely a necessary piece of the puzzle. This is the only way to make *us* evolve, too."

Cora narrowed her eyes. Technically the Kindred didn't lie, but she could still selectively twist the facts. Something still sat uneasy with Cora. She paced back and forth.

"So if your plan works, and the Kindred become powerful enough to stop the Axion, what's to stop the Kindred from attempting to become the most powerful race yourselves?" Her question was directed toward Serassi, but her gaze went to Cassian.

A quiet spread through the room.

"We have no interest in domination," Cassian stated.

"That isn't what Fian and Arrowal seem to think," Cora countered.

"Fian and Arrowal are Axion in disguise," Cassian said. "The real Fian is, at this very moment, risking his life in battle on the aggregate station."

"It's true," Leon added. "We saw it ourselves."

Cora made the mistake of meeting Cassian's eyes—so clear, so blue, so obvious in that moment that he wasn't entirely alien. "You have to trust me, Cora," he said. "I am not lying about this. My cards are all on the table. The Kindred do not wish for domination. Not I, not Serassi, not any of us."

He held out his hands palms up. She thought about their training sessions in the Hunt, when she had taught him how to lie. Right now, he wasn't bluffing.

Above the doorway, the timekeeper clock gave an audible click. Time was almost out. Any moment, the impostor Fian would come to collect Cora.

Serassi uncapped the syringe, eyes on the clock. "We can wait no longer. The effects of this paragon burst will not be immediate; it might take one or two puzzles before the effects settle. Until then, you may feel disoriented."

Cora glanced at the needle, then at the clock. Did she trust what Serassi and Cassian were saying? *Did she have a choice?*

"Wait." All eyes turned to Mali, who had been silent but now stepped forward. "I assume you have Nok and Rolf's DNA samples in that vial."

Serassi nodded.

Mali glanced over her shoulder at Leon. "But you do not have mine or Leon's." She began to roll up her sleeve. "The stock algorithm chose us because of our unique traits. Leon's strength and his artistic aptitude. My adaptability and keen senses." She held her bare arm out. "I want to contribute."

"Mali," Cora said, "we don't even know if this will work."

Mali shot her a stiff look. "I do not mean to offend you, but"—her eyes traveled from the bloodstains around Cora's nose to the bruises covering her body—"you need all the help you can get."

Leon snorted. He came over and shoved back his sleeve too. "Mali has a good point. That vial can't hold *all* of humanity's strengths if it doesn't have any of my DNA."

Cora rolled her eyes.

"Hang on," Bonebreak said. He rooted around in his pocket, then produced a tangled lock of dark hair. "Here's more. From, you know, the other one."

Cora stared at him. "From *Lucky*? You stole hair off his dead body?"

Bonebreak looked toward the ground sheepishly. "In case we needed money in a pinch. What do you call it? For a rainy day."

Cora made a disgusted noise in the back of her throat, but then she threw her hands up. "Fine." From beyond the door, she could hear footsteps approaching. She nodded to Serassi.

Serassi replaced the syringe tips with different, larger ones from the tool belt at her uniform's waist. Moving quickly, she sterilized Mali's and Leon's arms, then drew their blood and took a sample from Lucky's hair.

The footsteps outside the door stopped.

"Lift up your hair and turn around," Serassi told Cora. "Quickly."

Cora swept her hair to the side and felt the press of the cold needle at the base of her skull. There was a pinch as the needle punctured and then a painful warmth as the paragon burst spread through the blood vessels at the back of her head. She massaged the throbbing sensation, but it only seemed to latch harder onto her brain, searing her neurons with fire.

"It feels weird," Cora said. "It hurts."

Serassi had already taken apart the vial and syringe and was replacing it in her tool belt, as though nothing had happened, when the knock came at the door.

Cora's vision was starting to fade in and out of focus. A dull roar seemed to surround her, as if a stadiumful of people were cheering between her ears. She took a step and stumbled.

"Serassi, something's wrong."

"It is a new drug," Serassi explained. "This technique has

never been tested. I do not know the exact effects. Your body needs time to adapt to the compound."

"She doesn't have time," Cassian growled.

Cora felt hands shaking her. Everything moved suddenly too fast and then too slow. The roar increased. *Whispers.* How were there so many voices? Where were they coming from?

Someone knocked harder at the door.

The roar grew, and Cora clamped her hands over her ears. She realized the voices were coming from *inside* her head. From hundreds—thousands—of strains of human DNA in the injection Serassi had given her. It was as if her body weren't her own any-more. As if thousands of other legs were inside her feet. Thousands of other voices in her head.

Mali opened the door.

Fian waited on the other side, hand raised to knock again. No—not Fian. Now that Cora knew he was an Axion, the little glimpses of emotion he let slip seemed so obvious, like the trace of contempt he now wore when he tilted his chin to the lights. How had she ever believed this creature was a Kindred?

He smiled darkly when he saw her ashen complexion. "Time for round two, Gauntleteer."

31

Leon

LEON WATCHED CORA ENTER the Gauntlet with a sick feeling in his stomach. He hated the Gauntlet's claustrophobic rooms, and the central vestibule was the worst. All those monitors giving off a sickly light, that low hum that worked its way into his head until he thought he'd go crazy. Even worse was the way the four Chief Assessors stared so passively at the monitors' scrolling lines of coding, as though they were watching a weather report, not Cora's life-or-death progress. Now she was in there again, the portal door sealed shut, enduring God knew what. Puzzle five could be killing her. The injection Serassi had given her might have fried her brain. She could be writhing in pain, and those damn judges would just stare.

Mali rested a hand on his shoulder, as though sensing his worry. "There's nothing we can do for her. Cora is on her own until the next break." She dropped her voice. "Besides, we have our own puzzles to solve. Willa thinks she may have discovered something."

Leon glanced over his shoulder toward the Mosca recess room, where Cassian was standing in the doorway, staring coldly at Fian as though he were fantasizing about shaking the Axion until his disguise melted off. A sentiment Leon shared.

"Come on," Mali pressed.

Leon reluctantly returned to the recess room. Anya had left to see if she could overhear anything useful from the other delegations, but the Mosca and everyone else were congregated around the back wall, where Willa was scrawling on paper.

Leon looked over their shoulders at the note.

I learned much about the Axion while they were experimenting on me. They are sensitive to high-pitched frequencies—which is why the Intelligence Council ordered that their genetic implants be set to emit certain tones. But frequencies can do more than just announce when one is disguised. A high-enough frequency would disrupt Axion brain waves to the extent that they would no longer be able to shape-shift at all. It would force them into their true appearance.

Murmurs spread through the room as the various Mosca and humans read Willa's note.

"So we'd know immediately which ones are impostors," Leon said. "And then we arrest the bastards."

Serassi gave him an exasperated look. "It is naive of you to think it would be so simple." She went to one of the monitors, reached behind it, and extracted some equipment. She set it down on the desk in front of Willa. "Though it is still a good idea. Can you build a frequency emitter from this?"

Willa examined the wires, then started attaching them to the monitor's speaker.

The speaker suddenly let out a high-pitched squeal, and Leon made a face. "Try not to shatter all our eardrums in the process, okay, Queen Kong?"

He caught sight of Bonebreak coming in from the facilities room, looking over the coded monitor with its scrolling data. Anya hadn't yet returned, and the others were distracted with Willa's project. For a second, he was alone with Bonebreak.

"Listen," he said in a low voice. He quietly reached for the provision pack that he had stashed in his inside jacket pocket. "I know we've got bigger problems right now, but I got the delivery for you."

Bonebreak barely glanced at him. "Eh? What are you going on about, boy?"

"The special delivery," Leon whispered more urgently. "From the station. The provision pack you asked me to pick up." He opened his jacket, revealing the package.

Bonebreak tilted his head in a bewildered way. He scratched at his chin beneath the mask as his gaze went between Leon's face and the package.

"Come on, mate," Leon urged. Sweat was starting to break out on his forehead. Any minute Willa might look up from her work, or Mali might turn around, and the last thing he wanted was to be caught smuggling when he was supposed to be a goddamn hero. "If you don't want it anymore, too bad. We had a deal. I risked a lot for this."

Bonebreak grabbed the lapels of Leon's jacket and pulled him into the corner, to the side of the monitors where they'd have some privacy. "Listen closely, boy. I have no idea what you speak of. I requested no pickup. I made no deal with you."

"Yes, you did! *An easy job*, you said. On Armstrong, right after Nok killed the sheriff and all hell broke loose."

"On Armstrong?" Bonebreak sputtered. "As soon as that sheriff was killed, I ducked behind the dais to to save my own skin, like any sane creature. I most certainly didn't search you out for a *chat*."

"Then who did I make a deal with?" As soon as he'd spoken the words, it struck him. How, at the time, Bonebreak had seemed to disappear and reappear on opposite sides of the tent almost instantaneously. "Oh, shit." He swallowed. "An Axion."

An angry rumble came from behind Bonebreak's mask. "One of those bastards had the gall to pose as me, and you were too dumb to tell the difference?"

"Hey!" Leon snapped. "It was chaos and he sounded just like you. *Smelled* just like you, too!" But as soon as he said those words, he realized it wasn't true. The Bonebreak he had spoken to in the tent had lacked the Mosca's trademark odor.

Bonebreak shook him again. "What did you tell him? Did you say anything that will get us killed?"

Leon's mind turned back to the deal he'd made with the trader. "I, uh, might have told him about the plan to rescue Cassian from the station."

Bonebreak hissed his displeasure.

"But listen, what harm did it do? The plan worked. He couldn't have been impersonating you for more than a few minutes, tops. We got Cassian and the Axion didn't stop us. So no harm, no foul, right?"

For a second, Bonebreak was silent. Then, very slowly, his eyes dropped to Leon's jacket. "That depends, boy, on what is in that package you so obediently stole for our enemies."

Leon swallowed. He pressed a hand to the provision pack, feeling the hard edges. How had the Axion impersonator even gotten the package into the crate? It must have been one of the Axion already on the station, the one the fake Bonebreak had been communicating with. He slowly pulled the package out, holding it by the corner as though it were contagious. Bonebreak recoiled as well. On the opposite side of the room, Willa's emitter released an even higher frequency.

"Open it," Bonebreak whispered.

"*You* open it."

Bonebreak hissed a string of curses as he snatched the package out of Leon's hand and tried to tear at the edge, but he was unable to get it open. With a frustrated growl he pulled a knife out of his pocket and sawed at the corner.

Leon caught a flash of movement as the recess room door opened. Anya slipped in quietly. "I'm back." Her face looked grim. "I didn't find out anything useful. The Axion didn't say much about their . . ."

Willa adjusted the emitter's dial again, and a high squeal burst through the room. Leon clamped his hands over his ears, wincing. He was about to call to Willa to shut the damn thing off when he caught sight of Serassi's face.

She was staring at Anya. Or, rather, the place where Anya had been standing.

What the hell . . .

Anya was gone. The girl had simply vanished. No, not vanished. *Changed.* A completely different person stood where she had been standing, dressed in Anya's same white Temple menagerie clothes, a few inches shorter than Anya so that the pants hem brushed the ground. It was a man. He was about four feet tall, painfully thin, the bones of his face especially pronounced—with the telltale white stripe in his hair.

An Axion impostor.

"Shit!" Leon yelled.

Mali and Cassian spun around, going rigid as soon as they saw the spy dressed in Anya's clothes.

"Anya . . . ?" Mali started, but Leon pulled her away from the Axion.

"It isn't Anya!" he said. "It's one of those damn spies—Willa figured out how to expose them."

The Axion tossed a look over his shoulder, judging the distance to the door.

"Don't think about running." Cassian strode to the door and slammed it shut.

The Axion's eyes darted back and forth, his face scowling.

"How long have you been posing as her?" Mali demanded. "Where's the real Anya?"

"Kill me and you'll never know." His grinning lips pulled back over graying, uneven teeth. "You're too late, anyway. This plan has been generations in the making. We have forty lightships heading to the Gatherer home planet as we speak, and another hundred hunting down their mobile rovers. Twenty of our fastest cruisers are headed for Drogane and the other Mosca planets."

His cruel grin stretched wider. "We've already assumed control of four Kindred stations, including station 10-91. Its attempts to resist were pathetic. All those who fought us were killed."

Leon's stomach shrank. He thought back on the battle, Tessela and Fian fighting against the Axion intruders. His mouth felt suddenly very dry. Were they really dead? He swallowed down a lump.

"They could have gotten out," Cassian said, as though reading his thoughts. "They could be on a cargo shuttle to Armstrong."

"Armstrong?" the Axion sneered. "Then they've only bought themselves a few more hours."

Mali gripped his shirt hard, shaking him. "Why? There's no reason for you to attack Armstrong. It's just humans and dust."

"There are reports," the Axion said slyly, "of evolved humans who can use telepathy. That's the third phase of our plan—destroy any human settlements that show signs of evolution."

Leon sucked in a breath. Ellis had been telepathic. Maybe there'd been others, too. He bit back the worry rising in his throat. Nok and Rolf were on Armstrong. And Makayla and Shoukry too, and all the kids and animals from the Hunt, assuming their ship made it.

"Christ," he muttered, briefly closing his eyes.

The Axion started to let out a snicker at the distraught expressions on everyone's faces, until Leon strode up and slammed a fist into his grinning mouth. The Axion's eyes rolled back in his head and he collapsed to the floor, unconscious.

"Leon!" Mali said. "He's the only one who knows where Anya is!"

"I didn't *kill* him," he argued.

Cassian stood over the Axion's unconscious body. "This is bad. If the Axion have already spread as far as he says, then there isn't much that can stop them now. We might be the last hope. And if he has been posing as Anya even as far back as Armstrong, he knows everything. He must have told the other Axion that we're on to them."

"He couldn't have been posing as Anya as far back as on Armstrong," Mali said. "I was with her the entire time." Mali turned to Willa. "Anya left with you."

Willa's eyes widened. She scrawled a quick message on the back of one of her papers.

Theta.

"Theta?" Mali said, and then her expression went flat. "That's an Axion fuel station, isn't it?"

Willa nodded. She scrawled more.

Anya went inside, and when she came back she was acting different. I tried to warn Cora. But Anya convinced her it was just the Kindred's drugs.

"That was weeks ago!" Leon said. "She's been a spy this entire time?"

"We need to consider what this means and what to do about it," Cassian said.

Next to Leon, Bonebreak suddenly let out a snort of surprise. When Leon turned, the provision pack was open, and Bonebreak held a roughly spherical object with a glowing blue ring around it.

"What the hell is this?" Bonebreak said.

They all turned to him. Cassian and Serassi immediately went stiff. Cassian's voice was tight. "That," he said, "is a bomb."

Bonebreak squealed and tossed the orb to Leon.

"Shit!" Leon said. "What am I supposed to do with this thing?"

"It's ticking," Cassian said in a rush. "It must have been triggered when you opened the pack."

"That spy who posed as me was planning on getting you killed, boy!" Bonebreak said. "He got you to pick up a bomb that would blow up in the ship, killing you and Mali and Cassian before you could get back here. He didn't think you'd resist opening it!"

Cassian's lips moved silently, counting the ticks. His voice was urgent. "Ten more seconds until it goes off."

Willa and Mali and Bonebreak all leaped back. Leon glanced at the door. His arm was too wounded to throw, but he could run. He could make it to the central vestibule, at least far enough to protect his friends. . . .

As if sensing his thoughts, Bonebreak cursed.

"Idiot humans." He snatched the bomb out of Leon's hand and started charging toward the door to the vestibule.

"Brother, no!" Ironmage yelled.

Leon gaped. His heart was thumping hard, his adrenaline pumping. What was that stupid Mosca doing? If Leon knew anything about the black market trader, it was that he'd sooner let them all blow up than risk his own life to save even one of them.

"Bonebreak, what the hell?" he yelled.

"I always liked you, boy," Bonebreak called. "Never thought

I'd die for a weak human childs, but at least you could smuggle with the best of them. Break some bones for me, boy. Break some bones!"

Leon stared, agape, as Bonebreak ran toward the dais. That crazy Mosca was actually, for the first time in his life, going to do something heroic. The other delegations turned in surprise, not yet having noticed the bomb. Bonebreak turned back just once. He nodded toward his brother, touching his chest in a sign of solidarity.

Leon took a single, stumbling step forward. "Bonebreak, no—"

With a sudden blast of light, the central vestibule shattered into a chaos of smoke and fire.

32

Cora

CORA AWOKE IN A cornfield.

Her back was flat against black soil as she blinked into a blue sky. A gentle wind blew the ripened stalks, making a rustling sound like whispers.

Whispers.

She sat upright, crying out, and clutched the sides of her skull. She must have passed out when Fian pushed her back into the puzzle chambers. Voices flooded between her ears like a deafening roar. There had to be a mistake. This couldn't be what Serassi had intended. What if she'd been lying? What if Serassi had been one of the Axion in disguise and the injection was meant to kill her?

The ground rocked violently and Cora was thrown to her side. She cried out as she slammed into the ground. Her head rang. Half dazed, she looked around, but the cornfield was intact. Had it been the storm outside? Or had it just been in her head, the effects of Serassi's drug? She tried to stand, but her muscles were

263

spasming, and she collapsed back to the ground. She had to get out of this cornfield . . . this puzzle. Her friends were facing a danger none of them had anticipated. The Axion's takeover would mean the end of freedom for all species.

The breeze rustled more cornstalks, and Cora doubled over and clamped her hands over her ears. Confusing sensations flooded her body. Her hand seemed to reach out on its own. She grabbed it with her other hand, staring at it. The fingers twitched strangely. Her nails clawed against her own palm. Her muscles started spasming harder as her vision changed: first it took on a red tint, then a gray one.

Was this a panic attack?

Was she dying?

Fear blackened her mind as a series of visions assaulted her. *Driving a tractor through rows of corn with wrinkled old hands. Chasing a little boy through a corn maze. Planting seeds in freshly tilled earth.*

The visions felt like memories—but none of them were her own.

Cora dug her fingers into the ground, breathing hard. Whatever those visions were, they weren't real. She wasn't back on Earth. She was on Drogane. In the Gauntlet. Puzzle number five. The corn was simulated.

And the voices and visions . . .

"Stop it!" she yelled.

Cora shook her head, trying to rid herself of the contradictory voices, and then suddenly, as though she'd been hit by a sudden rainstorm, she straightened. Everything made sense. The voices were part of Serassi's injection. The paragon burst contained the best traits of all of humanity, and the voices represented all the differing human perspectives and memories. The paragon burst had worked—or it would, once she learned how to master the sensation.

And then a new voice cut through the whispers and images. A clear voice with a strange, flat accent she knew instantly.

Sing, Cora. Find a song.

It was Mali's voice. Cora jumped up, spinning around, but she was alone. The voice was in her head. It didn't have the same warm tickle as a telepathic message; it felt rounder, more hollow—like an echo. All Cora could think was that this must be how Serassi's drug worked: putting echoes into her head, memories of her friends. The real Mali probably had no idea her voice was now woven into Cora's DNA.

She took a deep breath.

Then she started humming a shaky melody, until the humming soothed her, and her thoughts became her own again, and her hands moved only at her command. She took another deep, shaky breath and forced herself to stand.

She had to focus. Solve the puzzle.

A low cry sounded to her left.

She whipped her head toward it too fast, and a wave of dizziness overtook her, but she blinked through it and took a determined step toward the cry. The corn pushed at her face, dry husks scratching her bare arms. She tried to stand on tiptoe, but the corn was too tall. She could only see a few feet in any direction.

The cry came again. High-pitched, like something in pain.

She started moving faster, following the sound among the rows. Maybe it was a corn maze, a physical puzzle—but no, there were no twists or dead ends, only row after row. Besides, the stock algorithm wouldn't hand anything that easy to her.

The cry came again from behind her. She spun and raced down the row, kicking up black soil. Was it a person? Someone wounded? It came again, a single sharp whimper, as she crashed through the corn into the next row.

She stopped.

A small bundle of white fur huddled in the middle of the row. A fox. Wet, sticky blood streaked down one of its legs and soaked into the soil beneath it. She started—it had a small gray patch on the top of its head, just like the Arctic fox from the Hunt menagerie. Surely it wasn't the same fox, right? That would be impossible. The stock algorithm must have reached into her memories to create it. She took a step forward cautiously. This could still be a physical puzzle in disguise—the fox might attack. But as she neared, it was clear that the fox couldn't even stand, let alone strike. Its leg was mangled, and a deep gash ran across its abdomen, as though it had been accidentally caught under a tractor.

Cora knelt, overwhelmed with sadness.

What if it *was* the same fox from the Hunt? What if, somehow, the stock algorithm had materialized it here, wounded it like this, just to test Cora? She felt suddenly sick at the idea that the Gauntlet might use something real, something living.

And then she understood what this puzzle was—a moral one. Real or not, she had to put the fox out of its misery.

No, don't, a small voice whispered in her head. It was Nok's voice. *Don't hurt it!*

And then:

Leon's voice: *Do it.*

Nok's voice: *But it could recover.*

Rolf's voice: *You aren't a veterinarian—you don't know what's best.*

Mali's voice: *It's suffering. Let nature take its course.*

The wind rustled again. She had no idea how long she'd been in this puzzle, but outside the walls Cassian and the others needed her.

The fox whimpered again.

And yet humanity was a complex thing, judging by all the differing voices in her head. Some argued the fox should live, others claimed killing it was the right thing to do. She ignored the voices all offering different viewpoints and sorted through them until she found the one she trusted most: Lucky's.

Everything that's alive must die, his voice said. She recognized the words as ones he had written in his journal: *If you can, give it a good life first. Honor it. Don't make anything suffer just because you can't stomach what needs to be done.*

She reached out and slid her hands over the little fox's back. Its fur was so soft, its little heart fluttering. In the Hunt it had been a prisoner, just like her. Before doubt had a chance to change her mind, she slid her hands to its neck, felt for the bones of its spine, and then drew in a sharp breath.

"I'm sorry."

She snapped the bones.

They broke as easily in her hands as twigs. She cried out as the fox slumped to the ground, then pressed her hands to her mouth. What if it *was* the real fox? Taking a life was taking a life. Eventually the voices in her head died down, but they didn't go away entirely. They sank into her mind, just as the muscle spasms eased too. Her friends' voices echoed as she stroked the dead fox.

It's at peace, whispered Mali's voice.

You did what you had to, Nok's said.

Tough call, said Leon's.

And, somehow, she felt comforted. She wasn't alone anymore, she realized. It wasn't just her running the puzzles now. With the paragon burst's voices of Mali and Leon and Lucky and even people she had never met, it now felt as though all of humanity were behind her.

The next door opened.

33

Cora

CORA ENTERED THE SIXTH puzzle chamber to find herself surrounded by plain walls with doors on every side, but when she tried to open one: *zap*. An electric shock. She jerked her hand back with a hiss. She tried again. *Zap*. She cursed—stronger this time. The smell of singed flesh filled the room. Try after try, shock after shock, she tried each door, wincing, only to realize there was no solution. The electric shocks *were* the puzzle: a physical puzzle to test her ability to withstand pain. After a dozen shocks she began to black out. One more and she'd faint—she simply wasn't strong enough. But then, just as her vision began to go, voices filled her mind. *Keep going*, Mali said. *Don't give up*, Lucky urged. And so, with bolstered courage from the paragon burst, she continued to touch door after door, suffering shock after shock, pushing herself far more than she ever thought possible, until at last a door opened and she crawled, sick and spent, into puzzle seven.

Heat bathed her skin as soon as the door closed. Burning

heat, like standing too close to a campfire. She was on a platform like in the treetops course, but there were no trees. No forest. Ten feet away, on the opposite wall, was another platform leading to the door to the next puzzle. Cora crawled to the edge of the platform, looked down, and immediately jerked back.

The floor was made of lava. Real, glowing-red, smoking lava. Sweat dripped from her forehead. There was no bridge. No rope to cross. There wasn't anything intellectual about it, so by the process of elimination she knew it had to be a perceptive puzzle. She crawled back to the platform edge and concentrated on the lava. *Maybe I can cool it.* But her reaching thoughts had nothing to latch onto, nothing to open or twist or lift. No way to change the temperature. *Maybe it's only an illusion—the trick is seeing past it.* She reached out a toe and, drawing in a breath, tried setting down a foot.

It sizzled.

"Ah!" She jerked her foot back, clutching it. Not an illusion. The lava was real. "So if I can't change the lava," she muttered to herself, "and there's nothing to telekinetically lift to build a bridge, then . . ."

Wait. There was something she could lift.

She could levitate *herself* across the floor. Of course—Bonebreak had warned her that one of the perceptive puzzles would require her to lift a heavy object. But *herself*? It would basically be floating. Flying. Just the prospect made her head throb. She'd already damaged her brain so severely. She didn't know how much strength she had left. But then she remembered training with Anya. Lifting the heavy potted fern, which had weighed about the same as she did.

What was it Anya had said? Something about pushing herself to the brink.

She closed her eyes and concentrated. What an unsettling feeling, to reach her thoughts back toward her own body. She let her thoughts surround her like a hug, cradling her below the armpits, and the knees, and around the middle.

Lift.

An uneasy lightness filled her. It felt like being on Fuel Station Theta again, where the gravity had been weaker, only there was something eerily unnatural about feeling that here. And then she felt a burst of pain, and she gasped, releasing her concentration.

She closed her eyes. She had to push past the pain.

Lift.

Slowly, wobbly, she rose an inch off the platform. Her bare feet touched air. She fought against the awful pain and concentrated on floating. *Forward.* Waves of heat radiated from below her. *Don't look down,* she told herself. *Don't open your eyes.* The pain was blinding. Her mind felt as though it were tearing faster and faster. She could almost hear a sound like flesh splitting, and fears nipped at her that she'd break her brain completely, she'd lose all her memories, but she pushed herself harder. None of that mattered if she didn't win. Blood dripped from her nose, sizzling on the lava.

To the brink!

She cried out as one final tear ripped through her head. Suddenly there was nothing there: No mental arm reaching out to hold her up. No psychic abilities. Without warning, she fell. She screamed as she plunged downward, snapping her eyes open. The air rushed out of her as her chest hit the opposite platform. She cried out, reaching for something to hold on to. She was halfway on the platform, her feet dangling over the edge. She dug her fingernails into the grooves in the platform. A toe brushed the lava and she cried out. The smell of burned flesh filled the room. Crying, dripping blood, she pulled herself the rest of the way onto the platform and collapsed.

Safe—she was safe.

Or was she?

Her body ached, but what frightened her even more was that her head *didn't*. Something had happened when she'd felt that tear. The pain in her head had vanished. She tried to tentatively push out her psychic abilities, but there was nothing there. It was just as though she'd suddenly lost her hearing or her sense of smell.

She had broken her mind *permanently* this time.

Fear made her breath go still.

She swallowed and frantically tried to remember something to see if her memories were still intact. Cassian—yes, she could picture him. She knew his name and how they'd met. Lucky—she remembered him too. She sighed in relief. It was okay; she remembered. She knew who Anya was, and Mali, and Nok and Rolf. She remembered waking up in the desert habitat of the cage. Before that, she remembered . . .

And her relief disappeared.

She remembered her first day in the cage clearly. The red sand dunes. Finding Lucky, and Yasmine's body. But before that was only a blank. She knew some facts: she'd been abducted from Earth, her name was Cora—but there were simply no *memories*. She must have had a family, but she couldn't remember them.

Couldn't remember going to school, or what she did for fun, or who her friends were. Couldn't picture her house. Couldn't even remember what state she was from.

She drew in a sharp breath. It had happened—exactly what Willa had warned her about. She had torn her brain and lost half her memories: every moment of her life from before the cage. She pressed her back against the platform, fighting a rising sense of panic. Was the damage permanent? What would happen if she never remembered? Would Cassian take her back to a planet she had no memory of? Would she have to rely on Mali and Leon and Nok and Rolf for the rest of her life? She couldn't even remember her mother or her father.

Tears started pooling in her eyes, and she pitched forward, burying her face in her knees. Around her, lava hissed and sizzled. Her breath came in uneven sobs.

Slowly, very faintly, voices came to her head.

Stand up, Rolf's voice said.

She didn't stop crying. At least tearing her brain hadn't affected the paragon burst, but what good was it now? Those voices couldn't bring her memories back. They couldn't tell her what she'd forgotten about Earth.

The voices began to whisper louder, voices of her friends and strangers alike:

Keep going.

Keep fighting.

She swallowed back another sob. Whispers of encouragement continued floating between her ears. And then:

Don't give up!

It was the echo of Mali's voice, practically shouting. Cora

opened her eyes at last. Swallowed back the rising panic. At least she remembered Mali. And Cassian, and Leon, and Serassi, and Nok and Rolf and Lucky. She might not remember her old life, but she remembered her new one.

Keep going, Mali's voice urged again.

The door opened, and it took the last of her energy to crawl through into puzzle eight. Bright lights blinded her. She blinked through them. She was on a . . . a stage. Stage lights shone from the ceiling, and she shaded her eyes to peer into row after row of empty theater seating. It was a concert hall. Beautiful and grand. Chairs of red velvet. Gilded theater boxes overlooking the stage. The only other thing onstage beside Cora was a grand piano.

From somewhere in the rafters, an intercom crackled to life. Cora tensed, apprehensive, mustering courage to fight if she had to. But then a slow song started playing.

> *All these years I thought I'd know*
> *All the places I would go*

An unfamiliar song—or had she known it once and was now missing that memory? She stood shakily and circled the piano. By the process of elimination, this had to be an intellectual puzzle.

> *And yet a thousand steps and still, I'm—*

The song on the intercom stopped abruptly as she reached the piano bench. She waited for the song to resume, but it didn't. She searched the piano, but there were no letters or numbers to rearrange.

Then an idea struck her. She sat on the bench and rested her fingers just above the keys. In the cage, there had been a music puzzle in the grasslands habitat. Three notes would play on the wind, and she and Lucky had matched them with identical musical notes. Maybe this puzzle was similar, only instead of matching the notes, she had to take it further and finish the song.

She touched a key hesitantly. A low C note reverberated through the room. Something about the familiar vibration washed over her skin, instantly calming her, as though she'd taken a deep breath of fresh air. She closed her eyes. It felt natural, deep down. She felt certain that back home—though she didn't remember—she must have known how to play. She tried to shut off that blankness where her memories should have been and play on instinct.

Somewhere deep, she missed music. She missed her memories. She missed *home*, whatever it had been.

Serassi's paragon burst flared to life too at the sound of the note. Music was one of the reasons Cassian had been fascinated by humans—an art form that the Kindred, in their sterile world, didn't practice. She could feel humanity's love of music humming inside her. All those voices, all those minds and hearts blossoming in unison.

She pressed another key, trying to remember the melody of the song on the intercom, and hummed a note to match it. She would need to get the rhyming just right, as well as the rhythm. The lyrics would have to make sense too with the rest of the song, not to mention the notes would need to perfectly match the ones that came before them. If she hit one wrong note or got one imperfect rhyme, she might lose the puzzle. And she couldn't lose now, not when she was so close to seeing her friends again. To stopping the Axion.

"I'm not just any girl . . ."

She hummed the words slowly, her voice raspy with lack of warm-up. She hit each key on the piano slowly, careful to match the melody that had played moments ago as her mind worked to finish the rest of the line. Even now, she could feel the paragon burst working within her. Her thoughts came faster than they ever had before. She was aware of so much more than she'd ever been. It was as though Serassi had downloaded an encyclopedia into her mind, not just of facts but of emotions, ideas, sensations.

"I'm not just any girl. . . . I have an iron will, and I will show you who I am."

She hit the last key.

The intercom crackled back to life—the puzzle wasn't over yet. Another song started playing.

Dreams are like stars, stronger at night

This second song was more complicated. There were more sharps and flats to the notes, the speed was more staccato, the words harder to rhyme. But she didn't care. The challenge felt thrilling. She kept playing, faster now and more confidently, not worried about stumbling over the notes.

Her voice rang out as she found just the right pitch: "Shining with promise, promising bright." The room took on another energy, almost as if the empty seats were all filled. Cora pictured ghosts of people in all the seats, not just attentive spectators but active participants in her song. She pictured Mali and Lucky in the front row, Leon and Nok and Rolf behind them. Because she wasn't the only one singing. It was their voices too, echoing in her head.

The voices of humanity.

Yo soy tan solo sin ti

Her fingers slowed to a stop. Was that Spanish? For a moment that beautiful flood of hope faltered. The voices in her head died down, as hesitant as she was. Her pulse started to pound faster. Her fingers were frozen over the keys.

She didn't speak any foreign languages.

She let out a ragged breath. *Dammit.* Just once, couldn't the stock algorithm take pity on her? Throw her an easy puzzle? But no, it had woven tricks and traps into every single one, making it impossible. She'd only managed to beat the others with the help of the paragon burst, or else with clues that Willa and Ironmage and Cassian had given her ahead of time.

The speaker crackled again, waiting for her to finish the song. Taunting her with its silence.

I don't speak Spanish, she wanted to yell. *I can't do it!* Suddenly anger filled her—she'd come so far. She wanted to kick the bench over, slam her fists over the keys, rip out the piano wires with her hands.

But then one of the echoing voices reached her:

But I do.

Lucky. Lucky's voice. He'd been born in Colombia. He spoke Spanish fluently. Cora scrambled to sit back on the bench, her shaking fingers poised over the keys. She could match the notes and handle the rhythm.

She just needed the words.

From deep down, the paragon burst stirred. She could feel it in her blood, her bones, almost moving her hands and her vocal cords for her. Lucky's spirit was inside her, putting words in her mouth.

"Pero tu espíritu," she sang, not understanding the words coming out of her mouth, *"es siempre conmigo."*

She struck the final note.

Tears streamed down her face. The stock algorithm couldn't know this—it was just a code and a machine—but it had given her a gift with this puzzle. It had stirred her blood and reminded her of what mattered. Of Lucky. Of hope. She didn't remember her family back home, but as she played, she felt them. Felt their love, even from afar. She felt the melody of the world, a planet that was a song in itself, and a people who wouldn't stop singing.

She pushed up from the piano.

The notes lingered in the cavernous concert hall. She looked out over the empty theater and smiled. Somewhere, deep down, Lucky would always be with her. As soon as the next door appeared, she'd be finished with this round. And she was ready: to see her friends, to face the final round—and most of all, to bring humanity the song it deserved.

34

Mali

A BOMB.

Mali threw herself under the worktable that was littered with Willa's frequency-emitter equipment, shielding her head with her hands. A bomb had gone off—a package that Leon had smuggled from the station. The explosion had ripped through the chambers of the Gauntlet. Torn apart the central vestibule, shattering half the control compartments.

Dust still rained down through the recess rooms. The bomb's boom echoed off the walls, making her ears ring and her head spin.

She blinked out of her shock.

Had she seen right? Was Bonebreak really . . . gone? *Dead?* That Mosca trader was the last person she'd expect to sacrifice himself.

Dust clouded as the wreckage settled. Dazed, she squinted through it, trying to find the others. Something was dripping, splashing her. Blood? Was it hers or someone else's? She held up her wet hands, relieved to find it was only water seeping through the walls.

She crawled shakily out from under the table. Willa was frantically trying to salvage the damaged emitter equipment, and from across the room Serassi was yelling something at her, but Mali couldn't make out the words past the ringing in her ears. She caught sight of a beam pierced through Serassi's leg, pinning her in place near the coded monitor. Her dark Kindred blood was soaking into the fabric of her left pant leg and mingling with the puddles of water on the floor.

Mali traced the lines of water up to the ceiling, still feeling dazed. Where was the water coming from? The Gauntlet modules weren't powered by any liquid fuel source. The water had to be external. . . .

The storm.

The realization hit her with a dark sense of foreboding. When they had entered Drogane's atmosphere, Cassian had warned of the planet's unpredictable weather. He'd said they were fortunate to land during the eye of the storm and that his instruments indicated the worst of the weather would most likely hold off until the Gauntlet was over.

But storms were anything but predictable.

"Mali!"

Someone was calling her name, but it sounded small and tinny, as though coming from miles away. She tilted her head, tapping her ear to try to stop the ringing, as she searched the room, coughing through the dust. Cassian had gone to Serassi's side and was trying to wrench the beam out of her leg with his bare hands.

Willa was still fumbling with the equipment like it was more precious than any of their lives. Ironmage was sprawled on his back near the bench, unconscious, a bruise on his temple where shrapnel must have hit him. She started to crawl toward him to make sure he was alive when someone streaked across her line of vision.

Anya's clothes—the impostor.

"Stop!" she yelled. The impostor was the only one who could tell them where the real Anya was. She tried to scramble to her feet, but her balance was thrown off from the blast. She careened first to the left, then to the right, until she managed to grab hold of a bench.

Leon was near the doorway, clutching the side of his face, blood streaked over his tattoos. The impostor was running straight toward him.

"Leon, don't let him get away!"

Dazed, Leon shook his head, stumbling as though he too were barely able to stand. Mali choked in desperation. She tried to take a step forward but tripped and fell.

"Please, Leon, I . . . I need you!"

She winced at her own words. Never in her life had she begged someone for help. And yet Leon didn't look at her with a gloat of superiority. He only blinked through his daze, eyes darting to the impostor, and nodded.

"I'll get him, Mali. I promise!" He took off after the impostor.

Mali sucked in a sob—leave it to Leon, a criminal, a smuggler, a lovable pain in her side—to be the one person in the world she could rely on.

She pushed to her feet, making her way across the room after them. She clung to the wall for support as she stumbled into the central vestibule.

She froze, gaping. The vestibule was even more damaged than the Mosca recess room. The floor behind the judges' dais was now a hole where the bomb must have exploded. There was no sign of Bonebreak's body, only a few pieces of torn rust-red jumpsuit. Her stomach twisted as she felt an unexpected hitch of sadness. *Sadness, for a Mosca?* But not just any Mosca. A Mosca from whom she'd never expected anything but betrayal but who had just saved all their lives.

The four Chief Assessors' chairs had been ripped up and twisted, the dais itself splintered in two. Monitors crackled and hissed, showing only static. For a second she remembered that Cora was trapped inside the Gauntlet puzzle chambers, and she ran to the portal door. Had Cora felt the blast? Had the bomb broken the puzzle modules? But the portal door was still sealed, a burn mark across the front the only sign of damage. Mali tried to pry the door open with her fingers, but it wouldn't budge. She let go with a frustrated sigh.

Cora was still on her own.

Half the overhead lights had shattered and the few remaining ones flickered uselessly. Bodies of Gatherer and Axion and Kindred delegates littered the floor, and she fought the urge to turn away at the sight of a severed arm wearing a Mosca sleeve, and a chunk of hair, and a single boot with the Axion crest.

She coughed, trying to clear the dust from her eyes. Where had Anya's impostor run to? Had Leon caught him? Some of the survivors were starting to rise out of the dust. It felt like eternity since the bomb had detonated, but Mali knew it must have been only seconds. The dust hadn't even fully settled. She heard moans. A scream of pain. And yet that high-pitched ringing was still in her ears.

She tapped her ears again as she stumbled around the remains of the vestibule. She let go of the wall and suddenly slid across the floor, catching herself on the broken dais. This wasn't just off-kilter balance from the blast. The room was actually leaning. Water was running down the floor, pooling against the back wall. And then the room shook and shifted again, and Mali and the others were thrown backward. She clung to the dais.

It was the storm, she realized as more water poured in through the ceiling. The bomb's blast must have compromised the infrastructure of the Gauntlet modules. The structure was no longer stable. It might have easily withstood the storm before, but now they were at the mercy of Drogane's raging tempests.

"Mali!" Leon appeared in the doorway, one hand clutched over his bleeding face.

"Where'd he go?" she yelled back. "Where's the impostor?"

"Forget him—behind you!"

She spun just as an Axion lunged for her. She ducked out of the way, twisting around the dais, using the off-balance room to her advantage. The Axion tumbled toward the back wall, hitting his head hard. Mali took a deep breath, steeling herself.

She flexed her muscles, ready to fight. The Axion was pushing himself to his feet again, but he was dazed from the blast too. She frowned, noticing his uniform. Beneath the thick coating of dust, he wore long, gauzy white robes that swept the floor. Gatherer robes.

She saw movement from the corner of her eye. Another Axion rose from the dust, coughing. He ripped a thick Mosca mask from his face. Confused, she caught sight of a Kindred uniform she recognized—Fian's uniform. Only now an Axion woman wore it, her gaunt frame too small for it, the sleeves dangling too long for her arms.

"It's the blast." Leon stumbled beside her, still clutching his face. Blood had stained the collar of his shirt a crimson red. "It somehow set off Willa's equipment and triggered the frequency that makes them drop their disguises. Now all those sneaky bastards can't hide anymore. They're exposed and they know it. There's no telling what they'll do—we should be ready for anything."

Mali drew in a sharp breath. *That* was the high-pitched ringing she still heard. The frequency that Willa had broadcast to turn Axion impostors back into their real selves. It had spread beyond the Mosca recess room into the full Gauntlet chambers, and now the impostor Fian was exposed, and all the rest. . . .

She swallowed hard as she took in the bodies. Despite the Gatherer and Mosca and Kindred uniforms, over half were, in reality, Axion.

"So many of them," Mali said, trying to keep the panic from her voice. Suddenly the room lurched violently to the side, and Mali grabbed Leon's arm to keep him from being thrown to the floor. "The structure isn't stable anymore!" she called over the din. "It could be ripped apart! We've got to get Cora out of there." She pointed toward the portal door.

"We can't." Cassian came out of the rubble, the flickering lights making his eyes look hollow and grim. "She's the only hope we still have. The Axion can try to impersonate us, but they can't impersonate the stock algorithm. They can't alter a computer program. Cora *has* to finish. She must win. It's the only thing that will give us enough power now to stop them."

"But they're exposed!" Leon said. "Their plan's shot to pieces. They'll try anything to stop her, even if it means ripping the Gauntlet apart with their own hands."

"That is why we have to hold them off," Cassian said. "We have to give her a chance."

Suddenly, the shrill frequency stopped.

Mali felt a swell of relief to hear herself think again, but it only lasted a moment. A growl sounded as a dusty shadow ran up behind Cassian.

"Behind you!" she yelled.

Cassian ducked as an Axion in a Gatherer's robes tried to slam a piece of debris at his head. Cassian straightened and stepped hard on the Axion's too-long robe and shoved the creature to the floor, then smashed his other boot in the Axion's face.

"Hold them off!" Cassian yelled. "Don't let them stop the Gauntlet!"

Mali needed no further encouragement. She exchanged a quick nod with Leon, who spun on an Axion delegate who was running toward one of the broken monitors. Leon grabbed a piece of broken glass and slammed it into the Axion's face.

The room lurched again, and more storm water poured through the ceiling. Mali slipped and fell just as an Axion loomed over her. She drew back her foot to kick the Axion off-balance, but a loose piece of debris flew over her head, slamming into him.

Mali jerked around to find Serassi already picking up another piece of debris to use as a projectile. Willa was next to her, leaping into the high rafters and kicking over an Axion with the momentum.

"Where's Ironmage?" Mali called to Serassi.

"Still unconscious," Serassi said. Maybe for the better, Mali thought, not to know yet that his brother was dead. Anger swelled in her blood. Bonebreak had saved their lives. He'd redeemed himself, he'd stayed and fought, he'd even sacrificed himself.

She squeezed her hands into fists.

He couldn't have died for nothing.

She tossed her head up and recognized a flash of white. Anya's clothes. The Axion who had been impersonating her was fighting with Redrage and another Mosca near the rear wall of monitors. The anger inside her concentrated harder.

For Bonebreak.

For Anya.

For everyone who wanted to be free.

"Willa!" she cried, catching sight of the chimpanzee swinging in the rafters. "Help me!" She jerked a finger toward the impostor Anya, and Willa gave a quick nod and hurled herself from rafter to rafter toward the Axion. Mali raced along below her, dodging the worst of the fighting. Willa reached the Axion first. She threw herself from the rafters, slamming into the Axion's back. The impact brought Redrage crashing down too.

"Go," Mali said to Redrage. "Help Ironmage in the recess room. Leave this one to me."

Redrage, limping hard on her right leg, gave a quick nod.

Mali turned to the Axion, who had been shoved to the ground by Willa. Mali smashed her fist into his face, as silver blood spurted down the front of Anya's clothes.

"Where is she?" Mali demanded. "Where's Anya?"

The Axion grinned his silver teeth, tight skin stretching over high cheekbones. "It doesn't matter," he hissed. "You won't leave this planet to find her. We'll stop the Gauntlet. We'll soon rule again, as we were born to do."

Willa huffed in anger and pinned the Axion's hand back as Mali slammed another fist into his face. He only laughed again, those silver teeth sparkling. Anger swelled in her until all she could see was red. She grabbed the closest piece of wreckage, one of the chair legs from the judges' dais. The end was torn and jagged.

"You aren't stopping the Gauntlet," she said. "Cora *will* win." She pressed the chair leg against his neck.

"She still has one break left," he said, coughing. "The moment she steps outside that door, she'll never step back in to finish round three. We'll stop her."

Worry made Mali hesitate—she glanced over at the Gauntlet door. He was right. Any moment Cora would finish round two. She'd be spit out straight into this chaos.

"Willa," she said, "find Cassian. Tell him he has to watch that portal door. Tell him when Cora comes out, he has to protect her."

Willa gave a nod and leaped onto the nearest bench. Mali searched the room for Cassian, and her stomach curled when she saw him. He and the Axion impostor who'd posed as Fian were facing off against each other, a chasm in the floor between them. Water filled the pit, crackling now with life, electrified by rogue wires.

The Axion who'd been disguised as Anya snickered beneath Mali's hands. "You see? You can't stop us."

"Like hell we can't." It was Leon. Mali's heart lifted. He crouched beside them. "And when we do, we're going to rescue Anya and everyone else you've kidnapped and replaced. And we're going to enjoy torturing their locations out of you."

He smiled at Mali and nodded toward the broken piece of metal in her hand. "Would you like to do the honor of torturing him, or should I?"

35

Cora

THE THRILL OF HAVING defeated puzzle eight still hummed
through Cora like the lingering notes of a song. The paragon burst
had made her feel light-headed at first, but now, as she made her
way across the stage toward the doorway that would take her back
to her friends, she felt focused. Strong. Complete—or as complete
as she could be without her memories. Humanity pulsed beneath
her skin, making her realize that being human wasn't just about
memories, but about feeling what all people felt—fear and desire,
hope and anguish. About finding one's own way to belong.

But as she approached the open doorway, the acrid smell
of smoke reached her. *An electrical fire?* A piercing, high-pitched
squeal made her clamp her hands over her ears. Her footsteps sped.
Something had happened. That jolt she'd felt in the cornfield—had
it been an explosion after all?

She raced across the stage toward the door. How long had
she taken to complete round two? An hour? A lot could happen in

an hour. And the stock algorithm had a way of making time move strangely. It could have been ten minutes or ten hours.

She reached the doorway and gasped. Beyond, the central vestibule was in pieces. Broken beams hung from the ceiling, wires sparking dangerously as water poured off them. The judges' dais was shattered in two, as if a fireball had swept through the room. *And the bodies.* Dozens of them, prostrate and unmoving. The delegates and aides who had survived were fighting among themselves. She pressed a hand to her mouth. Gatherer fighting against Mosca. Human against Axion. Kindred against Kindred.

It made no sense.

She cried out as she recognized the two figures fighting where the dais had once been. It was Cassian, his uniform ripped across one arm, and Fian. Or rather, someone in Fian's clothes. A woman. She was more than two feet shorter than Fian. Wiry and thin, with pronounced bones. Fian's clothes sagged off her small frame. Her stature didn't make her any less dangerous, though. She slammed her elbow into Cassian's ribs. He doubled over.

"Cassian!"

But he didn't hear her in the commotion. She stumbled forward, a hand still pressed against her mouth. Dozens of Axion impostors were now unmasked. Two Gatherers. A Mosca in a rust-red jumpsuit and shielding. Even, in the corner struggling with Mali, *Anya.* Cora stopped in shock.

Anya had been an impostor the whole time?

The false Fian grabbed one of the live wires while Cassian was still doubled over. She pulled down the wire, then crouched down, ready to spring toward Cassian. The woman was going to knock him into the water, then electrify it with the wire. . . .

"Cassian, look out!"

He still didn't hear her. Panic pulsing in her veins, Cora threw her hands out, aimed at the impostor.

Drop the wire, she commanded with her mind.

But her fingers didn't crackle with the sparking sense of telekinesis. There was nothing. She threw her thoughts out harder, panicking. Still nothing. She tried once more.

Drop the wire!

The impostor didn't flinch. Cora's abilities hadn't affected her at all. She tried again, more desperately, but whereas her abilities had hummed to life before, she felt nothing now.

Because my abilities really are *gone,* she realized. *Not even the paragon burst can boost abilities that are permanently broken.*

"Cassian!" she screamed instead, as loudly as she could.

He tossed his head up just as the impostor tried to shove him into the water. He dodged at the last second and the woman lost her balance and fell into the shallow puddle instead, the wire dangling and sparking out of reach. Cassian clutched his bleeding arm and climbed out of the water. Cora ran to meet him.

"What happened?" Beside her, monitors sparked and crackled.

"A bomb," Cassian explained, his breath heaving. "It set off a frequency that exposed all the impostor Axion. Now it's war. All the intelligent species against them. Their only chance is to stop you from finishing the Gauntlet, so that humanity, and the Kindred, will not become stronger than them."

"How are they going to stop me?"

"By any means necessary. They can't let you go back through those doors and start round three. Once that final round begins, there is no stopping the tests until the end. Everything will hinge on your ability to win."

The room suddenly bucked, throwing them to the left. Cassian grabbed her to keep her from tumbling toward the puddle that the Axion woman was trying to climb out of. Ironmage and Redrage, with their poor balance, tumbled in, though, knocking the impostor back into it. For a second they were a tangle of limbs and angry cries until the room righted itself again.

"The storm's getting stronger," Cassian said. "You're going to have to hurry through the last four puzzles before it tears these modules apart."

He started to help her back toward the doorway, but the impostor Fian yelled to Crusader and another Axion to block the portal door. Cassian twisted Cora away just as Crusader hurled a chunk of metal wreckage at her head.

"Redrage!" Cassian yelled. "Help us get to the door! And Ironmage—"

But it was too late. Cora pressed a hand to her mouth as she watched the Axion who'd been disguised as Fian grab hold of Ironmage's head in the puddle and, with a single jerk, break his neck. Ironmage slumped lifelessly into the water.

"No!" Cora cried.

Redrage let out a bellow of fury. She charged headfirst into the Axion, and Cora winced at the sound of a bone snapping.

Cassian pulled Cora into the safety of a corner. "As soon as the portal door is clear, we've got to run for it."

She grabbed his shoulder, kneading her fingers against his bone and muscle. "Wait. I can't. I can't go back in there."

His head lowered, confused.

"The last perceptive puzzle," she said in a rush, wiping the blood from her nose. "I won't be able to solve it. During the last round, I tore my brain so badly even the paragon burst can't help me. I don't know what happened. I was following Anya's instructions . . ."

His face went hard as stone. "Anya. You mean the impostor."

Cora tossed her head up and searched the fight for the Axion who'd been disguised as Anya, locking eyes on the creature with the white streak of hair. She pressed a hand against her forehead. "Oh, god, that was their plan, wasn't it? One of them posed as Anya so they could sabotage me. Everything she trained me in was only meant to hurt me, and it worked. I can't levitate anything now." She motioned to a small piece of rubble on the ground. Before, she would have been able to move it effortlessly, but now it didn't budge. "If I go back into the Gauntlet, I'll fail. I can't do it."

The wall of flickering monitors threw a harsh light against their faces. Behind them, the battle was turning. The Axion were getting the upper hand—there were simply too many of them. Cora thought about what must be happening on the aggregate station and all the other planets where the Axion were battling at the same time. When your enemy could be anyone, how did you stand a chance?

Cassian looked away. "You're the only hope we have. The Axion are spreading, attacking more planets and stations. The only thing that can stop them is the evolutionary jump. Kindred and human both taken to a level that can defeat them permanently."

Cora felt tears on her cheeks. "I know how hard you've all fought, but I can't."

He pulled her into his arms, holding her tight. She felt the warmth of his blood soaked into his uniform. The pulse of his beating heart. Was this what he'd imagined would happen when he'd first seen her on Earth? When he'd abducted her and trained her in the cage, had he ever thought they'd be standing here, all hope lost? Had he thought they would come to mean as much to each other as they did?

He ran a hand down her short, tangled hair. His heart was beating faster, and it spurred her own. More tears pushed at her eyes. He'd once been her enemy, but all that was far behind them. He had told her once that they could have changed the world together, and he'd been right. He'd seen potential in her that she'd never thought was there.

"You've gone further than any human ever has," he murmured. "I'm proud of you. Nothing will change that. Nor the fact that I love you."

The tenderness in his voice made her sob harder. Was this really the end?

She couldn't imagine what would happen now, or how they could possibly be together, after such a heartbreaking defeat. Would he always look at her with disappointment behind his eyes? Would she always feel as though she'd let him down?

Behind him, she watched Ironmage's lifeless body floating in the water. And beside the puddle were the remnants of Bonebreak's shielding. Oh, God, was he gone too? Littering the room were dozens of dead Mosca and Kindred and Gatherers. Leon, Mali, and Willa were holding their own, but they couldn't last long.

Movement caught her eye by the doorway. Serassi, limping, was using a broken panel to fight off the Axion guarding the portal door. She threw a look toward Cassian and Cora. "Come on!" she yelled. "I'll hold them off!"

Cora stifled a gasp.

Serassi still believed in her. She was risking her life to help. All the Kindred were, and the Mosca, and the humans, and Gatherers, and Willa. Could she really just give up? As if to answer, the whispers surged inside her, thousands of voices of humanity urging her not to stop.

She pushed the tears out of her eyes. "I want to do this."

Cassian looked at her in surprise. "But without your perceptive abilities . . ."

"I have to try," she said.

He looked as though he might protest again, but then he glanced at Serassi, struggling to hold off the Axion. The battle was nearly finished now. Only a few rebels remained to fight the Axion. His hand tightened over hers.

"All right. Go."

Fear and exhilaration filled her as they raced across the room. The hum of the paragon burst swelled inside her, all of humanity united in helping her win. Cassian shoved his elbow into the face of an Axion and then pulled her toward the portal door.

"When we go in," he said in a rush, "don't look back. Don't think about the battle—it doesn't matter who wins or loses out here, only what happens in there. If you defeat the final puzzle, the evolutionary jump will be triggered. It will spread throughout this room, throughout the galaxy. The Axion won't stand a chance."

They neared the portal door that Serassi was fiercely defending. More water poured in from the ceiling, and Cora remembered the storm outside. They didn't have long. Through the doorway, the ninth puzzle chamber was black. No telling what it would bring.

"Wait. You said *we*," she said. "You said when *we* go in . . ."

His eyes met hers, and she knew that he wasn't telling her something. She knew that *this* secret—whatever it was—was what he'd been keeping from her all along.

"That's the trick to the third round," he said quietly. "I knew you wouldn't agree to it if I'd told you before. The third round involves a much more personal challenge. The sponsor becomes part of the puzzles. The risk becomes greater."

She stared at him in disbelief. "I won't let you risk yourself."

But even now, Willa's words were flooding back into her mind. *Think hard about who you care about. The Gauntlet will test you on it—it tested me. It defeated me. Now I have nothing.*

But she hadn't thought *this* would be who the stock algorithm would pit her against. She thought Willa had meant it would be a hologram of someone from her past. Not someone real. Not someone who could die.

"That's why the sponsor is so important," Cassian continued in a rush. "A member of an intelligent species must be willing to sacrifice himself for the good of the lesser species. And that is how much I believe in you, Cora. In your race. I always have."

"But . . . but Bonebreak was going to be my sponsor."

"Yes, and if I hadn't returned, he would be here now. He knew the risks. And, apparently, he felt that the potential rewards were great enough that he was willing to risk his life." Regret flickered in his dark eyes. "He already did, just not the way he envisioned."

She glanced again at Bonebreak's torn shielding, fighting a

sharp wave of grief for the Mosca. She shook her head. "I won't let you do this."

"My life will be in your hands. And I trust you."

The room lurched again sharply. Someone screamed, and a terrible sound came from the rafters. Metal squealed. Wires sparked. The roof peeled a few feet away from the walls as wind and rain and sleet pelted them. The storm was snarling its way in.

"Come on!" Cassian yelled above the roar.

The central vestibule had almost entirely turned on its side now, with the Axion and others hanging on to the fixtures to keep from falling. One of the Axion tried to swing for the portal door, but Serassi gave him a sharp kick, and he tumbled down. Cassian helped Cora climb toward the door. She protested, shaking her head.

He met her eyes.

And then he threw them both into the Gauntlet.

36

Cora

THE PORTAL DOOR DISAPPEARED behind them.

For a second, Cora fought to catch her breath in the darkness. The door had sealed out the sounds of the battle, but the newfound quiet was an illusion. She knew her friends were just on the other side of the wall, fighting for their lives, and that the storm was tearing the structure apart.

"Cassian?" She coughed out smoke. She reached toward the darkness, fingers grasping nothing. "Cassian, where are you?"

"Cora? I'm here."

She stumbled toward his voice. "Where? I can't see you!"

The walls began to emit a faint light. It grew like a sunrise and she spun around, searching for him, fearful of what else might lurk in the room with them. There were tall pillars in the chamber, obscuring her view. Her senses felt heightened and more alert thanks to Serassi's injection, and as she wove around the pillars in the faint light, intuition told her that something about this chamber wasn't what it seemed. Then—there. A shape took form in the light. Tall, impossibly muscular. *Cassian.* He was on the opposite side of the room, clutching his hurt arm, his back to her as he searched for her amid the pillars.

"Cassian!"

He spun and their eyes met. She let out a sob of relief and ran toward him, weaving around the pillars. He held out a hand, and she reached for it. "Thank god. . . ." Her fingers brushed the warmth of his palm.

And then she was falling.

She screamed as her hand was wrenched from his. A panel in the floor had dropped open. It happened so fast that she didn't have time to grab for the edges, even with the faster reflexes the paragon burst gave her. She was plunging into darkness.

She slammed into a hard floor below, wincing.

Overhead, Cassian's face appeared in the opening. "Cora! Hold on—"

But the floor sealed before he could finish.

She was alone.

For a few moments, all she could hear was her own heartbeat in the darkness, thumping irregular and quick, as though there were many hearts inside her own. The lights in the new puzzle chamber began to gradually illuminate. Was she still in puzzle nine? Or had she fallen into a new puzzle altogether? The lights rose, casting shadows over a chamber that was bare except for a central table. She tried to remember everything Willa had told her about this round.

They will make it personal, Willa had said. *They need to know that the Gauntlet is real for you.*

Cora started to push to her feet, but the chamber suddenly lurched sidewise. She gasped as she crouched back down on the floor, steadying herself, heart pounding. The storm was growing stronger. She didn't have much time.

She waited a few seconds. Thankfully, the room didn't lurch again.

She went to the table. The lights were bright enough now to make out a three-dimensional model on the table's surface. It was a simple cube, made of glowing laser lines, just like the model of the Gauntlet that Cassian had once shown her. In that model, a tiny holographic runner had made its way through each of the puzzle chambers, demonstrating how the Gauntlet worked.

But this laser model was just a single cube. She waited impatiently for something to change. Seconds passed and nothing happened. She shook the table, trying to jar it into action.

"Come on! I don't have much time!"

Slowly, the laser outlines changed color. The cube started to expand. Cora stepped back, not wanting to accidentally get in its way. More laser lines appeared as the cube expanded, forming another cube, and then another on top, until there were twelve cubes in all: a model of the full Gauntlet. Each cube was a different color: red, blue, green, and yellow. Only it wasn't a generic model, like the one Cassian had shown her. It was *this* Gauntlet. There were tiny holographic stalks of corn in one of the cubes and a miniature piano in another. Three cubes were empty—the puzzles she hadn't solved yet—but otherwise the cubes' colors corresponded to the different types of puzzles she'd gone through so far. The first was red, a moral puzzle, which had been the temptation to cheat. The second was green, an intellectual one. She inspected the cubes until she found one with a tiny table—the very chamber she was in. It was green.

Another intellectual puzzle.

She drew away from the Gauntlet model warily. Why would the stock algorithm give her a hint, even one as simple as the type of puzzle she was in? Did she dare trust it?

As she watched, a tiny holographic runner appeared in the first cube. She leaned in, peering closer. The runner had buzzed hair, a torn uniform, and tiny holographic drops of blood dripping from his arm.

Her face paled.

The holographic runner was a model of Cassian. She looked around at the walls, wondering if he was still trapped in the chamber overhead.

A gray holographic line started to rise from the floor in the chamber where Cassian stood. She leaned closer, anxious. What did it mean? With the laser's imperfect representation she couldn't be sure, until she saw the tiny holographic figure lifting his feet and waving his arms. Almost as if he were . . .

Swimming, Leon's voice said in her head.

The gray line means water, Rolf's voice added.

Cora's eyes widened. The stock algorithm was flooding the first chamber with water. If this was a model of what was really happening in the other chambers, Cassian was going to drown.

And suddenly the puzzle made sense: Cassian *was* the puzzle.

She had to figure out how to save him.

She circled the table with quick steps, wetting her lips. The ceiling suddenly groaned and she glanced upward. A battle was raging outside, and a storm. She didn't have time for guessing games.

Think!

She studied the three-dimensional model, her thoughts whirling faster than ever. She could almost feel Rolf in her head, his DNA boosting her own intelligence. Her thoughts felt crisper, more analytical. The flooded chamber that Cassian was in was sealed except for a single door, which was above Cassian's head. He wasn't a strong swimmer, judging by the holographic figure's movements. He'd drown before the water rose high enough for him to reach the door. If there were only some way she could rotate the chamber he was in and put the doorway on the side so the water would drain out . . .

She reached out, fingers grazing the hologram, relieved to find it was solid. The laser lines hummed beneath her fingers as she carefully lifted the model, unsure if what she did to the model would actually change the Gauntlet itself. Slowly, she twisted the flooded chamber around so that the door was now on the bottom, letting the water drain, giving Cassian an escape path. The entire model moved with it—the cubes didn't move interchangeably. She watched with relief as the water drained and the Cassian figure stopped swimming, crouched as though to catch his breath, and then dropped down into the next chamber, the candy store. But that chamber began filling with water even more rapidly. She turned the model again, but the water just flowed through the one open door straight into the next cube.

It was a spatial reasoning puzzle: an enormous Rubik's Cube, with her friend's life at stake. She had to figure out a safe path for Cassian to get through each of the chambers without drowning, yet every chamber she twisted affected all the others. The more doors she opened for him, the more water would flow from one to another. He'd be drowned by the time he made it to the end.

Her mind raced as she looked between the different chambers. Rolf's analytical voice hummed in her mind. *There is the room with a floor of lava . . . the lava might evaporate the water if you can get Cassian that far.* But that was puzzle seven, and Cassian was only at puzzle two and already the water was rising high.

She needed something closer. . . .

The high ropes course!

Puzzle four was full of trees, bridges, and rope swings. If she could get Cassian to that one, he could climb the rope and exit through the top. Gravity would keep the water from flowing into the next puzzle, buying him some time. She twisted the model again so the door was on the side. Cassian climbed—or rather swam—into puzzle three, the hunting room. His arms were moving fast now—he was swimming as hard as he could, and the gray line was nearly at the top of the chamber. As quickly as she could she twisted the model again, opening a door in the bottom to puzzle four. Water poured out, taking Cassian with it, and for a second she held her breath as the tiny figure of Cassian free-fell into the trees, plunging toward the ground. At the last minute, he reached out an arm and caught himself on the rope ladder.

She let out a tense breath. "Come on, Cassian. Climb. Hurry."

The water was quickly filling the forest puzzle, but at least it would have to fill the entire chamber first before spilling into the next. Cassian climbed slowly, with his wounded arm, into puzzle five, the cornfield, which he was able to run through into puzzle six, the electric shock room. Judging by the gray line, there were a few inches of water on the ground, enough to make the electric wiring snap and smoke dangerously. If he touched the water, he'd likely be electrocuted. Cora bit her lip and shook the model hard enough for the electric wires to fall lose from the ceiling. Cassian used to them to swing jungle style over the floor, into puzzle seven, the lava room. Here, the rising water was for once a blessing, as it extinguished the lava so that he could dash across it. Cora's heart pounded as she twisted the model as quickly as she could, opening doorways for him as fast as he was running through the maze.

"Almost there," she muttered. A drip of water suddenly landed on her forehead and she looked up. She didn't know if it was from the puzzle or the storm.

She looked back at the puzzle. "Shit!"

In that one second of distraction, she'd made a mistake. She'd twisted the puzzle too far, opening a doorway that let a tidal wave of water flow directly into chamber eight. Cassian was paddling his arms furiously. The gray line was already at the ceiling. His arms slowed. His feet stopped kicking . . .

"No!" she cried. "Hold on, Cassian!"

She twisted the puzzle once more, turning it so that the opening was on the side, letting water rush out.

At the same time, the door to her chamber burst open.

She shrieked as a wave of water poured in, and she grabbed the table to brace herself. The laser model sizzled and shorted out. Water drenched her. It was rising. Three feet, now four . . . She trod water desperately.

And then another door opened on the opposite wall. The sea of water rushed out, carrying her with it like a deluge into the next chamber, chamber ten. She crashed to the hard ground, knitting her fingers in the floor slats. *Slats.* She sat up quickly. The floor of chamber ten was made of a grate that let the water drain straight through it. She nearly laughed with relief, until she caught sight of herself in the chamber's mirrored walls and saw how haggard she looked.

And then Cassian, soaking wet, came staggering through the doorway.

He was the real one, not the model. An eternity of Cassians reflected in the mirrors.

She jumped up, running across the grates. The sound of rushing water below echoed through the chamber. She threw her arms around him. He coughed hard, water thick in his lungs.

"You're alive!" she said as they sank to the slatted floor.

He coughed harder, water still pouring down his skin. She pressed a hand to his cheek, felt the warmth there. In her heart, she'd always known Kindred and humans weren't so different. It bolstered her with hope that they were in this together now, two species from the same ancestor and the same planet.

"It'll be okay," she said tenderly. "I can do this, I know I can. Serassi was right about the paragon burst. It makes me stronger, physically and mentally. It's like I have a little bit of Rolf and Leon and Mali with me."

But as soon as Cassian stopped coughing, he looked up with burning rage. He threw her hand off of him violently.

"Don't touch me," he hissed. "Where's Cora?"

She stared at him in incomprehension. And then she glanced in the mirrored walls and let out a ragged breath.

Her reflection wasn't her own anymore. She was looking at Fian—at the impostor version of Fian. The same wrinkle in his forehead. The same gray uniform. She gasped, touching her forehead and seeing the action reflected in the mirror.

The Gauntlet had made *her* into an optical illusion this time.

"Cassian, listen," she said. "It's me, Cora. This is just the next puzzle. The Gauntlet is trying to trick you."

Cassian rolled back the sleeves of his uniform. "You tricked me once, Axion. I don't know how you got in here, but you won't trick me again."

He balled his fist.

37

Rolf

ROLF'S PICKUP STIRRED CLOUDS OF sand as he drove a load of Armstrong citizens, packed together tightly and cradling their few belongings in their laps, toward the marron root mines. All morning he'd been making this trip, back and forth, as quickly as he could, as many people as he could fit in the truck bed. The way the mine's tiers overlapped one another made it the perfect place to hide out from an Axion attack. They wouldn't be visible from above, and the deep chasm would protect them from any explosions or chemical dust clouds.

He pulled up to the edge of the mine and cut the engine.

"Let's move," he said, lowering the back gate and helping the citizens climb out. "Remember, stay hidden until Nok or I come back to give the all-clear."

The citizens rushed for the mine ladders, disappearing into the chasm one at a time. The sun was merciless overhead. Rolf wiped the sweat from his forehead, scanning the skies.

Nothing yet but thin clouds.

When would the Axion attack come?

He jumped in the truck and revved it, heading back to town for the next load. The strongest citizens had stayed in the tent encampment to fight from the ground and were now disguising the weapons under tent canvas. He spotted Dane's dirty uniform amid the bunch, along with two of the mine guards, and he narrowed his eyes. Dane had wanted to side with the Axion. The coward.

Rolf checked his list of refugees and citizens who still needed to be taken to shelter. A pair of Mosca pilots, a wounded Gatherer, a dozen elderly citizens, eight loads' worth of wild caged animals.

A lion! he thought as he sped back to town. How was he supposed to get a lion to climb down the scaffolding into the root mine?

On the outskirts of the town, he spotted Nok, Loren, and two Mosca refugees loading the laser weapons into the back of the other truck.

"Go around the back of the general store!" Nok called. "The next group is waiting for you there."

He nodded and skirted the town. From here, the desert stretched out as far as he could see. The field where the forty refugee ships had landed was nothing but bare ground now, the ships all hidden beneath tent canvas or in low trenches. He felt eerily exposed, staring at that bare desert. His fingers knit against the steering wheel. He looked up into the empty sky again.

A group of fifteen wounded citizens was waiting for him at the general store. Makayla was with them, helping load the stretchers one by one. Rolf jumped out to help. "Hey, Makayla, let's start with the—"

A distant whine, like a mosquito, interrupted him.

There weren't mosquitoes on Armstrong.

He squinted into the sky again.

Nothing.

Nothing.

Then, out of nowhere, a droning squeal filled the sky.

Rolf's heart shot to his throat as a slick white ship rocketed overhead.

"It's the Axion!" one of the wounded said.

"They're here!" another cried.

Rolf whipped around to look at Makayla, whose face had gone slack. She let out a ragged cry and then started loading the citizens in stretchers faster. "Come on!" she called. "Let's hustle, people!"

Another Axion ship tore through the clouds, leaving a trail of white that crossed against the other line. Panic clawed up Rolf's throat. He clutched his neck, feeling as though he couldn't breathe. A third ship appeared. Its white line of exhaust crossed the other two lines, making a starburst of white.

"Rolf!" Makayla said. "Let's move, we gotta get these people to the mines!"

He jolted back into action. Screams tore through the air from the few remaining Armstrong residents who hadn't yet taken cover. Someone knocked over a stretcher, which landed hard against Rolf's leg, and he buckled with pain.

Two more Axion ships streaked the sky, leaving white trails of exhaust. They crisscrossed at the exact same point again. Seven lines of exhaust. Now eight. All of them intersecting in the same place, almost as though it were intentional, as though it were . . .

"Makayla!" he called urgently. He held up the keys. "Do you know how to drive?"

She nodded.

He tossed her the keys. "Take these people to the mines. There's something I need to check on."

She raised an eyebrow at the strain in his voice but climbed into the driver's seat, revving the engine, and then the truck sped away, tires kicking up dust, in the direction of the mine. Rolf glanced at the sky again as another Axion ship shot by overhead.

They weren't firing.

Not yet.

Only making that strange crisscross mark out of exhaust.

He started running toward the sheriff's office, hobbling on his hurt leg. He threw open the door and grabbed the map he'd made of the town, unrolling it in a hurry on his desk. He traced a finger over the approximate pattern of those crisscrossing exhaust lines, muttering the coordinates under his breath.

His eyes went wide. "Oh, no."

He grabbed the map and hobbled outside as fast as he could. His pulse pounded in his ears as he made his way toward the truck Nok and Loren had been loading with weapons. Nok was in the town square now, yelling orders for the citizens to uncover the hidden weapons and start firing.

"Get those pilots safely to the ships!" she yelled. "Cover them!"

"Nok!" Rolf's hurt leg buckled beneath him and he crashed to the ground. "Nok!"

She saw him and gasped. She started running toward him. She didn't see the Axion ship lining up directly behind her. Time seemed to slow as she ran. Rolf took in every terrifying half second.

A light turned on beneath the Axion ship. A laser weapon was powering up. They were going to fire. Nok was running as fast as she could, but not fast enough. The past few months flashed just as fast in his head: The first time he'd met her. Their first kiss. The moment she told him she was pregnant. Learning he was going to be a father of a little girl.

"Nok!" Rolf cried.

She wasn't going to make it.

At the same time, someone shot out from the awning of the general store, slamming into her, knocking her out of the way of the laser pulses. Time sped up again as sand blasted into the air. Rolf shoved to his one good leg, hobbling and coughing as he made his way to her. "Nok!"

She coughed out his name weakly. "Rolf?"

Thank god.

He hobbled through the scorched sand to where she crouched on hands and knees, dirt streaking her face, turning her dark hair sandy.

Dane sat up next to her, coughing. Rolf's surprise that Dane had been the one to save her was eclipsed by his worry. "Are you okay?"

"Yeah," she breathed. "Sparrow—I think she's okay too."

Rolf grabbed her, pulling her to him. He breathed in the smell of her hair, somehow sweet and strawberry even now.

He'd come so close to losing her.

"Come on." Dane grabbed at their jackets. "Up. Now. Take cover."

A shriek tore through the sky. Rolf pitched his head up to see the Axion ships circling back around for another attack. Dane helped both of them to their feet and threw one of Rolf's arms around his shoulders to help him hobble to the general store. Overhead, the whine of ships grew deafening.

The Axion ships fired again, hot blasts of laser pulses shattering the remnants of the dance hall. Someone screamed. An explosion ripped through the town as they flung themselves into the shade of the general store.

"They're targeting the town!" Dane said.

Rolf shook his head. "It isn't the town they're targeting."

"What?" Both Nok and Dane stared at him in confusion. The Axion ships had doubled back, firing again. Bodies littered the town square. Billows of black smoke rose from the smoldering wreckage.

"Firing on the town is just a distraction," Rolf explained through heaving breaths, "just like we tried to distract them into thinking the town was the place to hit." He pointed up at the white lines of exhaust that crisscrossed overhead. "That's their real strategy. They're making a bull's-eye." He dragged the map out of his pocket and unfolded it on the ground, crossing lines over it to match the white clouds of exhaust. "See?" he asked. "The target points to one place."

He slid his forefinger to the transport hub.

"We were so stupid," he continued. "Of course they knew about the reactor core. The impostor Fian was here, on the ground. He was even in that transport hub! Brother Paddal didn't know that, but we should have remembered. The Axion know they can take us out with just one blast, if it's perfectly targeted. That's what they're doing."

Nok gaped.

"We have to stop them," Dane said.

Anger suddenly flooded Rolf. "You wanted to *join* them, you bastard!"

Dane's face twisted in anger too. "I wanted to *save* us! I still do!"

Rolf paused, breathing hard. Was there a chance Dane really wasn't as bad as he seemed? He'd saved Nok's life a moment ago. Even at risk to himself . . .

"Shut up, both of you," Nok snapped. She pointed to the reactor core on the map. "We need to figure out how to keep them from blowing it up."

Rolf looked at her. God, she was beautiful. The badge glistening around her neck, her face streaked with dirt, her belly round.

He had once wondered what it meant to be a good father. Now, feeling such certainty in his chest, he knew. It meant love. Pure, radiant, encompassing love.

A love he would do anything for.

Overhead, the Axion ships let out another volley of pulses. Nok shrieked, and everyone ducked.

Rolf grabbed up the map. "There's only one way to make sure they don't hit the reactor core. You heard Brother Paddal. A manual shutoff."

Dane and Nok both stared at him. "The radiation's too high," Nok said. "If someone climbed in there, they'd be—"

"They'd be a hero," Rolf said quietly.

The look on Nok's face turned to one of dawning horror, which quickly turned to anger. He could see her brain working. See her put together that the only person who had studied the maps and knew enough about reactors to be able to shut it down was him.

She lunged for him. "Don't you dare!"

Dane grabbed her, holding her back.

Rolf had already snatched up a wrench from the pile of abandoned construction tools. His pulse was pounding in his ears. He felt dizzy, as though this were a dream. As though it weren't really he who was going to climb into that reactor core, but a dream-Rolf, a second self. The real Rolf wasn't brave. The real Rolf wasn't a hero.

And yet, for Nok and Sparrow, he'd be anything.

"Rolf!" Nok strained against Dane. "Don't do this!"

"Dane." Rolf met the boy's eyes. He was far from trusting him, and yet in this instant, he believed that Dane really did want to keep them all alive. Dane was a scared boy with something to prove, but not cruel. Just determined. And right now, Rolf could use him. "Keep her here. Don't let her come after me."

Dane paused, a flicker of doubt in his eyes, as though he too wanted to talk Rolf out of it. "You don't have to do this," Dane said.

"Yes," Rolf said. He pushed at phantom glasses he no longer wore. "I do."

He headed across the town square, his steps feeling too light, as though all the blood were rushing to his head.

"No!" Nok cried. "Rolf, you jerk, you bastard, you get back here, I love you, I need you!"

His breath came fast.

He wouldn't look back.

He wouldn't.

"I love you too, Nok," he whispered very quietly. "More than anything."

The general store door slammed behind him, and then he

was in the thick of battle. Armed citizens were firing on the Axion ships, trying to take cover in the wreckage. A laser pulse caught one in the head, and she screamed as she crumpled to the ground.

Rolf froze as the dead body fell at his feet.

He was really doing this crazy thing? *He* was going to shut down the reactor core?

He stumbled forward on his good leg, wincing through the pain. Yes. *He* was going to save the town, dammit. He was going to save Nok, and Sparrow, and do this so that they would have a place to call theirs. So that Nok would have a chance for happiness. So that Sparrow would grow into a little girl. So that many years from now, Nok would cradle their daughter in her arms and tell her bedtime stories about how their father had saved their lives. Another pulse of lasers exploded just a few paces away and he collapsed to the ground, breathing hard.

Ahead of him was the vent that led to the reactor core.

With shaking limbs, he crawled forward and tore off the vent grate. The sound of cries came from behind him: the pilots making a run for the ships.

He plunged into the darkness of the vent. Steam burned his skin, but he knew it was nothing compared with the burn of core radiation ahead. He crawled beyond the red warning labels. He could hear the battle raging outside. Laser pulses against laser pulses.

He kept crawling. He reached the inner core, and an alarm started droning.

Evacuate, the voice said. *Evacuate. Radiation levels high.*

Was it just in his head, or could he already feel his eyes burning? His vision went blurry, but there. Ahead. A small panel held together with screws. He crawled forward, slower now, his breathing strained. His stomach was heavy with sudden nausea, but he fought through it.

He used his last ounce of strength to open the panel with the wrench.

The manual shutdown.

He twisted the lever.

I love you, Nok.

He slumped in the warmth of the darkened tunnel. The hum of the reactor core slowly shut down and then stopped.

Silence.

I love you, Sparrow. I'll be looking down on you. I'll be your proud father, always.

The tunnel was growing warmer.

He could hear the distant sounds of the battle raging outside. Ships against ships. The Kindred and Mosca and Gatherers fighting off the Axion. The crash of lasers in the air.

Was it only in his head, or did he hear the town cheering too?

Arm-strong! Arm-strong!

His eyelids sank closed.

He smiled.

The cheers changed in his head. *Ro-lf! Ro-lf!*

Such a beautiful sound, them cheering his name. He pictured Nok, with their daughter in her arms, both of them pumping their fists toward the sky, smiles radiant on their beautiful faces, his name on their lips.

Ro-lf! Ro-lf!

His eyes did not open again.

38

Cora

"CASSIAN, STOP! IT'S ME!"

Cora scrambled away from Cassian's raised fist. The metal grates on the floor were painful on her bare palms, but all she could focus on was the awful realization that Cassian thought she was his enemy. In the puzzle chamber mirrors, Fian's angry face looked back instead of her own reflection. Her hand grazed the painted red circle near the edge of the room and an alarm blared. She jerked her hand back, and it stopped.

She noticed drawings of sparring pairs on the walls above the mirrors. Puzzle ten, she realized, was a wrestling ring.

A physical challenge.

Though she'd lost all specific memories of attending wrestling matches back home or watching them on television, she still vaguely remembered the rules. The first wrestler to push their opponent outside the red circle won. Though it was a physical puzzle, its true challenge was clear: Cassian didn't recognize her.

"Listen," she said, eyeing the red circle to make sure she stayed within it, "I know I don't look like me, but it's Cora." Her voice came out unnaturally deep. She gasped, clamping a hand over her mouth. Different words had come out.

"It's too late," her voice had said. "The Gauntlet's broken. We've caught the girl. There's no reason for you to live."

She gaped. The Gauntlet's illusions hadn't changed just her appearance—it had changed the very words she'd said. She searched her mind, calling on the paragon burst for a solution, but there was no answer. Humanity was as stumped as she was.

"Then try to stop me," Cassian replied. "Try to keep her from me."

He started forward. Cora let out a shriek. Her heart was raging as hard as the storm outside. But Cassian was moving slowly, not yet recovered from his near drowning. He blinked as though his vision was blurry. She scrambled away as he lunged for her, moving with sharper reflexes than she'd ever had before. Though she should have been exhausted, her muscles felt strangely powerful.

Leon, she realized. Thank god for the paragon burst. Without Leon's DNA to boost her physical strength, she wouldn't have stood a chance.

"You can't . . . get away . . . ," Cassian said, his movements labored. He doubled over and coughed up more water. A pang of both fear and sympathy hit her. She was, in a terrible way, grateful that he'd almost died. On any other day he'd be able to defeat her easily, but he was unnaturally weakened, and she was unnaturally strengthened. For the first time, they were well matched physically.

"Cassian . . . ," she started, but let her words fall. It was useless. The Gauntlet would just create an illusion around whatever she said. There was no reasoning with him. No convincing him of the truth. This was a physical puzzle, and the only way to win was to defeat it—to defeat *him*.

She nearly blacked out at the impossibility of getting him outside the red line through sheer strength. Cassian was exceptionally well built, even for a Kindred. He towered nearly a foot and a half above her, and he had to weigh three times her weight.

But she was desperate.

She took a deep breath, trying to focus. Blood still trickled from his left arm. He was trying to hide how much it hurt him, but she hadn't seen him lift it, not even ball his left hand into a fist. So he wouldn't be swinging any punches from that side, at least.

He wiped water from his face, then lurched forward.

She held her ground, breathing hard. He was slower than usual. His steps were sluggish and heavy, almost as though he were drunk. He grabbed for her as she darted to the left, and his right hand only grazed her bare arm. With both of them still soaking wet, their skin was slippery. She filed that information away as she ducked toward his left side again, knowing that arm was useless.

Use it, Leon's voice grunted. *Hurt him. You have to.*

Before she could stop herself, she shoved her elbow straight into the gaping wound on Cassian's left shoulder.

He screamed. She cried out too, wishing she didn't have to hurt him, but she didn't have a choice. She slammed her elbow into his arm again, shocked by her own enhanced strength. Was this how Leon felt all the time, so powerful? Cassian crumpled to the floor, catching himself with his right arm at the last moment.

Keep going, Leon's voice hummed. *Don't stop.*

She shoved her shoulder into his side, trying to throw him off-balance so she could push him out of the red ring. But she only managed to shove him a few inches before she tripped on the grate. Just that second of hesitation was all Cassian needed to grab her with his right hand, catching her by surprise, and swing her to the floor. Her head connected painfully with the grates as the wind rushed out of her.

"That's for Cora," Cassian hissed.

"I'm not an Axion," she said, though she knew it was useless. "I'm—"

"You're dead," Cassian said. "But I'm going to make you suffer first." He grabbed her wrists, twisting them over her head, and then straddled her middle, digging her back against the grates. She tried to pull her hands from his, but even with Leon's DNA, she was no match for a Kindred. With her arms pinned, she couldn't punch him in his wounded arm. She couldn't throw him off-balance like this, not while trapped underneath him. . . .

Wait.

A moment of déjà vu hit her, and her heart started to thump. This was the wrestling position Lucky had taught her in the cage's desert maze. He had explained how when an opponent was much bigger, she couldn't rely on any feats of strength. She had to use her own weight against him through momentum. The paragon burst projected visions into her head. *Her own sparring match with Lucky. Ancient tribes fighting in a desert. High schoolers in a gymnasium wrestling match. Leon beating up some poor kid in a movie theater parking lot.*

Now, she told herself.

She shoved her hips upward, catching Cassian by surprise. She shifted herself to the left, throwing him off-balance. Then it was simply a matter of using his own heavy weight to tip him forward, as she scrambled out from under him. He landed hard on his left arm, giving a ragged cry.

Cora winced at the sound of blood from his wounded arm dripping down to the floor below.

He tossed his head up, pure rage in his eyes.

Use his momentum against him. She heard the echo of Leon's voice in her head.

As Cassian stood, Cora balled her fists. She spared a quick glance at the floor—the red line was directly behind her. If she stepped back just one inch, the alarm would go off again. Two inches, and she'd lose. But now she realized the nature of the game worked in her favor. Cassian didn't care about winning a puzzle or wrestling matches. He cared only about killing her—the Axion he thought she was—and that meant he didn't care about stepping outside any lines.

"Come on," she goaded. The room was cold, and her soaked, clammy clothes made her shiver. "Come and get me."

For once, the Gauntlet didn't change her words.

"Gladly," Cassian replied.

He rushed at her.

She stood her ground. She waited as he barreled toward her, closer . . . closer . . . his right hand pulled back . . .

And then she ducked with quickened reflexes at the last minute, rolling away from the red line.

"Coward!" Cassian yelled, wheeling to a stop.

Cora landed on her back and kicked out her legs as hard as

she could, connecting with his knees. He staggered backward a single step.

It was enough.

He crossed the red line.

The alarm started blaring. It droned steadily as all the lights overhead turned red, tinting the room the color of blood. Cassian spun around as if this were some new danger. His eyes settled on Cora.

He froze.

She lay on her back in the middle of the room, panting. She tensed her muscles, ready in case he attacked again.

His voice was tentative, confused. "Cora?"

She turned to the mirror. The red light was cast down not over the reflection of an Axion impostor, but over a girl in black clothes, hair wild, eyes even wilder.

"Cora?" he said again. This time panic filled his voice. The alarm stopped blaring, but neither of them seemed to notice. Out of the corner of her eye, she saw a door open in the right-hand wall.

The puzzle was over. She had won.

"Cassian," she breathed as she rolled over onto her knees, "never try to kill me again, okay?"

A look of horror crossed his face. He shook his head vigorously. "I thought you were an Axion. It was him, he was here."

"It was the Gauntlet," she said, still fighting for breath. "One of its illusions. It made you think I was someone else so you'd fight me."

He took a quick step forward, thought better of it, and stopped. "I would never fight you."

"I know." She looked up at him. "And so does the stock

algorithm. It had to disguise me or else you'd never have willingly been my opponent. Willa said this was the trick of the third round: the puzzles become personal." She rubbed her aching wrists.

He knelt down to her level. "I'm sorry."

He pulled her into an embrace. She stiffened. Afraid of hurting him more, afraid to *be* hurt. But then she felt his warmth. He wasn't holding himself at a distance anymore. She then melted into him and wrapped her arms around him too. She breathed in his scent. He was a small flame of warmth in the cold room, kindling her hope.

Her love.

There was still a chance for them. A spark. One that would never fade.

"The door's open," she whispered. "We can go to puzzle eleven."

But his arms around her didn't release. "Not yet. Not after this. I don't dare continue, knowing what the Gauntlet is capable of making me do."

"We don't have a choice," she insisted. "The storm could tear everything apart at any second. And everyone outside could be getting slaughtered by the Axion."

He pulled back far enough to look into her eyes. "I'm afraid."

She touched her hand to his cheek. This close, she could see all those little details that made him so real—the bump in his nose, the wrinkles on the sides of his eyes, a small scar by his hairline. Even if she didn't know that humans and Kindred were related, hadn't she always felt it?

"We'll do this together," she said softly.

He covered her hand with his, and she felt a rush of strength.

She leaned forward, pressing her lips to his cheek. With the red light bathing them, she couldn't see the blood on his clothes or the dried blood from her nosebleeds. She could almost pretend that everything was okay.

"All right," he said at last. "But whatever happens, know that I love you."

She took his hand. Kissed his knuckles. "I do."

Together, they crossed through the doorway.

39

Cora

CORA DRIFTED TO A stop as soon as they entered the next chamber, puzzle eleven. It wasn't a bare cube this time. Her lips parted—it was the most beautiful room she'd ever seen. It was a ballroom like from a fairy tale, with gleaming marble floors and a three-tiered chandelier casting a warm glow over stained-glass windows and ornate molding. Soft instrumental music played from some unseen musicians. She pressed a hand over her mouth, overwhelmed with surprise. But then the door closed behind them, and she spun. There was only a wall, as if the door had never existed.

"Cora," Cassian said. "Your clothes."

She looked down to find that the Gauntlet had worked its illusions again. Instead of the sweat-stained black Gauntleteer uniform, she now wore a sweeping crystal gown that reflected the twinkling lights in rainbow colors. She ran her hands down her sides, feeling each individual crystal sewn into the heavy fabric, wondering how something that didn't exist at all could feel so real.

"Your clothes, too," she said, nodding at Cassian. His bloody uniform had vanished. He now wore a crisp black suit, all signs of the dirt caking his skin gone, and it stole her breath to see him like this, dressed so shockingly humanly.

He gently touched her hair, which was swept up on top of her head in an elaborate braid. "I didn't know the stock algorithm was capable of such complex illusions."

"I guess if everyone knew," she said, "then the Gauntlet wouldn't be a challenge. The stock algorithm has been keeping secrets even from its creators."

The room suddenly jarred, and for a second the illusions flickered. The music dropped out, and Cora and Cassian were standing in a bare chamber, both bloody and beaten and barefoot, and then just as suddenly the beautiful illusion flickered back on.

"What . . . what was that?" Cora gasped.

"Not part of the puzzle," Cassian said cautiously, looking up at the sparkling chandelier. "The storm outside, I think. It's interfering with the illusions themselves."

Cora turned toward the walls. "Then we have to solve this as quickly as we can. There's already been an intellectual and physical puzzle this round, so this one has to either be moral or perceptive." Her nerves started to prickle at the prospect of a perceptive puzzle. How could she solve it without her abilities? As much as she felt humanity's strengths humming within her, the paragon burst couldn't help her when it came to psychic abilities, not since she'd broken that part of her brain.

Cassian was silent. When she turned toward him, she gaped.

He had multiplied.

She blinked, not certain she was seeing correctly. There were six of him now, standing right where he'd been standing, dressed in identical black suits, of identical heights, and with identical buzzed hair. They were lined up three in the front and three in the back, standing perfectly still.

She took an involuntary step backward. "Cassian?"

All six turned their heads. She took another step back, unnerved by the sight of them. Her heart started pounding so loudly it almost drowned out the sound of the music, except the melody suddenly swelled louder. As if on cue, the six Cassians started walking. No, Cora realized, not walking. Waltzing. They strode around the room in time with the music, arms extended around imaginary partners, dancing far more gracefully than the real Cassian ever had. Cora stood in their midst, speechless.

What kind of a bizarre test was this?

She watched them spinning, feeling dizzy herself. Creating an illusion of a beautiful ball gown was one thing, but could the Gauntlet really make Cassian dance like that? Why didn't the real Cassian just stop dancing and tell her which one he was? Was the real Cassian even here anymore?

Then she remembered how in the last puzzle, no matter what she had said, the Gauntlet changed her words to different ones. This had to be a similar trick—the real Cassian must be trying to tell her who he was, but the stock algorithm was preventing him.

She took a step toward the closest Cassian, but he was moving fast. His face was eerily blank, and she pulled her hand back.

"There's only you," an unseen voice sang to the accompanying music. "In all the world, there's only you. I'd know you blind."

The voice kept repeating the same lyrics over and over until Cora thought she'd go mad. She pressed her hands to her ears. So this was the puzzle: figure out the real Cassian.

More sweat broke out on her forehead. This was the puzzle she'd most been dreading. A perceptive one. Whenever other Gauntleteers made it to this puzzle, it must have been a simple task of closing one's eyes, reaching out with one's mind, searching through all the decoys for the real one, and picking him. Days ago, it might have been easy for her too, even with the Gauntlet's illusions. Her mind and Cassian's used to find each other so easily, even from far away. But now, when she closed her eyes and tried to extend her thoughts, there was nothing.

Only pain.

She doubled over as an ache pulsed in the back of her head. It hurt so badly that her vision went black and she had to crouch to the ground before she passed out. She squeezed her eyes shut, trying to clear her mind. At last, the pain started to ease.

She opened her eyes and let out a sob.

It was useless. Her perceptive abilities were gone. The dancing Cassians all looked identical, swirling to the looped music. The room suddenly rocked again, and she shrieked and steadied herself on the floor. The music fluctuated, but the illusions didn't give out this time. None of the Cassians' suits became a blood-soaked uniform. She stood, wiping off her hands shakily on her dress.

The storm didn't care about her perceptive abilities. It was coming regardless.

And so was the war.

She took a deep breath and then ran alongside the first of the Cassians. She took hold of his extended hand and slid her torso between his other hand and his chest, trying to match his quick steps. As soon as she was in his arms, he looked down at her and smiled as if some spell had been broken, and her heart leaped. Had she found the real Cassian? But the smile remained on his face for an eerily long time, and her hopes began to sink. No, this Cassian was just acting however the Gauntlet wanted him to.

"Cassian," she said, searching his eyes for some clue that might tell her if he was the real one, "tell me about the necklace you gave me once. The charm."

"The dog," he said, holding her close as they spun faster and faster. "To remind you of a dog you had at home. Sadie. You told me once you couldn't sleep without her."

Cora's heart flickered with hope. She fought the urge to prod him for more information about her own past that she didn't remember. What else had she told him about her family, her life there?

But this might not even be Cassian at all.

She let go of him, stepping back out of his arms. He didn't stop dancing as his face returned to a static mask of normalcy. With a mixture of apprehension and distrust, she watched him dance away, then slid into the arms of the second one.

He smiled down at her in an identical way as the last one.

"Cora," he said tenderly.

She wanted to trust that loving look in his eyes, but she didn't let herself be influenced. "Tell me about the necklace you first gave me," she repeated.

"It was a charm of a dog," he answered on cue. "To help you sleep at night."

She let go of this one too, stepping back into the center of the room. Different wording, but the same answer. If she asked the other four, she'd doubtless get the same response.

A heavy jolt shook the room. She tossed a look up at the chandelier, whose crystals all trembled wildly. A sound rumbled beneath the music, like twisting metal. Something was happening just outside this chamber. Something was tearing it apart, either the storm or the Axion.

She ran to the third Cassian, wasting no time. She rested her hand on his left arm as they danced and squeezed the place on his biceps where he was wounded, hard. But the dancing Cassian didn't flinch. She let go of him and ran to the fourth, squeezing his arm, and he didn't react either. She ran to the fifth, but he too showed no reaction when she squeezed his arm.

She watched the last one, the sixth. If this one flinched, then it was the real Cassian. She moved into his arms, meeting his eyes. There was warmth there. Every inch of him was identical to the Cassian she knew. She moved her hand slowly down his biceps.

Squeezed.

He didn't flinch. He smiled at her as blandly as the others had.

She cursed and pushed him away, but he returned seamlessly to the dance. She raked her nails through her hair, pacing. *Think, think . . .* If she couldn't tell them apart by their wounded arm, and she couldn't tell by asking them questions, how was she supposed to figure out which one was him?

That's the point, she reminded herself. *It isn't about deduction. It's about being psychic.*

The room shook again and she balled her fists, pacing in the opposite direction from the dancers. They passed her in flashes, each one giving her an identical smile. Bile rose in her stomach. Solving the puzzle was impossible if she couldn't use her mind.

But . . .

She stopped pacing abruptly.

Maybe she could use her heart.

The idea took hold of her. The Kindred thought that perceptive abilities were about training one's mind to perform feats of telepathy and telekinesis, but intuition was perceptive too. Cora had always been especially intuitive, which was one of the reasons Cassian had first picked her. In those moments when she'd felt true intuition—like the time she knew Lucky was lying to her—she had felt it not in her mind, but in her heart.

Maybe humans were different from Kindred and the other intelligent species. Maybe this was one of her race's unique gifts: that they could be perceptive using their feelings, not just their thoughts.

She watched the dancing Cassians with renewed attention. Studying each one not with her mind, but with her heart. Instead of looking for any visual differences or trying to make them guess riddles, she just observed. Just *felt*.

She let her heart guide her—feeling her heartbeats in her core, waiting for some sign, some skipped pulse, some flood of warmth, that would lead her to the right one.

The music faltered again. For a few terrifying seconds, she heard the squeal of something metal close by being ripped apart. The floor beneath her started to rumble.

She looked among the Cassians quickly.

She had to pick one—now.

40

Leon

"QUICK," MALI SAID TO Leon. "Hand me that electrical cord."

Leon squinted in the direction she pointed. Almost all the lights in the central vestibule had shattered, casting everything in semidarkness. He found the black wire she was talking about a few feet away, flopping like a snake on the metal floor, shooting out sparks.

"Leon, hurry!"

They were hidden away deep in the corner of the Gauntlet's smallest control compartments, one of the few rooms that hadn't yet been destroyed. The Axion who had assumed Anya's identity lay on the floor beside Mali, still wearing Anya's clothes. His hands were bound with wire. His sharp eyes threw hateful glares between Mali and Leon. Gray blood oozed from cuts Mali had made on his arms.

"It's sparking," Leon said, eyeing the wire as though it would bite.

"Well, use something else to pick it up." Mali glanced impatiently toward the door. The sound of fighting continued in the central vestibule, though it had shrunk to just a few yells and clanks of metal. The Axion had all but won. When they did—any moment now—they'd come looking for any hidden survivors, like Leon and Mali, and the prisoner they were currently preparing to torture.

"Bloody hell," he muttered, and snatched up a ripped piece of jumpsuit from a dead Mosca and used it to grab hold of the wire. He held it at arm's length, grimacing, and passed it off to Mali.

"Tell us where Anya is," Mali threatened the Axion. "Or we go from the knife to the wire."

The Axion narrowed his eyes. "Even if I told you, you would never be able to reach her. You know as well as I do what is happening beyond that door. That is the sound of my people defeating yours. You'll be taken prisoner if you're fortunate, killed if you aren't. There will be no rescue for your friend."

A crash of thunder rumbled through the room, shaking the walls. Something cracked in the ceiling, and Leon tossed his head up just as a flood of frigid rainwater burst through the ceiling tiles and drenched him.

"Bloody hell!" he yelled.

"Shh," Mali hissed, jerking her head toward the door. "They can't know we're in here. Make sure no one's coming."

Ice water dripped down the back of Leon's neck. He gritted his teeth against the cold, wiping water from his eyes and off his clothes. He went to the door, keeping watch.

Behind him, Mali kept threatening the Axion. "You haven't won yet. This battle goes beyond that vestibule out there. Cora's still running the Gauntlet. There's still hope." She held up the wire. "Hope for *us*, that is. Not much for you unless you start talking." She lowered the wire to the side of his head. The closer she held the wire, the more the gray veins in the Axion's face stood out, as though drawn to the electricity.

Leon grimaced, watching. Mali could be a holy terror. And he loved it.

"Tell me where Anya is," Mali said. "Now."

Leon looked through the doorway, checking to see if the coast was clear. Three Axion were fighting with Serassi by the dais. The rest of the Axion were capturing wounded prisoners— a few Kindred soldiers, a tall Gatherer with silver blood trickling down her arm, Mosca with broken shielding, leading them to a back room. One of the Axion slammed a fist into Serassi's chest, hard. Leon flinched. It sounded as though something had cracked.

Leon muttered a curse and turned back to Mali. "Screw it. You're doing a good job, sweetheart, but we don't have time for this." He grabbed the wire from her hand and shoved it straight into the Axion's face.

The Axion started screaming.

"Leon!" Mali warned. "Keep him quiet!"

"Too late for that," Leon said, jerking his head toward the fight outside. "They've nearly won out there." He shoved the wire into the Axion's gaunt cheek. "Tell us!"

"Leon . . . ," Mali warned, looking toward the door. He could just make out the sound of heavy boots headed their way. The

Axion's screams had given them away. He shoved the wire harder against the man's face, his heart thudding in his chest. This had to work. He had to do this, for Mali. . . .

"Theta!" the Axion screamed.

Leon dropped the wire. At the same time, dozens of Axion grabbed him, pulling him backward. They'd gotten Mali, too.

"Let her go!" Leon went irate at the sight of their hands on her. He tried to fight off the ones holding him, but Mali shook her head.

"Don't. There are too many. It's over."

The Axion soldiers pulled them into wreckage of the central vestibule. Leon's stomach clenched at the sight of so many dead bodies. Many he didn't recognize except for their clothes, Kindred and Mosca and Gatherers who had been loyal to them. And then there was Ironmage, dead in the puddle of electrified water. And the scraps of shielding that were all that remained of Bonebreak.

Break some bones for me, boy!

Leon gritted his teeth. He couldn't even fulfill Bonebreak's dying request. What kind of a hero was he? He looked away, furious. The Axion shoved them into the recess room with the other prisoners. One entire wall had been torn away by the storm, and wind howled through the gap. The chill bit into his rain-soaked clothes, and he hugged his arms across his chest as they pushed him toward the wall, where the other prisoners sat in silence. Serassi, a bruise marring her face, her hair loose and messy, clutching her ribs. Willa, bleeding from multiple gashes. Redrage, wheezing through her shattered mask.

"Sit," an Axion ordered. "You try anything, you get shot."

He pushed Leon and Mali down next to Serassi.

Leon grumbled as he eyed the Axion guards. He couldn't stop his teeth from chattering. Rage made his muscles feel extra tight. He flexed his fist, desperate for something to slam it into.

Then, a soft hand touched his shoulder.

"Thank you," Mali said. "You did it. We know where Anya is." She gave a smile.

His heart leaped. He flexed his fist again, his tense muscles easing only slightly. "Lot of good it does us here," he muttered. "Theta seems damn far off right now, with those guns pointed at us."

"But she's alive," Mali said. Her hand tightened on his shoulder. Her eyes were so clear, so focused on him. Like she really saw him. A small pocket of warmth opened in his chest, and he stopped shivering quite as much. For the first time, he started to see what a future might look like for them, back on Earth. His family would lean on him hard to join up the smuggling operation, but with Mali's support, he'd resist that life. He'd do something better. Maybe own a bar. A pawnshop. He looked down at his muscles, flexing them.

A cop?

Bloody hell, had he actually just considered that?

He sighed—it didn't matter. They'd probably all die here anyway. The others looked terrible. Serassi winced as she leaned against the wall. He could tell from her eyes that she was uncloaked, and she hunched forward over her hurt ribs in a very humanlike way. So different from the stiff Chief Genetics Officer who had once told him to strip naked so she could perform tests on him.

In the central vestibule, the Axion were speaking among themselves. A pounding noise started, and he wrinkled up his face as he strained to see what was happening.

"They're trying to break into the puzzle chambers," Serassi explained. "It's the strongest part of the structure, the only part the storm hasn't completely torn apart yet." For a second, a ripple of dark pleasure crossed her face as she nodded toward the wall monitor. "They're worried. The last I saw before those monitors shorted out, Cora had made it to puzzle ten. She could be on puzzle eleven, or even puzzle twelve by now. They're getting desperate enough to physically break into the modules and stop her. Her winning is the only thing that still threatens them. That's why they haven't killed us yet—bargaining chips, in case their plan fails."

"*Can* they break in?" Mali asked.

"I don't know," Serassi said. She pointed to the Axion guards just beyond the doorway. One was speaking in emphatic words Leon couldn't make out. "He's updating his superior on battles beyond this planet. They've invaded Armstrong. They've taken over nearly ten percent of the galaxy, crippling the entire Intelligence Council system."

"That means they've won," Mali said flatly.

Serassi's face returned to its tight, passive look. But then she glanced to the side. "Yes. Unless Cora and Cassian come through. If Cora wins, it will trigger the evolutionary jump for humans and Kindred. Not everyone will feel it right away, but we're close enough that it'll be almost instantaneous for us. You'll feel it in your body: strength as if you could lift an entire shuttle. And in your minds. You'll be able to read the thoughts of everyone in this room. If the evolutionary jump happens, it doesn't matter that the Axion outnumber us. We'll be strong enough to defeat them here." She smiled. "And everywhere."

Leon decided he liked Serassi infinitely more like this, with her hair messy and a smirk on her face, than with that mask of indifference. He exchanged a look with Mali, who was staring at her scarred fingers. He reached down and took her hand, squeezing tight.

"How will we know if Cora loses?" he asked.

The smile faded off Serassi's face.

"We'll know she's lost," she said, "if the Gauntlet ends and the Axion kill every one of us."

41

Cora

THE SIX CASSIANS SEEMED to be spinning faster. Cora pressed a hand to her head, trying to stop the sensation that the room was moving. But it *was* moving, she realized—it was swaying back and forth, tossed around by the coming storm.

She was out of time.

She whirled toward the first Cassian, then the second, then the third. She let her mind clear of worries: about the storm and about the Axion just on the other side of those walls, waiting to kill her and everyone she loved. She ignored the throbbing pain in the back of her skull. She didn't think about how, if she lost, the entire known universe was doomed.

She focused instead on her memories of Cassian. The paragon burst spread through her as a warm sensation. The first time she had ever seen him, in her dreams, when he had been so beautiful that she mistook him for an angel. And then the time in the snow when he had made stars appear in the night sky to comfort her. And she thought about their first kiss. Standing in the ocean, the warm salty waves lapping at their thighs, as he had pulled her into an embrace. *I want to know what it feels like,* he had told her. And electricity had sparked between them as their lips touched, shooting straight to her heart.

She pressed a hand to her chest, holding on to that feeling, multiplied by ten by the warmth of the paragon burst.

Knowing him, as he knew her.

Knowing him beyond appearance, beyond name or rank, knowing him more deeply than the stock algorithm ever would. Knowing him as deeply as she loved him.

Her head jerked toward the fourth Cassian.

He looked in every way identical to the others. His black suit showed no signs of dust or tears or battle; his left arm was extended, not revealing any kind of wound. The look on his face was just as masklike as the rest.

And yet there was something different about him.

Her heart beat extra hard. A warm shock of feeling. A *spark*.

She crossed the room, grabbed his outstretched hand, and pulled him into the center of the room. "You," she said, staring into his eyes. "It's you."

The music stopped.

She was afraid it was the storm causing more interference, but then the other Cassians vanished, one by one. The chandelier overhead flickered and disappeared, followed by the ornate walls and the marble floor, until they were standing on a plain metal grid. Her dress faded into plain black clothes, and her hair fell loose around her face, once more tangled and dirty. His fine suit changed back to a torn uniform.

He suddenly clutched his left arm, crying out in pain.

"Cassian!" She caught him as he stumbled. She led him to the wall, which he leaned against for support. "Are you all right?"

"I couldn't move," he said, wincing in pain. "I had to do what the Gauntlet wanted me to do. I wasn't in control of my own body."

"It's okay now," she said. "I'm sorry I had to hurt your arm—I didn't know how to tell you apart from the others."

"How did you?" he asked.

She looked into his eyes. There had been a time when making eye contact with him had been nearly impossible. But now she felt a thrill at connecting with him on this level, of truly knowing him. "Remember when I told you that I wanted to know you as well as you know me?"

The corner of his mouth turned up. "You were lying. You were trying to trick me."

"I guess it wasn't entirely a lie," she said. "It turns out I do know you already. Your heart. The stock algorithm can't disguise that."

She pulled back, resting a hand on either side of his face, looking into those eyes that weren't so different from her own. He leaned in at the same time she did, and their lips met. She felt that familiar spark. Though they had touched often enough for her to be used to it, it still surprised her. She leaned closer, wanting to feel more of his warmth. He wrapped a hand around her back, holding her close.

"I love you, Cassian."

A rumble overhead made them both look up.

A door opened in the ceiling.

Her heart started thumping anxiously as her fingers

squeezed against his shoulders, wanting to hold on to this moment with him, this small moment of victory, of pure love.

Because there was only one puzzle left. And she knew it would be the hardest of all.

The ceiling was ten feet high, so Cassian made a stirrup with his hands for Cora to step into. "You climb up first," he said. "I'll be right behind you."

She rested her hands on his shoulders to steady herself and then placed a bare foot into his palms. He lifted her easily, even with his hurt left arm, and she reached for the doorway, catching the edge, pulling herself up with her improved strength.

She flexed her sore fingers, looking back down through the doorway.

"Your turn," she called.

He knelt down, preparing to jump—but the door slid shut.

42

Cora

SHE GASPED. "NO!" SHE slammed her hands on the metal floor. "Cassian!" She pounded her fists harder. She couldn't do this alone. She needed his confidence in her. She needed—

"It won't do any good," a voice said from behind her. "That door opens for no one but me."

She shoved up from the floor and spun toward the voice. It had had an odd quality to it, almost an echo. She found herself staring at an empty, plain chamber. The lights were faint, but it was clear that she was alone.

"Where are you?" she asked cautiously.

The room grew a few degrees colder. Air blew from unseen vents. Dust drew together, forming a sort of column in the center of the chamber. She stepped away from the phenomenon tensely, prepared to fight or flee to a corner. The column of air solidified into a hologram, made of the same glowing lines as the ones that had formed the Gauntlet model from puzzle nine. Slowly the lines rearranged themselves until she was looking at a person.

Well . . . not a person. The outline of a person. It was about her height, androgynous, with no hair or clothes or anything but the glowing hint of a face and body.

"Welcome to the final puzzle," the hologram said.

She took a step cautiously to the left, hesitant to trust her own eyes. "Who are you?"

"I am the stock algorithm."

Cora swallowed, staring at the glowing figure. The stock algorithm was a program, not an entity. And yet this hologram had referred to itself as though it were alive.

"I have taken on a form you will recognize, but I am formless by nature. I am not alive or sentient. I am merely a program developed by the Intelligence Council, designed to serve many functions. Here, my task is to test you and all lesser species."

Its voice was layered, as though there were many voices speaking at once.

"You aren't . . . real?" she asked.

"I am not alive, but I am very real. I can process information. I can govern and follow protocols. I can even reach into your mind and extract memories and fears. I am, by many definitions, more intelligent than any living species in existence."

She narrowed her eyes, her initial wonder fading. "Then why don't *you* stop the Axion? If you have superior morality, you must know the war they're waging is unjust."

The stock algorithm's glow slowly changed from green to red, then yellow. "I am merely a program. I do not have physical form. I cannot stop anyone or anything."

"But you could let me win," Cora said.

The stock algorithm changed to a blue glow. "Programs cannot cheat. Only sentient life can do that." It turned back to red. "There was a time you were planning on cheating me, in fact. I can see it in your mind. It wouldn't have worked. The evolutionary jump can only be triggered by a legitimate win."

Cora narrowed her eyes. "I don't need to cheat. I've come this far on my own, even without perceptive abilities."

"Yes," it said. "Impressive. But you are not finished yet."

The room rumbled again. Cora wasn't sure if the stock algorithm was causing the vibration or if it was the effects of the storm.

"It is interesting you bring up morality," the stock algorithm continued, oblivious to the effects of the storm, "as you must realize that this final puzzle is, by process of elimination, a moral one."

Cora reached involuntarily for a jacket she wasn't wearing anymore, a pocket she didn't have. Mention of morality had made her think of Lucky's journal. Lucky's words had helped her defeat the fifth puzzle, and it had helped her maintain her sanity in a crazy, impossible world. With him on her side, and with all of humanity's nuanced morality from the paragon burst, she felt she could solve anything.

"Go ahead, then," she said, glancing at the swaying chamber. "Throw whatever you've got at me. If you're going to pit Cassian against me again, I'm ready."

The stock algorithm cycled through the different soft colors again. "The final puzzle is personal, yes, but not in the same way as the others in the third round. I have already tested your relationship with another. It is time to test your relationship with yourself."

She swallowed down a bubble of worry. Her confidence wavered at the hologram's words, but she held her ground. The room rumbled louder, the shaking so hard it was threatening to unbalance her. She held her hands out for balance as the stock algorithm started to flicker like static.

"What do you mean?" she yelled over the roar of the storm.

"The ultimate show of a superior species," it said, flickering faster now, "is in selflessness. The Gauntleteer must symbolically prove that he or she is not more important than the species as a whole."

Cora's lips parted in confusion. The hologram was fading quickly.

"Wait! What does that mean, exactly?"

The room shook harder, throwing Cora back against one of the walls. The roar of wind poured in through cracks, chilling her to the marrow. The stock algorithm outline was growing fainter, its holographic body disappearing in the interference.

"What am I supposed to do?" she yelled.

The stock algorithm's voice filled the room, but the wind whipped it away.

"What?" Cora yelled. "What did you say?"

For a second, the face of the stock algorithm reappeared.

"Turn around," it said.

And then it was gone.

Cora clutched the wall, holding her hair back from whipping around her face. She squinted into the wind, turning toward the back wall. The plain metal grid was gone now. An illusion replaced it, though it flickered like static too, threatening to vanish as the storm grew. But even with the interference, the scene before her was enough to make her breath go still.

She took a shaky step forward, forgetting about the storm.

The back half of the chamber was now a scene of night on Earth. Rain poured from dark thunderclouds that blocked out the moon, soaking the pine trees below and forming puddles on the asphalt. She could hear the rush of a swollen river below her.

She was standing on a bridge.

Her eyes scoured every detail, head whipping back and forth. What was this place? She felt as though she was supposed to know it—it felt too specific to be random. But her memories were gone. She knew what a bridge was, even knew that pines like this grew mostly around the East Coast, but it meant nothing to her. Was this where she lived? Had something happened on this bridge, during this rainstorm?

She took a shaky step toward the edge, looking down at the water. Dizziness gripped her and she pulled back, breathing hard. Her pulse was racing. Sweat beaded on her forehead, and she wiped it away, staring at her hand.

Her body seemed to remember this place, even if her head didn't.

She closed her eyes. *Figure it out. Why would the stock algorithm show me this place?* But without her memories, whatever she was supposed to prove here was impossible. She paced, chewing on a fingernail, gaze darting from lamppost to lamppost.

Think. Remember. The bridge . . .

The squealing sound of car brakes suddenly echoed in her head. She dropped her hand and whipped around toward one of the lampposts. *Yes.* Those squealing brakes—that was a memory. *She remembered!* Something had happened here. An accident. A car . . .

And then it hit her.

Everything.

A car swerving to avoid another one in the wrong lane, smashing into the lamppost. The other car plunging through the guardrail, a man and a girl in the front seats, falling toward the river.

She raced to the guardrail, looking downward.

She had fallen here.

She remembered.

But something felt off. She glanced back at the lamppost—her memories were from that angle, watching herself, not from a car falling off the bridge. And then it hit her. The memories weren't her own.

They were Lucky's.

Her fingers gripped the guardrail, steadying her against this realization. They were Lucky's memories, coming from the paragon burst, not hers.

And yet . . .

When she looked down at the water, there was the slightest, faintest image in her head. A word: *Love.* Then more: *Cora, I love you. Hold on.* Somehow, she knew those had been her father's words as they plunged over the bridge, words that Lucky, far away in the other car, couldn't have possibly heard.

Could his memory have triggered her own? Was there a chance her memories *could* be recovered, in time? That they were still there, buried deep?

The storm raged harder overhead. She tossed her head up.

She needed to act—now.

The final moral test.

A whisper of what that might mean tickled the back of her head and she clutched the slick lamppost, feeling a panicky sort of laugh bubbling in her throat. In puzzle two, the candy shop, she'd had a foreboding feeling as she'd typed her own name on the anagram puzzle with the other names of the dead, as though she were somehow ensuring her own death. *And maybe I was.* Maybe it really had been a deadly promise that all led to this moment.

To the final moral test: selflessness.

This was what the stock algorithm had meant when it said an individual must prove a willingness to put the good of the entire species over oneself. Cora had to prove she valued humanity's existence more than her own.

At the cost of her life.

She sucked in a quick breath. There was nothing moral about taking one's own life—that was tragic, not selfless. But this was different, she realized. The Gauntlet demanded a symbol of her ultimate dedication to her species.

And there could be no greater symbol than self-sacrifice.

She had always wondered why there were no previous Gauntlet winners. This was why. They'd all completed this final moral test. The only ones who lived to tell about it were like Willa, competitors who had dropped out in earlier rounds. She pressed a hand to her head, feeling faint. The Kindred, the Axion, the Gatherers, even the Mosca—all had been willing to make this symbolic sacrifice.

But could she?

She let out a shaky cry.

She'd cheated death that time on the bridge.

Now, if she wanted to save humanity, she would have to let death win.

43

Cora

THE RIVER BELOW WAS dark and fast.

Rain streaked Cora's face as she stood on the bridge, clutching the lamppost, staring down at the precarious thirty-foot fall. Somewhere in the back of her head she knew the bridge wasn't real, just as the rain and the smell of pines wasn't real, but it didn't matter. The danger was real. Just as in the treetops course, if she fell, she'd crash all the way to her death.

She gripped the lamppost harder. She'd known running the Gauntlet meant putting her life at risk, and she had accepted that. But there was a chasm of difference between a calculated risk and certain death. Did Cassian know that this was what would happen? That she'd end up with this final, deadly test?

No. He couldn't have. She felt it deep in her core. He hadn't known how powerful the stock algorithm was, and even he had been surprised by the nature of many of its puzzles. He'd never have asked her to sacrifice herself willingly, not even to save the galaxy.

But now the stock algorithm *was* asking her. Did she dare say no? Did she dare say *yes*? *Maybe I can cheat it,* she thought in desperation. But no—the stock algorithm could see into her heart, just as she had seen into Cassian's in the eleventh puzzle. There was no cheating now.

A terrible ripping sound tore through the night, and she spun around. The rear half of the puzzle chamber was still the plain grid-pattern cube, though the stock algorithm's avatar had disappeared. The ripping sounded again and half the ceiling wrenched itself off. Her mouth fell open. Wind tore at the metal, pulling off panels and sending wires sparking. Cora hugged the lamppost harder, sheltering her face against it.

A gaping, angry hole yawned in the ceiling. Dark wind howled through it, and cracks of lightning sent jagged, dangerous flashes of light into the chamber. The storm was literally tearing the Gauntlet apart, piece by piece. Maybe it had already demolished the control rooms, where her friends were. Maybe it had destroyed all the other eleven puzzle chambers, including whichever one Cassian was in. Maybe this chamber—this puzzle—was the last intact structure on the planet's entire surface.

She tasted warm and salty moisture and freed a shaking hand to wipe away her tears. Panic was pulsing within her, punctuating each of her fears: *They're all dead. The Axion have won. It's too late.*

But it couldn't be too late. The bridge illusion was still there, which meant the Gauntlet's mechanisms hadn't been completely destroyed. If the illusion still worked, then the puzzle still worked, which meant she could still win.

All she had to do was jump.

She turned back to the rushing water below, trying to put the storm out of her mind. Carefully, with trembling limbs, she climbed to the top of the guardrail, balancing against the lamppost to keep herself steady. A wave of dizziness hit her as she looked down. Bile rose in her stomach. For years she'd had a fear of heights and a fear of deep water, both caused by what had happened on this very bridge.

You have no choice, she told herself. *You'll probably die either way. The bridge or the Axion.*

But her feet didn't move. Because deep down, she knew that she did have a choice. She didn't have to jump. She could forfeit the Gauntlet right now, just as Willa and countless other competitors had done, and she'd be free. She'd be returned to Cassian and Mali and Leon and the others, and if they were going to die at the Axion's hands, at least they would die together. Now, perched on the guardrail overlooking her worst nightmare, she had never felt so alone.

But I'm not alone.

The reassurance came with a flood of familiar warmth—the paragon burst. It warmed every cell, every blood vessel. The strength of humanity was always with her. And self-sacrifice wasn't a foreign concept to humans. People had sacrificed themselves for loved ones or causes they believed in for as long as humanity had existed. The paragon burst filled her with a flash of visions. *Soldiers dying in war. A mother dying in a difficult childbirth. A father working with toxic chemicals to give his children a decent life.*

And it wasn't just strangers. Lucky had sacrificed himself so that she and the others could escape the aggregate station. He'd thrown himself on that Mosca soldier, taken the knife to his gut to protect them. And there was Lucky's mother, who had spun the car on this very bridge so the driver's side would take the brunt of the impact, protecting Lucky.

Cora opened her eyes. Tears still streamed down her cheeks, mixing with the rain, but she knew she had no choice. If her friends were still alive, they needed her. In their own ways, they had each made sacrifices for her.

She heard more metal twisting behind her, but she forced herself not to turn around. She didn't want to see the storm tearing the rest of the chamber apart. She didn't want to know how bad it was.

She looked down at the rushing water.

"I'm scared—," she whispered to no one, her voice cracking. "I don't want to die."

Another sob slipped from her throat as her fingers loosened their hold on the lamppost. The rain fell harder, streaking her face, washing her tears away. She didn't want it to end like this. Maybe sacrificing herself in this way was noble, but it didn't feel noble—it felt terrifying, sickening, so very final.

She cried harder. Time seemed to telescope, and she was back on that bridge two and a half years ago, watching herself and her father fall into the water. She saw herself pounding on the closed car window. The slack look of shock on her father's face. And then him reaching out to her and holding her close as the car slammed into the river.

"This is my choice," she whispered. "My life."

And then one foot was off the bridge. More twisting metal squealed behind her. Wind from the storm pushed at her back. The illusionary night sky flickered once, then twice, showing nothing behind it but a grid on the wall before returning to the illusion.

The Gauntlet wouldn't last much longer.

It had to be now.

Now.

She jumped.

She suddenly felt no guardrail beneath her, no lamppost at her hand. Falling happened faster than she remembered from that night in the storm, the rushing water coming up at her so quickly, her stomach flying up to her throat and crawling out of her in a scream.

She hit the water.

The impact jarred her to the bone. At first she thought it had knocked the breath out of her, but then she realized she was gulping water. The river current was strong, dragging her down fast. Without the protection of the car, she was being swept straight into an eddy. A scream hurtled up her throat, erupting in bubbles. Time seemed to blur again and suddenly she was back in the ocean habitat in the cage, swimming hard against the current with Mali and Lucky and Leon. Down, down, toward the exit that she knew must be there, deep beneath the water. The exit that Cassian had promised her existed when he'd stood in the surf and kissed her.

Her eyes blurred with salt water—no, tears. She was in the river, not the ocean. The water was so very cold, colder than she had ever felt in her life, and felt impossibly thick. Her limbs were moving slower now. Her lungs screamed for air that wasn't there, and she felt so heavy, as though she'd swallowed a hundred gallons of water.

This was it.

She was really going to die.

A haziness filled Cora's vision as her arms slowed, then drifted to a stop. She let the current drag her down farther. She didn't seem to feel the cold anymore. Her lungs were at peace. Her thoughts sank deeper into the blackness of her memory. But this far into her mind—this deep—a tiny light shone. A flickering image like an old movie projector. It showed the big oak tree that she and her brother used to climb when they were little. *Happy shrieks of children finding a nest of wrens. Looking up at the sky through the branches. Charlie helping her jump down.*

With her final breath, she cried out.

"Charlie!"

She remembered. Deep down, her memories were still there. In her heart, she had never lost her family at all.

44

Mali

WIND WHIPPED THROUGH THE ruins of the Gauntlet's control rooms. Mali hunkered close to the wall of the recess room, her braids flying around her head. The other captives shifted anxiously as the last remaining support structures groaned precariously.

"This place isn't going to last much longer!" she called to Leon, cupping her hands around her mouth so the wind wouldn't tear her words away.

He jerked his thumb toward the Axion standing guard in the doorway. "Tell that to the guys with the guns."

Willa rested her hand on Mali's other arm, pointing toward the monitor, which was flickering between static and displays of the coded symbols. Willa shaped a few gestures with her fingers. Mali hadn't ever officially studied sign language, but over the years, trapped in different enclosures and cages with a variety of species that couldn't always speak the same language, she had picked up the basics. She recognized several of Willa's signs.

Axion. Storm. Clever. Watch screens.

Mali nodded. "I understand." She twisted toward Leon to translate. "Willa says the Axion aren't stupid—they know this place is about to go but don't want to leave until they're certain Cora has lost. That monitor is still showing some scrolling symbols, which means Cora's still in the puzzles. It isn't over. They're still trying to get into the chambers."

Willa's hand clenched harder on Mali's arm. Mali turned around with a questioning look. The chimp's wide eyes were riveted to the screen.

Serassi's eyes were on the screen too. "Fascinating," she said.

"What is it?" Mali asked, feeling a fresh twinge of panic. "Can you read it?"

"Yes." Serassi spoke in a hushed voice, eyes shifting nervously to the closest Axion guard, whose back was turned. "The storm is causing bad fluctuation, but I can make out most of it." Suddenly the corners of her mouth dipped in a smile. "Cora's made it to puzzle twelve."

Mali clamped her hand over Willa's, crying out with relief.

"That girl's a fighter, for sure," Leon said incredulously.

Mali squinted in the wind, trying to see through the doorway to the central vestibule. "It looks as though the monitors in the main room have all shorted out completely. I do not think the Axion know the extent of her progress."

The main support beam groaned again. Even the Axion guard looked over his shoulder to give it a nervous stare.

"What about Cassian?" Mali asked quickly.

"The coding reports that Cora is alone in the puzzle," Serassi said, keeping her voice low. Her brow furrowed as she tried to interpret the scattering of symbols on the screen. "It doesn't mean he's dead. The Gauntlet has been separating them and putting them together at random intervals. If he is in a different part of the Gauntlet, the monitor won't register that, since it is only following Cora's progress."

Leon eyed the groaning beam. "She'd better solve that last puzzle fast. . . ."

"Wait," Serassi said, focused intently on the screen. "There is new information. It is difficult to read, with the distortion. It seems Cora is in some sort of Earth-like scenario. I can read the symbol for trees. A road."

"That could be anywhere back home," Leon said.

"I'm trying to read more," Serassi said tersely. "The puzzle has the coding for the color red. Red means a morality puzzle."

"She's good at those," Mali said, hope in her voice. "It's the intellectual and perceptive puzzles that give her the most trouble, but she must have already passed those. She's been reading Lucky's journal as a moral guide." Mali swallowed, squeezing Willa's hand in her own and Leon's in the other. She couldn't tear her eyes off the screen, though the symbols meant nothing to her.

You can do it, Cora. Think of Lucky.

Serassi continued to focus on the screen. "Now I am reading the symbol for water. It's distorted. I can't quite make out more details. Rain, I believe."

"It's simulating somewhere back on Earth, with trees and a road and rain," Leon said. "And it's moral? What's she supposed to do, stop a flash flood or something?"

"Wait—another water symbol," Serassi said. "A river. There is distance between Cora and the water. She's above it. She's—"

Serassi's face went suddenly slack.

A dark premonition took hold of Mali. "What happened?" She grabbed Serassi, shaking her. "What about a river?"

"It's Cora," Serassi muttered, her eyes wide. "She . . . fell. She fell into the water below. It happened just now. The symbols are going crazy. They're coming so fast." Serassi swung her head around, meeting Mali's gaze directly. "She . . . she's dead. Drowned."

Mali's hand froze on her arm. Suddenly the wind didn't seem as loud. The puddles didn't feel as cold against her feet. She felt the blood draining from her extremities in a way that made her dizzy.

"She lost," Serassi stated.

An awful numbness spread through Mali's body. "No," she whispered.

She sank back against the wall, stunned.

She didn't know which piece of information was harder to process—that Cora was dead or that she had lost. Cora had been their last hope, and she'd gotten so far. They had traveled the galaxy to be here. They had learned to achieve things no human had before. They had fought their way to the very end of the Gauntlet.

She pressed her hand against her mouth, silencing a sob.

Willa started making a strange huffing noise that Mali thought might be how she expressed her grief. She glanced toward the Axion guard, but with the chaos from the storm, he hadn't heard their exclamations.

"Hey . . ." Leon pulled her into his arms, holding her tight. "Listen, she died for a cause. We're still here. We'll still fight, however we can. We won't go down easy."

But even despite Leon's reassurances, a blackness had appeared in Mali's chest. She heard Leon's words as only hollow sounds. Fighting was useless. They'd already fought and lost. They'd be enslaved now, not just humans but all the species, or else slaughtered. She stared at her hands, at the scars, and started shaking with anger. She had promised herself never to be a victim again. And yet here she was. Her fingers started trembling harder, tingling even. She shook them, thinking it must be the cold. But they tingled in a way that felt . . . strange.

She pulled away from Leon, looking down at her hands.

Why did they feel so different? Like energy was pooling in her fingertips. That energy spread into her palms and up her arms. She didn't dare touch Leon, fearing the energy, like he might shatter into dust if she touched him.

"I feel odd," she said.

Leon started knitting his fingers too, as though they were spasming. "It must be the cold," he said. "And the shock of . . ." He nodded toward the monitor that had reported Cora's death.

But the feeling was now spreading throughout Mali's body faster. She felt suddenly ten pounds lighter, as though she were barely even sitting on the ground anymore. It was a mix of euphoria and confidence so powerful it was almost scary. The sensation crept up her spine, her neck, into her head. A starburst of electricity radiated through her brain, and she gasped and clutched at a piece of the shattered wall.

"Mali, look!" Leon pointed to Mali's hand.

Mali glanced down at the piece of wall beneath her fingers. It was made of something strong, like steel. The power of the storm, even of the bomb, had only barely managed to dent it. And yet the portion in her hand was crumpled like a ball of paper.

She whipped her hand back.

"How'd you do that?" Leon said. "You bent metal!"

At the same time, Serassi's head slowly tilted up. Her hair hung in messy waves by her ears, but there was a different look on her face. One not of despair but of wonder. Serassi knit her fingers against the back of her skull, eyes wide. "Impossible . . ."

"You feel it too, don't you?" Mali said.

"What?" Leon asked in alarm. "What's going on? Why are my hands all tingly?"

"Because it's happening," Serassi said, her voice shaking. "The evolutionary jump. It's happening. It's strongest with me and Mali because our perceptive abilities are already honed, but it's starting with you too, Leon. It'll take more time with you and the others, but it's happening. You feel different, don't you?"

He looked uncomfortably at his hands. "Kind of strong. Like I downed an energy drink."

"Just wait," Serassi said, and then her face broke into a smile. "It will grow. It will spread. First humans will feel stronger physically, as you two are already experiencing. Be capable of running faster, greater strength. Then greater intelligence will come. A more sophisticated moral sensibility. Then, in time, perceptive powers will develop. Don't you see?"

She looked among them all. "It worked. The Gauntlet. I

don't know how Cora did it, but it worked." She glanced at the symbols scrolling across the screen, lips moving silently as she tried to piece it together. "If she had failed, the stock algorithm would have stopped broadcasting those scrolling symbols, but they're still going. Ah! I see my mistake now. I thought the symbol meant *fall*, but it didn't. It meant *jump*. Cora jumped intentionally. She . . . she sacrificed herself symbolically. She won the moral puzzle. She won the Gauntlet."

Mali gasped. *Cora won.*

Mali could barely process such a revolutionary concept, except that her mind seemed to be working faster than it ever had before. She scrolled quickly through what this meant—that the tingle in her fingers was the evolutionary jump. That she was one of the first humans it would happen to, and soon she'd be more perceptive, smarter, stronger.

But . . .

"But she's still gone?" Mali asked.

Serassi must have heard the uncertain tone in her voice. "I'm afraid so. The screen is very clear about the *death* symbol." She paused. "But she didn't die for nothing."

Mali felt dizzy again. Cora had won, but at such a heavy price. She glanced at the Axion guarding the door. His back was still turned. He hadn't seen the information on the monitor, and neither had any other Axion, judging by the repetitive thunking in the central vestibule as his colleagues still tried to break into the portal door, not knowing that it was futile now. Not knowing the Gauntlet was already over.

"Serassi, if you're experiencing the evolutionary jump too, if you're stronger, do you think you can free us?" Mali whispered.

Serassi smiled in cold determination. She stood, stalking silently toward the Axion guard. She ran her fingers through her loose hair, twisting it back into a fresh knot, looking even more powerful and deadly than she always had.

The other captured Kindred along the opposite wall were all glancing at one another, and if Mali had to guess, they were exchanging psychic messages.

"I don't get it," Leon whispered. "What's going on?"

"Watch," Mali said. "And wait."

Mali's heart thumped hard as Serassi moved behind the guard. The guard heard her a second before she attacked and he turned, but Serassi moved impossibly fast, knitting her fingers in the air as Anya had done. The Axion went rigid. Serassi continued to move her fingers. The Axion started moving in a swaying way, no longer in control of his own body. He took a swaying step toward the rear of the room, toward the wall that had been torn off. Then another. The captives moved back, letting him pass. Serassi guided him all the way to the end of the room, where the floor abruptly ended in a twenty-foot drop into twisting, sharp wreckage.

The Axion stepped off and fell to his death.

Serassi turned, staring at her hands. "I've never been able to do that before. Take control of another's mind and command their body. The evolutionary jump worked." She looked at the other Kindred prisoners with a steady gaze that meant they were exchanging messages telepathically. Almost as one, the other Kindred stood.

"You must still be quiet," Mali said. "The Axion will hear you."

"Let them." Serassi glanced over her shoulder as the Kindred prisoners strode purposefully toward the door. "We're done being captives. They aren't stronger than us anymore, and they're about to feel justice."

The Kindred started spilling out into the central vestibule. Redrage joined them, and even the Gatherer prisoner. Leon grabbed Mali, holding her back, but he needn't have bothered. She was too stunned by all this information, and the sensation in her body, to be able to fight yet. Was this happening to all humans, everywhere? To Nok and Rolf on Armstrong? Even to the ones back on Earth? They stopped at the door, watching as the surprised Axion tried to defend themselves from the Kindred.

The battle happened fast.

The Kindred were not vindictive. They were not bloodthirsty or after revenge. They were simply cold and efficient as they and their Mosca and Gatherer compatriots dispatched every Axion traitor in the room.

Throats sliced.

Skulls crushed through telekinesis.

"You know what this means," Leon said. "This means the same thing is happening throughout the galaxy. To all the planets and stations with humans and Kindred on them. The Axion won't last long." He wrapped an arm around Mali's waist. "It means we're free now. We can go to Theta and get Anya back!"

She thought of Anya—the real Anya. She'd finally be able to repay her friend for all the times Anya had saved her life. And even better, she'd be with Leon. Together they'd rescue Anya, just as they'd freed Cassian. She smiled, thinking of being trapped in the shuttle's lining with him, pressed so close. How she'd been so hesitant to trust him—to trust anyone.

Not anymore.

He leaned forward and pressed a kiss to her forehead. "Wherever we go, we'll go there together. I promise."

And she believed him. "We could go back to our solar system. Learn if Earth is still there," she said.

Leon looked down at her. The storm was making the structure shake violently, but Mali felt as though they were tucked away in some other place: the calm eye of the storm. She and Leon. And now there was a real future for them, where she might be able to find her family and return to the desert where she'd been born.

She laughed.

"What?" he asked.

"Despite your best efforts," she said, "you couldn't avoid being a hero."

He rolled his eyes, but the corners of his mouth curled upward. "Keep that to yourself."

They watched from the recess room as the Kindred soldiers dispatched the last of the Axion with deadly precision. Mali flexed her fingers. She had transformed into something new: a new type of human, one more capable and, she hoped, wiser.

"Everything is working out," she said, but felt that pang of darkness. "Except Cora isn't here."

Leon hugged her close, rubbing a hand down her back. He didn't need to offer reassuring words; they could feel each other's sadness and gratitude for Cora's sacrifice. No matter how much Mali knew Cora had done something world changing, she couldn't shake her sadness.

"I can't believe she's gone." She let out a sob. And then more.

She'd cried so rarely. Was this what it meant to be human? To feel such sorrow?

Leon kept rubbing her back as she rested her forehead against his chest. Then his hand stopped, and she felt his breathing go still as footsteps approached.

Mali jerked upright, wiping away the tears.

Cassian stood in the ruins of the central vestibule.

Blood streaked down one of his arms. His fingers were shredded as though he'd climbed out of the jagged wreckage of the puzzle chambers with his bare hands. The lines of his face were heavy with exhaustion, but there was determination written there too, along with a sheen in his eyes—the evolutionary jump.

"Cassian, you're alive!" she said.

He gave a single nod. "Come with me. This isn't over yet."

Mali frowned as she and Leon pushed to their feet. "You mean the battle?"

"The battle will continue until the Axion are defeated—but in the meantime, we have something just as important to do."

Cassian motioned for them to follow him as he stepped over the uneven floor. His movements were quick, anxious. Mali scrambled behind him as he led them through the devastation of the central vestibule, toward the place where the portal door had once been. Now it was broken, crumpled in on itself, the opening crunched to only a foot high. Cassian dropped down to his stomach to crawl through.

"We're going into the puzzle chambers?" Mali asked in alarm.

"Yes, and we must hurry," Cassian said, "before the storm does any more damage." He was already crawling through the narrow space. His head disappeared into the chamber, then his torso, then his feet. Mali glanced at Leon.

He shrugged and dropped to his stomach.

They followed Cassian through the damaged portal door. Mali's heartbeat thumped as she spilled out into a room with gridlike panels on the walls, the ceiling halfway torn off, lights flickering. Her breath stilled. She knew the puzzles were over. Yet for years she'd heard rumors about the Gauntlet, and she still expected some shocking illusion to appear at any moment.

"We're going after Cora, aren't we?" she asked.

Cassian nodded. "This way."

"But she's dead. Serassi saw it on the monitors. It was real. It had to be or else the evolutionary jump wouldn't have happened."

"It was real," Cassian confirmed as they climbed through a maze of identical chambers, each one more devastated than the last. The wreckage sliced Mali's hands, bruising her knees as they dropped down from trapdoors and crawled through broken wall seams. Sparks snapped and popped as the storm continued to rage outside. "Cora did sacrifice herself," he continued, moving quickly to try to beat the storm. "She fully believed that she would die when she jumped, which is what the morality puzzle required."

He shuffled through a torn wall seam, then dropped to his knees, leaning over something on the floor. Mali and Leon pushed their way through the seam behind him, spilling out into another wrecked puzzle chamber. Mali froze.

"Cora," she breathed.

Cassian was leaning over Cora's body. She lay in a puddle of dark liquid that was slowly draining from the cracks in the chamber's floor. Her blond hair, soaked, clung to her pale skin. Her Gauntleteer uniform was tangled around her lifeless limbs. She wasn't breathing.

Mali looked away with a quick inhale.

"It's okay," Leon said, rubbing her shoulder. "She knew what she was doing. It was her choice."

Hesitantly, Mali glanced back at Cora's body. Cassian was lifting each of her eyelids, then feeling along her skull as though to check for broken bones. His movements were quick, anxious.

Mali frowned. "She's dead, Cassian. She isn't breathing."

Cassian parted Cora's teeth to look inside her mouth, then quickly picked her up in his arms, carrying her back to the broken wall seam. "You are correct," he said. "She is not breathing." He squeezed through the wall seam with Cora's body and then hurried back through the course they had taken through the Gauntlet wreckage. "But it doesn't mean she's dead."

Mali drew in a sharp breath as she ducked under a fallen beam. "She's *alive*? How?"

But the storm had made another beam fall, blocking their path. Cassian changed course and plunged into another chamber, then stepped carefully over a shattered wall panel and bent down to open a trapdoor in the floor.

It revealed a dark pit.

This was not part of the official module.

He grabbed a few sets of goggles hanging from a hook. "Put these on so you can see." He pulled one pair over his own eyes and then climbed into the pit. Mali and Leon hurried to do the same. The temperature was cool. Storm water made the stone walls slick, but the floor was well trodden.

A cave.

When she came around the corner, unused to the red tint that the Mosca goggles gave everything, she stopped.

A small cavern had been converted into a makeshift medical room, with a bed and beeping equipment. Cassian laid out Cora's body on the bed and began hooking up the equipment, affixing sensors to Cora's arms, pressing a tube into her throat. Thick blue liquid started to flow out of the tube.

Slowly—impossibly—Cora's chest rose and fell.

Mali ran to the bed.

"What is this? How is this possible?"

The anxious set to Cassian's expression eased. He leaned over the bed, blood still trickling down his arm, and rested a gentle hand on Cora's forehead. Her chest rose in another breath.

He looked at Mali and gave a weary smile.

"Cora taught me how to cheat," he explained. "And I paid very close attention."

45

Cora

HER LUNGS WERE THICK with water. An icy blackness coated her skin. Her memories were hazy, but she remembered sinking deep into the swollen river. A sense of peace had surrounded her as she'd melted into the dark muck of the riverbed. But now she didn't feel peaceful at all. Now her lungs burned as though someone had clawed them with jagged fingernails. Her head throbbed, and her entire body felt violently, painfully alert.

Was *this* dying? This awful, terrifying, electrifying pain?

She awoke with a gasp. Air flooded into her nose, rushed down her irritated throat, and coated her screaming lungs. She sucked in another breath, and another, greedily, as though she weren't sure she'd ever have enough air. The pain was so acute she nearly blacked out. She tried to sit up, only to have a wave of dizziness knock her back against the pillow.

She cracked her eyes open, but a golden sort of light stung them, and she recoiled. She tried again gradually, blinking hard.

There was a soft humming in the room, maybe a radio or a juke-box, she couldn't be sure. Her vision was swimming as she tried to take in the blurry shapes in the room. She blinked harder. The walls were brown. Wood. A dirty window let in mottled sunlight.

A baby suddenly wailed.

She jerked her head around as the humming stopped. The movement drew the attention of someone sitting in a rocking chair by the window, cradling a baby.

"You're awake!" Nok pushed out of the rocking chair, clutch-ing the baby to her chest as she came to the side of the bed.

Cora stared at Nok as though she were a ghost: there were dark circles under her eyes and a listlessness to her skin, as though she'd been ill too.

"Nok?" Cora's voice was creaky with disuse. "What . . . what happened?"

"We're on Armstrong. You're safe." Nok clutched the baby tighter. "You've been unconscious for almost two weeks. Cassian says that's a normal recovery period when it comes to ingested sta-sis fluid."

Ingested stasis fluid? Recovery period?

Cora tried to sit up. "Where's Cassian? Where's Mali?" Her eyes fell on the baby as she realized with relief that Nok must have given birth safely. "And Rolf?"

Nok's eyes, heavy and dark, started to rim in red. She blinked a few times, struggling against tears. Cora leaned forward, worried. "Nok?"

"Rolf . . . he . . ." Nok swallowed, stumbling over her words. "Rolf protected all of us. He left plans to rebuild this whole town. We owe him so much. . . ."

Cora's breath stalled. "Why are you talking about him like that?"

"He's gone," Nok choked out. "He crawled into the transport hub's reactor core to shut off power so the Axion couldn't blow up the town. He . . . he died. Once the power was off long enough and the radiation levels lowered, Keena sent some guards in there to get his body—she's been sick too, but she's getting better. We buried him yesterday. In the valley by the river."

Cora drew in a sharp breath. *Oh, no.* Now the dark circles under Nok's eyes made sense. Nok *had* been ill. Her heart had broken irreparably.

Cora swallowed back her own grief. "Oh, Nok. I'm so . . . I'm so sorry." She reached out, catching Nok's wrist, pulling both Nok and her baby into a hug. Nok didn't try to hold back tears. She shook with sobs as Cora squeezed her shoulders, fighting an urge to sob herself.

The baby started wailing.

Nok pulled back, patting the baby's back gently, wiping away her tears. "I gave birth to Sparrow a few days ago. She came early, but she's a fighter. Like her father. Anyway, I'd better get Cassian. He asked me to tell him the minute you woke." She paused at the door. "I'm glad you're okay, Cora. Rolf would have been, too."

Cora nodded her thanks.

Alone, Cora stared at the ceiling, groggy, trying to process it all. *Rolf was gone.* The pain in her head was gradually dulling, but it still throbbed hard enough that she felt she might pass out again. Her lips were dry, and she looked around for water, dimly taking in a wooden table next to the bed; but when she felt for water or a bottle, her hand only grazed paper. A journal. Lucky's journal.

Someone must have found it and saved it for her.

She forced herself to sit up, rearranging the pillows to form a backrest. She touched her sleeve. She was wearing a soft cotton shirt that went down to her knees and was draped in a cozy felt blanket. The wooden walls looked like they belonged in a cabin or hut, but everything was clean, and there was a fresh smell of new paint.

She heard faint voices outside. The sunlight was too bright to look directly through the window, but she thought she saw dusty red ground, maybe the hazy shapes of other cabins or huts, and some people moving.

The door opened again.

Cassian took one look at Cora and sank onto the edge of her bed, reaching out to run a hand through her hair.

"You're awake."

"Cassian." She squeezed her eyes closed again but reached out to hold on to him, needing to feel him. "I heard about Rolf."

"Yes. He died a hero."

She took a deep breath. "And . . . and I don't understand. *I* died, too. I remember."

He shook his head. "You only thought you did. You had to believe you were truly sacrificing yourself in order for the Gauntlet to register it. But you're crazy if you thought I would let you die."

She squinted at him in incomprehension.

"The river," he said. "It wasn't water. It was a stasis fluid that is breathable to humans, like amniotic fluid. Though it usually results in a partial shutdown of secondary biological systems, which is why you lost consciousness for so long. Your body had to purge all the stasis fluid and learn to breathe air again."

She pressed a hand to the base of her scratchy throat, thinking of that impossibly heavy feeling in her lungs, how the water had felt too thick, too solid. "But . . . how?"

"Bonebreak and Ironmage. They weren't about to let you die, not when their trading rights were on the line. They made the bargain with you, and they were afraid if you died, no one else would uphold it. So they bribed the Mosca Chief Assessor to change the settings on the Gauntlet. They couldn't influence the stock algorithm or its puzzles, but they could tweak the raw materials it had to work with. We knew the Gauntlet often pits runners against their nightmares, and I knew water was one of your greatest fears. So they swapped out the water supply it used with stasis fluid, and ensured the Gauntlet would be positioned over a cavern they could use to revive you in secret." He paused. "Unfortunately, neither of them survived to see their plan work. I went through with it on my own."

"You mean you cheated." She stared at him. "But the Kindred don't cheat."

He smiled. "I had a good teacher. She showed me that there's a place for cheating. That sometimes cheating is necessary."

She started to feel a twinge of panic. "But if I won by cheating, if I didn't really sacrifice myself, then it didn't work. . . ."

He stroked her hair, calming her down. "*You* didn't cheat. I did. You still won." He took her hand carefully, rubbing some life back into her fingers. "Don't you feel it? The evolutionary jump?"

She stared at his hands on hers, and she *did* feel a twinge of something different. She felt as though she had greater control over her movements. As though her hand had twice the number of nerves, twice the muscle. In a way, it was similar to the paragon burst: as though she had enhanced strength. And yet she didn't feel the echo of other humans' DNA any longer, boosting her own. This extra strength was all hers.

"And the Axion?"

"Kindred troops are still fighting them in the farthest provinces. Most of the immediate battlegrounds have been reclaimed. Station 10-91. And here, on Armstrong. Nok said the fighting was bad. They lost a lot of people at first. They would have lost everyone if Rolf hadn't shut down the reactor core they were targeting."

She took a deep breath.

Cassian nodded quietly. "The damage is great everywhere. It will take years to rebuild everything, and to establish a new system to govern the reality that the evolutionary jump triggered. The Kindred are more powerful now, and that makes the Mosca and the Gatherers nervous. We must decide how to balance our power fairly and, of course, determine what to do with the Axion. And then there are humans. You're an intelligent species now. The Intelligence Council made it official when the stock algorithm declared you the winner of the Gauntlet."

He looked to the window, and she followed his gaze. Her vision was clearing, and she could now make out some of the figures. There were Mali and Leon, standing in the town square outside, working on rebuilding the sheriff's office, which must have been damaged. Willa was there, too. And then Anya skipped up to join them.

Cora sat straighter. "Anya! You found her?"

Cassian nodded. "Mali and Leon brought her back from Fuel Station Theta. It turns out, perhaps unsurprisingly, she had already managed to free herself. They found her trying to rewire a shuttle. Another few days, and she would have escaped on her own."

Cora smiled. She felt, for the first time in a long time, a flicker of hope.

Cassian took her hand. "When you are ready, there are many people who want to see you."

46

Cora

IT WAS A WARM afternoon on Armstrong, three days after she'd regained consciousness, when Cora was finally strong enough to get out of bed. Her lungs still burned whenever she took too deep a breath, but as soon as she stepped through the doorway into the breeze, she felt renewed.

She looked down at the paper in her hand. Cassian had printed out the stock algorithm's file on her that contained the basic facts about her life on Earth.

> *Name: Cora Mason. Age: 17. Birthplace: Richmond, Virginia. Last known Earth location: 39.0276° N, 83.9197° W. Intelligence per human IQ: 126. Unique talents: Gifted at vocals and song construction.*

Most of her previous life was still a haze or else blackness entirely—but slowly, like single frames in a movie, memories were coming back one by one.

Charlie.

Sadie.

An oak tree outside her bedroom window.

Nok saw her in the doorway and came over, balancing her baby on her hip. "Ready for the tour? I'll show you the renovated town first." The sheriff's badge hung around her neck, glistening in the sunlight. "We renamed the town. The moon is still called Armstrong, but it isn't a preserve anymore. We're free to govern ourselves now, no Intelligence Council oversight. We've named this place New London." She gave a guilty smile as they strode into the town square. "We should have put it to a vote, maybe, but I was partial to the name, since London was where both Rolf and I lived before coming here."

"I thought Rolf didn't like London," Cora said, shading her eyes from the sun. She had to move slowly, her muscles still weak.

"He didn't. Which is why the name is perfect. *New* London. A new start. That's his legacy." She wore a look of pride, mixed with grief, as she gazed out over her town. Her fingers touched the smooth metal of the sheriff's badge. "I decided I'm going to keep my title. *Mother Sheriff*, that's what they've started calling me. The people here are excited to have a baby around, and with Rolf gone, everyone's pitched in to help me with her. It feels like a family. Keena's getting stronger each day, and even from the hospital she's teaching me how to work with the governance council. We've modified the role of sheriff. It isn't a dictatorship anymore." Nok smiled as Sparrow gripped the badge, getting her sticky fingerprints all over it. "It's a position of spiritual leadership. Of guidance. Of family."

She smiled proudly.

And there was much to be proud of, Cora realized. The artificial village they had first stumbled upon had seemed so idyllic at first glance, until they had realized that the outdated posters and fake flowers meant it was only a sham. But now real flowers adorned each freshly painted building. A carpenter's workshop had been set up at the far end of town to make repairs to all the buildings and expand the town to accommodate its several hundred residents. Men and women of all ages worked together, as the sound of saws and hammers filled the air, along with the murmurs of chatting in the distance. She caught sight of someone waving from the roof of a schoolhouse and shaded her eyes.

"Is that . . . Makayla?"

Makayla waved harder. She was perched on the shingles, hammer in hand, with a big grin on her face. Jenny and Christopher looked up from the other side of the roof, waving as well.

"It's the kids from the Hunt," Cora said incredulously.

"Oh, yeah," Nok said. "They've been a huge help around here. You can catch up with them tonight at the party . . . hang on. Hold Sparrow for a minute. I have a surprise for you."

Before Cora could object, Nok hoisted the baby into Cora's arms and turned to one of the faded posters advertising a town square dance that had never happened. Cora looked down at the baby in her arms. She had Nok's dark hair and Rolf's small mouth. As the baby yawned, Cora felt a thrill for Nok and everything she and Rolf had done to change Armstrong to a proper colony. Humanity's first colony. And Sparrow was the first human born there.

Nok ripped off the old poster, then unrolled another paper and hammered it to the post, stepping back to admire her work.

"About time we had a real celebration," Nok said. "I've been staring at those fake old posters for so long." She paused, her face growing serious. "It's been so hard without Rolf. I'm glad we finally have something to celebrate." She took Sparrow back, cooing to the baby. "Come on. You've got to see the farm we're building to hold all the animals from the menagerie."

Nok walked her through the settlement, explaining the governance system they had established. The evolutionary jump hadn't happened instantaneously, as Serassi had warned, and some of New London's residents were experiencing it sooner than others and struggling to deal with the changing sensations of increased intuition and enhanced strength. So Nok had set up volunteer counselors to help them cope, a sort of mentor program. When they reached the mines, Nok explained how Rolf had envisioned Armstrong mining with machines, not human labor, but the explanations were so technical Cora only shook her head. Even with the evolutionary jump, she wasn't smart enough to understand Rolf's logic.

"These people are lucky to have you," Cora said.

"We have big plans for this place," Nok added as she turned toward the horizon. "There are more resources than Ellis ever made use of, trees and minerals, that we have plans to extract sustainably. We have a chance here to do something Earth can't: start over without the shadow of the Industrial Revolution, without pollution or environmental degradation. Generations from now, when Sparrow's grandchildren have spread as far as those mountains in the distance, this planet will be just as well cared for as it is now."

Cora caught the message in Nok's words, though Nok hadn't

spoken it outright: even with Rolf's death, Nok hadn't changed her mind about Earth. She wasn't going back. And though it filled Cora with a sadness to think of her friend so far away, she was proud of Nok.

"You'll do a good job here," Cora said. "Sparrow will grow up well."

Cassian appeared in the distance, crossing the desert toward the mining operation. Cora gave Nok a long hug and then turned and met him halfway, where the afternoon sun cast their shadows across the sand.

"You shouldn't overtax yourself," Cassian said. "You're still weak."

"I'm feeling better. You forget that the evolutionary jump makes us stronger. Heal faster, too." Cora glanced back at the mine. "They've done so much good here. It's heartening to see."

They headed slowly back toward town.

"Armstrong is fortunate to have good leadership," Cassian said. "Not all of the colonies have been so blessed. Even with the five intelligent species working together, it will be a long time before the universe returns to a stable system of governance."

Cora interlaced her fingers with his as they walked. The spark tickled her palm, making her smile. She'd come to expect it, crave it even. A reminder of their connection. She squeezed his hand, but then her smile wavered. How much longer would she feel that spark? Now that the Gauntlet was over, what future would the two of them have?

"Is everything okay?" he asked.

She nodded quickly. "It's . . . nothing. I've been meaning to ask, how's Willa?"

"Recovering. She was hurt badly in the fight."

"I was thinking about her," Cora said, "and about the lesser species. It's good that humanity has been elevated, but I still worry for the animals' welfare."

"Animals would never pass the Gauntlet," Cassian said. "They aren't equipped to govern themselves. They aren't all advanced like Willa."

"I know, but they deserve proper care and better oversight than they had before. Even among the Kindred, they were never treated as they deserve to be."

"What do you suggest?"

"I was thinking of an honorary delegate to the Intelligence Council. Not a sixth representative, but a corollary one to advocate for the rights of animals and all the lesser species. Sort of like what Nok does here, consulting with the governance council in her new role as sheriff. Willa is perfect for a similar role with the Intelligence Council. She's an animal, so she understands their needs, but she can articulate and reason."

Cassian nodded thoughtfully. "I'll pass that idea along to the other delegates in our next meeting."

While Cora had still been unconscious, Cassian had been appointed the new Kindred delegate to the Intelligence Council. A new Gatherer delegate had also been appointed, since Brother Magga had died in the battle. There was even a nonvoting Axion delegate, who had no official power but was still a representative.

"There's something else we discussed in our last meeting," Cassian said, slightly hesitant. "The fifth seat on the Intelligence Council. It belongs to humans, and it's vacant. Naturally, you're the first person the other delegates suggested. As winner of the Gauntlet, it's your right."

Cora couldn't say it came as a complete surprise. Willa had told her long ago that if she won she'd be a natural leader among humans, something she wasn't certain she had wanted at the time.

"What do you think?" she asked.

He smiled. "I'd like nothing better than to be at your side, helping establish humanity in the proper position it should hold."

The sun had started to set, and the air grew drastically cooler. Cora hugged her arms around her jacket, studying the sandy path. They were almost back in New London. The sound of saws and hammers had stopped for the day, and she smelled the sizzle of marron root and roast sand-rabbit, as well as the sounds of soft chatter.

"Wait," she said, stopping outside town.

He turned back.

She took his hand again. The spark leaped between them, warming her heart.

"I can't be the delegate," she confessed. "I've never been a natural leader, not really. The Gauntlet was one thing, but sitting around a table, negotiating trade deals and voting on rules . . . it isn't me." She took a deep breath. "I read my file in the stock algorithm. I still don't remember all my life at home, but I know the facts. My father was a senator. I guess that should mean I would be good at politics, but I don't have any passion for it. You need someone who cares deeply about fairness for the species, who's clever when it comes to that kind of thing. Who *remembers* home."

"It sounds like you have someone in mind."

"I do. Anya. She's young, I know, but before the Axion captured her, she was able to do incredible things. Stir human uprisings. Inspire humanity. *The wolves are strong, but the rabbits are clever.*" Cora smiled. "And she won't be alone. Other humans can coach her until she's ready to govern from the Intelligence Council. Keena has already agreed to help mentor her. And there's something else." She reached into her pocket and took out Lucky's journal. "This will help, too. Between these pages is everything Anya needs to know about what makes for a good, fair mind when she grows up."

She handed him the journal, letting it go almost reluctantly. But Lucky's words were already seared into her mind and her heart.

"And you?" Cassian asked quietly. "What will you do, if not sit on the Council?"

She squeezed his hand harder. The spark ignited her palm, warming it, making her think of all the things they had been through together.

Cora glanced toward the setting sun, watching the final sliver disappear behind the high mountains. The first stars were appearing in the purple-black sky overhead, and she felt their pull.

She took a deep breath. Held his other hand too. The spark between their clasped hands traveled back and forth, one heart to the other.

What future was there for them?

Cora wasn't sure. But she knew, in her heart, where she had to be.

"I'm going home. Back to Earth."

"You are so certain it is still there?"

She squeezed his hands. "I know it is."

47

Cora

"IF I NEVER RIDE on another spaceship," Leon said, "it'll be too soon."

Cora rolled her eyes as she took a seat opposite him and cinched the buckle. The ship rumbled to life sooner than she'd expected, and she shot out a hand, grabbing hold of Mali's.

"Fine," she admitted to Leon. "I see what you mean."

The music and laughter from Armstrong's Independence Day party still rang in her ears. Through the ship's view screen she could see New London shrouded in solar lights, filled with dancing couples and groups of people laughing. It had been nearly impossible to say good-bye.

"You know we'll never see each other again," Nok had said.

"Give humanity a few years," Cora had answered. "Once the evolutionary jump fully settles and we're all even more brilliant, we'll have built a teleporter, I'm sure." They had embraced as hard as the first day they'd met, both scared and clinging to each other in the face of a confusing new world. Then Cora had kissed Sparrow on the forehead and said her good-byes to Willa and the kids from the Hunt before boarding the ship.

Now, it felt unnaturally quiet with only Mali and Leon in the passenger hold, especially as the two of them whispered to each other about plans for their lives on Earth, Leon extolling the virtues of cheeseburgers and cold soda, Mali asking him to teach her more curse words. Cora had imagined there would be so many more of them to make this journey back home. Lucky. Nok. Rolf. Makayla and Shoukry and the others. Cassian had explained that eventually, the Kindred would return the animals to Earth and any human wards who wanted to go back. But they were too malnourished now to make the trip, and besides, they had to verify Earth still existed. It would be this first, exploratory trip back—Cora's trip—that would prove it did.

After the shuttle leveled off, Cora unbuckled and climbed to the front. She sat in the empty copilot's chair next to Cassian.

She glanced at him from the corner of her eye. They hadn't spoken much about what would happen next. Their talk had stuck carefully to the logistics of the trip, the probability of Earth's existence, the possibility that the evolutionary jump had already spread to Earth humans. No words had been exchanged about what Cora's decision meant—for them.

"The voyage takes a full rotation," he explained. "Two human weeks. We will have to stop for fuel and supplies on Fuel Station Omega, which is Mosca-run, and is located twenty thousand miles outside of your solar system. The ship has cloaking abilities; once we approach Earth's atmosphere, we will not be traceable by any satellites or reconnaissance equipment. We will use Earth's moon's gravitational orbit to keep us in place. Then the ship's hologram technology will re-create your desired location here, in the hull. Once we have verified those coordinates, the dematerialization process will transport you to that exact location on Earth."

She listened to his explanation halfheartedly.

"I still have this fear," she confessed, "that we'll arrive and only see a hole in the sky where Earth used to be."

"According to probability, Earth is there," he reassured her. "The percent chance that Earth has been destroyed is only thirty point one, not ninety-eight point six. I confirmed it myself with the stock algorithm."

"But there's no guarantee."

He moved his hands slowly over the controls. "No."

The spark from his touch tickled her skin, and she drew her legs up into the chair, hugging her knees. When were they going to have to say what they both were thinking?

"I suppose even if it's there, it's still dying, isn't it? Humans won't be able to live on Earth forever. We might have a generation left, or ten, but not eternity."

"You forget that the evolutionary jump has been triggered. It will take time to spread to all humans, especially those who aren't as aware or advanced as some of those off the planet. But it will spread eventually. Once some humans begin the change, even if they are far away, others will follow. So perhaps it is not too late for humanity to alter its practices and preserve Earth." He switched on a few buttons and the ship rumbled more quietly. "In any case, humans are no longer Earthbound. There's Armstrong. And there are other human colonies spreading to other planets, from the humans in the menageries and enclosures who have been freed.

There's Anya and her mentors to advocate for them." He laid his hand over hers. "Whether Earth lasts a hundred generations or not, humanity *will* survive."

She interlaced her fingers with his, studying the contrast of his almost glowing skin against her own pale hand. The spark warmed her palm.

"What's going to happen when we get there?"

"I will rematerialize you one at a time to your target location. As far as how to explain your disappearance, I would advise avoiding the truth. A few humans have returned after living with us in the far reaches of space, and it has not gone well for those who try to tell the world about our existence. The ones who fare best are the ones who simply claim no memory of their disappearance."

She gave a mirthless laugh. "I *don't* remember much."

He gave her a sympathetic look. "I am confident that your memory will fully recover in time. In the meantime, you will make new memories. Your family and friends will formulate other explanations for your disappearance—a kidnapping, a runaway situation, a blackout caused by drug use. Then, when humanity has evolved sufficiently, they might be able to hear the truth."

She nodded slowly. "Yeah. But that isn't exactly what I meant."

She hadn't been asking about the logistics of how he'd transfer them to the planet, how she would find her family again, or how she'd explain her absence. She wasn't talking about her plans to visit Lucky's granddad's farm in Montana, to sit with the old man and hear his stories of Lucky from before she had known him.

"I mean, what will happen between us?"

He was quiet for a moment.

Then his hand tightened around hers, flooding her with warmth. "I told you once that you staying with me was the only thing I wanted."

She nodded, staring at their clasped hands.

"You showed me sides of humanity I never knew. Forgiveness. Music." He smiled. "Even the virtues of cheating."

She smiled too, but a well of sadness was forming behind it.

"But what you showed me most of all," he said, "was your determination. You didn't let anything stop you, and I won't stop you now. I still want you to stay, more than anything. I want you to continue the work we're doing, together, and I want to have a chance to get to know you as true equals." He took a deep breath. "But your heart isn't here. I know that."

She felt the sting of tears behind her eyes.

"My heart's always with you," she whispered.

"But your feet are on solid ground," he said, "not among the stars."

She shook her head, because he was right and they both knew it. He had shown her a world she never would have known otherwise. He had taught her to believe in herself despite the odds, he had pushed her to be the best version of herself possible. She couldn't imagine that anyone on Earth would ever understand what she'd been through. How could she ever love anyone else who didn't make her skin spark at just a touch? Who could give her the stars?

And what about him—would he ever love another human? Would any other girl ever feel the spark of his touch warm her as much as it had warmed Cora?

She held in a sob, turning away. From Earth, she'd never

know if Cassian would continue to draw pictures of stars, of dogs, and of her, in his notebook.

"I don't want to say good-bye," she admitted.

He reached over, brushing away her tears, and then leaned across the controls and kissed her gently on the cheek. "It won't be good-bye," he said. "And you won't be alone. I'll be watching, in case you need me. Or in case I need you."

She tilted her head, pressing her lips to his. In the quiet of the cockpit, it was just the two of them and the stars. Cora rested her head on his shoulder, listening to his heartbeat.

She closed her eyes and let the spark of their touch flood her. She wanted to remember this exact moment forever. Remember the feel of him, the warmth, the radiating love. The beating of his heart, almost like repeating notes of a song. The rush of his blood, like a melody. The hum of the ship, like a singing voice . . .

She opened her eyes and cocked her head.

"Do you hear that?" she whispered. "That music?"

Cassian leaned forward, pressing a few controls on the panel. He twisted a dial and the sounds that Cora had heard magnified. Not a beat and melody and song in Cassian's blood, but *here*. In the cockpit. An actual song. Actual music. It filtered in through a speaker on the ship's control panel.

The song was something with an old-fashioned, lazy melody. The hint of a clarinet. A woman's sultry voice humming. Cora pursed her lips in confusion. "I don't understand. Where's it coming from?"

Cassian pressed more buttons on the panel, checking the ship's equipment. Cora glanced behind her at Mali and Leon, but they had fallen asleep in each other's arms. Maybe they didn't hear the music, but there was a smile on their lips just the same.

"It's a radio signal," Cassian said.

He continued to check his readings. The song kept filtering through the speakers, the notes wrapping around Cora, soothing her, making her heart beat with longing for home. *Music.* It was what had given her strength in an alien world. It was one of the things that had brought her and Cassian together.

Cassian's hand paused. "It's a signal coming from a transmitter in the Delta sector. A young signal. It can't have been traveling for more than a few months."

Cora's lips parted. "You mean . . ."

He smiled. "It's a signal from Earth. Broadcast to the universe in the hopes that some other form of life will hear it."

She broke into a smile and pressed her hands to her face, unable to hide her joy. A signal that recent meant that Earth had to still be there. It couldn't have been destroyed when the stock algorithm had predicted.

Earth lived.

Its song still played.

She leaned back in the chair, sinking into Cassian. He wrapped an arm around her shoulders. Together, they listened as the song grew in strength. The notes punctuating her heartbeats. The melody slow and soulful, reminding her of her own bittersweet feelings. Leaving Cassian. Maybe never seeing him again. And yet that spark—she'd never forget that spark.

Her eyes stayed on the screen.

Watching for a blue-and-green planet she knew was there.

Watching for home.

ACKNOWLEDGMENTS

THAT'S IT, MY FRIENDS. Cora and Cassian's story has come to a close. And what an amazing journey it has been.

After every book and series I write, I get a flood of questions from readers asking if there will be more volumes set in the story's world. As hard as it is to part with Cora, Cassian, Leon, Mali, and all the characters I've come to adore in the Cage series, this is my good-bye to them. But it doesn't mean *you* can't continue to imagine their next adventures. I hope they all have a long future in your hearts and dreams.

I owe thanks to my agent, Josh Adams, and all of Adams Literary, as well as to the wonderful team at Balzer + Bray, particularly my editor, Kristin Rens, for seeing this series through from the first glimmer of an idea to the final page. Special thanks as well to Megan Miranda. I am so fortunate you have you as my beta reader.

Lastly, thanks to the readers who make these books come alive through their artwork, passion, and fandom. Keep your heads amid the stars.